NO SECONDD CHANCE

(DS Pete Gayle Crime Thrillers, Book 14)

By

Jack Slater

A rumour on the streets. A courier caught in the act. Somewhere in or close to Exeter, someone is making guns and selling them on the black market. Someone secretive enough to cover his tracks by any means necessary and ruthless enough to kill without compunction.

DS Pete Gayle and his team must work with the National Crime Agency to catch him before he can spread any more death and destruction across the streets of the UK's major cities as well as closer to home. But how can they track down a ghost who works in the shadows and leaves no witnesses when all they have to go on is a cryptic nickname?

For Pru

CHAPTER ONE

Pete settled into his chair in Interview Room Two in the custody suite of Exeter police station. His boss, sitting next to him, nodded for him to start the recorder.

'Shane,' he said to the man seated opposite them. 'I'm DI Colin Underhill. This is DS Peter Gayle. We've been asked to talk to you by the National Crime Agency's National Firearms Targeting Centre and the National Ballistics Intelligence Service.' His tone was dry, his words clipped as if he wasn't in the habit of talking much. Which he wasn't, Pete acknowledged silently. For Colin to string two sentences together was unusual.

The way he'd brought Pete into this was typical. Pete had been at his desk in the squad room when his phone rang barely half an hour ago. He'd picked it up and Colin had said, 'Come to my office.'

'Guv?' What's...?' By the time he got the second word out, he was already talking to a dial tone.

'This interview's being recorded, both audio and video,' Colin was telling the male seated opposite them.

In his mid-twenties, dark hair falling over his forehead, Shane Gallagher was leaning back in his chair, arms folded across his narrow chest, legs spread, staring at the wall behind them, completely disengaged. Partly, perhaps, because he was wearing a white overall provided by the custody suite, his own clothes having been removed and sent to forensics for testing. Those overalls were bad enough when you were wearing something under them. When that consisted of just your underwear, they'd be positively uncomfortable, Pete guessed.

Which, maybe, was partly the point: to throw the wearer off their game even if they were accustomed to the system, as Shane was, having been in and out of custody since he was ten years old.

'So, why'nt the National what-its-name do it themselves? Stead of you recording it for 'em?'

He speaks, Pete thought. That was a good sign.

'Not the way they work,' Colin responded. 'They're London-based. Just an administrative centre. The real work is down to us coppers out in the field.'

Which is where the big, burly fifty-eight-year-old DI looked like he belonged in his khaki trousers, check shirt and tweed jacket, Pete thought: in a field or at the cattle market. But looks could be deceptive. He might not say much, but his mind was sharp as a tack.

'Do you still live in St Thomas?' Pete asked Gallagher.

The slightest hint of a twitch of the top lip was all the response he got.

'Ferndale, right? Is that one of the old houses or one of the newer ones?' Pete already knew the answer, but the point was to engage the man, get him talking, regardless of the subject, and progress from there.

'Old 'uns.'

Pete nodded. 'Handy for the station.' It was only a few hundred yards from one of the three main railway stations in the city. 'Use them much, do you? The trains.'

Another twitch of the upper lip.

'I gather you were there yesterday. Been anywhere nice, had you?' Again, he knew the answer, but it didn't hurt to look less competent than you were in these circumstances.

'Not really.'

At least he hadn't denied having been somewhere. Pete raised an eyebrow. 'Why go, then? Visiting rellies? Or mates?'

Gallagher paused, frowning. 'What's this about? You pull me in here, take my clothes, ask these damn fool questions. What for? What am I meant to have done?'

'That was quite a chunk of change you brought back with you,' Pete said. 'Twelve grand. Where did it come from? Or who?'

Fear took over Gallagher's features, his eyes widening, sweat breaking out suddenly on his face. 'You...? That was money?'

'What did you expect it to be?' Pete asked.

'I didn't know. It was sealed up. And meant to stay that way. And now you've got it?'

Pete dipped his head to one side. 'It's evidence.'

'I'm... You've fucking killed me. Literally.'

'We could return it,' Pete said. '*If* you're willing to work with us.'

Now the sneer was fully formed. 'Yeah, right. Fat lot of good that'll do if he already knows it's tainted goods. That I was picked up by you lot.'

'Why would he? And, even if he does, if you've been released without charge due to lack of evidence...' He spread his hands in a shrug. 'The fact you were picked up doesn't even have to be related, does it? Given your usual source of income. Occupational hazard, isn't it? Then, we just wait and watch.'

'He's careful. He'll know if you're watching.'

'So help us catch him. If he's locked up, he can't come after you, can he?' Pete said, playing on Gallagher's fear.

'I can't. I don't know his name, where he lives. Nothing.'

'Do you know what he looks like?'

'No.'

Pete caught the tilt of Colin's head in his peripheral vision. He glanced sideways. The senior man was looking distinctly dubious.

'Then how do you contact him?' he asked.

'I don't. He contacts me. I just follow instructions.'

'You sound like this is a regular thing. How often have you worked for him?'

'Once before this.'

And never again, Pete thought. *Whatever the outcome here.* 'How does he contact you?'

'Note through my door.'

So he knows where you live. 'Have you still got any of them?'

He shook his head. 'They say to burn them.'

'And you do as you're told, despite not knowing this person?'

'Yeah.'

A spark of defiance again, finally. Good. 'So, how did you first connect with him? If it is a "him".'

'I was… Working. He come up to me. He'd got a black beanie pulled down, a Covid mask on. Gloves. Asked me if I wanted to make some easier money than what I was doing. A one-off deal first. Trial run, like. More if I did it right.'

'So, is he white, black, Chinese, Indian?' Colin asked.

'Job to tell. It was dark. But not black or Chink.'

'When you say you were working,' Pete said, 'You mean dealing, correct?'

He nodded.

'Where?'

He paused.

'We know where you deal, Shane,' Colin said. 'DS Gayle just meant which one of your spots?'

His lips pressed together as he thought about that. 'By the Railway Club,' he said reluctantly.

Pete knew the place. A wide area of pavement tucked into a corner where the railway went over the main shopping street in the St Thomas area of the city, where the social club sat next to a pub and trees dotting the pavement made the lighting poor, at best.

'We're not concerned with the dealing here, Shane,' Pete told him. 'We've got bigger fish to fry.'

'Yeah, it's the frying bit that bothers me,' he grunted in return. 'And not you doing it.'

Pete nodded. 'I understand that. But like I said, he can't do anything to you from inside, can he? You help us put him there and we'll make sure you're protected.'

'I can't tell you what I don't know.'

'Which is no doubt why he operates the way he does. To protect himself. But there's got to be a way of reaching out to him. Otherwise, how could he do business?'

He shrugged. 'Dunno. And I don't care.'

Pete held back his instinctive response. 'Have you got any family, Shane?'

'No.'

'Anyone you care about?'

His lips moved to make the same response, but he held it back. Sat silently watching. Waiting.

'A girl?' Pete pressed.

Still, Gallagher sat stoically.

'You want her to be safe, don't you? We're the same.' Pete nodded towards Colin, sitting beside him. 'We've got people we care about. It's why we do this job. For now, as far as you know, and as far as we know, his products are going away from here, to the big cities: Birmingham, Manchester, Liverpool, London. But what happens when he sells to someone here, in Exeter? There are people here who'd buy from him if they knew about him. The people you deal with, for instance. Not the users, I mean: the suppliers. The county lines gangs. And others. Pimps and other crooks. What happens when they're let loose with something like that? They don't give a damn about the consequences if they get something wrong, do they? And that puts you and your girl directly in the firing line. Literally. And that's why we've got to find him. Shut him down. So anything you can tell us – anything at all that helps us put him away – makes you and your girl so much safer, Shane. You understand?'

He gave a small nod.

'What about the second time you dealt with him? How did he contact you then? And where?'

'Like I said: note under my door.'

'So you've only ever met him that once?'

'Yes.'

'So, how do you pass the payments on to him?'

'He lets me know where and when to drop it.'

'And where and when was that, last time?'

'Behind somebody's hedge on School Road at midnight.'

School Road was a couple of streets away from where Gallagher lived, Pete knew. 'And you never asked him, "Why me?"'

Another shake of the head. 'Didn't care, did I? Just glad of an easy few quid. But now...' He fixed Pete with an intense stare. 'That's screwed, isn't it? And so am I if he knows I've been talking to you lot.'

'What makes you so scared of him?' Colin asked.

'His reputation. He's known for being a ruthless bastard.'

'Tell us about that,' Pete said. 'Who talks about him? What do they say? What do they call him?'

'It's just stories. Bogey-man type stuff. He pays well but cross him and he'll kill you and your body will never be found.'

'So, it's known on the streets that he's out there, supplying guns?'

'Yeah.'

'Only a matter of time, then, until someone local gets hold of one.'

'Except he don't shit in his own backyard. Only sells away from here.'

'So, what do they call him?'

'Just "The Gunman".'

Pete exchanged a glance with Colin, who nodded. With pursed lips, he turned back to Gallagher. 'All right. People say he'll kill you if you cross him. Is there anything to back that up? Any examples of it happening?'

'Have you got any unexplained vanishings? Or bodies?' Gallagher countered.

'People come and go all the time,' Pete said. 'Especially in certain lifestyles. Sometimes they just don't want to be traced.'

'Yeah, right,' he retorted with a sneer. 'Certain lifestyles meaning you don't look too hard for them. Like mine, for instance.'

Pete shook his head. 'Everybody's got a mother, a father, someone they care about or that cares about them. Even you. We'll search, whoever they are, if only for the sake of those loved ones.' He saw Gallagher's expression. 'I can quote cases if you want. But the point is, can you quote cases to support what you say about this Gunman?'

'Me? No. It's what I've heard on the streets or in the pub, that's all.'

'Heard from who?'

Gallagher's head pulled back, a look of mixed horror and incredulity on his face. 'Are you serious? You want me to give you names so you can go to them and say, "Shane Gallagher tells me you've been spreading rumours about The Gunman. What can you tell me about him?" Not a chance. I'd be finished in this city, if not on this earth.'

Pete sighed and leaned forward, elbows on the table. 'We work with informants all the time, Shane. It's part of the job. We know how to keep them safe.'

'What, so now you want me to be a snitch? No chance.'

'I haven't asked you to snitch on anybody. Only to tell us where you heard the stories on the street about this gun maker. Just so we can track them back, maybe to a reliable source. That's all. And your name won't be attached to anything. Guaranteed.'

He shook his head. 'I dunno.'

Pete decided to give him the benefit of the doubt as to the meaning of that phrase in this instance. 'What context did the subject come up in? What brought it up?'

'I dunno,' he repeated, his meaning clear this time. 'Just chatter, wasn't it?'

'You remembered what was said enough to be scared of the man,' Colin pointed out.

'Yeah, but... I'm not a video recorder, am I?' he said, nodding towards the digital recording device on the end of the desk. 'I don't recall every detail.'

Colin sighed. 'Maybe you need time to think on it. We've got you for twenty-four hours, at least.'

Gallagher's eyes flashed wide with horror. 'That'll guarantee it. He'll definitely know I've been in here.'

'You'd best hope we catch him, then. If you're not going to tell us anything useful, I'm not going to waste time sitting here.'

'I said before – I can't tell you what I don't know!'

Colin shrugged and sat up straighter. 'If that's your final answer, interview concluded.' He nodded to Pete, who checked his watch and quoted the time and date before reaching for the recorder.

'Think on,' Colin said to Gallagher then stood up and turned to the door.

*

'So, what's the next move?' Pete asked as they walked along the corridor from the custody suite towards the high glass atrium that connected the two wings of the police station on the edge of the city.

'Plan B,' Colin said. 'Keep an eye on the cash.'

'What – it's still there?' Pete demanded.

They'd let Gallagher believe that they'd removed it from where he'd stashed it in his flat. In fact, Colin had let Pete believe that, too.

'Yes. They searched his place when they arrested him. Found it, checked the contents, added a tracker.'

'Jesus! You could have told me that before.'

'Worked, didn't it?' Colin countered. 'Scared him into talking.'

'Risky, putting a tracker in there. If our mystery man knows Gallagher's been arrested, he'll check for one, surely? He seems to be the careful sort. And if he finds it, he's likely to take it out on Gallagher and then go into hiding; go quiet, at least for a while.'

'NCA's plan, not ours. And he'll still need an income. He'll pop up again eventually.'

'Even more cautious than before, though. Which reduces our chances of catching him.'

Colin shot him a glance. 'So, what do you suggest instead?'

Pete could see from the glitter of Colin's narrowed brown eyes that he was treading on thin ice. 'Have we got Gallagher's phone?' he asked.

'Yes. There's nothing on it.'

'But we could put a bug on it. And a tracker.'

'We need to track the money, not the courier.'

'Yes, but he can lead us to the target. As soon as he moves, we follow at a safe distance. He goes to a meeting place, we close in. No need for any apparent connection. Observe the hand-over or drop-off, whatever happens, and go from there.'

Colin paused, thinking. 'It'd need at least two – one to hold back, though not too far. But yes, if we can get a warrant…'

'How long will that take?' Pete glanced at his watch as they stepped through into the back of the huge glazed central atrium. It was now 4.20 in the afternoon.

'I'll go straight up.'

'It's getting late in the day to find a judge still in chambers,' Pete said.

'I'd best get a wiggle on, then.' Colin angled away from him, towards the lifts as Pete approached the wide stairs behind the station's reception desk. Colin would be going up to Chief Inspector Christine Naylor's office on the top floor while Pete returned to the squad room on the first floor. She would need to OK the warrant before it went to whichever judge was available to sign it off.

CHAPTER TWO

Pete put his phone down and looked up, meeting the gaze of each of his team members in turn. 'We're on surveillance duty.'

'Oh, ah?' said Detective Constable Dave Miles, sitting alongside DC Jane Bennett who was opposite Pete in their six-desk workstation. 'What about all this?' He waved a hand to indicate the papers spread across his desk, which related to the cold case they were currently reviewing.

'On hold, for now,' Pete said. 'We're on this exclusively until the contact's made, and we go from there. Eight-hour shifts, in pairs.' He looked around at his team 'Jill, you're with Dick, Ben with Dave, Jane with me.'

'So, when do we start?' the spiky-haired PC Ben Myers asked from the far side of Dick Feeney, who was seated next to Pete.

'Pack up your desks now,' Pete told them, sitting back in his chair. 'We meet in Incident Room One in half an hour with the guvnor. He's lead on this.'

*

'So, what's the story, guv?' Dave asked, arms folded across his chest as he half-sat on the front edge of one of the desks in IR-1.

Colin looked around as if checking that he had the full attention of the whole team – as if he wouldn't have, Pete thought. There was no doubting it as they clustered near the front of the big room, facing the DI, who stood before the whiteboard.

'Someone on our patch is manufacturing firearms,' Colin said. 'Selling them on the dark web.'

Dave's head jerked back as his eyebrows rose in surprise. 'How do we know he's on our patch?'

Pete straightened up. 'The guvnor and I were just interviewing the courier he used to take one of his weapons up to Birmingham and bring back the payment for it. In cash,' He took a step forward, placing himself alongside Colin. 'A local drug dealer. Small-time chap from over the river, in St Thomas. Shane Gallagher. He was arrested with the money at his flat this afternoon, having been followed back there by Transport Police working on behalf of the NCA.'

'NABIS picked up chatter about a maker down this way a few months ago,' Colin said. 'Someone was arrested with a weapon in Birmingham that matched one recovered in Manchester last year. Phone work on the male in Brum led to intelligence that he was trying to get hold of a replacement. They have them for a reason, generally. The hand-over was observed and the courier followed back here.'

NABIS, they all knew, was the acronym for the National Ballistic Intelligence Service, an independent office-based organisation within the national police service, based in Birmingham.

'So, what now?' Dave asked.

'We're getting a bit of extra software added to Gallagher's phone. We can track him with it and listen to his conversations. We could charge him but then again, he could lead us to the bigger fish so we're going to release him and stay close, see what happens. He said he was waiting to hear what to do with the package he brought back with him.'

'The payment,' Jane clarified.

'Yes, but he supposedly didn't know that,' Pete said. 'It was wrapped up and taped inside a lunchbox.'

'He must have guessed, though,' Jill declared.

Pete shrugged. 'He was paid to take a package to Birmingham and bring another one back. He wasn't told what was in either of them – on the basis, I suppose, that what you don't know, you can't tell. And you're not tempted by.'

'Yeah, right,' Jill retorted. 'A sealed package that you're not tempted by?'

Dave chuckled and gave the immaculately uniformed little PC a nudge. 'So that's why you joined the job, Titch. You're a natural-born nosey-parker.'

'When you're paid five hundred plus expenses to take it somewhere, you resist,' Pete said before she could reply. 'If you've got any sense. Plus there's this "Gunman's" reputation. He's not known to be a nice man. Especially if you cross him.'

'Gunman?' Dick asked.

'That's what he's known as on the streets, apparently.'

Dick frowned. 'Have we heard of him?'

Pete turned to Colin.

'Uniform say there's only one report of the name being used to their knowledge.'

'So, yes, we have,' Dave concluded, sharing a glance with Dick. 'But it wasn't followed up?'

Colin shrugged. 'Too vague and tenuous.'

'Until now.'

Colin nodded.

'When's Gallagher being released?' Jane asked.

'As soon as we get his phone back from Tech,' Colin said, meaning the technical team at the force HQ, which was adjacent to the station they were currently in.

'It's Friday today,' Pete said. 'Hopefully, none of us had plans over the weekend. But I'd have thought our man would be in touch with Gallagher soon. I can't see him wanting to leave an amount of cash like that out there on the loose for too long, even if he is the cautious type.'

'How much are we talking about?' Dave asked.

'Trust you,' Jill said.

'Twelve grand.'

Dave gave a low whistle in response. 'Not cheap, then, these weapons. And they're home-made?' He looked from Pete to Colin and back.

'Partly 3D printed, partly engineered,' Colin confirmed. 'A lathe, a drill-press and the right bits are about all you'd need, apparently, other than what you or I would have in our garage.'

'Easy money, then. He can afford to be careful.'

'Organise the shifts amongst yourselves,' Colin said. 'But he needs twenty-four-hour cover as long as he's in possession. Then we follow the package. But this is a covert op. We stay out of sight.' His stern gaze moved from one member of the team to the next, impressing on them the importance of that.

'We'll handle it, guv,' Pete told him.

Colin nodded once and stepped away from the whiteboard. 'Custody will let you know when he's being released.'

*

Pete's phone rang, abruptly breaking a long silence in the car, during which he realised he'd started to nod off. He jerked upright in the driver's seat. Beside him, Jane grunted and snuffled awake as he picked up the phone from the central console.

Thumbing it open, he couldn't help noting the time on the screen. It was 11:53pm and the call was being automatically forwarded from Shane Gallagher's number. He picked it up quickly, lifting the phone to his ear in time to hear Gallagher's voice.

'What the fuck? Now?'

'Now,' a muffled male voice confirmed and the line clicked dead.

'Dammit,' Pete muttered, leaving the phone on and connected as he reached for the door handle.

'What's up?' Jane asked, rubbing her eyes with her knuckles. 'Sorry. I must have nodded off.'

'You did. Sounds like Gallagher's on the move. But I missed the start of the conversation, where he must have been told where to go.'

'Shame. Not a perfect system, then. About time, though. Which is what, by the way?'

'Nearly midnight.'

She blinked. 'Two and a half days since he got back. The guy's certainly cautious.'

'Yeah. Let's go. I'll walk, you drive. Take it slow, one junction at a time. I'll call you up when it's clear to move.'

'OK.'

He stepped out of the car. A warm summer day had given way to a muggy night, the coolness that he'd expected for their second night shift parked on a side-street that led off from around the corner from the end of Ferndale Road, yet to materialise. As they were on surveillance, he was wearing jeans and trainers, a T-shirt and a sleeveless denim jacket so, although he had a pair of cuffs tucked into an inside pocket of the jacket, he had nowhere to carry a police radio. He would have to rely instead on his mobile phone for communications. The situation was a lot less than perfect, but it was the best they could do on short notice.

He walked to the end of the street and crossed the one it met at an angle towards the inside of the corner it formed with the end of Ferndale Road, opposite the RAF cadets' hut in the corner of Cowick Barton playing field. Looking along Ferndale, he saw a figure in the distance, walking away from him on the far side of the road. From around three hundred yards away, and under street lighting, he couldn't be sure that it was Gallagher, but it was a male of about the right height and build. He set off after him, keeping his pace steady and unhurried, sticking to the left side of the road and deliberately not focussing on his quarry as he left it a few seconds before taking out his mobile phone and placing a call.

'Boss?' Jane said when she picked up.

'Come on through,' he said quietly. 'He's heading for the far end of the street, on the right-hand side. Take it steady and pull in again somewhere around the corner, before you get to Alphington Road, so you can see which way he goes. I know we've got the trackers, but it's best to have eyes on as well, as much as possible.'

'Right.'

She ended the call and moments later, he heard an engine behind him. Then headlights rounded the corner behind him and the black Ford Focus they'd been sitting in rolled past him. He didn't acknowledge it, in case anyone was watching – just stayed focussed loosely on where he was going, keeping the figure in the distance in his peripheral vision.

Before Jane caught up with him in the car, the male reached the right turn at the far end of the road and went from sight around it. Pete passed the house where Gallagher lived in an upper storey flat. A quick glance told him there were no lights on, but that was all the notice he took of the place. Again, he had to maintain his cover, in the unlikely event that the flat was being watched.

He had almost made it to the corner when his phone rang again.

'He's turned off,' Jane said as soon as he answered. 'He didn't go down to Alphington Road. Turned into Prince's Road instead.'

'OK, stay put. I'll be with you in a minute.'

'Will do.'

She hung up as he picked up his pace, walking briskly now. They weren't going to be able to follow Gallagher into Prince's Square at the far end of the street he'd turned into without being spotted if that was where he was headed. They'd have to either rely on the trackers they'd installed in his phone and the heel of his shoe as well as amongst the tape wrapping of the Tupperware box containing the cash or find another way to stay close.

He rounded the corner, a quick glance telling him that the footpath coming into the road on his left was clear. Just a few yards down, another road led off to the right. He crossed it and, to his left, the new-build houses gave way back to older terraces. He lifted his phone, unable to pick out the black Ford amongst the cars parked down both sides of the road that stretched away in front of him.

'Boss?'

'Where are you?'

'A few yards past Prince's Road on the left.'

'I'm crossing now. Get ready to start the engine. I've got an idea.'

'I'm ready. I can see you in the mirror.'

He caught a flash of red light. 'Was that your brake lights?'

'Yes.'

'Got you.'

He hung up again and, back on the narrow pavement between the parked cars and the tiny brick-walled gardens of the Victorian houses, maintained his long, swift stride. It took just seconds to reach the black car and, as he did so, Jane leaned across and opened the door for him, turning the key in the ignition as he sat in beside her.

'So, what's the plan?'

'Go on down here and take the next right into Queen's Road, then up towards the square. That way, we'll come into it from a different direction than Gallagher, so no obvious connection.'

'If he gets that far,' she cautioned, signalling to pull out.

Pete shot her a look.

'As opposed to going into one of the houses along Prince's Road,' she said.

Pete grunted, sitting back in his seat as she pulled away, driving swiftly but without racing the engine. 'We'll cross that bridge if we get to it. We've got the trackers in place.'

He took out his phone again and brought up the app. The concentrated red dots blinked steadily together as one, as he'd expected them to, moving along Prince's Road on the little map.

'He's still in motion.'

Jane flicked on the signal again and turned right into another street of old red brick terraced houses, similar to the others around them. Again, she pushed the car as hard as she could without making too much noise and soon she was turning right once more, into another side-road, this one much shorter. Facing them at the far end, Pete could see a larger, more modern house, one of a pair of semis build in the 1970s, he guessed, with one car on the drive and another parked across the front.

Almost immediately, Jane was slowing again, braking for the junction.

'Which way?'

He checked the app on his phone for a location. 'Right.'

Driving more slowly now, in keeping with the location, she pulled out as Pete's phone buzzed again. He picked it up quickly enough to hear Gallagher's voice asking, '…Now?'

'West,' came the reply.'

'Stop,' Pete ordered and Jane quickly complied.

'All right,' came the response from Gallagher.

The call ended.

Pete waited for a count of ten, then said, 'Go ahead.'

They started forward again. It was only a couple of houses along to the sharp left-hand bend of the square street layout. She made the turn.

'Straight on,' Pete said. 'He's going to the west side.'

The trackers confirmed that Gallagher had emerged from the end of Prince's Road and turned right, followed the road around the next corner and was now stationary. Pete saw a gap at the kerbside between parked cars. 'Pull over there,' he said.

Jane complied.

'Come on.'

He stepped out of the car, Jane following suit, and they headed up the pavement in front of the houses on the outer side of the small square, the centre of which was filled in with houses now, though originally it would probably have been an open grassed area.

'Where to?' she asked quietly as they headed towards the corner.

'The west entrance,' he muttered. 'He seems to have stopped again.'

'Meeting the guy?'

'I expect so.'

'We don't want to spook him.'

'We'll cross over and head up, around the corner into Regent Street,' he said quietly. 'Just keep going as if we belong around here.'

'Right.'

'Here.' He reached for her hand as they approached the junction. Even as long as he'd known Jane, it felt strange to walk hand-in-hand with someone other than Louise. But it was for the sake of their cover.

'Odd, right?' he said, speaking more normally now and turning to look at her as they reached the corner.

She gave a low chuckle. 'Yeah, just a bit.'

'Never mind. We'll get over it. At least Dave isn't going to take the piss.'

'Oh, Christ! Don't even think about it!' she retorted. 'Where is he?'

Pete knew what she meant. She was talking about Shane Gallagher, not Dave Miles. 'Don't know,' he admitted as they reached the far pavement and started along it, away from the square. 'Hold on.' He took out his phone, glanced quickly at the screen, which was open at the tracking app, then pretended to tap and swipe with his thumb before raising it to his ear. 'Hello,' he said into it. 'Yeah, where are you?' He paused as if listening. 'Seven? OK.' He lowered the phone.

'Any the wiser?' asked Jane.

'Yeah. Just round the corner.'

'So, why did we park back there?' she asked, maintaining the role.

'You know what these places are like. You find a space, you grab it. There might not be another. And anyway, it's good to get your legs moving,' he added, nudging her playfully.

They reached the end of the short street and rounded the corner to the left. Once out of sight of anyone behind them, he stopped and turned to face her, releasing her hand. 'We've passed him,' he muttered. 'Back there on the other side. The first house.'

'That big one with the green door and the oversized hedges?'

'Yes.'

It was the only property other than the garages at either side of the end they'd just emerged from that actually opened onto the short linking street. At either side of the front door, the windows were protected by variegated privet hedges that were thick and dense and at least seven feet tall.

'OK. How precise is that thing?'

'About ten feet, they said.'

'He'll be inside, then.'

'Hmm.'

'Not for long, though, I shouldn't think.'

'And with a bit of luck he'll come out this way. It's shorter than the way he came.'

'One of us will have to fetch the car, though,' she pointed out.

'I'll do that while you keep an eye out,' he offered.

'Gentleman to the last, eh?' she teased with a grin.

'Practical,' he retorted. 'My legs are longer.'

She sighed. 'You know how to let a girl down.'

'At least I do it gently.'

'Has he moved yet?' she asked, changing the subject.

Pete checked his phone. 'Nope.'

'What's taking him?' she demanded with a frown. 'How long does it take to hand over a sarnie box and say, "Thanks and goodbye,"?'

'Not this long,' he agreed. 'We'll give it a minute more.'

'I didn't see anyone else coming or going or hear an engine. Did you?'

'Nope.'

'So, either they were bloody quick, they're still there or they doubled back on us.'

'Given how cautious the subject seems to have been up to now, I can't see him inviting Gallagher in for a coffee and a chinwag. And if he's gone, why's Shane still there?'

'Yeah… Do you reckon we might have a problem?'

Pete pursed his lips. 'It seems likely, doesn't it?' He checked the app on his phone. 'Still no movement. Target or package.'

'Time to break cover?'

'Head that way, at least,' he agreed. 'If needs be, we can bluff it out.'

They headed back around the corner and across the road, towards the property where the app suggested Shane Gallagher still was. Moving quickly but quietly, Pete was glad that Jane wasn't wearing her usual short heels. The trainers she now wore with jeans, a white T-shirt and a short leather jacket were much quieter.

He could hear nothing except the distant hum of traffic from the main road, around two hundred yards away beyond at least four rows of houses.

He reached the gateless entrance between the hedges of the property they were focussed on and stepped in towards the door. Caught the soft gleam of something pale, low down to his left and glanced across as his hand lifted towards the door.

A shoe.

The sole, in fact, of a trainer. To one side of it was another, this one flat to the ground, and attached to them were a pair of legs clad in dark jeans. His gaze lifted. Shane Gallagher's face was turned away to the side, his body slumped and still.

'Shit.' Pete stepped quickly across. Dropping to a crouch, he reached out to the slumped man's neck, feeling for a pulse. The skin was still warm, but totally still beneath his touch. He glanced over his shoulder, saw Jane peering around the hedge at him. 'He's dead.'

CHAPTER THREE

'Christ,' Jane muttered. 'I don't envy you telling the guvnor.'

Pete grunted. 'Thanks.'

'We must have walked right past the murdering son of a...' She shivered. 'He must have been crouched in here, waiting for us to go past and out of sight, then come out and gone into the square. Assuming this isn't his house,' she added, looking up at the door.

'Yeah, right.'

She shrugged. 'Just saying... It wouldn't be the first double-bluff someone tried on us.'

'No, but it would take some balls. And why?'

'Saves having to get rid of him. Get us to do it for them.'

Pete chuckled dryly. 'True.'

He turned back to the body, taking out his phone to use it as a torch. Instantly, he could see the cause of death, even against Gallagher's dark clothing. His lower abdomen and the top of his jeans were soaked in blood which appeared to have flowed from his central torso. A stab wound. A quick, hard thrust with a knife, up under the ribcage into the heart, Pete guessed. He would have been shoved against the wall, stabbed, held in place until the killer was certain he was going to remain quiet – moments, only – then lowered into the position he now occupied.

A quick search around the body revealed the sandwich box that had held the cash Gallagher had been delivering. It lay under the hedge, now open and empty.

Had the killer been onto them? Or had Gallagher been disposable all along?

Pete let the breath sough out through his mouth. Either way, they were up against a cold and ruthless killer. And, as of now, they had no clue as to who he was or where he'd gone. He stood up and reached over the body to checked the latch on the tall wooden gate in the fence that stretched across from the house to the hedge. It seemed to be locked.

He stepped out onto the pavement. 'Call control, get forensics and the pathologist into gear. I'll call the guvnor.'

Jane gave him a nod and stepped away to comply.

Pete had Colin Underhill on speed dial. It was answered on the second ring.

'Yes?' More of a grunt than a question.

'Guv, it's Pete. We've lost him. And Gallagher's dead.'

'*What?*'

'Gallagher got a call. We missed the destination but we followed him. Carefully. Around into Prince's Square. We must have been just yards away when our guy stabbed Gallagher, but he got away. We're guessing into the square, but we don't know for sure.'

'Then find out.'

'Guv.'

The line went dead in his hand. No accident, Pete guessed, and he wasn't about to call back and make things any worse than they already were. Instead, he made another call.

'Control.'

'It's Pete Gayle. I need any and all CCTV footage from Alphington Road, covering the stretch from Queens Road to Waterloo Road from ten minutes ago and continuing for the next hour. Also Cowick Street, covering the Cecil Road and Old Vicarage Road junctions.'

'What are we looking for, sarge?'

'A killer. Other than that, I don't know until I see it – and maybe not even then,' he admitted.

'Right, we're on it. Do you need me to mobilise…?'

'That's all in hand,' Pete interrupted. 'My DC's on it. Except, we'll need some uniforms to cover the area while Forensics do their stuff.'

'I'll arrange that.'

'Thanks.' He hung up.

'Forensics and Doc Chambers are on route,' Jane told him.

'Right. Best knock 'em up, then.' Pete nodded towards the dark green door of the house whose garden was now a murder scene.

'They're not going to be happy at this time of night if they're innocent.'

'What are you – channelling Dick Feeney, now?'

She grinned. 'You knock, I'll stay back here in case they try and do a runner, shall I?'

'Better yet, I'll ring the bell.'

He reached for the white button at the side of the door and pressed it. Instead of the expected regal chime, it was a harsh buzz. He pressed it again, just in case. Moments later, with no response, he tried it a third time. This time, a light came on upstairs.

'Ah, here we go.'

The light was followed by another, in the hall. Then locks and latches began to click. One, two, three, four, Pete counted. They were certainly security conscious, whoever they were. He took out his warrant card in readiness.

The door finally opened, held close to the frame by a chain. An eye peered through the gap beneath a tumble of tousled grey hair. 'Do you know what time it is?' the raspy male voice demanded.

'Twenty-six minutes past midnight,' Pete replied. 'And I'm no happier at being up and about at this time than you are, sir. Police.' He held up his warrant card to confirm it. 'I need a word.'

'What, now?' He blinked several times, trying to banish the sleep from his eyes and his brain.

'Exactly now, sir, yes.'

'What for?'

'I'm what you might call the advance party. In a few minutes, this place will be swarming with uniformed officers, forensic investigators and a pathologist, so if you don't mind…'

'Eh?' The man shook his head, confused. 'Why? What's…? Pathologist? What's happened?'

Pete nodded towards the hallway beyond the still mostly concealed figure. 'This might be easier inside. And more comfortable.'

'Huh. Well, I'm awake now, I suppose.' He shut the door, then opened it again more widely, the chain now hanging behind the doorjamb. He was almost as tall as Pete, but twice as broad with a substantial belly under his white vest and striped pyjama bottoms. His feet were clad in slippers. 'Come in. But be quiet. The Mrs is still asleep.'

'No problem.' Pete beckoned Jane forward as he stepped over the threshold into a large hallway with black and white checkerboard tiles covering the floor at a forty-five-degree angle beneath deep brown skirtings and walls that were an equally dark green, almost matching the door.

'In here,' the man said, leading the way into the room on the left, under the window of which Shane Gallagher's body now lay. It was a lounge, decorated in dark, Victorian colours and furnished with old-fashioned dark oak and a green velour three-piece suite ranged around the fireplace. There was no TV, Pete noticed.

Closing the front door, Jane followed them through.

'This is my colleague, DC Bennett,' Pete said. 'I'm DS Gayle, Exeter CID.'

'CID. Pathologist. Forensics. Sounds like there's been a murder.' He plonked himself down in one of the armchairs and waved them towards the sofa.

'There has,' Pete told him. 'You and your wife live alone here?'

'Yes. Have done for forty-three years. Not alone, I mean, but the kids have long-since left to build their own lives. Why is a murder relevant enough to us to justify waking us up at this time of night?'

'Because it happened in your front garden. What should I call you, by the way?'

'In our...! My God! When? Who?' He half-stood but slumped, blinking, back into his chair. 'Riley. George Riley.'

'Thank you. The victim's name is Shane Gallagher. He lived on Ferndale Road, so not far from here. As for when – just a few minutes ago. What time did you and your wife go to bed?'

'Nine, like always. Hot chocolate with a slug of brandy and off we go. She's dead to the world. I am normally, too. Was until you started leaning on the doorbell.'

'In that case, do you mind if we quickly check the premises? Make sure it's all secure, given the circumstances?' Pete suggested.

'Check the…? You think he might have broken in here?'

Pete gave a shrug. 'We don't know, Mr Riley, but its best to check. For your safety and your wife's. We'll be quiet and careful, obviously.'

Riley grunted. 'I suppose, then.'

'Oh, before we do that, the gate out there that opens onto your back garden.' He nodded towards the outer corner of the room. 'You keep it locked, do you?'

'There's no lock but it's bolted, yes.'

Pete nodded. 'OK. That's the only way into the back, is it?'

'Yes.'

Still, the suspect could have scaled the fence and broken in at the rear of the house, Pete thought. He stood up. 'Right, let's get this done and we'll get out of here.'

*

The uniformed officers arrived first. They taped off an area that included the short street that the house emerged onto as well as the arms of the square that led from it, all the way to the nearest corners. Then, working inwards towards the centre point, they began to search under cars, in the small front gardens and beneath the drain covers in the gutters, looking for anything that might have been discarded by the killer as he left the scene: gloves, blood-stained outer clothes, the weapon, even fresh cigarette stubs, chewing gum or wrappers that might hold fingerprints or DNA.

They'd barely started on this when the anonymous white van of the forensic investigators arrived. Tape was untied to allow them access to the scene then replaced behind them. The van pulled up a few yards further along the street, on the far side, and Pete stepped forward to greet the team leader as the passenger door opened and he stepped out. For once, it wasn't the short, rotund Harold Pointer with his round, wire-framed glasses, but a taller, dark-haired male who Pete had worked with a few times before, Andrew Creswell.

'DS Gayle. Here already?'

Pete's lips tightened. 'We were looking for the victim when he was killed.'

Creswell grimaced. 'Ouch. That's going to be uncomfortable, back at the station.'

'Tell me about it.'

The back doors of the van opened and two more CSIs emerged, already suited up, to join the driver in unloading their equipment.

'The victim's over there, in the front garden,' Pete told them. 'His name is Shane Gallagher. You'll find his details on the PNC.'

Not that his having a criminal record would affect the way they treated the body or the efficiency of their work but it would affect their search, in terms of what they might look for.

'Weapons? Drugs?' Creswell asked.

'He was a dealer, but that's not what he was doing tonight.'

Creswell nodded. 'All right. We'll see what we can find,' he said as an engine sounded behind Pete and he turned to see another vehicle approaching – a black VW estate car.

For some reason a faint wave of relief swept through him.

The Passat drew up behind the forensics van, the engine was switched off and the door opened.

'Peter,' said Doctor Tony Chambers. 'I'd say, "Good morning," but that's probably not appropriate,' he said with a quick grin, then nodded to Jane, his buzz-cut silver hair glinting beneath the streetlights. 'DC Bennett.'

'Doc,' Pete and Jane said together.

'Sorry to fetch you out of bed,' Pete continued. 'But we've got a body for you. Behind the hedge, over there.' He nodded towards where Gallagher lay, undisturbed until now. 'We think a stab wound, on the basis that nothing was heard and he's leaking a lot of blood from his abdomen.'

'How come the two of you are here so quickly?' Chambers asked. 'And in civvies.'

'We were working. Surveillance.'

'Ah.' Chambers opened the back of his car and drew out an overall similar to those worn by the forensic investigators. Pulling it on, he donned nitrile gloves, took a pair of shoe covers from a box in a corner of the boot and picked up his bag. Closing the car, he led the way across the street.

'To the left,' Pete told him as he approached the Riley house.

'Ah-hah.' Chambers set his bag down in the gateway, donned the shoe covers and took out a torch. 'I see what you mean.'

It looked to Pete like even more blood had leaked from the body since he examined it earlier.

Crouching beside the body, Chambers reached for the bottom edge of the dead man's blood-soaked T-shirt and carefully stretched it out. 'Unusual,' he said.

'What's that?' Pete asked, looking over his shoulder.

'The weapon. Rather than a knife, it appears to have been more like an ice-pick. You can see that the tear in the T-shirt is round, rather than a slit. Around five or six millimetres in diameter. A sharpened screwdriver, perhaps. Something adapted for the purpose. Or, as I said, an ice-pick. They can come with a sheath.

Safer to carry around if that's what you want to do. I'll see the depth and direction of the wound at post-mortem and do all the other usual checks, of course, but that certainly appears to be your cause of death.'

'Thanks, Doc. We'll leave you to it, then. Let me know when you're going to do the PM.'

CHAPTER FOUR

'What the bloody hell happened?' Chief Inspector Christine Naylor slammed both open hands on her desk.

It was barely 8.00am and just two minutes since Pete had answered his desk phone to her brusque demand, 'My office. Now.'

'He must have seen or heard us coming,' he said, determined to stay calm in the face of her anger. 'Hidden until we were out of sight and slipped away into the square and off from there, ma'am. There are several ways he could have gone from...'

'I know all that,' she snapped, green eyes flashing, the sun gleaming off her tied-back blonde hair and the silverwork on the epaulettes of her white blouse from the window behind her. 'I mean, how did you let it happen? A man died on our watch, Detective Sergeant. Under your bloody nose, for God's sake! You were supposed to be keeping an eye on him, weren't you? Following him.'

'Yes, ma'am. But we didn't know his destination and we were keeping our distance in order not to spook the man he was going to meet.'

She sighed heavily. 'You've got his phone records, at least, I hope?'

'Yes, ma'am. But the call came from an unregistered mobile. We're following it up.'

'How?'

'We can't track the phone, but the SIM inside it had to be bought from somewhere. We're tracing that. Hopefully, it'll give us something on who bought it. Maybe a CCTV image or a credit card receipt.'

'Hopefully? Maybe?'

'Ma'am,' he said, cutting her off before she could build up another head of steam. 'We're onto the provider. They're checking records to find out where the SIM would have been sold. As soon as we get that information, we can check the retailer and their surroundings – shopping centre, carpark, whatever – for CCTV. It was probably bought for cash. They're not expensive. And for all we know, he may have already dumped it, but it's not in the area between Alphington Road and Cowick Street. We've already searched all the likely routes of egress. No phone or weapon has been found. We're still checking CCTV for vehicles and pedestrians leaving the area in the hours following.'

'And what if he lives within that area?' she demanded.

Pete grimaced. 'Then where would he do his work, ma'am? He'd want somewhere isolated, where he wouldn't be seen or overheard. That's a pretty densely populated area. Mostly old Victorian and Edwardian terraces with a bit of modern infill. And even if he uses 3D printing for the bulk of his product, he'd still need a lathe and so on for the bits that have to be metal, unless he buys them in. And would he risk that? Especially to his own address? He seems to be both careful and intelligent.'

'But also arrogant and daring,' she countered. 'As demonstrated by the killing of Shane Gallagher almost under your noses last night.'

Pete tipped his head. 'Fair point. But we've got to start somewhere, so we're working to eliminate the easy possibilities first. If we can't find him leaving, then he either holed up somewhere until morning and slipped out with the rush-hour or, as you say, he lives there. And if that's the case, he's going to know we're coming for him long before we get there and have plenty of time to clean up and get rid of anything incriminating. Assuming he doesn't live within sight of where he killed Gallagher, in which case he already knows we're looking for him.'

'Hmm.' She pursed her lips. 'Then you'd better hope you're right, and he doesn't.'

'Exactly, ma'am.'

'Which leaves me with the unpleasant task of speaking to the National Firearms Targeting Centre and explaining how we lost the prime lead they provided us with.'

'Ma'am. He had no family so there's no-one to notify of his death in that sense. He did have a girlfriend, though. He didn't tell us anything about her and we've yet to track her down. We'll do a search of his phone, his flat and, if nothing pops up, ask around for her, starting with his downstairs neighbour and the pub on Cowick Street that we know he frequented.'

'You'd best get on with it, then. And hope there aren't any repercussions from the NCA over his death,' she added heavily.

Pete bit back his response. He knew better than to tempt fate. 'Ma'am.' He nodded stiffly and turned to the door.

*

'Anybody got any good news?' he asked, pulling out his chair in Incident Room 1 and dropping into it.

'We've got hold of all the public CCTV there is from Cowick Street and Alphington Road last night, into this morning,' Dave said. 'There might be some private stuff out there. Doorbell cameras, dashcams, private security cameras and so on, but that's a matter of getting out there, knocking on doors. We had to wait for you to come back before doing that. How's your backside?'

'Not as sore as it might be. But we're on shaky ground, as of now. We need to get some backsides on some of those seats over there and eyes going through what you've got so far,' he said, nodding towards the classroom-like array of individual desks that occupied the far end of the big room. 'Or else we do that and get some uniforms out searching for the private stuff you mentioned.'

'From what the guvnor said when we were setting this up, it'll be the latter, I should think,' Dick said from beside him.

'You could always volunteer to go out there with them,' Dave said to him. 'Act as liaison and team-leader, feed back to us with anything that's found. Save your old eyes the strain of staring at a screen all day. What d'you reckon, boss?' he asked Pete.

'I reckon Dick's right. The guvnor will want to keep things tight – get a team from Ops Support out there canvassing while we look through what you've already got ourselves. And while they do that, we need to knuckle down and do what there is to be done. I say, "we," but that doesn't include me, at least for a while. I've got Shane Gallagher's post-mortem to attend.'

'Slipping out from under the yoke again?' Dave teased.

'Do you want to go instead?' Pete asked, knowing what the answer would be.

'No, you're fine. I'll stay here and keep the troops in line.'

'Yeah, right,' Jill snorted.

'Thought so,' Pete said, ignoring her. 'Jane, get the guvnor to ask Ops Support to send a team out and see what they can find. Ben, get onto Gallagher's network supplier as soon as they're open, and get the details of that number that called him last night. Then get onto its supplier and find out where it was sold. I want anything we can get on who bought it, when and where, including CCTV from the shop, the street outside it or preferably both. We need to ID the purchaser and track them down ASAP. I'll be back as soon as I can.'

*

'Hey, Doc, what have I missed?' he asked pushing through the double doors into the mortuary with disposable shoe covers on his feet, disposable gloves on and a lab coat over his suit.

Chambers looked up from the post-mortem table, where he was laying out his tools at the side of a body which was still covered with a white sheet.

'We're about to start, Peter. You couldn't have timed it any better.'

Pete grunted. 'If you only knew.'

Chambers raised a grey eyebrow.

'I'd have preferred to be here twenty minutes ago.'

'Trouble in paradise?'

'It might still be new, but I don't think I've ever heard it called that. And no more trouble than I was expecting, I suppose, given the circumstances. Still, I could have done without.'

'I dare say. Anyway, if you're ready…?'

Pete nodded.

When Chambers folded back the sheet, he saw that the body beneath had been undressed and cleaned. The puncture wound was an obvious dark spot about the width of a biro, placed centrally on the torso, just beneath the tip of the sternum.

'Given the position of the wound, we won't start with the normal Y-incision,' Chambers said. 'And, as you know, we no longer use a probe to indicate the direction and depth of the wound. Too prone to causing more problems than it solves. So, instead, an overall external examination, followed by a visit to Radiology for a CT scan of the victim's torso. That'll confirm the track and depth of the wound as well as exactly which organs were damaged by it. Then we can transect the wound itself in order to find and identify any foreign matter that may have been introduced by the weapon.'

'Sounds like a long job that I don't really need to be present for,' Pete said.

'Indeed. From the amount of blood-loss noted at the scene and in his clothes when they were removed here, this morning, my guess would be that, as I said last night, it was a single upward thrust through the soft tissue of the solar plexus and into the heart. If you look carefully, you can just make out the early stages of discolouration from bruising on the lower face as well.' He pointed to the area as he spoke. 'Probably a hand over the mouth and nose to prevent him crying out. The weapon was used, the victim held in place for a few moments then lowered to the ground where you found him. That would be my working hypothesis at this stage, but as I say – to be confirmed. Or not, as the case may be. I'll keep you updated if you need to get off and do what you do to find the perpetrator.'

'Thanks.' Pete raised a hand and headed for the doors.

*

'Bloody hell, that was quick!' Dave and Jane had both looked up from their desks, which faced the door, as he stepped into the incident room. 'Started without you, did he?'

'No, but he'll finish without me,' Pete said, hanging his jacket over the back of his chair. 'What have you lot been up to while I was out?'

'Ben's tracked down the number of the incoming call on Gallagher's phone.'

Pete glanced across as he pulled his chair in.

'Pay-as-you-go, as we thought,' Ben confirmed. 'Cheap two or three quid job from the supermarket just down the road from here.'

'What, literally?'

Ben nodded. 'Rydon Lane.'

'Is he taking the piss or what?' Dick said, the expression on his dry, greyish features even more sour than usual.

'Hmm.' Pete wasn't convinced. Supermarkets almost guaranteed anonymity. There were so many people passing through, how could you pick one out unless they used a credit card? That was more likely to be the reason for the location of the purchase, he imagined. 'Cash purchase, I suppose?'

'Haven't got that far yet, but I expect so,' Ben said. 'Shall I go down there and find out, and see what CCTV they've got?'

'I'll go. My engine's still warm and you're on a roll here.' He pushed his chair back again. 'What about Ops Support?' he asked Jane.

She flicked her ginger hair back. 'The Guvnor was going to get onto them. We haven't heard any more.'

He nodded. 'All right. I'll ask him when I get back.'

Rydon Lane was a completely inappropriate name for the busy dual carriageway that led south from the roundabout in front of the Devon and Cornwall police headquarters, next-door to what was still thought of as the new police station. Pete hooked a left onto the main road and had just a few hundred yards to drive before exiting at the slip-road that gave access to the supermarket, a retail park, a park-and-ride carpark and an edge-of-the-city housing development.

Entering the huge store, he saw no security staff so went to the customer service desk and asked for the manager. Showing the assistant his warrant card quickly ended her almost automatic delaying tactics. 'I'll get her for you,' she said, picking up a phone on the desk in front of her.

Moments later, a short, stocky woman in a charcoal skirt suit walked briskly towards them across the shop floor. She stopped at the counter beside Pete and looked from the assistant to him and back. 'How can I help?'

Pete showed her his warrant card. 'DS Gayle, Exeter CID,' he said. 'I wouldn't have bothered you, but there's no security staff around so... Firstly, are there security cameras over the tills here?'

'Not individually. You can see the number of tills.' She nodded towards the line of checkouts that stretched away along the front of the store from behind the customer service desk where they stood. 'There are two covering the self-checkout area and another one covering the walkway coming away from the tills. We find that's enough to serve the purpose and as many as one person can sensibly cover in the screen room.'

Pete nodded. 'Right. We've got a purchase that occurred at one of the tills. I've got the date and time. I'd imagine it was a cash transaction, but either way, I need to find out who bought the item. A SIM card.'

'How do you know it was bought here?'

'From the provider.'

'OK. So you'll want to start with the CCTV.'

Pete nodded.

'This way.' She held out a hand to indicate direction and set off, her pace as brisk as it had been earlier. She led him along behind the tills to the far corner of the building where toilets and baby-changing rooms stood opposite a door marked Staff Only. She used her ID badge to unlock it and pushed through with Pete staying close behind. A set of stairs led up in front of them. At the top was another door with ID badge entry. This opened to a corridor that ran along the side of the building with doors off at intervals on the left. She stopped at one of them, knocked and entered, letting Pete follow her into a darkened room with several screens on the opposite wall over a long desk with a keyboard at its centre, a man in a dark uniform seated before it.

'Tony,' she said. 'This is DS Gayle from up the road. He's got a couple of questions for you.'

Tony was middle-aged, greying and broad-shouldered but without the gut that Pete might have expected, given his job. They nodded to each other.

'I'll leave you to it,' the woman said.

'Thanks.' Pete turned to the seated man as she stepped out, closing the door behind her.

'So, what do you need?'

'If I give you a date and time, I need anything you've got from the till area to help me ID someone making a purchase.'

'OK.'

'We're looking at the twelfth, so just over a week ago, 09.48.'

'No problem. Dodgy purchase, was it? Nicked card or summat?'

'No, we just need to identify the person and speak to them. The item they're purchasing was linked to a crime.'

'Oh, ah? Carving knife, was it?' he asked with a grin.

'A SIM card. A call was made with it that led to a crime being committed. I can't say too much at this stage. On-going investigation. We haven't decided yet what to release and what not to. You know how it goes.'

He had no idea of Tony's background or how much he knew about police procedure, but it wouldn't hurt to let him feel included.

'Right.' He turned back to his keyboard and screens. 'Let's see what we can see then, eh?' A few taps at the keyboard and the image on the central screen immediately in front of him changed and went still. 'Here we are. 09.48.'

Pete leaned closer. The camera lens he was looking through was close to the customer service desk, not far from the main entrance. He could see several of the tills had customers at them, but there was no way of seeing too much of the more distant ones. Even gender wasn't obvious in all cases. 'Can you zoom in at all?' he asked.

'Only digitally when it's not live feed. Sorry.'

'All right. Let's let it run a minute, see if any of them come towards us. Without the actual receipt, I don't suppose it's going to be possible to tell which till the card was bought through.'

Tony looked up. 'It should be. They're all digital. Everything that gets swiped through is recorded. When, where, if there was a discount or deal linked to it. Helps with keeping track of turnover as well as stock.'

Pete's eyes widened in surprise. 'Ah. Now you're talking. How do we get hold of those records?'

Tony nodded towards the side of the room opposite the direction Pete had approached from with the store manager. 'Two doors down. They'll have it. I'd come with you, but I can't leave the cameras. Hang on.' He picked up the radio that had stood unnoticed in the shadows beneath the screens at the back of the desk and keyed the mike. 'Tony to Charlie. You got a minute, mate? Got a little job for you. Escort duty.'

The radio hissed and a tinny reply came through. 'From where to where?'

'Camera room to stock control. Non-staff-member.'

'Eh? What's...?' He stopped, not wanting to ask the question in public, Pete guessed.

'Copper,' Tony told him. 'Detective Sergeant.'

'OK, I'm on the way.'

Tony glanced up.

'Meanwhile, can we run that footage, see if we can't get a face or two from those at the tills at the time of the transaction and save time later?' Pete asked.

'Yeah, course.'

He pressed play and people started moving around on the screen. A woman in a flowery dress with narrow straps over the shoulders and dark hair pulled up into a ponytail was first to leave her till and walk towards them.

'You looking for a male or female?' Tony asked.

'I don't know,' Pete admitted. 'The user was male, but that doesn't mean he bought it, does it?'

Tony grunted. 'Fair enough. You want a picture?'

'If she's not the buyer, she might be a witness.'

'True.' As Tony reached to pause the footage a young male in a dark orange T-shirt with a logo on the front that wasn't readable from this range stepped away from another till, almost bumping into the woman as she passed. She stepped quickly around him and they walked towards the camera almost together until she picked up her pace to get away from him.

He paused the image. 'How's that? Two for the price of one.'

'Nice,' Pete admitted with a smile. 'Which order are the tills numbered in?'

'You don't shop here, then?'

Pete shook his head. 'Not often. Too far from home and the wrong direction.'

'Number one's at the far end,' Tony told him.

'Right. Thanks.'

The door opened behind him and another man stepped in, in a similar dark uniform to Tony's.

'Charlie, this is DS Gayle from up the road,' Tony told him.

'Charlie Harper. You want to talk to the stock control folks?'

'Seems like they might be able to help,' Pete agreed.

'Right. Well, if you're ready...'

'Yes.' Pete turned back to Tony. 'See you in a bit.'

'I'll get those customers imaged for you and mark 'em as to which till they were at.'

'Brilliant. Thanks.'

Charlie opened the door and stepped out, leaving Pete to follow.

'DS Gayle, you say?' Harper checked, stepping out along the corridor.

'That's right.' Pete took out his warrant card to confirm it.

'You nicked a cousin of mine, a couple of years back. Possession with intent.'

'Really?' *Here we go,* he thought.

'Yeah. Best thing that ever happened to him,' Harper said with a grin. 'Straightened him out at last. We'd been trying for years but done no good. Seventeen months inside was the shock he needed.'

Pete smiled, relieved. 'Good.'

'Here 'tis.' Harper stopped outside a door that was exactly the same as that of the camera room. He knocked and used his ID badge to open it, stepping in without being invited.

'Cass, Mand, I've got a visitor for you.' He stepped in far enough to allow Pete room to enter too. The room was a lot brighter than the one he'd just left, but not much bigger. Two women sat at desks that faced each other and were side-on to the door. The one on the left was in her forties, Pete guessed, and chubby with more makeup than she really needed and greying blonde hair that she wore down onto her shoulders. Across from her sat a younger, slimmer dark-haired woman with hard features and hair scraped back into a bun. Both wore the store uniform.

'DS Gayle,' Pete told them. 'Exeter CID. I'm told you might be able to help me out.'

'Is that so?' asked the blonde with a smile.

'I'll leave you to it,' Harper said. 'Don't eat him will you?'

'Thanks,' Pete said and turned back to the two women.

The blonde looked him up and down and shifted in her seat. 'So, how can *I* help *you*, Detective Sergeant?' she asked, her tone making it clear exactly what she had in mind.

CHAPTER FIVE

'How'd you get on?' Dave asked when Pete stepped back into the incident room, heading for his desk.

'I kept my trousers on and the zip done up.'

Dave laughed. 'Oh, ah? Found a groupie, did you?'

'She was keen to help. And she did. With the case.'

'Oh?' Dave's eyes widened and Pete saw Jane and Jill look up from what they were doing at either side of him.

'How?' Dick asked.

Pete took a thumb drive from his jacket and put it with a half-dozen sheets of A4 paper on his desk, turning the pages face-up to reveal that they each held a full-page print of a photograph. He fanned them out. 'Each of those is a person who was at a till at the time in question. And our lady of the eager libido identified which one of them bought the SIM card we're interested in from the till receipt data.'

'So, who's the lucky winner?' Dick asked.

Pete spread the printouts wider and slid one out of the middle. 'There you go,' he said, tapping the image with his forefinger.

'Well, she didn't kill Shane Gallagher.'

'Keep on like that, we'll make a detective out of you.'

The image was of a woman who looked to be in her seventies, at least. Small and slender, she had curly grey hair and a stooped, shuffling gait. Pete picked it up and held it up for the rest of the team to see.

'And it was a cash transaction?' Jane asked.

He nodded.

'Have we got her car reg?' Dave asked.

Pete shook his head. 'She used the bus.'

'But they have CCTV on, so do we know where she got off?' Jill asked.

'Not yet. But seeing as you asked, you could get onto them and find out.'

The smartly uniformed little PC grimaced. 'Me and my big mouth, eh?'

Dave chuckled. 'I'm saying nothing. Ow!' He rubbed his upper arm where she'd hit him. 'Workplace violence. What was that for?'

'I didn't see a thing,' Jane said.

'You wouldn't. You're the wrong side of me, as well as…'

'You're not about to make a sexist comment there, are you?' she cut in.

His eyes shot wide. 'Would I?'

Jane chuckled. 'Definitely.'

'Anybody got any news for me?' Pete asked.

'We're still ploughing through CCTV footage and Special Ops have got a team out there looking for more to add to it for us,' Dick told him.

That saves a conversation with Colin, Pete thought.

'And we've heard from the girlfriend,' Dave said. 'Gallagher's, I mean. She called in to report him missing. The guvnor went to see her, seeing as you were busy. Called us when he got back a few minutes ago. She thought he'd probably been arrested when she saw the police tape on his door, but when he didn't come back after twenty-four hours, she called Custody and they put her through when she gave them Gallagher's name. She knew he'd made a trip, but she didn't know the details. He'd told her nothing about it – just that he was going to take her out for a nosh-up once he got paid for it. And then he never showed, so she went round there next morning to give him what for and...' He shrugged.

'Saw our tape instead,' Pete finished.

'Yes. So, anyway, the Guvnor said she was pretty cut up about it when he told her Gallagher was dead. He was convinced. She's going to stay with her folks for a few days while she gets over it. I don't know if he told her it was for her own safety or just for the company while she gets over the shock, but she's going, apparently.'

'Where to?'

'Tiverton.'

Pete nodded. It wasn't far, but it should be far enough. At least, she wouldn't be at home if Gallagher's killer wanted to make sure of her silence too, assuming he even knew of her existence. Which, to be fair, they had no way of knowing.

'What time was the bus the old lady caught back to Alphington Road?' Jill asked, picking up her desk phone.

'10:10. It's on a loop from the station. Leaves there at a quarter to.'

'Right.' She made the call as the others resumed their work and Pete got up to put the photo of the woman they were now looking for on the whiteboard. Underneath it, he wrote, "SIM card purchaser."

'We can go and collect it anytime,' Jill announced. 'They'll have it ready for us.'

'Go on, then. I'll take over what you were going through on the CCTV.'

She raised an eyebrow. 'OK. Thanks.'

He gave her a quick grin. 'The rest of us get coffees first. You haven't got time.'

*

By the time Jill got back from the bus station in the city they'd finished going through the CCTV from the council-owned cameras on Cowick Street and Alphington Road and come up empty. Their man either lived in the area between the two main roads or had stayed put there for several hours until he could merge with the work crowd.

'You never know,' Dick had said when they finished. 'The bugger might even have been watching you and the Doc and the forensics team from somewhere, tucked away in the shadows, probably grinning like a Cheshire cat at how clever he is.'

'There's nowhere he could have hidden that's in sight of the crime scene,' Pete said. 'But the idea of it makes me even more determined to catch him.'

The door opened behind them and they both turned to see Jill enter.

'You took your time, Titch,' Dave declared.

'But I've found out where our lady of the SIM card got on and off the bus,' she countered as she approached the cluster of desks, taking a thumb drive from her pocket.

'Where?' Pete asked.

'Alphington Road. The bus stop just north of the railway bridge.'

'Ooh. Did she, now?' he felt a grin spreading across his face. Maybe their man was local to the crime scene, after all. 'Did you see which way she went from the bus stop?'

'She turned south when she got off.'

'Towards Prince's Square.'

'Yes.' Jill pulled out her chair and sat down.

'Among other places,' Dick cautioned.

'Obviously,' Pete agreed. 'But it's a good start. Now, how do we find out where she lives?'

'The tyre place by the railway bridge has got CCTV cameras,' Ben said. 'I've been looking at the footage from them this morning.'

'The cross-roads at the end of Sydney Road hasn't got any,' Jane said. 'But the hotel just up from there has.'

'Yeah but there's another bus stop just there,' Jill pointed out. 'If she was going that far, she'd have got off there.'

'There's a junction on the other side of Alphington Road, down by the railway bridge,' Dave said. 'Big place on the corner.'

'Yeah, fogey-farm, isn't it?' said Ben. 'They might have cameras in case of escapees.'

'They have,' Dave confirmed. 'But nothing facing the main road.'

'And no, it's not a fogey-farm,' Dick said. 'It's a nursing home. For ill people.'

'Well, sorry for breathing,' Ben said. 'Either way, if she was going up past it, they'd still pick her up.'

'There's a car-sales place up there, too,' Jill said. 'It's where I got my Renault from – the car before my current one.'

'They'd definitely have cameras,' Dave said. 'They'd have to, for security.'

'Right. That's three places to check. Don't get comfy, Jill, you can come with me. Print us off a copy each of the old lady's photo to take with us.'

*

Pete was driving past the County Council offices on Topsham Road when his phone rang. He used the touchscreen of the in-car comms system to accept the unlisted call.

'DS Gayle.'

'It's Nick Grosvenor, Ops Support. We've finished canvassing the area around Prince's Square, out to Alphington Road and Cowick Street. Got quite a bit of footage for you to go through. Most of it's from Cowick Street, to be fair, though there are quite a few little businesses in the area, given that it's basically residential.'

'OK, thanks for that,' Pete said. 'It didn't take you anywhere near as long as I expected. I'm out following up on another lead, but I can send someone down to the main reception desk at the nick to collect it.'

'Right, I'll be there in a few minutes.'

'Perfect. Thanks again.' Pete touched the red icon to end the call, catching a glimpse of the angular stone apse of a church through trees to his left as he started down a hill between high stone walls.

'I bet the others will appreciate that,' Jill said. 'Not. They'll have square eyes by the time we get back there.'

'Find the guvnor's number on there and give him a call,' Pete said, nodding to the screen.

Jill raised an eyebrow but complied.

It rang once and was answered with a brusque, 'Yes?'

'Guv, it's Pete. I just heard from Ops Support. They're bringing in a load of footage for us from around the crime scene. Someone will need to collect it from Reception. Any chance of getting some extra eyes to help us go through it? The sooner we can identify a suspect and track him down, the less chance he's got of doing a runner or getting rid of evidence.'

'I made it clear this is a quiet operation. We're on delicate ground with the NCA already, after what happened last night so no. Just use your time intelligently.'

Pete couldn't hold back a sigh of disappointment. 'OK.' He reached for the screen and ended the call.

'It wasn't unexpected, but I had to try,' he said to Jill as they approached a pedestrian crossing with traffic lights outside a low-rise block of 1960's-built flats faced with pale brick and dark hanging tiles.

'Use your time intelligently?' she said, looking across at him. 'What's that supposed to mean?'

'Mostly getting Uniform to do things like we're doing now without telling them anymore than we can help, I imagine. And collecting all the evidence we can, but not going through any more than we absolutely need to, to find what we're looking for.'

'So, standard procedure, then.'

'Pretty much.'

Minutes later, with the railway bridge over the road just yards ahead and an MOT and tyre replacement centre on their right, he slowed the car and signalled to turn into their destination.

'Oh, Christ,' Jill said. 'I'd forgotten that. I don't know who came up with it as a road name or when, but it's a good thing Dave's not here. We'd never hear the last of it.'

Pete saw what she meant. The nameplate on the road he was turning into, tucked low on the wall at the base of the railway bridge, read Willeys Avenue. 'I don't suppose they even thought of that, back in the day.'

'Maybe not, but I bet it gets some piss-taking now.'

As Dave had said, what stood on the left-hand corner was a big building; four storeys of dark brick with, for some reason Pete couldn't fathom, bright blue window- and doorframes. The side facing onto Alphington Road was obscured by dense foliage but as Pete drove up the hill and turned into the small parking area at the rear, he saw what they needed above the main entrance on the corner of the building – a prominently positioned CCTV camera.

He stopped the car. 'You go in and get what you can. I'll walk up to the car-dealer's and see what they've got. Then we can go down onto Alphington Road. You go right, pop into the few shops along there, I'll go over to the tyre place and left, up to the undertaker's. How's that for intelligent use of our time?' he added with a grin.

'Almost as intelligent as not bringing Dave to Willeys Avenue,' she replied, opening her door to step out. 'See you back here?'

'Yup.'

Pete locked the car and, as she headed for the entrance to the nursing home, he turned left out of the entrance and walked up past a modern block of low-rise apartments towards the car dealership further up on the other side of the road where it curved around to the left, out of sight.

Rounding the bend, he saw that he was on the edge of another extensive-looking area of Victorian terraces. Ideal territory to hold an elderly lady who went shopping on her own, using the bus from close to the bottom of the street.

He crossed towards the open field-type gate in the metal fencing around the display area of the dealership and went in, heading for the low white building with its corrugated roof in the rear corner. Stepping inside, he found himself in a small reception area more suited to a workshop than a sales environment. A low counter stretched across the space, dividing off the back section, where a door led through to the actual workshop. Two rigid plastic chairs stood to his left. A keyboard and computer screen on the desk faced away from him, a brass bell beside it.

He hit the bell and waited.

In moments, the door of the workshop opened and a tall, skinny male in his mid-forties came through. He was wearing grease-stained red overalls and wiping his hands on a rag that was filthier than they were.

'Morning. What can I do for you?'

Pete held up his warrant card. 'DS Gayle, Exeter CID. I've just got a couple of questions relating to a case we're working, if you've got half a minute.'

'OK.'

'I see you've got cameras out there. Do they cover the gate and the street beyond it?'

'Yes.'

'And how long's the footage kept on the system for?'

'A couple of weeks.'

'Great. Could I see what it recorded on the morning of the twelfth? Or, better yet, get a copy of it?'

'The boss ain't here, but I don't see why not.'

'OK. And lastly, do you recognise this woman?' He pulled out a copy of the photo of the woman who'd purchased the SIM card. 'You may have seen her walking past here.'

The man looked down at the photo and grimaced. 'No.'

Pete's lips tightened in disappointment. 'You're sure?'

The man shrugged. 'I'm in the workshop mostly, so I wouldn't tend to see anyone passing by.'

'All right. Can I get that footage, then?'

He grunted and lifted a hinged section of the counter between them, then leaned down to fire up the computer as Pete stepped through. He brought up the CCTV on the screen and glanced up. 'Do you know how to use it?'

Recognising the screen layout, Pete said, 'I'll manage.'

As the man stepped back, Pete took the one seat, pulled it up to the counter and slid a thumb-drive into the slot on the front of the hard drive. As it loaded, he keyed in the date, start-time and duration he wanted. 'If I go from 8:00am to 11:00, that'll cover it,' he said and, with a few more taps at the keyboard, started the copying process. It took no more than a few seconds. He pulled out the thumb drive and stood up from the desk. 'All done. Thanks.'

He left the man to his work and headed back down the road.

Traffic was light at this time of day and he was able to cross immediately, heading into a much cleaner, tidier and more pleasant reception area at the MOT and tyre centre on Alphington Road. A male in a suit and tie looked up from a desk behind the counter at the jingle of the bell over the door and stood up to approach the counter.

'Hi, how can I help?'

Again, Pete held up his warrant card. 'DS Gayle, Exeter CID. I've just got a couple of quick questions relating to a case we're working.' He took out the photo of the old lady and held it up. 'Do you recognise this woman?'

The man frowned, peering it at for a stretched moment. Then his expression cleared. 'Yes. She catches the bus out there.' He nodded towards the road outside. 'I've seen her at the stop. Quite chatty. Talk to anyone who gives her half a chance. I've been caught once or twice with her.'

'When did you last see her?'

He frowned again. 'Is she all right? Nothing's happened to her, has it?'

'She's fine, as far as we know. We're trying to find her, that's all. We need to speak to her as a potential witness.'

'Ah.' He nodded. 'Right. I see. Well, let's see... Must have been... Day before yesterday she was out there, bright and early as usual, waiting for the bus.'

'You don't happen to know whereabouts she lives, I suppose?'

He shook his head with a grimace.

'Which direction she comes from?' Pete pressed.

'Down the road, I think, towards town. But where, exactly, I don't know.'

'OK, well, that's a start, at least. I don't suppose you remember if you saw her on the twelfth?'

'Twelfth... Last Wednesday? Probably, but I can't say for sure.'

'Could I see your CCTV? Or download the footage from the morning of the twelfth?'

'Sure. I'll do it for you now. Won't take a minute.'

Pete dipped his head and handed over the thumb drive he'd used earlier. 'Stick it on there for me, that'll be perfect.'

'What times?'

'Eight to eleven should do it.'

The man nodded and stepped away, back to his desk. 'Coming up.'

In no more than a minute he was holding out the thumb drive. 'Here you go. All done.'

'Thanks.'

'Is that it?'

'For now, yes. If there's anything else, we'll come back.'

The man reached out to shake his hand and Pete accepted and returned a firm grip. An automatic gesture, he guessed. Heading back out, he glanced down the road and saw Jill heading towards him along the pavement. He raised a hand to her and waited, stepping clear of the entrance.

'You got anything?' she called as she reached the end of the property he was standing in front of.

'Our lady lives down that way somewhere,' he replied, nodding towards her. 'Don't know exactly where yet.'

Jill grinned. 'I might.'

He raised an eyebrow. 'Really?'

She nodded, stopping beside him. 'There's a little jewellery place down there. Not a shop-front, more a front-room business. Nothing expensive, more your new-age style stuff. The woman in there recognised her.'

Pete grimaced. 'I didn't peg the old dear as the hippy type.'

'She isn't. But the woman says she sees her coming and going from the place across the road. The fogey flats. Retirement home,' she corrected herself with raised eyebrows.

'Ah. Is that what got Ben confused, earlier?' Pete wondered aloud.

'Could be. Do you want to go and see what we can find out?'

'Sounds like an intelligent use of our time while we're here,' he agreed.

Stretching northward from the MOT centre was a row of what would, in their time, have been more expensive and up-market three-storey terraced houses, the first of which housed a small bakery. They used the crossing outside it and walked the few yards along to a smart-looking newish block of apartments, the ground floor faced with pale stone while the upper levels were of dark brick – a modern version of that used to build the terraced houses opposite.

Pete led the way in though the pillared portico entrance and over to a reception desk behind which sat a woman in her fifties, he guessed, with carefully coiffed grey hair, immaculate make-up and a flowery silk blouse with matching scarf over a cream skirt.

She looked up and her imperious expression shifted as she saw Jill's uniform. She straightened in her seat. 'How can I help, officers?'

Pete showed her his warrant card. 'We're with Exeter CID,' he told her. 'We're looking for this woman.' He held up the photo of the female from Tesco's.

The woman's eyes widened in recognition. 'Mrs Tranter? Why? What's happened?'

'We just need a chat with her. She may be able to help with our enquiries. As a witness.'

'I see. I believe she's in. Just a moment...' She flipped quickly through a ring-bound pamphlet at her elbow. From what Pete could see, it looked like a list of residents. She stopped, held her finger at one entry and used the other hand to tap the keys on the switchboard phone in front of her. She then flipped the booklet closed and picked up the receiver. Paused briefly. 'Mrs Tranter? It's Marjory on reception. You have some visitors down here.' Another brief pause. 'Police officers. Apparently, you witnessed something... Well, they seem to think you may have. Would you like to come down and speak to them...? Very well.' She hung up. 'She'll be down in a few moments. I don't think there's anyone in the lounge at the moment, if you'd like to use it.' She held up a well-manicured hand towards the room that opened off behind them. It was laid out with comfy-looking armchairs and sofas grouped around coffee tables, all in pastel shades with an emphasis on dusky pink.

'Thanks,' Pete said. 'If Mrs Tranter's happy with that...'

Moments later there was a gently 'ping' from somewhere out of sight and the sound of doors sliding open. The woman from the photograph that Pete had returned to his jacket pocket stepped briskly around the corner, a slight frown marring her neat features.

'Mrs Tranter?' he said, holding out a hand.

'Yes.' She took it briefly with just the tips of her fingers and thumb.

'I'm DS Gayle. Pete. This is PC Jill Evans. We've just got a few questions we'd like to ask if that's OK.'

'I can't imagine what about.'

'Should we have a seat?' He lifted an arm towards the lounge.

She nodded. 'Yes.'

She led the way across to a cluster of chairs at the far end of the spacious room and sat facing away from the reception desk.

Waiting for them to settle across from her, she leaned forward and said, in a low voice, 'No need for Marjory to know any more than she has to.'

Pete smiled. 'Quite right.'

'So, how can I help the police?' she asked, sitting upright.

'I understand you went to Tesco's last Wednesday morning,' Pete started as Jill took out her notebook and pen.

'Yes. I always do. Not that I need much, but it gets me out and about, you know.'

'And you bought a SIM card for a mobile phone.'

She eyes widened in surprise. 'How do you know that?'

He smiled. 'It's what we're trying to find out about. It wasn't for yourself?'

'No!' she said, 'I've no need for such a thing. Why would I, here?'

Pete tipped his head in acceptance. 'So, who did you buy it for?'

'Oh, just a young man I met over the road. I was waiting for the bus and he was perched on the little wall in front of the garage over there, looking depressed, so I asked him what was wrong. He said that he'd been going to see his aunt. She's in a hospice in Torquay. He lived in Clyst Honiton, I think. Or St Mary. One or the other.' She gave a quick shake of the head. 'Anyway, he was coming through town and he had a problem with his car, so it was in dock and he was stuck there until it was finished, so he was going to be late and he couldn't phone her and let her know because there was a problem with his phone. It needed a new one of those little cards. He asked if I was going to Tesco's.' She gave a quick smile. 'He'd seen my bag. When I said I was, he asked if I'd get one for him. Just a cheap one, he said. He wasn't really into mobile phones like most youngsters are these days – just wanted it for the occasional phone call or text message, so anything would do.' She drew a breath. 'I don't really understand the things. I don't have one myself, as I say. No need. She raised her hands to indicate their surroundings. 'I've got everything I need here so the landline's perfectly sufficient for me. But that's what he said, and he gave me a ten-pound note, said it shouldn't cost more than two or three and I should use the rest to get myself a cream cake or something nice, so I agreed.'

'Did you get his name?' Jill asked.

'I think it was John. I don't remember a surname. I don't know if he ever said it. And it wasn't as if he was asking me for anything. I was taking his money, not the other way round, and I was going there anyway. I got the thingy and a cream donut each for us, did what I'd gone for and came back.' She raised her hands again. 'That's all I can tell you, really. Why? What's happened?'

'We need to get hold of this John,' Pete told her. 'He might have some information we need. You didn't know him at all? Recognise him from anywhere?'

'No,' she said, shaking her head. 'I'm sorry I can't be more help.'

'That's all right,' Pete said. 'You've been a great help. Thank you.'

'Would you like a cup of tea while you're here?' she asked, looking from Pete to Jill and back.

'No, thank you very much,' Pete responded. 'We need to be getting on. People to find, criminals to catch and barely enough of us to do it all, you know.'

'Oh.' She looked disappointed. 'Yes, I see. Well, I hope you find him and he can help.'

'Yes. Thank you.' Pete stood up. 'Have a good day, Mrs Tranter.'

'Thank you,' she said with a nod.

As they stepped out into the sunshine that had broken through the clouds while they were inside, Jill said, 'Back to the garage, then. Find out who their customers were that morning.'

'Presuming he was one,' Pete said.

She grunted. 'Now who's following in Dick Feeney's footsteps?'

'I know from the look on your face when she said he was called John that you were thinking, if he did give a surname it'd have been Smith.'

Jill laughed. 'Guilty as charged, m'lud. But weren't you, too?'

CHAPTER SIX

Pete keyed up the CCTV footage from the MOT centre on Alphington Road to the time that the bus should have arrived to take Mrs Tranter towards the supermarket. He could see her on the screen, waiting at the stop while a figure in a beige jacket and dark trousers sat on the low wall in the foreground, his back pressed against the low metal fencing atop the wall. He tapped the keys to start the playback in reverse, drawing him back in time at six times normal speed.

Mrs Tranter moved quickly backwards across the road, stood beside the male, chatting with him. He appeared to take something from her. A cigarette stub flew up to his hand from the pavement at the base of the wall. Mrs Tranter crossed the road away from him and disappeared from the frame, top right. Pete's hand reached for the keyboard again and hit pause, then play to run the footage forward. She entered the picture again, approaching the bus stop at the far side of the road. Paused there a moment. The man seated outside the MOT centre nodded to her. Something was said. She crossed the road towards him and he tossed away his cigarette.

Pete hit the pause button harder than necessary. 'Yes.'

'Got something?' Dave asked, looking up from across the cluster of desks.

'Yes, maybe. Jill, when we met outside that MOT centre, did you notice any dog-ends on the ground?'

She grimaced. 'Not really, but I wouldn't be surprised if there were. Why?'

Pete's glance shifted back to Dave, beside her. 'Get your leathers on and get down there,' he said. 'Take some evidence bags and gloves and see if you can bring us back a sample of our man's DNA.'

'Eh? How? Where from?'

'Come round here, I'll show you.'

Dave quickly got up and came around the desks to lean over Pete's shoulder. 'There he is,' Pete said, pointing to the screen, and to the figure, his back to the camera, semi-obscured by the low fence he was sitting against. It showed his position in relation to the entrance of the MOT centre though. 'I don't know yet how long he was there, but he was smoking and dropping his dog-ends.'

'That was over a week ago. Are they still going to be there?' Dave protested.

'We don't know until we check, do we? But the quicker we do that, the more likely they are to still be there.'

'All right. I'm going.'

'I'll run the footage back further while you're on the way and let you know how many you might be looking for. And while I'm at it, I'll email you a picture of him and you can ask if the guys in the MOT centre remember him.'

*

Here he comes, Pete thought as a male in a beige jacket jogged across the road into view on his screen. *Cheeky sod.* He paused the footage and ran it back further. Moments later, he had his man approaching the scene, pedalling easily along the far side of the road, heading south from the direction of the twin bridges and the end of Cowick Street. Or the city centre, on the far side of the river.

He let the footage play.

The male went from sight at the top right of the screen. It took him about a minute to leave his bike somewhere out of sight of the camera. Probably chained to the railings at the bottom of Willeys

Avenue, Pete guessed. Then he crossed the road, glancing back the way he'd come, and settled on the wall of the MOT centre, took a pack of cigarettes from inside his jacket and tapped one out. With a lighter from his trouser pocket, he lit it and sat waiting.

Pete checked the time at the bottom of the screen.

It was ten minutes until the bus was due to arrive. Long enough to be sure of being in position before most regular users would turn up at the stop, Pete thought. So this was carefully planned. Was Mrs Tranter targeted specifically? Did he know her? Or know of her and her habits? She'd said she didn't recognise him, but that didn't mean he didn't know about her. Or was he simply stopping for a rest on his way out to the supermarket, saw her bag with its prominent logo and took a chance?

He shook his head. There was no way of knowing until they tracked him down and asked him.

He hit fast-forward and let the footage run on until the bus arrived, Mrs Tranter got on and it moved away, out of frame. Slowing the replay back to normal speed, he waited and watched to see what the male would do.

He didn't rush. Sat for a few moments – no doubt until the bus went from sight, Pete thought – then stood up, checked the road in both directions and sauntered across, back towards where he'd left his bike. Leaving the frame, he was not seen again. Pete let the footage run on, but there was no sign of him. Had he headed out of town along Alphington? Or up Willeys Avenue? There was no way of knowing. He hit fast-forward, running the footage forward to the point where the bus would have returned. Nothing. He ran it forward another twenty minutes and sure enough, his man was back. Wherever he'd been, he'd come back and resumed his place on the wall outside the MOT centre to wait for the old lady's return.

Pete hit pause, ran it back to where the male was crossing the road to approach the low railing. Before sitting down, the subject had glanced directly into the MOT centre. He hit pause again and took a screen grab. It was far from perfect, but it was the best image of the man he was going to get. He saved it and emailed it to Dave with a message. *"He wasn't a customer that day. Rode a push-bike. But they might recognise him. And there should be 3 dog-ends."* Then he closed the video screen and picked up his desk phone to place a call.

'Camera room,' came the brief response.

'Graham, it's Pete Gayle. Can you get hold of some footage for me from the twin bridges, last Wednesday morning, 08:30 to 10:30? Traffic cameras, council ones, whatever you can find that'll tell me which way someone went from the top end of Alphington Road.'

'I reckon one of your lot should be seconded down here permanently, the amount of work I do for you.'

'It's worth a tub of cherries if we track him down.'

'It's track him down now, not just see which way he went?'

'A large tub.' Pete knew how fond the little blond man was of glace cherries.

'You'll get me fat.'

Pete laughed. 'Way too late for that, mate. Might add an inch, but who's going to notice?'

'Ouch! I thought you wanted a favour.'

'Truth hurts but it's still the truth.'

'Well, all I can say is, what I've got's all bought and paid for, or at least legitimately earned.'

Pete heard the slap of his hand on his paunch over the phone line. 'I never doubted it, mate.'

'I suppose you want this miracle footage like yesterday?'

'Or before, if possible.'

Graham sighed heavily. 'No-one's got any patience anymore. Whatever happened to the relaxing pace of life the West-country used to be known for?'

'I blame the motorways,' Pete told him. 'Bringing all these in-comers down here.'

'Oi! I'm only from bloody Bath.'

'See what I mean?' Pete persisted with a grin. 'Damn near foreign. Call me when you've got something?'

Graham grunted. 'Don't know why I should, all these bloody insults.'

'You love it and you know it. Anyway, we're the ones who've got to sit through it all and stay awake.'

'You know how I feel, stuck in here every day, then.'

'It's not exactly Starsky and Hutch out here, you know. And you're safe and comfy while we're out there, facing down the dangers of life on the streets.'

Graham chuckled. 'You'll be putting on a New York accent next.'

'They were San Fransisco, weren't they? Or LA?'

'Who?'

'Starsky and Hutch.'

'Oh. Well, at least you ain't trying to be the Sweeney.'

'What, with their reputation lately? Not likely.'

'Yeah, I know what you mean. This is for that quiet op DI Underhill told me about, is it?'

'You think I'd be allowed to say if it was?'

'Right. OK, I get it. I'll see what I can find for you.'

'Cheers, bud.' Pete hung up and turned to Dick, beside him. 'All right. What did Ops Support bring us? Where should I start while he does that for us?'

'We've got footage from last night into this morning from several businesses on Cowick Street, including St Thomas pharmacy,' Dick replied. 'Plus the railway station, the tyre place you've just been looking at on Alphington Road and the one further out, past Queen's Road, the grocery shop across from Waterloo Road, a pedestrian crossing just north of that. There's also the primary school on School Road and umpteen doorbell cameras.'

'Did they say how many?'

'Fourteen,' Jane said. 'And you've got the two pharmacies, the pub and the little supermarket on the other side of Cowick Street as well. Then there's one on the Indian next to the church; the ink cartridge shop; the electrical shop; the hospice shop, believe it or not. That's all before you get to Cecil Road. Then there's a traffic camera on the crossing there; another private one on the estate agent's a few doors down from there; one at the bank on the other side of the road and another at the little post office across from it. Another traffic camera on the crossing between them, just before the railway bridge.'

'All right, all right,' Pete said, holding up his hands. 'I was only asking.'

Jane shrugged. 'And now you know. Eleven, plus two crossing cameras on the stretch of Cowick Street that we're interested in.'

'And fourteen doorbell cameras, five more business ones and another crossing,' Pete retorted. 'So thirty-three cameras in all. If we get nothing from that lot, I reckon we're looking for a ghost.'

'I didn't know you believed in them, boss,' Ben said.

'I don't.'

'So…'

'Let's find him.'

CHAPTER SEVEN

'Where've you been?' Jill demanded, looking up from her screen as the door of the incident room opened.

'It's rush-hour out there,' Dave said.

'And? You were on a bike.'

'And… How many fag-ends did you say I was looking for, boss?' he asked.

'Three,' Pete said as Dave approached the cluster of desks, his leathers exchanged once more for a charcoal three-piece with a black shirt, making him look like an Italian mobster.

'There were nine. Two of the guys in the MOT centre smoke. I had to persuade them both to give me swabs for elimination purposes. They didn't recognise our man except that they'd seen him there that morning. I dropped the whole lot off at Forensics. They'll be on it first thing, they said, and results should be through in thirty-six hours from then. So, what have you been achieving while I was out, Titch?' He nudged her in the back and dropped into his seat.

'We've been slogging through the grunt-work, if you must know. Somebody's got to and we're not getting any outside help.'

'What we have established with CCTV that Graham got hold of for us is that your smoking cyclist came from the city side of the twin bridges and went back over there after his meeting with Mrs Tranter,' Pete told him. 'We'll follow that up in the morning. I think it's probably best if we knock it on the head for the night pretty soon. You can only concentrate on this stuff for so long before you start missing things, regardless of training and practice.'

'So you get off light again, Dapper,' Jill said, giving Dave a dig with her elbow.

'God smiles on the righteous,' he said with a grin.

'And the Devil looks after his own,' she retorted.

'And you look closer to the latter in that get-up,' Dick added.

'Jealousy will get you nowhere, Grey Man,' Dave told him.

'Consistency is important in police-work,' Dick said, more than used to the nickname that resulted from his consistently grey attire, which matched his hair and even, to a degree, his smoking-toughened complexion.

'So's adaptability,' Dave shot back.

'And discipline,' Pete added. 'And the ability to concentrate.'

'I thought you were packing it in for the night,' Dave said, unrepentant.

'I said soon, not now.'

'Right. Anyone need caffeine before I knuckle down and rejoin the fray, then?'

*

Colin Underhill got up from behind his desk and started pacing as Pete closed the door behind him and stood just inside it.

The clock on the wall read 08:12.

'I don't know if it's because they don't trust us to do a decent job after what happened Sunday night,' the senior man said with a sideways glance at Pete. 'But the NCA and West Mids. arrested the gun buyer at six o'clock this morning, searched his place and confiscated the gun, along with two zombie knives and a flick-knife. They're interrogating him, but the plan is to release him on bail. He obviously wanted the gun for a reason – whether to use or to re-sell – so they're hoping he'll order a replacement again and we can track it better than we did last time. The order and the weapon.'

'Jesus! Already? What's the matter with giving us half a chance to track the bloke down?' Pete demanded.

'Things like this move fast,' Colin told him. 'There isn't time to hang around. He might have shifted it on, if that was the plan. Or used it.'

Pete sighed. Obviously, the DI was right, but it felt like they were being put under more pressure than was necessary, especially as it was being presented now as a fait accompli, without any prior consultation or even information that he was aware of. 'And how do they reckon we're going to track it?' he asked.

Colin smiled. 'That's up to us.'

Pete grunted. 'There's a surprise. To clear up their shit, you mean.'

Colin shrugged. 'Same as it ever was. But they've got to maintain the buyer's credibility with the maker, haven't they? And if they do that by blaming a dead man, he can't argue the toss.'

'I suppose,' Pete admitted. 'So, what now?'

'Keep doing what you're doing and we wait to hear from Birmingham. Where are you with it?'

'Snowed under with CCTV from Sunday night, Monday morning, and more to come from Graham, from the city centre, from the Wednesday morning when the SIM card was bought, to see if we can find where the cyclist who asked Mrs Tranter to buy it went and try to ID him. We could have his DNA tomorrow afternoon, but there's no guarantee he'll be in the database, of course.'

'Good chance, though, if our gunman runs true to form.'

'Hmm,' Pete agreed, tipping his head. 'We could do with finding out what his form *is* for finding couriers, though, before anything comes of the NCA's games up north. Shane Gallagher must have been a one-off, surely? Meeting him on the street like that.'

'Who knows?'

'Exactly. That's the trouble. But our man seems to be too careful to rely on a method as random as that.'

'So, why that time?'

Pete shrugged. 'Who knows?' he said, throwing Colin's own expression back at him. 'Urgency? An unexpected order? His usual man wasn't available?'

'All his orders would be unexpected, surely? He's not running a bakery or a garage.'

'Then how does he receive them?' Pete posed. 'He might get known about by word of mouth rather than advertising but potential customers have to contact him somehow.'

Colin's mouth pulled down. 'Dark web?'

'Hmm. I don't see how else. It's not like drugs, with dealers on the streets. Have the NCA got anything on that side of it?'

'Not that they've told me.'

'Should we ask? It could be useful to know. There can't be that many sources for illegal guns in this country. They're mostly imported, I'd have thought. Either with drugs or legal machine parts or something of the sort.'

Colin nodded slowly. 'Most come either direct from the States or from Eastern Europe. Turkey, Bulgaria, Albania, Romania. We only get thirty-odd shooting deaths a year in the UK for now, but that'll rise if guns get easier to get hold of. We need to keep a lid on the market somehow. Put this guy out of business and let it be known we're coming after anyone else involved in it – and coming hard.'

'Agreed. Which brings me back to the how and where of the marketing. If we can find that and set up a buy of our own, without risking letting a weapon get into criminal hands…'

Colin shook his head. 'The NCA say no. Blow it and you risk driving the offender underground, losing whatever contact network you've built.'

'So they do nothing?' Pete demanded.

'No. They pass the job off to the likes of us.'

'Yeah, without most of the information they've got. Tying our hands, setting us up for a fall while they sit back and moan about us when it happens.' Pete shook his head. 'All that achieves is to screw up our credibility and leave them sitting pretty in their offices in London and Brum.'

'Well, if you're that pissed off about it, get out there and do something. Throw it in their faces.'

'And let them take all the glory for our work.'

'I didn't think you were a glory-hound.'

'I'm not. But I do appreciate justice when I can find it. Legal and moral.'

Colin chuckled. 'What's the saying? Life's a bitch and then you die.'

Pete grunted.

'Go on. Get out of here and catch us a gun-maker. Or at least his courier, which gets us one step closer to him.'

'Right.'

*

'We're closing in,' Ben announced when Pete returned to the incident room. 'We've got him on Holloway Street, on the security camera on the Freedom Hall and the crossing camera just up from there, which shows him turning off up Roberts Road.'

'You've kept that quiet,' Jill accused.

'Now, now, kids,' Pete interjected, pulling out his chair.

'There's a nursery school up there,' Jill said. 'They might have security cameras.'

'Find out,' Pete told her. 'What else is up there?' He looked around the assembled team.

'Nothing much but a load of little old terraces,' Ben said.

'All right. Jill, it's over to you to find his direction then. Meantime, I'll check if we've got anyone who lives up there on the PNC.' He fired up his computer, went onto Google Maps and noted the street names that ran off from Roberts Road, then went into the Police National Computer system. Before he could start his search, Jill was putting down her desk phone.

'They've got two cameras facing across the front of the building,' she said. 'It's a council requirement, these days, for their licence.'

'Excellent. Off you go and fetch the footage, then.'

'Right.' Shutting down her computer, she got up to leave as Pete began his PNC search.

It didn't take him long to find four possible suspects living within the area accessed via Roberts Road. Only one of them, though, would pass the nursery school on his way home. The other three would turn off before reaching it. Still, the cyclist's presence or absence on the footage would add weight to the other evidence against him.

Not that the man had necessarily committed a crime, he reminded himself. But he was certainly involved in the preparations for one.

With four faces to look at, he brought up the first one. The subject looked like little more than a boy with short, dark hair. Give him a sweater and tie instead of the T-shirt he was wearing, he could have been looking at a school photo instead of a mugshot, Pete thought. His description put him at five-foot-five. Too short to be the cyclist.

Pete moved on, calling up the next name on his short list.

'Hello,' he said as the file opened on his screen.

'What?' asked Dick from beside him. 'Oh. He looks familiar.'

'Doesn't he?' Pete agreed.

Lean and lanky – a quick glance down at his stats showed he was five-foot-ten – with stringy hair that was dyed blond, the mugshot looked just like the less-than-clear image they'd got from the MOT centre footage.

'And his record shows a list of suspected thefts, burglaries and minor drug possessions going back to when he was fourteen, though no actual charges, somehow. So, Dale Gordon, you're definitely on the list. I'd best check the remaining candidates, just in case.'

The last two names on the list, including the one who lived beyond the nursery school, were quickly discounted by their descriptions and Pete picked up his radio. Keying the mike, he said, 'DS Gayle for PC Evans. DS Gayle for PC Evans.'

'PC Evans. What's up, boss?'

'Are you there yet, Jill?'

'Not even half-way.'

'Carry on as you were, then. Dave and I are on the way to join you after you've collected the CCTV. We've got a target address.'

'Yes?'

'Franklin Street.'

'He won't have passed the nursery, then.'

'No, but that fact itself is evidence that he's our man.'

'OK.'

'See you soon.' He switched off his computer and stood up. 'Come on, Dapper. We're up.'

*

'He's not here.'

She stood belligerently in the door of the little terraced house, arms folded across the front of her yellow vest top, dyed blonde hair tied back in a ponytail that Pete imagined was meant to make her look younger than her mid-forties age. It didn't.

'Since when? What time did he leave?'

'I dunno. I'm not his keeper.'

'Well, technically no, now he's over twenty-one, but you are his mother. And it is your house.' He sighed. 'Look, we're not here to arrest him. We just need to talk to him, that's all. Ask him a few questions.'

'And what if he don't want to answer them?'

Pete pursed his lips. 'Let's cross that bridge when we come to it, eh? It's not going to do him any harm to talk to us. It's not about his business. We're looking for information on an associate of his.'

'Associate?' she asked with a sneer. 'He ain't a bloody business executive.'

'And here I thought he was self-employed,' Pete said with a grin. 'All right. It may be a friend; it may just be someone he met on the street. We don't know. Yet. But either way, this person is trouble. Associating with him could put your son in danger, Mrs Gordon. Serious danger.'

'He can look after hisself. And I ain't Mrs. I raised Dale on my own.'

Pete tipped his head. He knew from Dale's police file that her name was Cathy, and there was no entry in the file for Dale's father. 'Then you'll value his life. Another associate of the person we're talking about was killed a couple of days ago.'

'Yeah, right,' she sneered.

'It's true. We knew the victim.' Pete glanced at Jill, standing beside him outside the woman's front door, which opened directly onto the pavement. 'In fact, I attended the scene.'

'And what makes you think this bloke killed him?'

'It's who he was going to meet.'

'And my Dale knows him? Deals with him?'

Pete shook his head. 'Not as a customer, as far as we know. Although the victim, the other night, was in the same business as Dale.'

'Well, who is this bloke? I can warn him off.'

Pete grimaced. 'We can't divulge that, Ms Gordon. But we do need to talk to Dale as soon as possible.'

'Can't divulge? You'd rather leave him out there, in danger, than break some petty rule?'

'Rules and laws are what hold society together. Without them, there'd be anarchy. Chaos.'

'Huh! Nothing wrong, as I can see, with a bit of anarchy. Bloody need it, the shambles we've got for a bloody government these days.'

'We're not here to discuss politics, Ms Gordon. We're here to speak to your son. How long's he been out and when's he likely to be back?'

'He left about an hour ago. Be back for his lunch, I expect. Usually is.'

'Any idea where he went?'

She shrugged.

Pete's radio hissed and Dave's voice came urgently over it. 'Boss, he's doing one. South on Roberts.'

Pete reached for his radio but Jill was quicker as it was on the outside of her uniform.

'Received,' she said.

'If you can get hold of him tell him to come and see us. Urgently,' he snapped to the woman in the doorway. 'I'm DS Pete Gayle.' He turned away before she could respond. 'Let's go,' he said to Jill.

He ran across and down the hill towards his car, using the remote to unlock it as he approached. By the time he'd got the engine started, Jill was jumping into the other side. He screeched away, hitting the blues and twos. Sirens echoed loudly off the close-packed houses around them as he sped away, slowing for the junction then accelerating again, leaving Dave standing at the next junction down. Understanding why, Dave raised an arm to point. Dale had turned right onto Topsham Road, across the traffic. Risky, on a bike and in a hurry, but at least it was down-hill, Pete thought as he braked for the junction and pulled out.

There was no sign of Dale Gordon or anyone else on a bike.

He left Jill to glance left up a footpath into the rear carpark of a block of flats and slowed again for the crossroads in the dip beyond. Glanced right while Jill looked left but, again, there was no sign of their man. Had he gone straight on up the slope onto Holloway Street?

Pete went for it. At the top of the short slope another road led off to the left. It immediately curved right to run parallel with Holloway Street but, just on the curve was another left turn. With no cyclist in sight ahead of them, Pete took the junction. Still no cyclist ahead of them. He took the left again. Just yards ahead, an alleyway led off to the right. He kept his speed down so he could glance up it.

'There he is, boss,' Jill said, pointing straight ahead.

Pete gunned the engine. Past the alleyway entrance, where the road they were on bent left, it ran straight for a stretch past cream-rendered houses down to a little nameless square where several narrow old streets met. Pete could see a figure, pedalling furiously, approaching the square. He gunned the engine, speeding after him. They were into a maze of tiny streets here, little more than one car wide, that twisted around each other, meeting hither and thither, some of them dead ends perhaps connected by footpaths. A lad who knew the area could end up anywhere with the advantage of two wheels over four.

Pete shed his seatbelt, anticipating the need for a quick exit from the car.

'Dave, we're on Melbourne Place,' Jill said into her radio. 'Heading for Colleton.'

Short for Colleton Crescent and several of the little streets and alleys that surrounded them now, Pete knew.

Ahead, the cyclist rose up off his seat, legs stilling for a moment as he hit the square.

'Colleton Hill,' Jill reported over the radio as Pete accelerated again, sirens echoing loud off the enclosing buildings.

Cars were parked down one side of the narrow lane, in front of more pastel-painted houses on the left, across from a stone wall that fronted a long public garden that overlooked the quay and the river.

'On route,' Dave responded over the radio. 'But I'm on foot.'

'Tell him to come up Melbourne Street,' Pete said. 'Might catch him doing a loop.'

With a nod, Jill keyed her radio mike again. 'Dave, come up Mel...' She stopped as, with the noisy car closing rapidly on him, the fleeing cyclist made a hard left turn partway down the hill – or tried to. As he leaned into it, the bike's tyres slid out from under him. It crashed noisily into the white-rendered side wall of the house on the far side of the alleyway he was trying for, dumping him in a rolling tangle of flying limbs on the tarmac.

Pete braked hard, stopping the car. Uncaring that he was blocking the road, he was out and running around the bonnet as Dale Gordon scrambled to his feet and took off running in the direction he'd been aiming for on the bike, which lay now in a tangle of buckled rims and randomly thrusting spokes.

Feet slapping on the concrete, Pete was after him.

Behind him, he heard Jill's voice. 'Melbourne Street,' she shouted into her radio. 'He's left again into Colleton Grove.'

Down between the two white-rendered old houses, they were quickly surrounded by high brick walls. Gordon ran to the left, Pete following past a pair of modern mews houses, their lower halves bare brick, upper halves rendered off-white in an attempt to blend with their surroundings. Past them, Gordon turned left again, following the little road back up towards the square they'd crossed just moments before.

Pete could hear Jill's shoes slapping the tarmac only three or four paces behind him. He put on a further spurt, pounding up the hill after the younger man, glad that he wasn't wearing full uniform with all the heavy accoutrements that involved.

'Dale,' he shouted. 'Stop. We just need to talk. No arrest involved.'

Gordon glanced over his shoulder. 'Yeah, right.'

Pete's lungs were beginning to burn from the steep hills as Gordon broke out into the square just twenty yards in front of him. Twenty yards could as well have been fifty, though, as Gordon surged away, now on level ground and wearing trainers and tracksuit against Pete's suit and formal shoes as well as the age difference between them.

But Pete wasn't one to give up. With the slope decreasing under his feet, he surged on.

Gordon went straight across the square, focussed on speed rather than agility, into Colleton Crescent.

Pete reached into his pocket for his car key. 'Jill, fetch the car,' he called and tossed the key high into the air and slightly backward.

'Jesus!' she squawked. He heard her pace change. 'Got it.'

He gave a puff of relief. The prospect of a smashed key-fob on the tarmac wasn't one he'd relished, but they had to catch the lad somehow.

He ran now under an arch of trees, between stone walls – the grounds of a big house on his right, the public garden to his left. From behind, he heard a short spurt of sirens as Jill started the car then the whir of rapid reversing.

Around the curve, the wall on his left lowered to shin height, topped now by black iron railings, and the trees gave way to open sky, grass stretching down towards the steep cliff-like escarpment above the quayside.

Pete recalled the last time he'd been along here, several years before, on another case, but there wasn't time to dwell. He could hear Gordon's panting now over his own but somehow, despite the spill from his bike, he kept going.

'Give it up, Dale. There's no point,' he called and heard a car engine behind him. He quickly moved across to the pavement on his right.

Gordon didn't respond. Just kept running, though he was starting to slow.

Pete gained another yard on him, then another. His unmarked silver Ford passed him. The horn tooted quickly. Instinctively, Gordon moved over, though staying on the left, where there was no pavement. Jill passed him. Then, closer to the Georgian Crescent itself, with cars parked along both sides of the road, she pulled over, nose-in, tight behind a parked SUV, cutting him off so he'd have to go around. But she was out of the car and heading him off before he could adjust his trajectory.

'Police. Stop,' she shouted.

But Gordon didn't. He put his head down and charged the diminutive constable.

Jill was no fool, though. She used her agility to side-step, grabbing his arm and sticking her foot out to tangle with his as she swung him around her and into the side of the Ford.

His balance gone and too exhausted to resist, his knees failed under him and he ended up kneeling, his face and chest pressed against the rear door of the car as Jill pulled his arm up behind him and snapped on the cuffs. Pushing him to the floor, she cuffed his other hand while kneeling on his back.

'Dale Gordon, you're detained for questioning in relation to the murder of Shane Gallagher,' she told him as Pete stopped at the rear of the car, one hand resting on the boot as he leaned over, panting hard. 'You do not have to say anything but it may harm your defence if you do not mention when questioned something which you later rely on in Court. Anything you do say may be given in evidence. Now, get up.'

She stood up off him and hauled him to a sitting position.

'I thought you said you didn't want to arrest me,' he said, looking up at Pete.

Pete took a breath. 'I didn't. But you didn't leave us a lot of choice, did you?'

CHAPTER EIGHT

Pete stepped up to the side of the car and opened the rear passenger door. 'Come on. In you get.'

'What, you're taking me to the nick? What about my bike?' he demanded as Jill helped him to his feet.

'You should have thought about that ten minutes ago, before you took off on it. And I can't see anyone nicking it now, can you, bearing in mind the condition it's in?'

'That's a valuable bike, that is.' He stepped around the open car door with Jill's hand clutching the cuffs at his back.

'Was,' Pete corrected. 'Now, it's not much more than a pile of junk. 'We could charge you with littering, now I think of it, for leaving it there on the street. Hazard to road users.'

What happened to not wanting to arrest me?' he complained.

'You did. Fleeing from officers.'

'You never identified yourselves. Could have been anyone.'

Pete shook his head. 'You were seen from down the street, Dale. You saw PC Evans' uniform and turned round and ran as if you wanted to hide something from us. Maybe we ought to search you, while we're at it. For our safety, if nothing else.'

'On what grounds?'

'Reasonable suspicion under PACE that you may be in possession of illegal items or substances. In fact, given the circumstances, and that you're about to enter a police vehicle, there's no maybe about it. We should. You haven't got anything to hide, have you, Dale? Anything sharp, for instance, that might harm either you or me as I search you?'

'No. Look, what is this? First you don't want to arrest me, then you do. What's it about, eh? What am I supposed to have done?'

'It's what we know you've done, Dale. You're on Candid Camera doing it.'

'Weren't me. Could have been anyone who looks a bit like me. I ain't unique.'

Pete shook his head. 'It's you, Dale, and any jury will see that, if it comes to it. But the point is, we didn't want to charge you with anything. Not unless it turns out you were deeper into the situation than it looks. You were just going to be a helpful witness.'

Jill chuckled. 'That'd be a new experience for you, wouldn't it, Dale?'

He turned to sneer at her. 'Yeah, funny. What situation?' he asked, returning his attention to Pete.

Pete stepped forward. 'Don't move.' He patted him down quickly and, finding nothing amiss, nodded to the car. 'Get in. We'll talk about it.'

Gordon complied and Jill shut the door on him and moved around to the far side of the car while Pete opened the driver's door and climbed in. Starting the engine, Pete parked the car more neatly so that it didn't block the road. Then he switched it off and turned in his seat to face the younger man, who had visibly relaxed when he saw what was happening.

'Ah. Our colleague's about to join us,' Pete said, seeing Dave approaching through the rear window.

'Another one? How many does it take for little old me?'

'Depends if you're likely to run or not, Dale.' Pete buzzed down his side window. 'Hop in, DC Miles,' he called.

Dave reached the car and complied, closing the door and pulling his seatbelt across. 'Ready when you are, boss.'

'OK. So, Dale, a week last Wednesday, you were down Alphington Road, outside the MOT centre by the railway bridge, killing time and smoking cigarettes. DC Miles collected them, so DNA will confirm what was seen on CCTV and described by witnesses.'

He frowned, saying nothing.

'While you were there, you spoke to an old lady, who you gave some money to, to purchase a SIM card for a mobile phone. Which she duly did, and returned it to you.'

'So? Nothing illegal in that.'

'True.' Pete dipped his head, accepting the point. 'So you won't mind telling us who you were purchasing it for, will you?'

'Me.'

'You?'

'Yeah. I wanted it.'

Pete pressed his lips together. 'Well, now, that's where you get into some serious trouble, Dale. Because that SIM card and the phone it was inserted into, were used in the commission of a crime. A murder, in fact.'

'Eh?' Gordon interrupted.

Pete went on, ignoring him. 'To entice the victim into the offender's reach. So either you're a cold-blooded killer or you're associating with one and protecting him. Which is it?'

'Murder?' Gordon demanded. 'Are you taking the piss? No way. I'm no bloody murderer.'

'Then, who did you pass that SIM card on to?'

'What, and you go pick him up and tell him I said so? No, thanks, mate.'

Pete shook his head. 'Not the way it works, Dale. We don't divulge information like that.'

'Maybe, but he can put two and two together and guess where it came from, can't he?'

'Not from anything we'll say to him, no. And if we've got enough evidence to hold him, it won't make a difference anyway, will it? He can't reach out and grab you from inside a prison cell.'

'Can't he?'

Pete sighed. 'He might be a bad bugger, Dale, but he's not supernatural. If he's inside, you're safe as houses.'

'That's a bloody big if to hang my life on.'

'What makes you think he'd come after you anyway?'

'You just said he killed somebody, didn't you?'

'Yes, but...'

'So, what's to stop him doing it again? In for a penny. He gets done for one, you can't give him two life sentences, can you? He's only got one life.'

Pete gave a brief smile. 'A bit of an oversimplified view, Dale, but I get your point. Mine is that, with your help, he'll get the full term and you'll be safe. If you don't help, then chances are our boss will want to make an example and you'll go down too, for conspiracy. In which case, you'll be in there potentially with him. And revenge isn't something the prison system can guarantee to protect you from, once you're in there.'

'So, I've got to stay out and be a good boy, is that it?'

Pete shrugged. 'You put yourself into this situation, Dale. I didn't.'

'But you're making the bloody most of it.'

Pete tipped his head, his lips pushing upward. 'I'm just playing the cards I'm dealt, Dale. You're the one that dealt them.'

'So, who is he?' Dave asked from beside the handcuffed youth.

Gordon shrugged. 'Dunno. And that's the truth. Not his name, anyhow.'

'So, what do you know?' Dave demanded. 'Bearing in mind that the sooner we catch him, the safer you'll be.'

'Eh? What's... Shit.' He looked distinctly worried now. 'Look, man, I can't... I need protection. And my mum.'

'From who?' asked Dave.

'Whom,' Jill corrected with an arched eyebrow.

'I don't give a shit about vocabulary. I want safety,' Gordon declared.

'Then tell us what we need to achieve it for you,' Pete urged. 'Whatever you can about this man.'

'There isn't much. I met him on the street. It was dark. No streetlights where I... Anyway, he was wearing a Covid mask and dark glasses, had a hoodie on, pulled up tight. You could tell he was white, but that was only from his voice. He had gloves on, too. Like surgical ones. Light blue, you know?'

'So, what about his voice?' Pete asked. 'What did he sound like, apart from white? Posh? Local? From away? What?'

'Hard to tell. Not posh, but no accent as such. Just ordinary.'

'So, he approached you on the street. Where was this?'

He grinned. 'By the old cop-shop.'

'Heavitree Road?' Dave demanded.

Gordon nodded.

'Cheeky sod.'

He shrugged. 'It's all boarded up, innit? No lights or nothing, back from the road a bit. Perfect.' He grimaced. 'Was. Expect you'll be keeping an eye on it now, won't you?'

Dave shook his head. 'Not us, matey. We're CID. Serious crimes. We don't piddle about with the likes of you.'

'Oh, thanks.'

'When did he approach you?' Pete asked.

'Night before. Tuesday.'

'What time?'

He shrugged. 'I don't clock-watch, mate. I just do what I got to do and clear off.'

'But you must know roughly. After dark, for a start. By how much?'

Another shrug. 'Hour or so, maybe. Like I said – I dunno. I don't wear a watch, do I?'

'How old was he? Roughly.'

'I dunno. I told you: I could hardly see anything of him. He was all covered up.'

'But you must have got an impression. From his voice, the way he moved and so on.'

He grimaced. 'Older than me. And you, prob'ly. Fifties, maybe? I dunno.'

Pete rocked his head from side to side. 'OK. What colour hoodie was he wearing?'

Gordon's gaze switched back to him. 'Hard to tell. Grey, mebbe. Blue.' He shrugged.

'But not black or red, for instance?'

'No.'

'And plain. No logo or stripes, anything like that?'

'No.'

'What else was he wearing? Jeans? Joggers? Chinos?'

'Jeans and trainers. But cheap ones, not fancy. Plain.'

'What about the hand-off?' Dave asked. 'How did that go down and when?'

'Same. Next night, he turned up, same sort of time, dressed the same as the night before except he had one of those black cloth Covid masks instead of the cheap blue ones on. Took the SIM and off he went.'

'Which way?'

'Towards town.'

'Why didn't you fetch the SIM yourself?' Pete asked.

'I thought about it. But he'd said to get someone else to do it and, for one thing, I wasn't going to cross him. And for another, I reckoned, if he wanted to get hold of it undercover like that, he was bound to be up to no good in some way and I didn't want to get tied up in that. I've got enough going on without his shit, whatever it is.'

'So, how did you come by Mrs Tranter for the job?' Jill asked.

'I'd seen her there before with her Tesco bag. She goes regular. Don't know why. I think she just likes the trip out, as much as anything. I thought, nice old lady, she'd do me a favour if it didn't cost her anything. So…' He shrugged.

'What takes you down Alphington Road at that time of the morning, to have seen her before?' Dave asked. 'Lad like you'd normally be in bed till way after that if you're not at work or college or on the way to the dole office.'

'I did work, as it happens. Got laid off, didn't I? Covid. Had to make some money somehow while everything was shut down, so I found another career.'

'You worked where?' Dave demanded.

'At the bakery next to the MOT place. So I ain't a stranger to early mornings. Used to see the old dear stood out there, waiting for the bus.'

'You said you weren't going to cross him – the man in the mask,' Pete said. 'Why not?'

Gordon fixed him with a wide-eyed stare. 'Cause he was fucking scary, that's why. You deal with some bad buggers in what I do, but he's on another level.'

'How?' Dave asked.

'People make threats all the time, but it's generally just talk. Bluster. With him, it wasn't. You could tell he was serious. He'd do it, and he'd enjoy doing it. It was like… You could hear it in his voice. And he knew where I live.'

'What did he say?' Pete asked.

'He…' He hesitated. 'He said, if I crossed him, he'd come round to Franklin Street and visit my mum. And my sister.' He swallowed. 'Said mum obviously had an iron. That he'd set it on high and hold it to their faces until they… Until they sizzled like bacon in a pan.' His voice got thicker with the horror of what he was saying.

'Jesus,' Jill breathed.

'And all for a two or three quid SIM card,' Dave said.

They knew from his PNC file that he had an eleven-year-old sister who attended the school just a few hundred yards further along Topsham Road from where they lived.

Pete nodded. 'All right, Dale. We'll check on all this. If you're lying to us – about anything – we'll be back for you. We know where you live, too. And we know who your friends are, as well. We'll find you and have you in. So, are you sure you've told us everything you can about this male?'

'Yeah.'

'And that everything you've told us is true?'

'Yeah.'

'OK. Jill, let him out, will you?'

'Hey, what about my protection? Now I've talked, he'll...'

'How's he going to know that?' Dave broke in.

'Can you see anyone round here, watching us?' Pete added.

'No, but...'

'There you go, then. You're as safe now as you were an hour ago.'

'And what about my bike?'

'You'd best take it home and fix it, hadn't you?'

'How'm I supposed to do that with the wheels all fucked up?'

'Phone a friend?' Dave suggested.

'Funny sod.'

Dave gave him a quick grin. 'I try.'

Jill opened the door for him and Gordon stepped out.

'Keep trying. You might make it one day,' he said to Dave and turned around for Jill to take the cuffs off his wrists.

'Remember, Dale,' Pete called. 'Stay out of trouble and you stay out of danger.'

'Yeah, right. Cheers for nothing.'

Jill pushed the rear door shut behind him and Gordon set off back the way he'd come along the street, crossing to the pavement this time.

'So, what have we gained from all that?' Dave demanded as Pete started the car.

'Well, you're a little bit fitter than you were,' Jill told him.

'And we've confirmed that, if Dale was telling the truth, our man knows more than the average person about where to procure drugs in the city,' Pete added. 'And he's probably old enough to know better.'

'And where he was a week last Tuesday night,' Jill added. 'And Wednesday night. We might even be able to pick him up on the cameras.'

CHAPTER NINE

'Hello. How's it going?' Pete closed the door on the semi-darkened room with its bank of screens covering most of one wall.

'Busy-busy, as usual. What's up?' Graham spoke without turning away from the screen he was concentrating on.

'I thought I'd best come down here and do my own scouting for a change, instead of leaving it all to you,' Pete said.

That made the rotund CCTV operator turn around, his too-long curly blond hair gleaming like a 1970s halo in the light from the screens behind him. 'Eh? You ill or what?'

'Well, that's nice. Here I am trying to do you a favour…'

'Yeah, right. Trying not to ask me for yet another one, you mean. How come? You haven't suddenly grown a conscience, have you?' he asked with one eyebrow arched behind the rims of his glasses.

'Don't be silly. What would I want with one of those?' Pete countered. 'Especially in your case.'

'Well, what else am I supposed to think? That you don't trust me, now you've gone all covert and secretive?'

'Hey, that's not our choice. Orders. And you're on the inside, so what's your problem?'

'Overcrowding. You could have sent young PC Evans down here instead. She's a site smaller and I enjoy winding her up.'

'You be careful you don't over-wind her,' Pete cautioned. 'One of these days, her spring will break and she'll snap you in two like a dead twig.'

Graham laughed. 'I know when it's getting too dangerous to carry on,' he said. 'Years of practice.'

'Be careful, that's all I'm saying,' Pete warned. 'I was with her this morning when she got hold of a young lad who'd pissed her off just a tiny bit. She might be little, but she knows how to hurt a bloke.'

Graham grimaced. 'So, what are you after, anyway?'

'Footage from around the old nick, a week last Tuesday and Wednesday nights, to start with.'

'What, they had some break-ins or something? I hadn't heard anything.'

Pete ignored the dig. 'It's being used by the local dealers, now there's no lights or security anymore. Good spot for them. Out of the way, but still handy. And our suspect was there on both occasions, apparently. I need to confirm that, get an image of him if I can and try to find out where he came from and went to from there. See if I can identify a vehicle or anything else that might lead to his name.'

'How come you're doing it, not one of your minions?'

'They're all still busy with what Ops Support brought us from Sunday night. There's a lot to get through. This is a side-line that might let us off that particular hook if we're lucky.'

'Well, obviously, our cameras on the building aren't working anymore, but there's still the traffic light cameras at the end of College Road. Crossing cameras at the end of Denmark Road. The leisure centre's got 'em, just past there. And there's traffic cameras on the roundabout on Western Way.'

'I'll take whatever I can get,' Pete said. 'Can we access any of it direct from here?'

'Yeah, if I want to. I can patch in direct to all the council ones from here, now the new system's up and running.'

Pete's eyes widened. 'You never told me that before.'

'You never asked. And I don't want to make it seem easy, do I? You'll take advantage, else.' Again, he took his eyes from his screens and turned to face Pete. 'And don't you go spreading it around, either.'

'As if I would,' Pete said, wide-eyed with false innocence.

Graham grunted. 'Park your arse over there and I'll bring something up for you.' He nodded to a spare chair at the side of the room where a desk held a single screen that was currently dark. 'Twelfth and thirteenth, you said?'

'Yes.'

'Evening?'

'From let's say 21:00 hours.'

'You'll have twenty or twenty-two and be happy with it.'

'All right. Twenty it is. I'll plough through. Are those traffic cameras on constant or red-light-activated?' Pete asked, taking the offered seat.

'They vary. And some can be switched manually from one to t'other when we want to monitor something.'

'But the two we're talking about…'

'Up the road, by the college, is on constant because of the kids. The one at Denmark is just for the crossing, so it's red-light-activated. But the leisure centre ones are on full-time and so are the ones at the roundabout.'

'Right.'

'You'll want to work outward from the nick, I suppose?'

'Might as well.'

Graham started typing on his keyboard. He hit return with a flourish and said, 'There you go. Fire up the screen and it's ready when you are.'

'Thanks, bud.' Pete turned to the desk, powered up the screen, settled the keyboard comfortably and reached for the mouse.

*

'Anything?' Pete asked, stepping back into the incident room nearly two hours later.

'Not a sausage,' Dick replied. 'You?'

'The same. It's like he disappears. Walks away from the old nick and into the ether. All we know is, he went downhill, towards town. But he didn't get as far as the leisure centre.'

'So, he must have gone up Denmark or Clifton, 'cause Higher Summerlands is a dead-end,' Ben said. All there is up there is a few garages and the back end of Saint Matt's.'

'Doesn't mean he didn't go up there,' Dick said. 'Kip for a few hours and drive away in the morning. Same as he must have round by Prince's Square.'

'So, we need to look for cars that match between the entrances of Higher Summerlands and Clifton Roads on the mornings of the twelfth and thirteenth and the routes out of Prince's Square on Monday morning,' said Jill.

'Yeah,' Dave chuckled. 'Good luck with that, Titch. How many weeks have we got?'

'None,' Pete told him. 'What we have got is West Midlands and the National Crime Agency already pushing our quarry into making another deal.'

'How?' Dave demanded.

'By taking the last weapon off the gang-member who bought it so he'll want to replace it ASAP. They hope.'

'And from the same source. They hope,' Jane said.

Pete nodded. 'Exactly.'

'And if not?'

'We're royally screwed.'

'Which they'll say is our fault for losing Gallagher.'

'Yup,' he agreed.

'Surely, this is a job we could farm out, though,' Ben suggested. 'I mean, all they're looking to do is match one vehicle – or pedestrian – with another. They don't need the context.'

Pete tipped his head. 'I can try.'

'You're assuming he came out of Clifton or HS,' Dick said. 'What if he went another way? There's plenty of possibilities, especially starting out on foot. He could have gone up Denmark and down onto Magdalen or along Barnfield. Or out the back along Clifton. Endless possibilities from up there.'

'You're right,' Pete admitted. 'Except for Denmark Road. He'd have been picked up on the Leisure Centre cameras if he'd gone up there. But we've got to start somewhere and Heavitree Road is as good a place as any. In fact, the place to start is with a list of vehicles and pedestrians coming out of the Prince's Square area Sunday night into Monday morning. A complete list with images so we've got something to compare the Heavitree Road data with. Then identify and eliminate all those we can. What's left is what we'll need to compare new data with. So everyone start on that and I'll go and try again with the guvnor for some help with it all.' He pushed his chair back to get up.

'There'll be hundreds. Literally,' Jill protested.

'Thousands, if you include the connection through to Cowick Lane,' Dick said.

'You can't get across to there with a car,' Jane pointed out.

'But you can on foot or with a bike. He could easily stick a folding one in the back of an SUV. It'd only take a few seconds.'

The whole idea was a daunting prospect, Pete admitted to himself, but it had to be done 'So, the sooner you start looking for him, the sooner you'll finish,' he said. 'I'll be back and join in as soon as I can.'

*

'So he likes to use small-time drug dealers he's picked up off the street as couriers and intermediaries,' Colin said a few minutes later with Pete settled into the spare chair in his office.

Pete nodded.

'And he does his research on them before approaching them.'

'So it seems. He knew about Gordon's mum and sister.'

'How? Did he follow the lad home and pick up information by watching or did he ask the neighbours or Gordon's clients? Or suppliers?'

'Long-term observation wouldn't be easy,' Pete said. 'It's a narrow street of old terraced houses with no front gardens. They open directly onto the pavement.'

'He could sit in a car.'

'And questioning the neighbours could get back to Dale. Or to his mother.'

'So? He's not going to introduce himself as the local gun dealer, is he? Might even claim to be one of us. CID. Making enquiries.'

'I can't see Dale telling his life-story to his clients. He'd want to keep them as far away as possible from his family, in case one of them got greedy and got ideas about not paying their dues.'

'Depends how long he's been dealing. Or how long the clients have known him. He's not that old. He might have got started, small-time, at school. A lot of them do.'

Pete tipped his head. 'True. He's certainly been getting into trouble since then. Or it could have come from his supplier. They're in a position of power over him. Could ask questions and expect to get answers. Maybe our gunman's got links to them?'

'He might have.'

'Even if he's no longer part of that picture, he could still have connections. People he could call on.'

'So, how do we find out which it is?'

Pete drew a breath. 'We can start by asking the neighbours. Even Dale and his mum. She wasn't exactly helpful last time we spoke to her, but you never know until you try.'

'That'll tell you if he took the direct approach. But if not?'

Pete grimaced. 'We can call on our CIs, find out if anyone's been asking around about street dealers in general or for information on specific ones. If that doesn't pan out, then we'll need to talk to clients and suppliers. But how? Dale's not going to tell us who his supplier is, that's for sure.'

'Not if he's got any sense,' Colin agreed.

'So... Dale could do it for us, if he's willing. Which I'm sure he would be, if I put it to him the right way. He's already scared of the gun-maker.'

Colin nodded. 'Get Gallagher to find out if anyone's been asking around after him to start with. Meantime, ask his neighbours and his mum if anyone's been snooping around there, asking questions or sitting in a car that doesn't belong up there.'

'OK. We can do that. What we can't do in anything like the timescale needed is track down the gunman from the two locations and three times when we know where he was. We need help, collating data.'

'I've already said: this op's got to stay on the down-low,' Colin grunted.

'I know, but they don't have to know why they're looking: just what they're looking for,' Pete argued. 'We've got the locations. We know the routes in and out. It's just a matter of matching a pedestrian, a cyclist or a vehicle from one to the other within the known timeframes. Anyone can contribute to that without having to know why. The assumption would be that it's because of Shane Gallagher's murder. If we leave it at that...' He shrugged. 'There's literally thousands of houses in the area around Prince's Square and multiple exit-points. The same for the old nick. My team could do it, but it would take weeks and we haven't got weeks if West Mids. have already gone off half-cocked with the buyer.'

'They have,' Colin confirmed. 'They bugged his phone and more – they didn't go into details – and let him go an hour or so ago.'

Pete's lips tightened at the phrase, "They didn't go into details." It was not a good feeling, not being trusted by colleagues, even from a different force. He could see the logic from their point of view, but even so... He sighed. 'So we need to get this gun maker identified as soon as we can. And, apart from through Dale and Shane, I can't see how we're going to do that before he makes another weapon to put out onto the streets. Doing it through them is bad enough, but just by going through the CCTV just isn't going to happen fast enough without help. If we could concentrate on questioning Dale Gordon, his mum and his and Shane's neighbours, that'd either give us a next step or eliminate the possibility while a team of people plough through the CCTV, making lists… If they do it digitally: then they can be compared automatically. That'd only take seconds to find any matches.'

'They'd need the incident room to do it in,' Colin argued. 'And they can't be allowed to see what you're up to.'

'So we move out and take the stuff off the white boards with us. We'd need it anyway.'

'To where? The other incident rooms are occupied and I can't have you back in the squad room.'

'Then we go somewhere else. Set up an incident room off-site. It still happens for more distant cases. Used to for us, if it was appropriate. The RAF cadets hut along the road from Gallagher's for instance. I don't know which days they use it, but it'd be easy to find out and borrow it while they're not in residence.'

'Mondays and Thursdays,' Colin said.

'What – the cadets meet?'

Colin nodded. 'I checked before setting up the surveillance on Gallagher.'

'It's Tuesday today, so if it can be arranged, we'd have today to move, tomorrow to use it, and clear out Thursday. It's not ideal, but if we can get Dale on-board, that leaves us a day's work with the two sets of neighbours. Going through all that CCTV will take a lot longer than that, bearing in mind that people go out to work at different times, so we've got no definable cut-off time. By the time they've paused the footage to make a note of each sighting, with the best will in the world, they're not going to be any quicker than real-time getting through it, are they?'

'So twelve hours per camera, midnight to noon.'

Pete nodded.

'And how many cameras?'

'Thirty-three.'

'For a team of twelve, that's a week's work.'

'Exactly.' *And there's only six of us.*

Colin grunted. 'I'll see what I can do. Leave it with me.'

CHAPTER TEN

'Ms Gordon.'

'You again?' She leaned with one hand high on the doorframe, hiking up one side of the striped halter top she was wearing with navy shorts to show her midriff.

'Me again. I need another word with Dale. And this time, I'll need to talk to you, too.'

'I'd have thought you'd seen enough of him this morning.'

'You know what he does to earn his money, don't you?'

Her lip curled. 'I'm not talking about that.' She cocked her hip to one side, emphasising the curvature of her body.

'And I'm not interested in it, any further than it's going to help with my enquiries. You may not have noticed, but I'm not in uniform.'

'So?'

'So, I don't care about a bit of weed or a bit of blow. I deal with serious crimes. Rapes and murders. Missing people. Things like that.'

She frowned. 'What's any of that got to do with my Dale? He's not a rapist or a killer.'

'No, but in his line of business, he meets them. Can't help it.'

'Well, he ain't no grass.'

'I haven't asked him to be. And I'm not going to.'

'So, what d'you want to talk to him for?'

'For his safety. And yours and your daughter's.'

'What? Are you…?' She stood upright, shoulders rising as defensive anger drew her neatly defined brows closer.

'I'm not threatening you,' Pete said. 'Maybe Dale ought to explain. Where is he?'

She stood back from the door and turned towards the stairs. 'Dale!' she shouted. 'Get down here.'

'What?' a muffled male voice came from upstairs.

'You got a visitor.'

'Who?'

'Come and find out.'

Glancing at Pete, she tipped her head for him to enter.

He stepped straight into a small front room set with a dark three-piece suite, coffee tables and a TV that was too large for the room above a gas fire that looked like it came straight out of the 1970s.

Footsteps thundered on the stairs behind a wall that divided the lower floor in half, front from back, and Dale appeared around the corner. His expression and his shoulders slumped at the sight of Pete.

'Oh, it's you. What do you want now?'

'Your help, Dale. But first, one of us needs to explain the situation to your mum. Do you want to do that, or should I?'

He looked warily from Pete to his mother and back. She was a good six or seven inches shorter than he was, but he was clearly under her thumb.

Which was as it should be, Pete reflected.

Dale looked back to his mother, who was standing now in the middle of the room with her arms folded. He sighed. 'I did a job for a bloke the other week,' he said. 'Nothing illegal. Just got him a SIM card for his phone, that's all. Thing is, he's a bad bast... Bugger. And he knows where we live.'

'What? How could you be that bloody stupid?' she demanded.

'*I* didn't tell him. He knew before I even met him. And he... Threatened you and Becks if I screwed him over or talked to his lot,' he said with a nod towards Pete.

'But you didn't, did you?'

'No, but...' He looked scared and confused, his gaze flicking one way then another.

'But what?'

'Well, if he knows where we live, does he know *he's* here now?'

'He can't be everywhere at once,' Pete said. 'And we're on his tail now, so he's got that to contend with. He hasn't got time to be worrying about the likes of you, Dale. No offence. But you did what was asked of you. Why would he?' He turned to the woman in the centre of the room. 'So, the upshot is that we need to find this male. Because the SIM card Dale got for him was used in the commission of a serious crime. A murder. And Dale can help us.'

'Like you said, why would he? The bloke's not interested in him anymore. He should stay out of it and let things be as they are.'

'For your safety, Ms Gordon, that's why. And that of your daughter. And Dale. The male we're after has killed before with no good reason to. There's nothing to say he won't again if he feels threatened. Your safety comes with us getting him locked up and off the streets.'

'Bollocks. Our safety comes from staying the hell away from you and him,' she declared.

Pete nodded. 'I wish that were true, Ms Gordon. But sadly, as I said, it's not. He seems to believe in a clean house. No possible ties. And, like it or not, Dale is a tie.'

'What do you want?' Dale asked, his tone heavy and resigned.

'I want to catch him. But first, I need to identify him,' Pete said.

'Don't you go dropping us in it any deeper than you already have,' she broke in.

'I'm not planning to,' Pete told her. 'But for that, I need your help, Dale. I'm not going to ask you to drop anyone in it,' he added quickly, holding his hands up.

'What, then?'

'Well, you said this man already knew about you. That raises the question of how, doesn't it? I mean, if you didn't recognise him, then how did he get to know so much about you?'

Gordon frowned. 'Yeah.'

'Well, there's a few possibilities. He could have followed you home one night and sat watching the place.' He glanced from Dale to his mother and saw her horrified shiver. 'Or he might have been talking to your customers or your supplier. He might have some sort of connection there. Or he may have been impersonating a police officer to add a bit of authority, but anyway, asking questions about you. And that's where you come in, Dale. Instead of us hauling in all your customers, charging them with possession and questioning them, all of which takes time that we haven't got, you could ask them, in the course of conversation. Your supplier, too. Has anybody new been sniffing around lately, asking questions about you, or about street dealers in general?'

'I do that, they won't come back. They'll think I'm tainted goods – under observation from you lot or something,' Dale protested.

'Not necessarily. It depends how you put it.'

'Like how?'

Which wasn't a straight-up refusal, Pete noted. 'Maybe like some damn weirdo's been sniffing around, looking for potential easy marks,' he suggested. 'People who won't go to the cops.'

'How would I know he ain't one?' Gordon asked, playing along.

'He could be,' Pete acknowledged. 'But there've been no arrests so it's more likely he's looking to rip you or the people around you off. And it's not like you're asking them for anything but information that'll help protect them, too, once you find it.'

'How? Other than passing it on to you, which makes me a grass.'

'Knowledge is power,' Pete said. 'Once you've got it, you can figure out who he is and what his game is. Then, with friends in low places like you've got, you can arrange for something to be done about him. At least, that's what you tell anyone who asks,' he added. 'In fact, the last thing I want is for anything outside of our control to happen to him. I want him nicked so I can question him. Find out who he is, where he's from and what he's been up to.'

'Huh. What happened to, "No comment"?'

'Nothing. It's still as much of a pain in the backside as ever. But there aren't many who can keep it up for long with a good interrogator. There's ways of tripping people up, getting them to say something. And lies or truth, once you start talking, it's hard to stop.'

'What good does a bunch of lies do you?' Gordon asked with a confused frown.

Pete gave him a quick smile. 'Lies can be as useful to us as the truth, Dale. Once you're locked into them, if we can prove they're lies, then your credibility in court's out the window, never to return. Put that with other evidence and here comes a conviction as sure as a train on the tracks. But first, we need to know who he is. So, will you help us? For the sake of your mum and your sister…'

He looked from Pete to his mother and back. Hesitated. Then nodded. 'OK. I'll give it a go.'

Pete nodded. 'Good. Let me know as soon as you learn anything, yes?'

Gordon grunted.

'Ms Gordon.' Pete turned to face her. 'Have you heard or seen anything unusual on the street here recently? A man sitting in a car? Or knocking on doors, asking questions, looking like a copper or a Jehovah's witness?'

She shook her head with a grimace. 'No, but I mind my own business, don't I? I'm not a curtain-twitcher like some of 'em up here.'

'Some like who, specifically?'

'There's one a couple of doors up on the other side, for sure. Mrs Turnbull. Nosy old bat.'

Pete nodded. 'All right. I'll leave you to it. Thanks for your time.'

*

Pete took the ninety-degree turn at the northern end of Ferndale Road and pulled over to park. Stepping out of the car, he looked around. Ahead, on the left, the run of old terraced houses stretched away from him, one of which had been Shane Gallagher's home. On the right, they were faced by a row of new-build terraced houses of similar size with little square porch roofs sticking out over the front doors. Turning around, he saw a pair of red-brick new-builds tucked into the corner with just enough room in front of each for a single car to be parked. They would have a perfect view along the road in front of them.

And in front of the one on the left was a little white hatchback.

He headed across to the one with the car in front. Pressed the bell on the white UPVC doorjamb. Moments later, the door was opened by a female in her twenties with dark hair in a messy bun on top of her head and no make-up, wearing miss-matched pink and blue sweatshirt and jogging bottoms over bare feet.

'Yes?' Her voice was hoarse and dry, her red-rimmed eyes matching the end of her nose.

'Hi.' He held up his warrant card. 'I'm DS Pete Gayle with Exeter CID. I just wanted to ask you a couple of quick questions, if that's OK.'

'What about?'

'Well, you seem to have a pretty good view along the street from here. I was wondering if you might have seen anything unusual or out of place, maybe on Sunday evening.'

'What time of the evening? I close the curtains as soon as it gets dark. Don't want the neighbours peering in.'

'Any time, really. A car or a person on foot, someone hanging around. Anything that stood out to you.'

She shook her head with a grimace. 'Not really. I don't spend a lot of time peering out at the street. And I haven't been exactly bouncing off the walls, the last few days.' She coughed as if to emphasise the point. 'Some sort of bug I picked up at work, I reckon. Been like this since Saturday.'

Pete nodded. 'OK, well thanks anyway. Do you know if your neighbour's in?' He nodded towards the house that was attached to hers.

She shook her head. 'Went out as usual, about half-eight.'

'Keep warm and get better soon then, eh?' he said, suppressing the slump of disappointment as he stepped away. He'd thought he might be onto something there. But long practice had taught him to take these minor let-downs in his stride.

To his left a footpath led up past a row of more modern houses towards the next street, but they wouldn't have a view of the street leading towards Gallagher's home. Heading along the street, he soon caught movement in the distance. Saw Ben Myers, in his dark uniform, stepping away from a door along the other side of the street. Then Dave Miles emerged from a house almost opposite Ben. They exchanged nods and perhaps words – Pete couldn't tell from this distance.

He raised his fingers to his lips and pushed out a powerful whistle. Saw both of their heads turn towards him and gave a beckoning wave.

Ben waved back and they both started towards him.

Minutes later, the whole team were crowded into his car, apart from Dave Miles, who crouched on the pavement, elbows on the bottom of the window opening beside Dick Feeney. Pete turning in his seat to see them all.

'What have we got?'

Heads were shaken. 'Nothing, boss.'

'Nowt.'

'Sweet FA,' Dick summarised. 'Nobody saw anything, nobody heard anything, nobody knows anything.'

'On the plus side, I suppose, nobody had anything to say against Gallagher,' Dave added. 'Seems like he stayed out of trouble around here, at least.'

'Not that that helps us find the bloke who killed him,' Jill pointed out.

'Have we talked to everyone we need to?' Pete asked.

'Not everyone's in, boss,' Ben said. 'Some are probably at work.'

'So we come back and finish the job when they're at home,' Pete concluded. 'Meantime, let's repeat the exercise over on Franklin Street. It shouldn't take long with all of us there. It's only a short street. We can't all fit in here so Dick, take your car over there. Take Dave with you. Leave your notebooks with Ben. While I drive, Ben, you can compile a list of...' His phone rang abruptly. He paused, checking the screen. An unlisted number. '...the addresses here where we haven't spoken to anyone yet.'

He tapped the screen to accept the call.

'DS Gayle.'

'I've got you a team of fourteen to help with the CCTV,' Colin Underhill said without bothering to introduce himself. 'And I've heard from Brum. They've got a bite. The buyer's reached out for a replacement firearm. They managed to clone his phone. The message stream ended with one from this end, saying, "One week".'

CHAPTER ELEVEN

'Shit,' Jill muttered.

Pete agreed with the sentiment. There was no way they were ready to pursue their man yet, with still no idea who they were looking for.

'If we'd managed to do that with Gallagher's phone...' she said.

'He'd still be dead,' Pete said, cutting her off.

'But we'd have the gunman in a cell.'

'So, our man will be looking for a new courier,' Pete said, aiming the comment at the still-open phone line. 'What do you want us to do, Guv?'

'Find him,' Colin said.

'Huh,' Dick grunted.

'Stick with the plan,' Colin said. 'I'll get onto uniform, get the word put out that he's going to be around, looking for a courier, and we need to know about it. You and your team contact your CIs and tell them the same.'

'Doesn't that kind of fly in the face of trying to keep things on the down-low?' Pete cautioned in spite of feeling nervous after Jill's comments.

'They've pushed it on. They can't have everything.'

'So, does that change things with the team doing the CCTV work for us, too?'

'No reason for it not to.'

'Not that I can see, but what does the Chief say?'

'She hasn't yet.'

'We'll hold off for five minutes then, shall we? Let you run it past her.'

Colin grunted and the next thing Pete heard was the dial tone.

'Are you trying to get sacked?' he demanded, staring at Jill in the driving mirror.

'No, but's true, isn't it? All this would be moot.'

'Well, we are where we are so let's get to it.' He drew a breath. 'We'll check with the neighbours on Franklin Street and, to be thorough, Roberts Road too, where it backs onto the Gordons' place, then go from there.'

'It's a bit of a turnaround,' Ben said as Jane and Dick both stepped out of the car. 'All secrecy and stealth to suddenly flooding the streets with the fact that we're looking for him.'

Jane climbed into the front passenger seat and buckled up.

'Like the guvnor said, they can't have it all ways,' Pete replied, starting his engine. 'They either want to take it slow and stealthy or they want to push it forward. They pushed, we didn't.'

He swung the car into a three-point turn as Jane passed her notebook back to Ben, who flipped it open and gave it to Jill to hold along with her own. He began scribbling as Pete completed the turn and headed back towards the main road.

*

Pete was driving under the bridge on Frog Street, heading away from the twin bridges over the Exe when his phone rang again. With the big multi-storey block of student accommodation on his left and open parkland stretching away on his right towards the low, stone Medieval Exe Bridge, he gave Jill a cautionary glance in the mirror and reached for the comms screen to accept the call.

'DS Gayle.'

'Stick to plan A,' came the response in Colin Underhill's deep, dry voice. 'Do not mention guns to anyone.'

'The chief didn't go for it?'

'Politics,' Colin grunted.

'So, we need to arrange an alternative to the incident room while the uniform team are in there?'

'Yes.'

'We'll be an hour or two. More doors to knock on. Then we'll get back there and clear out the incident room.'

'I'll tell them 15:30. They can get themselves installed and up-and-running, at least.'

Pete checked the time on the dash and blinked. 'That's forty minutes from now.'

'You wanted a rush on it.'

'Yeah, but...' he stopped as the dial tone cut in. 'Shit.' He cut the call and dialled Dave Miles.

'DS Miles speaking.'

'Dave, it's Pete.' He stopped behind a small box-van at the traffic lights on a wide open junction surrounded by trees and low-rise blocks of flats set well back from the road. 'You and Dick need to get back to the nick instead of Franklin Street. We've got to clear out of the incident room. Quick.'

'And put it all where?' Dave demanded.

The lights changed and Pete followed the van forward, easing across into the right-hand lane to make the turn off Western Way, heading south. 'Don't know yet. The RAF cadets hut on Ferndale was mentioned, but nothing's been arranged.'

'Is there time?'

'Not really. Just photograph the white boards and then box everything up and we'll deal with it when we can.'

'How long are we out of there for?' Dave asked.

'I don't know for sure, but there's a week's work there for them if they don't find anything sooner.'

'The cadets will want their hut back at least twice in that time and we've only got that long before we need a strategy in place for the target.'

'Yep.'

Dave sighed. 'All right. We're on the way.'

Jill grunted as Pete hung up again. 'As the guvnor said: politics. They don't think about the realities of the situation, do they? Or the consequences for real people. Like us.'

Pete saw Ben swap one of the notebooks she was holding for another.

His lips pursed. He didn't know what her problem was today, but nor did he have the time to deal with it. 'Life's a bitch, as they say. Maybe you can figure out where we can decamp to for a week, if not the cadets' hut.'

'Well, not my place, that's for sure,' she said. 'There isn't room. We need a conference room or something like that, that can be locked while we're not in it.'

They passed the end of the street they'd chased Dale Gordon into earlier, opposite the high wall fronting the Jehovah's Witness' meeting hall with its arched entrance closed off with a pair of ornate black iron gates.

An ideal space, Pete thought, if it weren't for the current occupants. Like the RAF cadets, they would no doubt want to use it for their own purposes. And unlike the RAF cadets, they might not have the discipline to stay out of it when required to.

'Yeah, the question is, where?' he said. 'We can't turf Jim or Ronnie out of the other two incident rooms.'

'Why did we give up the old mobile incident rooms?' Jane posed.

'Too expensive to maintain. Or too much trouble,' Pete replied.

'Hmm. The RDE's got a conference room. I went to a meeting there once.'

'That's a thought. Get the guvnor to get onto them, find out if we can use it.' He flicked on the indicator and took the tight left turn into Roberts Road. Passing the first junction on the right, he pulled into a space on the left, just before the next one – the one they wanted. 'Right, we'll split up. You go along here, Jane, check with the three properties that are closest to looking over the back of the Gordon place, then come and join us up there.' He nodded towards the end of the side-street as he released his seatbelt, the two houses either side of it standing out in stark white render against the bare red brick of the majority of properties surrounding them.

They stepped out of the car and started up the street.

'You start at the bottom,' he said to Jill. 'I'll go up and work back down.'

In fact, his intention was to start, on the way up the street, with the woman that Cathy Gordon had mentioned as a likely witness. Passing the Gordons' house on the far side, he stopped at the one three doors up where he could see a slight yellowing on the edge of the net curtain at just below what he guessed would have been Jill's shoulder height from the inside. He rang the bell and the door was opened almost instantly by a tiny woman with curly grey hair, dressed smartly in a pleated skirt and pink cardigan over a white blouse. Her only concession to the fact that she was indoors and at home were the tartan slippers on her feet.

'Yes?' she asked, her voice stronger than she looked.

The two steps up from the pavement to the doorway beside the bay window put her almost eye-to-eye with him, despite her size.

'DS Gayle, Exeter CID,' he said, holding up his warrant card. 'I wonder if I could ask you a couple of quick questions, Mrs…?'

'Turnbull. Melanie Turnbull. Detective Sergeant, eh?' she said, peering at his ID then up into his eyes. 'Sounds important. You'd better come in.'

She stepped back. The door opened directly into the front room of the little house. She raised a hand to indicate the two armchairs that faced the window, beyond the sofa that stood with its back to him, facing the fireplace on the far side of the room.

'Take a seat.' She gave an apologetic smile. 'I'm sorry, I missed your name. I got all hung up on the Detective Sergeant bit.'

'It's Peter Gayle.' He moved around the sofa towards one of the chairs.

'Would you like a drink, Mr Gayle?'

'No, thank you. I'm fine. I won't take up much of your time.'

'Very well.' She stepped through to take a seat on the far end of the sofa, sitting forward attentively and peering at him, birdlike. 'So, what brings you to this neck of the woods?'

'We're looking for a male who may have been along here asking questions – maybe pretending to be one of us – but in fact is a very dangerous individual,' he said, taking out his notebook and pen despite the fact that he didn't expect to need them. 'If he was around here, it would have been early last week, probably. Do you remember anything unusual around that time? A person knocking on the door, asking questions? A car that you hadn't seen before? Anything like that?' He clicked the nib of the biro out, ready.

She nodded slowly, her eyes still fixed on his. 'A stranger on the street? Asking questions?'

'Or just watching and waiting.'

'I see. And he's dangerous?'

'Very.'

'Hmm.' She cocked her head, thinking. Then blinked and focussed on him again. 'No. I've seen no-one like that, Detective Sergeant.'

Pete's lips pressed together as he closed his pen and pad.

'I did see a Jehovah's Witness. They come up here sometimes. I didn't speak to him, though. I used to enjoy winding them up. Trying to convert them to atheism or sun-worship or something, but they don't seem to knock here anymore. This one did, but I was busy so I didn't answer the door.'

Pete smiled and popped out his pen again. 'When was this, Mrs Turnbull?'

'Sunday afternoon. I was in the middle of baking, got my hands all covered in flour and dough, so I let him go.' She gave an impish smile. 'There's always next time.'

'And what did he look like?'

'Like they all do. Smart. He wore a dark suit a lot like yours. He could have done with a haircut, but otherwise…' She shrugged.

'Dark hair or light?' Pete asked.

'Dark. A little darker than yours, probably.'

'And how old do you think he'd have been?'

'Oh, I don't know. Forties, perhaps? I'm not very good on people's ages.'

'OK. And he came up the hill, did he, or down?'

'Up,' she said, nodding.

'You didn't see his car or anything?'

'No. He wouldn't need one, though, if he was coming from the Kingdom Hall, would he?' she replied with a tilt of her head.

'True. Did you get a decent look at his face, Mrs Turnbull?'

'Not really. The nets, you see… All I can say is that he was a white man, a little shorter than you, and possibly a little heavier. Not thick set, quite, but not slender, if you understand?'

Pete nodded. 'Yes.' He made a quick note in his own form of shorthand. 'Is there anything else you can tell me about him?'

Her lips pushed downward. 'No. He waited a few seconds after ringing the bell and moved on. I didn't see him again. Must have been busy when he came past, I suppose.'

'You don't know if he spoke to your neighbours?'

She shook her head. 'I'm not sure. I didn't hear anything, but I generally have the radio on when I'm baking, so I might not have.'

'Well, thank you for your help, Mrs Turnbull.' He put away his notebook and pen and stood up. 'I must get off and leave you to it.'

*

He went on up to the bend near the top of the street. The last house on the far side looked back down the hill. Like the one he'd visited a few minutes ago on the other side of the river, an ideal vantage point to see most of the street – certainly the Gordons' side of it – though the downstairs window had a venetian-type blind behind the glass. He rang the bell.

Waited.

There was no response. No sound from within, following the doorbell's chime.

He turned away, crossed the street and started back down.

He pressed the bellpush at the first house on the left, heard the harsh buzz of the bell from inside and the faint old-style rock music cut off. Sounds of movement were followed by the snick of the latch and the door was opened by a man with short grey hair and a salt-and-pepper beard, dressed in a paint-spattered polo shirt and grey joggers.

'Yes?'

Pete held up his warrant card. 'Hi. DS Gayle, Exeter CID. We're conducting some enquiries in the area. Have you got a couple of seconds?'

'I suppose.'

'Were you in a week ago Sunday afternoon?'

'Yeah. We generally are.'

'Did anyone knock on your door, asking questions?'

'Not that I know of.'

'You didn't see anything out of place around that time? An unusual vehicle on the street? Anyone hanging around that you didn't recognise?'

The man shook his head. 'Too busy to take much notice. Redoing the bathroom.'

Pete's phone buzzed in his pocket. He took it out and checked the screen Nodded to the man in the doorway. 'OK, thanks for your time.' He turned away and tapped the screen to answer.

'DS Gayle.'

'It's Jane. The guvnor said no to the RDE. Too many people with potential access while we're not there. Cleaners, porters, maintenance staff... And we don't know what risk any of them might pose to the case.'

'Hmm. He's got a point. So, we still need to find a venue.'

'Yeah. I've got nothing on Roberts Road so I'm coming round.'

'No, stay down there. Our suspect was definitely here on the Sunday afternoon, togged up like a Jehovah or Mormon, according to the woman Dale's mum mentioned at number fourteen. She couldn't give me a facial description, but if he had a car, he left it somewhere down that way. Maybe where we did. We could use a VRN or even a description. When Ben finishes what he's doing, he can help you try and find one. Check the nursery school and the flats opposite the end of Radford Road for CCTV, for a start, then see if any of the residents saw him or, better yet, picked him up on a doorbell camera.'

'OK.' She hung up and Pete put away his phone and went on to the next house down.

CHAPTER TWELVE

He was about to knock on the last door before Mrs Turnbull's when his phone buzzed again in his pocket. He lowered his hand and took it out. Tapped the green icon.

'DS Gayle.'

'Boss, it's Dave. We're all packed up in the incident room. Jane tells me the guvnor knocked the hospital idea on the head, so have we got an alternative to go to?'

'Not yet, no.'

'Wherever it is, we're going to need it for up to a week, right?'

'Yes.'

'So... I was talking to Grey Man and we thought... You know I only moved house about a month ago. I haven't really settled in fully as yet, but... It's got a fair sized through lounge-diner that we could use, if the rest of you give me a hand putting curtains up and so on.'

'You've been there a month and you haven't got curtains up yet?' Pete demanded, incredulous.

'I have upstairs. And how much am I there?' Dave countered.

'Right...'

'It wouldn't take much. A trip to the DIY store in Dick's car, get three sheets of Conti-board and some two-by-two to make a whiteboard with. He's got the tools to put it together. Hang some curtains. The table seats six. An extension lead or two to power the laptops and we're good to go. I'm not providing the coffee, mind!'

Pete chuckled. It was true they could get through a lot of coffee in a day, between the six of them. 'I dare say you can get supplies from the nick. Are you sure you're OK with the idea?'

'Yeah, well, everyone else has got family at home that we'd be in the way of, apart from Ben, and we're not all going to fit in his place, are we? But there's no-one in the way at mine. And it's not like it's an established home as yet that we'd be disrupting.'

'Well, it sounds like a plan to me, but run it by the guvnor and see what he says.'

'All right. I'll let you know. You all know where it is.'

He saw Jill emerge from a house a few doors down and waved her towards him.

'Yes. OK, thanks, Dave. I've got to go. We'll talk soon.' He hung up. Indeed, they did all know where Dave's new house was. They'd helped him move from his flat just outside the city centre to the 1970s three-bed detached on a small estate in Pinhoe, on the northern edge of the city.

'Jill. Have you got anything useful yet?' he asked as she approached up the hill.

'I've found one person who spoke to him.'

'Good. Did you get a description?'

'Male, forties, dark hair and suit. Clean-shaven. No accent – local or otherwise. They agreed to sit down with a police artist tomorrow, if we can set it up.'

'Excellent. Mrs Turnbull in number fourteen saw him, but only through the nets, so couldn't give any more than a general description, which matches what you've said. She did say he seemed to be coming from the bottom of the street, though.'

'Yes, Jane told me a few minutes ago.'

'I've just got this one to check on this side, then we'll have a walk down the other side of the street, see if anyone's got a doorbell camera. I already checked the house at the top, that looks down here from the bend. They're not in.'

'You taking the top half again? I can start from the bottom side of the Gordons' and work down.'

'OK.'

She turned away to continue what she was doing and he reached up to the bell beside the door he was standing by. Was about to push it when his phone rang again. With a shake of the head, he took it out and answered it again.

'DS Gayle.'

'Boss, it's Ben. We struck out at the flats across from Radford Road. They've got a camera, but it's tucked under the far end of the archway so it just sees people walking past or coming in or out of the actual courtyard.'

'Shame.'

'Did better at the nursery school, though. They've got three cameras facing each way along Roberts and down the side, along Temple Road.'

'You know I'm saving up all these wind-ups, don't you?' Pete said. 'There will be payback one day, when you're not expecting it.'

'Sorry, boss. I was just... Anyway, we've got the footage from there so we can check it later and we're going along Roberts Road now to see if anyone actually saw the male or his car.'

'And how did you get on with the Ferndale addresses?'

'We've got nine to go back to, including the one in the corner that you tried.'

'All right. We'll meet back at the car when we're done.'

Pete hung up again and finally got to press the bell-push next-door to Mrs Turnbull's.

A male in his sixties, Pete guessed, snatched open the door. He couldn't have been more of a contrast to his neighbour – scruffily dressed in a dirty white singlet and baggy jogging bottoms, he looked irritated and impatient.

'Don't you lot talk to each other? I already spoke to one of you, a week or two ago.'

'Really? What was that about?' Pete asked, keeping his tone even.

'Young Dale Gordon, of course. It's a wonder you haven't arrested him yet.'

'I see. Well, sorry about that, Mr...?'

'Paris. Jim Paris.'

'Well, Mr Paris, I wasn't aware that there was a case pending against... Dale Gordon, you say?'

'You... Well, what are you here for, then?'

Pete raised his warrant card at last. 'I'm DS Gayle with Exeter CID,' he said. 'What I'm here about is reports that someone's been impersonating a police officer in the area. You say a week or two ago. Can you be more specific?'

'Impersonating?' His balding head drew back sharply. 'You mean he wasn't one?'

'No.' Pete shook his head. 'Was he in uniform?'

'No, a suit, like you are.'

'And he had ID?'

'Well, yeah... I mean...'

Probably not, Pete thought. *You just made the assumption then, the same as now.* 'When exactly was this, Mr Paris?'

'I'm... Sunday. Afternoon. The racing was on.'

'This last Sunday?' Pete checked, knowing the answer would be negative.

'No, no. The one before. I was just starting to nod off, as it happens. Not that I do that very often, but... Anyway, the bell went, startled me, I come to the door and there he is, all suited and booted. Wanting to know young Dale's comings and goings, saying he's under investigation on drugs charges. Distribution or some such.'

Pete nodded. 'I see. Did he give you a name?'

'I don't recall. I expect so, but like I said, I was half-asleep, so...'

'OK. What did he look like?'

'A bit like you. Not so tall. Dark hair, dark suit, neat and tidy, you know?'

'Age?'

'Forties, I suppose. Somewhere there. Bit more tanned than you, but...'

'If I sent a police sketch artist round would you be able to describe him enough to create an image, do you think?'

'Why? What's he done?'

'Apart from impersonating a police officer, we're talking about blackmail, at least.' Pete didn't want to scare the man off by talking about murder.

'What do you mean, "At least,"?' he demanded.

'There are other possibilities, but they're not confirmed yet.'

Paris grunted. 'Well, I suppose. I ain't making any promises as to how good it'll be, mind.'

Pete tipped his head. 'That's between you and the artist, Mr Paris, but I'm sure it'll be worthwhile, if you can manage it.'

'Huh. Well, I suppose, then. When?'

'They'll be available tomorrow, if you are. We'll have to confirm the time and get back to you.'

'Right.'

'If I can take a phone number...?'

Pete took out his notebook and pen. Paris quoted the number and he wrote it down along with the name and address. 'Thank you. We'll be in touch.'

'Right,' he repeated.

Pete nodded and turned away. Jill was crossing the narrow road a few yards away. He called out and hurried to join her. 'Have you got in touch with the sketch artist yet?'

'No.'

'All right, I'll do it. I've got another one for them to visit.'

'That should be enough, then, shouldn't it?'

He nodded. 'We'll check for doorbell cameras while we're here. A photo's always better than a sketch or e-fit when it comes to people recognising a face.'

*

It didn't need all of them to knock on nine doors so, while Jane drew the short straw and took the doorbell camera footage home to go through so that, if anything was found, it could be passed on to the Ops Support team in the incident room in the morning, Pete, Jill and Ben returned to Ferndale Road at 6.45pm, once the rush-hour had calmed down a little and everyone was likely to be home.

The narrow streets were a lot fuller now with cars parked nose-to-tail along both sides. They'd agreed which addresses each would take before leaving Dave's house to each return home briefly. Pete's first call was to the house that looked directly along Ferndale, past what had been Shane Gallagher's flat. He parked on the street leading up towards it from the main Alphington Road, as soon as he spotted a space. Ben, he noticed, had done the same. He passed the young PC's bright blue Skoda as he walked towards the corner. He was still several yards short of his destination when his phone buzzed in his pocket. He took it out and checked the screen. The caller's number was unlisted. Work.

'DS Gayle,' he answered.

'It's Jane. I've found our subject and his car. But he parked in almost the same spot as you did, earlier, so it's too distant to make anything out, apart from the fact that it's a silver hatchback.'

'Have you run it forward to see if he comes any closer to turn around when he leaves?'

'He doesn't. Turns it in the end of Radford Road.'

'OK. Grab some stills as he turns it. Get side, front and back views. I know they're distant, but they can be blown up enough to recognise a make and model, at least.'

'Right.'

'Thanks, Jane. Let the guvnor know and drop them off at the nick before you come to Dave's in the morning, OK?'

'Will do. Night.'

In theory, he thought as he continued along the street with the noise of traffic drifting up from behind him, it could speed up Ops Support's search of the CCTV from the other locations. A quick scrub for whatever breed of silver hatchback it turned out to be could be much quicker than a blind search for vehicles that matched from one to the other. Though on the other hand, there were an awful lot of silver hatchbacks on the roads. Assuming it was his own vehicle, rather than one he'd borrowed, stolen or hired for the purpose.

He grunted. 'One bridge at a time, Pete,' he muttered.

Reaching the property he was heading for, he stepped up the short drive – occupied now by a small silver hatchback, he noted with a raised eyebrow – and rang the bell.

While he waited, he made a quick note of the registration, make, model and address.

The door was opened by a male around Pete's own age. Similarly slim with short dark hair, he was clean-shaven and dressed in a T-shirt and jeans.

'Yes?'

Pete held up his warrant card, watching the man closely. 'DS Gayle, Exeter CID. We're conducting enquiries following the death of someone who lived along the street here.'

'Really? Who's that?' The man seemed genuinely surprised and interested.

'A male who lived in one of the old houses along there.' Pete jerked a thumb over his shoulder. 'A Mr Gallagher.'

The man's lips pushed upward. 'The name's not familiar.'

'That's OK. Can you tell me if you saw anything or anyone unusual on the street on Sunday?'

He shook his head. 'I wouldn't have. I was out all day, visiting family.'

'What time did you get back?' Pete tried to recall if the car had been outside the house when he walked past on Sunday night, following Gallagher, but he wasn't sure. It hadn't been a priority at the time.

'About eleven. I was coming from Camborne,' he added when he saw Pete's eyebrows rise. Yet, he had no west-country accent, Pete noted. No accent at all, in fact.

'Ah. Right. That's a long old way for a daytrip.' It was getting on for a hundred miles. Even at night, it would take a couple of hours on what was mostly a standard A-road.

'I was there for the weekend. Went down Saturday morning.'

'OK. Well, thank you for your time.'

The man nodded and stepped back to close the door as Pete turned away.

He opened his notebook again and wrote next to the man's car details, *Check traffic cams, Sat/Sun, here to Cambourne.* Then, putting away the notebook and pen, he moved on to the next address on his list.

He met Ben and Jill at the corner of a new-build side-street almost opposite Gallagher's address around fifteen minutes later.

'Anything useful?' he asked.

'Nope,' said Jill.

'Nothing, boss,' Ben added. 'You?'

'Not sure. Need to check with Graham tomorrow. Or get Jane to do it while she's there.'

CHAPTER THIRTEEN

'Morning all,' Jane said, stepping in through the lounge door, in front of the jerry-rigged whiteboard which had been laid out in exactly the same way as the much larger one they'd had in the major incident room, back at the station. 'The good news is that I've got a make and model on that silver hatchback.'

'And the bad news?' Dick asked, looking up from the dining table at the far end of the room where he was working on his laptop, along with the rest of the team.

'One: the rumour mill's flying. I got quizzed by a couple of Jim Hancock's guys in the corridor while I was there, wanting to know what we're up to. I told them to ask the guvnor.' Jim Hancock was another of the four detective sergeants under Colin Underhill. 'And two: it's a Golf.' She stepped around the sofa that was set across the room as a divider between the dining and lounge areas, approaching the table as Pete felt the slump of disappointment. The man on Ferndale wasn't their target. His silver hatchback was a Nissan.

'So that doesn't narrow it down to more than a few thousand,' Ben said.

'And it came and went from Topsham direction, rather than the city,' Jane added, further reinforcing Pete's disappointment as she pulled out the one empty chair at the table.

'So, no go on the Kingdom Hall camera,' Pete concluded, shaking off his feelings about the man living along the road from Shane Gallagher.

Jane shook her head as she sat down. 'And the only public cameras between there and Rydon Lane are pedestrian crossing ones.'

'So probably no use to us whatsoever,' Dick added.

'So, we need to get out there and see if we can find any private ones,' Pete countered. 'Domestic or business.'

'There's no businesses along there until you're pretty close to Rydon Lane,' Dave pointed out. 'There's some biggish houses, mind. One or two might have security cameras.'

'Otherwise, he could have turned off any-bloody-where along there,' Dick said. 'There's no way of knowing and no way of tracing him that's not just guesswork.'

'Well, before we get depressed about it, how about you take Jill out along there and find out for sure?' Pete suggested. 'You drive, she can keep her eyes peeled. Go out as far as the Rydon Lane roundabout. There's the filling station there and the pub across from it. They'll both have cameras so, if he got that far, we can see which way he went and take it from there. If not, at least it narrows things down for the Ops Support team going through the Alphington Road and Heavitree footage for us. Might speed them up.'

Dick grunted, looking less than convinced.

In his mind, Pete had to admit, it could well be a waste of time, but they wouldn't know until it was done. 'Sooner it's done, the sooner we can cross it off the to-do list.'

'Come on, Grey Man,' Jill said, closing her laptop. 'Look on the bright side. You get me alone for half an hour, at least. Dave's been trying to do that for years.' She shoved an elbow into Dave's ribs, beside her.

'Don't go tempting him, he's happily married,' Dave countered.

Jane laughed. 'This is Dick Feeney you're talking about, Dapper. He's not happily anything. It's not in his nature.'

Dick closed his laptop and stood up. 'I'm a realist, that's all.'

'Well, realistically, you're probably right,' Pete said. 'But we all know probably's not good enough for the Crown Prosecution Service, so let's prove it, eh?'

*

Jill's estimate proved over-ambitious. It was almost an hour before they returned. Following Dave back into the room, Dick dropped a thumb-drive on the dining table beside his laptop while Jill moved around to the other side, next to Jane, taking another from her pocket.

'How'd you get on?' Dave asked.

'As expected, the County Council offices' cameras don't cover the main road,' Dick said. 'And two of the three cameras on houses along there are fakes.'

'The third one, on a big old place on the other side of the road, a bit further along from the Council place, shows the road in the top left of frame,' Jill added. 'It probably won't give us a registration, but it could confirm if the suspect went along there.'

'And that's it until you get all the way out to Countess Wear,' Dick said. 'You'd think a funeral parlour would have cameras, wouldn't you? But no. Legally, they're only required to have them on the inside, so that's all they do. That one, anyway. And the computer repair shop next-door has got one, but it's at such a tight angle across the front of the shop that it doesn't get anything of the road.'

'The vet's on the other side of it has got one,' Jill broke in again. 'It faces out of town. No point doing anything else, seeing as there's a bloody great shrub between them and the computer shop that nothing would see through anyway. I don't know if it's got anything useful on it yet, but I collected it. Luckily, it keeps two weeks' worth. And then there's the pub and the petrol station at the roundabout. I went to the pub. One of theirs looks across the junction towards the petrol station, another across the end of Bridge Road.

I've got footage from them, just in case. Dick went over to the petrol station.'

'Two cameras,' Dick said. 'Well, two that are relevant. One looks back across towards the pub, the other across Rydon Lane so they're covering both exits.'

'Let's divide them up and see what they give us, then,' Pete said. 'Download what you've got and pass it around. It won't take long if we take a camera each.'

*

It took less time to go through the footage than it had to collect it.

Pete hit pause on his keyboard and looked up to find the rest of the team watching him, waiting. He shook his head with a grimace. 'Nothing on Bridge Road.'

'Hmm. So we've got an unconfirmed possible at the house across from the County Council offices and that's it,' Jane summarised. 'So, as Dick said earlier, he could have gone anywhere.'

'We had to try,' Pete said as his phone buzzed on the table near his hand. He turned it over to check the screen. The caller was unlisted. Work. He picked it up to answer. 'DS Gayle.'

'Hi, it's Francesca. I've got an image for you.'

'*An* image?' he checked.

'Yes. I went to the two witnesses individually and drew something up with each of them. Then, because they were very similar, I merged them into one and went back to the witnesses with that. A couple of tweaks and they agreed it was him. Mrs Galloway even admitted it was better than the one I'd done with her in the first place. I've just emailed it to you.'

As if on cue, the phone in his hand as well as his laptop pinged with the arrival of a new message.

'Sounds like I just received it,' he said. 'Thanks, Francesca.'

'So, what's this male done?' she asked.

'He's wanted for questioning in a murder. A guy was knifed in someone's front garden a few nights ago.'

'Ooh. Right. Well, I hope that helps you track him down, then.'

He thanked her again and hung up. Going back to his still-open laptop, he closed the video playback and opened up his email. There, as expected, he found an email from Francesca Thompson, Facial Imaging Officer.

He opened the attachment and sat back in his chair.

'And there he is.'

The face that stared back at him was unremarkable in many ways. Not someone you'd look twice at in the street. His hair was dark, as they already knew. He looked around Pete's own build and age, but with thinner lips in a broader face.

'Let's have a look, then,' Dave said from across the table.

Pete picked up his laptop and turned it around. 'I'll email it to everyone and you can print it out, Dave.'

'Are we sure that's not you, boss?'

Pete pressed his lips together.

'There you go! Perfect.' Dave looked from Jill to Jane with a broad grin. 'You must have really made an impression there.'

'This is a compilation of two images, from two witnesses, one of them female, who I didn't speak to – Jill did – and the other a male in his sixties,' Pete told them. 'And no, Dave, he's not gay. At least, not that I could tell.'

'So, what now?' Jane asked as Pete returned his laptop to the table in front of him and forwarded the email to the rest of them as well as to Colin Underhill. 'Seeing as we've got to keep this whole thing on the down-low,' she continued, 'so it can't go onto the PNC and find out if anyone in the job recognises him.'

Again, Pete's lips pressed together at the implied lack of trust from their colleagues. 'We find a way around what the NCA insists on. I've got an idea. I'm going to see the guvnor. Run it by him in person. Meantime, you lot can run him through the PND with facial recognition, see if he's got a record.' He closed down his laptop and stood up. 'Is there any hope you can stay out of trouble while I'm gone?'

'Really?' Jill demanded.

'My house, my rules,' Dave said with a grin.

'Not on work time,' Pete shot back.

'Spoilsport.'

'Yup. See you shortly.'

*

'Guv.' Pete stepped into Colin's office and closed the door behind him as the senior man closed the folder on his desk and put away his pen. 'Did you look at the email I sent you about fifteen minutes ago?'

Colin's eyes narrowed briefly. 'I don't know how many emails I get a day. Most of them I'm not interested in.'

'This one, you will be.' Pete tipped his head towards the spare chair with a raised eyebrow. 'It's a picture of our suspect.'

Colin's eyes widened. He nodded for Pete to sit and reached for the mouse of his desk-top computer. Moments later, he looked over at Pete. 'An e-fit.'

'From two witnesses. And we know he drives a silver Golf. Jane told the team downstairs, this morning. We haven't got a VRN yet. Our only sighting of it, so far, was too far away. But if he was using the same vehicle on Sunday night or on Heavitree Road, the other week, they'll pick it up.'

Colin nodded. Paused for a moment, then pushed back his chair and stepped around his desk. 'Come on.'

'Where to?'

'Upstairs.' He opened the door and stepped out into the corridor, leaving Pete to follow.

'What does she want?' Pete asked, closing the door behind them and taking long strides to catch up with the DI. *Upstairs* could only mean one thing: the Chief Inspector's office. 'I can't see that what we've got so far justifies wasting her time.'

'She'll explain,' Colin said as they reached the end of the corridor and he pushed through onto the landing.

They climbed the stairs in silence and Colin led the way towards the front of the building. In the wide foyer, he strode across towards the secretary's desk. 'The Chief wants to see us.'

She nodded, lifted the phone at her elbow and pressed three numbers. 'I've got DI Underhill and DS Gayle here for you, ma'am.' Putting the receiver down, she said, 'Go ahead.'

Colin reached for the door handle near her left elbow and opened it without knocking.

'Ma'am.'

Following him into the big corner office, Pete closed the door behind them.

Chief Inspector Christine Naylor turned away from the expansive view across fields and trees, over the industrial estate and the motorway beyond it to face them. 'Gentlemen. I've been speaking to the team at the National Crime Agency about this case and they have a proposal.'

The vague feeling of unease in Pete's chest solidified into a lump of dread.

'They want us to try to insert someone into the gunman's circle, undercover. We know he's accepted another order from the buyer in Birmingham. He's got only days to produce the item and arrange its transport. If we can find a way to make sure that courier is one of us...'

You're joking! Pete thought, horror replacing the dread. 'I thought they wanted us to keep all this on the down-low, ma'am? Who are we supposed to try to get close to him with? And how, when we don't yet know who he is? Neither Jane nor I can do it because he might well have seen us on Sunday night. And none of the rest of my team are trained for undercover work.'

She pursed her lips. 'I am aware of the limitations we're working under, Peter. But the National Crime Agency has its own undercover section.'

'I dare say they do, ma'am, but a cockney or a Brummy will stand out like a sore thumb down here. As soon as our subject spoke to them, they'd be blown. I know this is a university town with all the diversity that entails, and some of those students have some pretty dodgy ways of supplementing their incomes, but that's not going to run. No way.'

She pursed her lips, considering what he'd said. 'You're right. It would need someone local. Someone who could play the part of the suspect's usual demographic: involvement in the drugs trade or something similar. Someone young enough to fit the part. Like PC Myers, for example.'

'He's not trained for that sort of thing, ma'am. And you said yourself, there isn't time to do that. And we know what the target's like: if he smells a rat, he attacks. How are we going to protect Ben, if he's even willing to try?'

'It'll take some careful planning, obviously, but what alternative can you propose?' she countered.

'We're getting closer. We've got his face. We've got his car – at least, make, model and colour. Birmingham know the destination of the piece. Can't they keep a close watch on the purchaser and bring him in once he takes delivery?'

'If our target's waiting for confirmation of delivery and doesn't get it, he'll go underground faster than you can blink,' she said. 'So, no, that's not a practical answer, unfortunately.'

'I can't see that putting Ben Myers' life at risk is, either, ma'am,' he argued. 'I'm sorry, but...'

'Perhaps we should put the idea to PC Myers himself before we dismiss it out of hand,' she said with a deceptive softness to her tone that Pete knew from experience was a harbinger of bad things to come.

Still, he shook his head. 'I'm as keen as anyone to get this male off the streets, ma'am. Keener than most. But I can't support this.'

Her brows drew together. 'Well, unless you can provide a viable alternative, Detective Sergeant, this is the way it has to be. As long as PC Myers is willing, of course.' She switched her gaze to Colin. 'Call him, Colin. We'll speak to him in person.'

And we all know which way that's going to go, Pete thought. A constable wasn't going to say, "No," to his chief inspector. Not if he had even the slightest trace of ambition.

'Ma'am.' The big man took out his phone and scrolled through the contacts list. Chose one and lifted it to his ear. 'It's Colin

Underhill. Get yourself in here ASAP. Just you.' He hung up. 'He's on the way.'

She nodded. 'Good. Then let's discuss our options while we wait.'

There are options now? Pete thought sourly. He took a leaf from Colin's book and remained silent.

She pursed her lips. 'If we publicise the suspect's image in the hope of someone coming forward with a name for him, and he sees it, we'll lose him. What are the chances that he'll use that car again, if it's even his, not a stolen one? Slim, I'd say, at best. As you said yourself, DS Gayle, he's not a stupid man.'

'But he has got a job to do and limited time to do it in, ma'am. He's under pressure. Which is when people make mistakes. And we have got a team searching CCTV for that car or whatever other one he may have been driving on Sunday night and/or when he met with Dale Gordon. We have approximate times. If there's anything to find, they should find it pretty soon.'

'That's a big *if*, Detective. And what help will it be if the car was stolen or cloned?'

'If he uses it, it won't make a difference. All it'll take is for a camera or a traffic car to spot it and we'll be onto him. He can be stopped and arrested in a controlled situation by officers in the appropriate PPE and we go from there. And anyway, the two cases we know of, of our suspect approaching someone to do the courier job for him, were on opposite sides of the city. How are we going to have any hope of making sure he even approaches, never mind uses, our man?'

'By limiting his options.'

To one? How? Pete raised an eyebrow and waited for her to expand.

'Clearly, we can't shut down all the dealers in the city for a week, but we can get to them,' she said. 'Granted, maybe not all of them, but I'm sure, between your team, you have enough confidential informants to reach most, at least.'

'Maybe.'

'Then, we put the word out, with the suspect's picture, through your CI's, that he's dangerous enough not to be dealt with at any cost.'

'There's bound to be some, even amongst those we can get that message to, who're greedy, awkward or desperate enough to ignore it.'

'Obviously. But we're all adults here. We know there are no guarantees in life. And if you put it the right way, you can at least optimise the odds. Don't tell them to give him a flat, "No." They might think that's dangerous, in itself – or not profitable for them. But if you give them an alternative suggestion. "You can't do it, but you know a man who can." And he'll split any profits with them…'

Again, Pete raised an eyebrow.

'*We* know there won't be any profits to split, but they won't, until it's too late.'

'Which risks losing the CI's street-cred,' Pete pointed out.

Again, her lips pursed in annoyance. 'Then I'm sure there's some sort of petty cash fund somewhere that can afford to dole out fifty quid to whatever deserving cause gives us the actual "in".'

Pete tipped his head. 'It might work, if the subject approaches the right person in the first place,' he admitted. 'But it still puts Ben in a dangerous spot. This guy checks up on his prospective couriers. Thoroughly. We know that from Dale Gordon.'

'Then we give him everything he needs to pass muster. A safe house to live in for the necessary time. A record under whatever alias we decide upon. A new means of transport. If we spread the word about him effectively, then everyone the suspect approaches will have heard of him, at least.'

Pete nodded. 'OK...'

'And he's a trained officer with several years of experience, is he not?'

'Nine, up to now.'

'Then he can handle himself. And he has the advantage that he knows he'll need to: to expect trouble.'

'True.'

'Then let's leave it up to him, shall we? If it was legal, I'd have him carry a concealed Taser, but it isn't, so that's out of the question. What we can do is make sure he carries a Parva spray and have the team constantly on-call and close-by so that, when any meeting does occur, he has backup at hand.'

Pete managed somehow to keep his expression neutral. 'We thought that about Shane Gallagher, ma'am.'

She slapped her desk with both hands, eyes flashing. 'Enough! Anybody would think you don't want to catch this male, DS Gayle.'

'I want him all right, ma'am. More than you or those guys up in Birmingham, I can promise you. What I don't want is to risk the life of one of our best officers in the process. I don't believe this operation's been thought through thoroughly. It's rushed and it's too risky.'

'That, Detective Sergeant, is for PC Myers to decide.'

Yeah, standing here in front of you and his guvnor, he thought, but managed to keep to himself.

CHAPTER FOURTEEN

'Are you taking the piss?' Dave demanded, seated at the dining table in his living room, the lights on and curtains drawn at either end, when Pete and Ben returned and told the rest of the team what had been decided. 'What kind of half-baked, damn fool stupid idea is that?'

Pete shrugged. 'It came from the Chief, herself. I don't know if it was hers or the NCA's, mind.'

'And you went for it?' Dave demanded, switching his gaze to Ben. 'You're an idiot.'

'How does she imagine, in her wildest drug-fuelled dreams, we're going to get it to work?' Dick added, setting down his pen and leaning back in his chair.

'One of my several questions,' Pete acknowledged. 'Which all combined to piss her off enormously, in the end. Enough that I won't be taking over from the guvnor when he retires, that's a sure bet.'

Dave chuckled. 'It was anyway, wasn't it? But back to the serious stuff. How are we supposed to swing this stupidity, for Christ's sake?'

Pete sat down at the table and leaned forward, elbows on the polished surface. 'Her suggestion was that we all get out there and talk to all of our CIs. Tell them to spread the word about our subject – how dangerous he is to anyone who's stupid enough to work for him – and suggest that, rather than piss him off by saying no, they should point him towards a guy that, although *they* can't help on the day, they believe probably will.' He raised a hand towards Ben, who was still standing in the gap at the end of the sofa, facing the dining area. 'A guy who's known to be able to shift pretty much anything to or from pretty much anywhere, with a specialisation in the less-than-legal. The Chief's setting him up with an address – a safe house – a vehicle, a new mobile phone with all the necessary gadgetry installed, a bank account, DWP details and a criminal record in the name he's going to assume for now.'

'And she reckons that'll work, does she?' Jill demanded. 'In what dream-world?'

Pete saw Jane's lips purse. 'We don't have to get to all of them.'

'What, you like this bloody lunacy?' Dave demanded.

'No, but it looks like we're stuck with it. Ben's going along. So, what choice have we got, except to make the best of it?'

Dave grunted, his expression as sour as Jill's.

'We'll have to do whatever we can to make it work,' Jane said. 'Because, if it doesn't, we know who's going pay the price and who's going to get the blame – and it's not the Chief or the National Crime Agency.'

They all absorbed that for a moment.

'So, what's your new name?' Jill asked, turning to Ben.

'Spike Bennett.'

'Really?' she demanded, her gaze switching from Ben to Jane, to Pete. 'That's a bit close for comfort, isn't it?'

Pete raised his hands, looking from her to Jane and back. 'Not my choice. But the best lies are based on truth.'

'Yeah, but... I don't like that too much. And how's he supposed to protect himself when it comes to meeting the suspect? He can't go tooled up, can he? And a stab-vest's going to be a bit obvious under a ripped T-shirt.'

'Again, as I pointed out to the Chief before Ben got there,' Pete agreed. 'Which is about the time I came within an inch of getting fired.'

'So, what was her answer?' Dave asked.

'No ripped T-shirts,' Ben answered. 'Leather jackets with that new flexible Kevlar sewn in. The jeans, too.'

Finally, he stepped through into what was intended to be the dining area and took his place at the table. 'It's a chance to do something I've always wanted to,' he said. 'Go undercover. There aren't many opportunities in the country – and certainly not in this county – so it'll be good experience.'

'Well, I don't like it,' Jill declared. 'Not even a little bloody bit. Out there with no back-up against a man we know is dangerous and completely ruthless.'

'So why don't you go with him?' Dave suggested. 'Be his back-up. Play the part of his girlfriend or something.'

'What?' She turned on him, eyes flashing. 'Are you even crazier than I thought you were? What about my kid, Numpty? I'm not a free agent like you and Ben. Where's she going to go for a week or however long it takes? She's ten years old, for Christ's sake.'

Dave shrugged. 'Just a thought.'

'Yeah, and about as half-baked as the idea of Ben going undercover in the first place.'

'He's doing it, though,' Dave pointed out.

'Doesn't mean the rest of us have to be as bloody stupid as he and the sodding Chief are.'

'One thing at a time,' Pete said, breaking into the exchange. 'Whether we like it or not, it's happening, so we've got to deal with it. Let's get out there, find our CIs, and spread the word.' He reached into his pocket and came out with a handful of scraps of paper which he handed out.

'What's this?' Jill demanded.

'The phone number for Spike Bennett. Make copies to hand out. Ben's already got the phone in his pocket, so he's ready to go. The story is that he's out of town on a job, but he'll be back tomorrow. By then, his new threads will be ready, in case we get a bite.'

'It's not a bite we're worried about,' Jane said. 'You saw Shane Gallagher.'

*

'I can't step outside for a chat like we used to, Mr Gayle.' The redheaded twenty-something finished wiping the glass in his hand and put it under the bar he was standing behind, rather than in front of, where Pete was used to seeing him.

'So I see,' Pete acknowledged. 'How come?'

Darren shrugged. 'I'm a married man now. Got responsibilities.'

'Yes, I haven't had a chance to congratulate you, have I? Or send the men in white coats round to check on the lady in question.'

'Oi.' Darren frowned. 'There's no need for that.'

Pete grinned. 'Just joking, Darren. I hope you're both very happy. Not that it helps with what I've come to see you about.'

'And what's that? Hold on,' he added, looking along the bar.

Pete followed the direction of his gaze. 'While you're here, give me an orange and lemonade,' he said.

Darren raised a hand to the other customer, then filled Pete's order before moving along to serve the other man.

Pete watched him draw a pint and set it on the bar. He took the payment, gave change and came back.

'So, what's up, then?'

'There's a male who appears to be targeting drug dealers in the city. He approaches them, asking if they'll do a courier run for him to another city: Birmingham, London, whatever. They take the package, bring back the payment, hand it over... And the last one, he stabbed to death.'

'Ooh. That's not nice.'

Pete tipped his head in agreement. 'And we know he's going to be looking for another victim in the next few days.'

'Well, if you know all that, why can't you arrest him?'

'Because we don't know who he is yet. We've got a description. A picture, even. But not a name.' Pete took a copy of the e-fit from his jacket pocket and placed it on the bar. 'Do you recognise him?'

'I'm not a dealer, Mr Gayle. You know that.'

'No, but...' Pete shrugged and picked up his drink to take a sip. 'Worth asking. You never know, eh?'

'Well, I don't.' He slid the picture back towards Pete. 'Sorry.'

'No problem. Thing is, as I say, he's a dangerous man. And you may not be a dealer, but you know several, Darren.' He gave the redhead a brief smile. 'So you could help us and help them at the same time.'

'How?'

'Put the word out. He's dangerous. Don't deal with him. But, for their own safety, they can offer him an alternative, rather than just a flat, "No." If they say, "Sorry, I can't do it, but I know a guy who would…"'

'And you've got someone in mind, yeah?'

Pete nodded. 'A chap called Spike.' Reaching into another pocket, he took out a crumpled piece of paper. 'That's his number. I could give you a few, if you can spread 'em around.'

'I don't know. I've got a full-time job here, now, Mr Gayle. I don't see that much of the old street scene anymore.'

'Not even to save a life? Now you're a responsible adult.'

'So, who is Spike?'

'A professional courier,' Pete said, passing on the story they'd agreed on. 'He transports drugs, cash, papers, weapons… Whatever pays.'

'As opposed to being one of you lot, undercover., right? And he's willing to take the risk, is he, knowing what this bloke's like?'

Pete shrugged. 'All I can tell you is what I have, Darren. Except that we know this guy does his research. Once he decides on a target, he'll find out where they live, how they're vulnerable… In one case, he threatened a target's eleven-year-old sister with a hot iron to her face if he didn't comply. So, are you going to help?' He raised his glass and took another sip.

Darren grimaced. 'Sounds like the kind of bloke we'd all be better off not knowing.'

'And yet he's out there, right now, preparing to target someone. Maybe a friend of yours.'

'You know as well as I do, Mr Gayle, there's no friends in the drug world. Just associates. People you meet, maybe hang around with for a bit. But no-one gets close enough to be called a friend.'

'Yeah, but that's the drugs. The desperation for them. Take that away and you're left with a bunch of desperate, vulnerable people who need little more than real friendship.'

Darren shrugged. 'Maybe, in a parallel universe. But in this one, most of 'em would knock their own granny on the head for a fix. And the dealers are no better.'

'True, but not the point here,' Pete admitted. 'I'm trying to save lives. Are you in?'

Darren's lips pushed up in a grimace. 'I'll do what I can, Mr Gayle. But like you say, there's some desperate people out there, who'd do anything for cash, no matter what the risks are.'

Pete tipped his head. 'We can only affect our own little section of the universe, Darren. I'm just trying to shift the odds in our favour, that's all. Make the city a little bit safer for everyone in it.'

Darren chuckled. 'A noble cause, but you and who's army, Mr Gayle?'

'The King's, if needs be.'

*

Pete left Darren with half a dozen copies of the phone number they'd set up for the purpose – a SIM bought from a bargain store near the edge of the city, in a second-hand phone from a pawn shop in the Guildhall shopping centre just around corner from the snooker hall they were standing in – and moved on. Darren wasn't the first of his confidential informants he'd spoken to this afternoon and he had three more to speak to before the day's end.

Walking down the hill towards the river, he wove between the shoppers on the narrow pavement, the hum of traffic constantly in his ears, and turned right, heading for the old half-timbered pub on Tudor Street. Its landlord was a man with several of the kind of connections Pete needed right now.

He was walking past a small carpark in front of a plumbing supplier's in an old stone-built warehouse building opposite the rear of the Holiday Inn when his phone rang in his pocket. He took it out and checked the number but didn't recognise it. He tapped the green icon, regardless. 'DS Gayle.'

'You need to get your fuckin' act together, man. I was just nearly killed.'

He thought he recognised the voice but wasn't certain. 'Who is this?'

'Who is this? Oh, great. Forgotten already, am I? Just another bloody mug amongst hundreds, I suppose.'

'Is that Dale?'

'Yeah, it bloody is. And some bastard just tried to run me off the bloody road. And I can't see as it's anything other'n something to do with you and your bloody snooping around.'

Pete was tempted to point out that, in his chosen profession, Dale could have any number of enemies and people who'd be happy to see the back of him. But it wouldn't be helpful, so he kept it to himself. 'Are you OK?' he asked instead, stepping over the low railing that divided the footpath from the carpark and across to the far side, where he'd be out of the way of passers-by.

'Yeah, ish. But not for the want of him trying.'

'Him? Did you see him?'

'Not his face. He came from behind me. But I got a good gander at his motor.'

'What was it?'

'A silver Golf.'

Pete felt the thrill of recognition, and of a possible breakthrough just a hair's-breadth away. 'Did you get the registration number?'

'Too bloody right, I did. I might not have a degree, but I ain't bloody thick.'

A grin spread across Pete's face. This could be the break he so desperately needed. The way of preventing the need for Ben to be put at risk, going undercover, up against a vicious killer. 'Hold on a sec.' Wedging the phone between his ear and his shoulder, he took out his notebook and pen. 'What was it?'

Gordon reeled it off swiftly and Pete wrote it down.

'Thanks. That's the one hole we still had in our information on him. Apart from his name, of course, but the car registration should give us that. Now, I'd suggest you use some of the proceeds of your less-than-legal activities while you've got the chance and take your mum and your sister away to Butlins or something for a week or so while we track this guy down and get him off the streets.'

'We can't just up-sticks and bugger off, just like that. It'd terrify my mum, apart from anything else.'

'So will you getting run off your bike, won't it?' Pete pointed out. 'And so would an unexpected visit to your house by someone we know has killed at least once before. Because I'm not exaggerating when I say we're talking about the ultimate psycho here, Dale.'

'Well, like I said, you better do your bloody job, then, hadn't you?'

'And while I do that, you need to do yours as the man of your household. Keep your mum and your little sister safe. And yourself, of course.'

'Huh. Nice.' The line clicked as he hung up.

Pete quickly went onto the DVLA website. Entering the registration, he hit return. The response was almost instant. The registration was, indeed, attached to a silver VW Golf. The registered owner was listed as Terence Anthony Burgess of an address in Shillingford Abbot. With his grin broadening, Pete took down the details in his notebook and called Colin Underhill.

'Yes?'

'Guv, it's Pete. I've got a name and address attached to that silver Golf. I'm in the middle of doing what we talked about in the city centre and the details I've got are for Shillingford Abbott, but…'

'How'd you find that?'

'He tried to run Dale Gordon off the road. Dale's not hurt, but he was pissed off enough to remember the registration.'

'Get out there. I'll put a patrol car on Gordon's address in the meantime. You told him to go on holiday for a while?'

'I did. I don't know if he'll go along with the idea, though. He seemed a bit reluctant.'

'Best hope our suspect's gone straight home, then.'

'Yeah. I'm a few minutes from the car, but I'm on it.'

There was a click and he was holding a dead phone. He put it away and started back the way he'd come.

*

Shillingford Abbot was a loose, well-spread-out cluster of houses, bungalows and farms that didn't seem to have a centre or focus of any kind. Not even a church, despite its name. It was just the other side of the A30 trunk road from the city, little more than a mile from the Marsh Barton Industrial Estate, yet it felt like a different time and a different world. Driving into the village, Pete found the address he was looking for down a semi-tarmacked lane with grass and moss up the middle, off a side-road that itself was barely wider than his car.

The house, when he got there, was an old redbrick detached property with a few outbuildings that suggested it might once have been a farm, though there was little sign of that now.

Disappointingly, he noted, there was no Golf in the yard, but space for one beside an old Range Rover that was parked facing the front door.

He parked beside the big dark brown 4x4 and approached the house with its black door under a peaked timber and slate overhang porch. There was no bell, so he used the heavy iron knocker.

In moments, the door was opened by a woman in her fifties, he guessed. Her blonde hair was flyaway, whisps floating around her round face, blue eyes questioning. 'Yes?'

Pete held up his warrant card and introduced himself. 'Is your husband at home, Mrs Burgess?'

'No, he's out at work. Why?'

'I'm trying to get hold of him. I need to ask about his whereabouts around half an hour ago.'

'Why, what's happened?'

'There was an incident reported, involving his car. The Golf.'

'That would be with him.'

'And where does he work, Mrs Burgess?'

'At McKay and Davis on Marsh Barton. They're steel fabricators,' she added when he looked slightly blank.

Pete nodded. 'I see. Do you know the number for them?'

He took out his phone.

'Of course.' She reeled it off quickly. 'Not that I phone it very often, but you do, don't you? Know how to get hold of your husband. Or wife.'

'As a rule, yes,' he admitted with a nod. He tapped in the number.

'McKay and Davis. How can I help?' asked a female voice after only one ring.

'Hi. This is DS Gayle with Exeter CID. Do you have a Terence Burgess working there?'

'Yes.'

'Can you tell me if he's there now?'

'Yes, I… Yes, he is. Why? What's this about?'

'Has he been there all morning?'

'Yes. He arrived at about ten-to-nine, as usual.'

'Right. Thank you. Could I have a quick word with him, please?'

'Um… Yes, I… Hold on, please.' There was a clunk and a pause. Then a male voice.

'Hello?'

'Is that Terence Burgess?'

'Yes.'

'This is DS Gayle with Exeter CID. Can you confirm that your car, the silver Golf, is there with you? And that it's been there since nine o'clock this morning?'

'Yes, of course. Why?'

'You can see it, can you?'

'No, but…'

'Then, would you just set the phone down and go and check on it for me, Mr Burgess?'

'I suppose.'

The clunk was repeated. Another pause. Then the phone was picked up again. 'Yes, it's there.'

'OK. Thank you.'

'So, what's all this about?'

'It seems your car might have been cloned. A false number plate, the same as yours, put on a similar vehicle to disguise its real origins.'

'Yeah, I know what it means. Mine's been done?'

''Unless a witness made a mistake which, in this case, I doubt.'

'Jeez. You don't ever think it'll happen to you, do you?'

'Well, at least, now we know. It might mean that you'll get stopped once or twice until we find the other vehicle, but if you've got your papers with you, it shouldn't be a problem.'

'Ah, for you, maybe. Be a pain in the backside for me, if it happens.'

'Hmm. Well, we won't take any longer than we absolutely have to, sorting it out, I can assure you. Meantime, I'll let you get back to work.'

Pete said his goodbyes and hung up. Turning back to Mrs Burges, he said, 'One last thing, Mrs Burgess.' Taking a copy of the e-fit from inside his jacket, he held it out. 'Do you happen to recognise this man?'

She looked at it and her lips pushed upwards. 'No. Who is he?'

'He's the person who appears to be using your husband's registration number on another vehicle.'

CHAPTER FIFTEEN

Pete woke abruptly to the buzz of his mobile phone on the bedside cabinet. He snatched it up, too late to prevent it waking Louise, who rolled over with a soft moan to face away from him. As he reached for the phone, he saw the digital clock beside it. 1:10am.

What the hell was going on at this time of the morning? Had Traffic found the cloned Golf? Having checked with Burgess's neighbours and people around his workplace that he wasn't their suspect and was telling the truth about his whereabouts at the time that Dale Gordon had been knocked off his bike, he'd reported the cloned car and flagged it as wanted in the murder of Shane Gallagher before he came home for the evening. If they'd found it... The thrill of possibility woke him up fully as he tapped the screen to answer the call.

'Yes?'

'It's Jill. I'm going to have to do it, aren't I?'

Pete shook his head in confusion. 'Do what?'

'Go in with Ben. No-one else can. It wouldn't look credible.'

Pete sucked in a breath. 'You don't have to do anything of the sort, Jill. Ben put himself into the situation. He's an adult. It was his choice, albeit under pressure. And like you said earlier, what about Katie?' he asked, picking up on the response she'd made to Dave less than twelve hours ago about her daughter. She was a single mother, after all, with all the responsibilities that entailed.

'It's a few days, at most. Jane said she can stay with her and Roger.'

'You woke Jane up as well?'

'No,' she snapped. 'We talked about it earlier. Met up after we'd finished doing the rounds of our CIs.'

Yet it took until one in the morning to talk to me, he thought. 'So, what finally tipped the balance?'

She sighed. 'I dunno. Guilt? I've been turning it over and over in my mind. Couldn't sleep for the life of me. In the end, it comes down to the fact that we can't let him do it on his own and none of the rest of you would look right with him, except maybe Grey Man as his grandad. So I'm the only one who can go in as his backup.'

She was right. They both knew it, though neither of them liked it. 'No-one's asking or expecting you to do this, Jill.'

'I know, but...' He could almost hear her shrug as her voice tailed off.

'Well, you'll get all our support if you do, you know that. Do you want me to go to the guvnor with the idea, or go with you when you do, or...?'

'I don't mind talking to the guvnor. Only thing is, I don't know how long it takes to do anything with that Kevlar cloth stuff. If there's off-the-peg kind of things with it or it's got to be made bespoke, like.'

'You can get some of it on Amazon,' he said. 'I looked it up earlier, seeing that we were talking about it for Ben. There's jeans, leggings, hoodies and some other stuff on there. No doubt, more's available at specialist outlets. I don't know where, or what kind of range there is for women. Something for you to look at on-line. Maybe get next-day delivery and put it on expenses. I'll counter-sign it. You'd best make sure the guvnor approves of you doing the job first, though. And don't phone him now. You'll get fired rather than approved.'

'A day might be a day too long. If what we've done so far even works.'

'Well, there's nothing we can do about it at this time of night. Get some sleep. We'll sort it in the morning.'

'I'll have a quick look at what PPE I can get hold of first. Amazon and a Google search.'

'If you're going to do this, you'll need to be sharp as a tack. On your A-game, not groggy from lack of sleep.'

'OK, Dad.'

'Hey – you phoned me, remember. I didn't choose to be talking about this at a quarter past one in the morning.'

'Yeah, sorry, but worrying and lack of sleep can do funny things to your head, can't they?'

'Exactly. Go to bed. Look at Amazon and so on in the morning. Then phone the guvnor when you've got your head on straight and your facts lined up.'

'Right. Night. And thanks, boss.'

'Good night, Jill.' He ended the call and fell back onto his pillow with a sigh.

'What's she talking about Amazon at this time of night for?' Louise asked.

'Because it seems like idiocy is contagious. I've got the Chief coming out with the most hair-brained, half-baked stupid idea I've ever heard in all my years on the job, then not only does Ben decide to go along with it, but now Jill wants to jump in alongside him. And all I can do is hope that neither of them gets killed in the process.'

*

'Guvnor.' Pete closed the door of Colin's office behind him. The big clock on the wall, which Colin had brought with him from the squad room at Heavitree Road when they moved here three years ago, was just ticking around towards 8:00am.

'Pete.' His dour expression didn't change.

'It looks like it's catching.'

'What is?'

'Stupidity. Have you heard from Jill Evans?'

'No.'

'Well, you will. She called me last night. Wants to go undercover with Ben as his backup.'

'Makes sense.'

Pete resisted the urge to turn around and walk straight back out again.

'She's the right age to play his girlfriend or sister. She's small, so non-threatening. Might even be seen by the suspect as possible leverage in dealing with Ben. A vulnerability. He seems to like them.'

'So, you'll support her in it?'

'She's a grown woman. An adult one, anyway. And perfectly capable, as you've said yourself many a time.'

The phone started to ring on his desk. He reached over and picked it up. 'Yes?' A grunt. 'Was just talking about you.'

Pete's eyebrows rose. '*Jill?*' he mouthed.

Colin nodded. 'Yes. OK. All right. Give me a few minutes, I'll call you back.' He hung up and, with a glance at Pete, picked up the receiver again and dialled an internal number.

'DI Underhill,' he said and paused. 'Ma'am, it's Colin Underhill. One of Ben Myers' colleagues, PC Jill Evans, is volunteering to go undercover with him to provide backup and additional credibility.' The chief inspector asked a question. 'That's right,' Colin said. 'We think also, it would encourage our man to use Ben. Gives him a possible weak point the suspect could plan to take advantage of, if he feels the need, once the initial meeting happens.'

If it happens, Pete thought, still struggling with the idea.

'OK, I'll tell her,' Colin said and hung up. Again, he picked the receiver straight back up and dialled from memory.

Pete raised an eyebrow in surprise that he could remember all the numbers of the four teams of detectives he had under his command.

'Jill,' he said when she picked up. 'You've got full backing. Make whatever arrangements you need to.' She said something Pete couldn't hear. 'All right.' Colin hung up and looked up at him.

'It's done. She's sourcing her own PPE for the job. It's quicker that way. We don't hold stock of things like that. Kate will stay with Jane and Roger. It's only a few days.'

'I hope she gets herself a hoodie while she's shopping for Kevlar clothing,' Pete said, feeling faintly sick. 'She'll need some protection for her neck without it being obvious, as well as her upper body.'

'She knows what she's doing. How've the rest of you got on with your CIs?'

'We've spread the word as far as we can. And Traffic are on the lookout for the silver Golf as well as the camera team. We could do with widening that to Uniform, though. It's a legitimate enquiry, not related to the firearms as far as anyone else is concerned.'

Colin's lips tightened. He shook his head. 'Best to keep it as tight as we can, just in case, for now.' He raised a hand to silence

Pete before he could protest. 'I know what you're saying. And why. But we don't want to drive the suspect underground or force him to swap cars when we've only just ID'd this one. As faint as the possibility is, we're under scrutiny from above. Way above. Any screw-ups will be noted and reacted to, so best play safe.'

'So, we're stuck. Relying on the faint possibility that this plan will work – and that Ben and Jill can pull it off and stay safe in the process. Unless we can find that car.'

Colin tipped his head. 'Way it goes sometimes. You do all you can, then wait for a response. You know that.'

Pete sighed. 'Yes. But I don't like it. Especially not in this case. Are we sure there's no way to trace his web traffic?'

Colin shrugged. 'It's encrypted from here to Christmas. One of those ultra-secure VPN's as well as going through the dark web, with the additional security systems that entails. They've tried. Got nowhere.'

'What the hell are we paying all those so-called cyber-experts for?' Pete demanded. 'It's a program. Or a set of programs. Written by people. Surely, other people can figure out what they've done and how to get round it? They managed it with Operation Eternal on EncroChat in 2020.'

'That was the French. They found some of the servers and managed to install some sort of hardware devices that let them intercept and decode the messages going through them.'

'OK. But, even so, you'd think with all the hackers in the world, someone would be able to come up with a way around what our man's using.'

'Most of the hackers are on the side of the people writing and using that sort of software, not those trying to crack it.'

'Most, but not all,' Pete countered.

Colin grunted. 'Still, they haven't done it yet. Not that I know of.'

'Hmm. All right. I'll get back to the team – what's left of it – and we'll see what we can do to find this guy.'

*

Pete phoned Dale Gordon as he drove down the long drive between grassy banks, heading out of the police station after agreeing that Ben and Jill would have twenty-four-hour monitoring, provided by Pete and his remaining team members, with Colin's help, until contact was made, at which point a surveillance team from the National Crime Agency would step in.

Gordon picked up on the second ring.

'Dale,' Pete said. 'Where are you?'

'Who's that?'

Pete sighed. 'Now who's not recognising who? It's Pete Gayle. Where are you?'

'Working.'

Pete's lips pursed as he reached the end of the drive and flicked on his indicator to turn north, towards Dave's new house. 'Which part of knifing a man in the guts and trying to run you off the road doesn't spell danger to you, Dale? When I told you to clear off for a few days, I meant it for your own safety. And your mum's and sister's.' With the traffic clear, he pulled out.

'I can't just drop everything. I've got customers who rely on me. And you might be well enough off to grab an 'oliday at two minutes' notice, but we ain't. Plus, you might say it's safer for 'em, but it'd scare the crap out of my mum and Becks if I walked in and told them to just pack a bag, we're going. Like, now. How would your missus feel, eh?'

'She'd be worried, but she'd do it because she'd know there was a good reason for me telling her to. You need to wake up and smell the roses, Dale. Until we catch this guy, you are in danger. For your life. And he's already told you, so are your mum and your sister. He's many things, most of them not nice, but a liar isn't one of them. Not in that sense, anyway. We've seen the proof.'

'So, where are we supposed to go, eh? And how long for? We can't afford Benidorm. And Becks is due back at school soon, anyway. What is it? Two, three weeks?'

'Our plan is to have him in custody by the end of this week.'

Gordon grunted. 'Yeah, right. In your dreams. It's Thursday now.'

'Then you shouldn't need to be gone long, should you? Have you got no family you could visit for a few days? Grandparents that haven't seen you for longer than they'd like? Or an uncle or aunt, maybe?'

'Huh. Don't know any of my dad's family. Never met 'em and don't want to. And my mum's an only child. And local. My gran lives up Fairpark Road.'

Literally a couple of streets away from where Dale and his mum lived, Pete realised. He sighed. 'And your grandad?'

'Died in 2020. Covid.'

Pete's lips pursed. 'I'm sorry to hear that. All right, if you're determined to stay put, at least stay safe. And make sure your mum and your sister do, too. Send them to visit your gran. It might only be a couple of streets away, but it'd be enough that they're not at home, hopefully.'

'What do you mean, *hopefully*?'

'Well, if he's already watching them when they leave…' Pete let that sink in, letting the young man's imagination do the rest.

'Then you better fucking catch him! I've got to go.' And he hung up.

Go where, to do what, Pete was left to wonder. But he didn't bother calling back. He'd done all he could in that direction.

CHAPTER SIXTEEN

With Ben and Jill having gone to the station, Pete left Jane and Dick at Dave's, checking the Police National Database for unsolved cases that might fit the profile of their subject while he headed out with Dave following on his big black Norton motorbike.

Turning into Roberts Road, he drove steadily along its full length to the T-junction with Radford Road where he turned right, heading back down to complete the loop, in the process passing both ends of the street where Dale Gordon lived. As he drove, a copy of the e-fit of their suspect lay beside him on the passenger seat while his eyes roamed both sides of the street, searching for silver Golfs or anyone who looked out of place or even slightly familiar.

Spotting nothing and no-one of interest, he pulled over behind Dave, who had come up Radford Road from the bottom end, then ridden down the length of the street they were focussing on and completed the loop to park on the bend halfway down.

Pete switched off his engine and stepped out, approaching the leather-clad detective constable.

'Anything?'

'Nope. You?'

Pete shook his head.

'So, if he's coming, he's not here yet.'

'Unfortunately, there's three different ways in and out of here and nowhere that you can see all three from.'

'No, but if you stay here and keep your eyes peeled, I can have a run up past Dale's gran's house and see what I can see.'

'OK. But don't approach him if you do see him. Call me.'

'Yes, Mother.'

Pete shot him a stern look.

'I'm not daft,' Dave said. 'And I've only just moved house. I've got a lot still to do before I pop my clogs.'

Pete grunted. 'Go on, then. As long as you remember that.'

Dave kicked the big Norton into rumbling life and Pete returned to his car and sat inside. From here, he could look down the hill to the junction with Roberts Road where Dave's brake light was just coming on and, in the mirrors, see back up beyond the junction with Franklin Street, marked by the white-rendered house on the far corner, and up towards the top end of Roberts Road.

He sat patiently, one eye on the far end of the road, the other on the mirror as Dave turned the corner and went from sight.

*

'Damn.'

He was sure that was a silver Golf that had just passed the end of the road in front of him, going left-to-right – towards the Gordons' address. Reaching for the ignition, he checked the side mirror as he slipped the car into gear. And cursed again. Another vehicle was coming down the hill towards him. If the road had been wide enough, he'd have pulled out anyway, but with cars parked down both sides it left barely more than a car-width of clear road and he needed to reverse towards the on-coming car.

He let it pass, then pulled out, changed gear and used the mirrors to reverse quickly up the hill towards the junction with Franklin Street. Passing it, he stopped and drew forward into the junction and around the bend at the top of the street. Pulling over, he looked down the street, but could see no-one on foot and only one silver car, which he knew had been there earlier, when they arrived.

A glance at the clock as he reached for his radio told him Dave had been gone no more than ten minutes.

'DS Gayle for DC Miles. Where are you, Dave?'

'Fairpark.'

'Can you come back along Roberts, past the nursery school, and up into Franklin? A possible target vehicle just came in off Topsham Road. I'm at the top of Franklin but it's not here.'

'Will do.'

Pete switched off the ignition and waited for Dave's return or for their target to come into sight at the far end of the short street.

Dave appeared first. He turned into the end of the street and came slowly up towards Pete, stopping alongside him. Pete rolled down the window and Dave flipped up the visor of his helmet.

'Couldn't see him on Roberts. He might have gone into one of the side-roads, though, if it was him.'

'True. I'd have thought if he'd parked up, though, you'd have seen him on foot by the time you came along. It took me a minute to get into position and call you.'

'Maybe a false alarm, then. I'll go back and keep an eye on the gran's place, shall I?'

Pete nodded and Dave flipped his visor down, gunned the engine of the big bike and swung it around to head back down the hill. He'd barely straightened the bike up and got into motion when a figure on foot turned into the bottom end of the street.

Dave let the bike roll, acting normally. Had he seen him? Pete wondered, focussing on the approaching man. Clad in dark cargo trousers and a check shirt under a short denim jacket, he was too far off, as yet, to pick out his features, though his hair was dark and his height and build matched the man they were looking for.

Although that applied to untold thousands of males in the city, Pete admitted to himself.

Still, he watched with tension gripping his innards as the man walked up the hill towards him, his gait determined and purposeful.

Dave passed him and kept going, but Pete saw his head turn before his left hand left the handlebars and pointed over his head, jabbing twice towards the man on the pavement.

It was him.

Tension clamping his hands onto the steering wheel, Pete forced himself to wait and watch until the man stopped at the Gordon's dark brown front door and reached for the bell.

That was it.

He flicked off his seatbelt and got out of the car. Crossing the road, he started down towards the man. Beyond him, Dave had pulled over into a space on the same side of the road and stopped the bike. They had their man in a pincer with Pete only four doors up from him and Dave just two doors beyond.

He glanced up, saw Pete and instantly seemed to recognise him, or at least realise what he was. He turned. Started to run back down the hill. Hesitated as he saw Dave looking back at him, then surged forward, towards the leather-clad man, who started to cock his leg over the bike to get off it.

The man jumped up and right.

The pavement was only two feet wide, the houses opening directly onto it with no front gardens. It looked to Pete as if he was going to try to jump around Dave, despite the lack of space, but his right foot hit the sill of a window and pushed off and up. His left kicked out, hitting Dave on the upper arm. There was a shout, muffled by Dave's helmet, as he seemed to collapse over the bike, which tipped to the left, away from the kick-stand, taking him with it as the fleeing man bounced off and forward, landing squarely back on the narrow footpath, his speed increased by the move.

Pete hoped Dave wasn't going to get trapped under the big bike, but he couldn't stop to help him. He pounded after the target, feet slapping on the grey tarmac, gaining speed and momentum with every step, now only three paces behind his man.

How the man planned to stop at the bottom, he had no idea. Or would he just keep going and hope that no cars were coming along Roberts Road as he angled across into the end of Temple Road, down the side of the nursery?

Pete's mind flashed an image of the man running into the path of an on-coming car, the impact, bonnet crumpling under his torso as his head snapped across to crack the windscreen.

His only other option would be to grab for the telegraph pole that he was now only a few steps short of and hope that it didn't pull his arm out of its socket in the process. But then Pete would have him.

If he could stop, himself.

But his man had another idea.

Again, he jumped up and right, his foot landing on the windowsill of the last house in the row, launching him across to the left. There, his left foot hit the spare tyre bolted to the back door of a small SUV. The car's alarm squealed as Pete ran past, unable to stop in time. There was a metallic crunch as the man landed on the bonnet of the black hatchback behind the SUV, crumpling the thin metal and setting off a second alarm.

Pete's feet slapped loudly on the tarmac as he tried to stop himself. The door of the white-rendered corner house opened and he yelled out, 'No! Stay inside.' Then he made the only move he could: grabbed for the thick, wooden trunk of the telegraph pole just inches from the wall on the inner side of the footpath, wrapping his right arm around it in a hug that felt like it might have dislocated his arm, but he held on as his feet left the pavement, body swinging up almost to the horizontal as it came around to crash painfully into the white-rendered wall and the meter box just beyond the pole. He quickly let go of the pole and landed in a crumpled heap on the pavement, half-rolling towards the gutter.

'What the...' The female voice cut off as he scrambled up to his hands and knees with barely a pause, feet slipping and scraping on the tarmac as he fought for purchase to head back up after his man.

Just a car-length now separated him from...

His head made it far enough back up the hill to see behind the 4x4.

Empty space.

The little hatchback's bonnet was crushed and ruined, crumpled like cling-film over packaged meat, he saw as he darted through the gap in case his quarry was hiding on the far side of the cars.

He wasn't.

Pete turned back, spinning on the pavement, trying to see which way his man had gone.

There was no sign.

'My car! What the fuck's going on?' The woman had stepped outside now, just two paces from him. In her forties, her hair greying, dark red lips pulled back in a snarl.

Pete had no time for her. He snatched out his warrant card. 'Police,' he snapped. 'I was chasing a murder suspect. Which way did he go?'

She blinked, lips going round in shock as her hand came up to point. To the right of the telegraph pole was a painted door-like gate and, beyond it, the wall continued up to the smaller metal gate of the first house, its door set back from the pavement on the front of a small side-extension. She was pointing at that gate.

Pete stepped across towards it, saw it had a spring closer on the hinge side. Beyond it, the side-extension was taking up most of what had anyway been no more than a small courtyard with the usual single-storey rear extension that thousands of these Victorian terraces had been provided with in the early part of the twentieth century blocking off the far side and a low garden wall coming across from that. Most of the remaining concrete courtyard was taken up by a pair of wheelie bins. The man he'd been chasing was gone from sight.

He glanced to his right, up the hill, and saw Dave was on his feet, struggling to pull the heavy motorbike back up onto its wheels.

He was tempted to call for a helicopter or at least a drone to help find the man who'd gone who-knew-where amongst the little gardens that stretched away up behind the houses of Franklin Street and Robets Road. There was no telling where he'd be amongst them by now, hopping over fences or hiding in someone's shed. But as soon as he heard the blades above, he'd be into the nearest house and before they knew it, they could easily have a hostage situation on their hands.

Pete sighed, defeated.

At least Dale's mother and sister were...

'Shit.'

One of those gardens the suspect had just gained access to was theirs.

He stepped quickly into the end house's courtyard, glanced over the wall into the neighbour's garden, checked the bins and that the front door was locked, then headed up the hill, ignoring the renewed protests of the woman behind him.

'Are you OK?' he asked Dave, who was just settling the bike back onto its stand.

'I think so.'

'Good. Find his car. He's garden-hopping. I need to check on the Gordons.'

'Right.'

With his right arm, shoulder, hip and calf all sending pain signals to his brain at every step, he went on up the hill. By the time he reached the brown door, his left hand was clasping his right arm against his side. He released it to push the doorbell. It was answered in moments.

'Ms Gordon,' he said, ignoring her changing expression, which went from sour to horrified. 'Dale's still out, is he?'

'Yes. What the…'

'And Becky?'

She shook her head quickly. 'At a friend's. Why?'

'Good. You need to lock your back door and leave. Now.'

Her expression shifted again. 'Why? What's going on? What happened to…?'

'Now, Cathy.' He stepped forward. 'Is the back door locked?'

'Yes. I keep it locked unless we go out there.'

'Then grab your bag, your phone and your keys.'

'But…'

'Move!' He raised his hands to usher her inwards and winced at the pain that shot down his right arm.

She stepped back. 'What's going on?' she demanded again.

'Did Dale tell you he was knocked off his bike yesterday?'

'He said he fell off it.' She crossed the tiny sitting room and picked up a handbag from beside one of the easy chairs.

'Well, he had help,' Pete told her as he heard Dave's bike rumble into life and roar off down the road. 'From the male I told you about before. Who's currently somewhere amongst the back gardens here.'

She froze as she reached for the phone sitting on the coffee table in the middle of the room. Looked up at him. 'How...?'

'I nearly caught him at the bottom of the street, but he got away.'

'So...' She straightened, phone in hand, automatically slipping it into the bag.

'You're safer somewhere else until we get our hands on him. Call Becky and Dale when you get there and tell them to come to you, not back here.'

'But how did you...?'

'There isn't time now. Keys.'

'In my bag.'

'Right, let's go.' Careful to use his left arm, he lifted it towards the front door.

*

He waited until he'd got her into his car before saying, 'I'll take you to your mum's. It's not far, but it's away from here.'

'How do you know where my mum lives?'

'Dale told me,' he said, starting the engine. 'Have you got a spare key to your house?'

'No, but Dale's got one.'

'I'll need to borrow yours, then, before you come back. Make sure the suspect hasn't broken in or anything.' *Make sure the house is safe for you,* he thought, but didn't say.

She shook her head. 'This is doing my head in. What's going on, exactly?'

Pete glanced at her as he drove down the hill. 'I can't tell you everything, but a man who Dale did a little job for – a perfectly legal one – has turned out to be dangerous. We're trying to apprehend him on suspicion of another crime. And he seems to have taken into his head that Dale either ratted him out or might do, so he's coming after Dale by any means necessary. Hence the danger to you and Becky.'

'Jesus! Who is this bloke?' she demanded as he stopped at the bottom of the street and turned right.

'That's the part we haven't got an answer to. Yet.'

His radio hissed. 'DC Miles for DS Gayle. I've found it.'

He reached for the radio and pressed the transmit button. 'Where?'

'Tucked round behind the nursery.'

'Can you keep an eye on it discretely? I've got Mrs G with me. Taking her to the other address.'

'OK.'

'And get Dick and Jane over here. We need to flush this guy out before he does anything we don't want him to.'

'Will do.'

'I'll drop you at your mum's and get back here,' he said to the woman beside him. 'Just make sure your kids don't go back to yours until we give you the all-clear, all right?'

She nodded.

'Can you do that?' he pressed.

'Yes.'

'OK.'

Pete wasn't sure he believed her, having spoken to Dale himself a few times now, but as long as she believed it, that was a start. The question now was, how were just the four of them going to make sure of the family's safety without endangering anyone else in the process?

CHAPTER SEVENTEEN

Pete got on the phone as soon as he was alone in the car, his movements delicate and careful with his aching right arm and his leg beginning to feel sore as he performed a three-point turn so he could head back along the narrow street.

'Guv, it's Pete,' he said when Colin answered. 'We've got a situation and I can't see how the Chief can say, "No," to us this time.'

'What is it?'

'The suspect turned up at Dale Gordon's place. We spooked him and he got away from us, but he went into the gardens behind the row of houses where Gordon lives. He knows which is theirs, but I don't know if he'll stick to his plan and go there or try to find some other way out. Which would mean going through someone's house or coming out the way he went in. Dave's found his car and he's keeping an eye on it, but we don't want him endangering a random member of the public, do we?' As he spoke, he finished turning the car around and started back along towards the junction with Roberts Road.

'Where are the Gordons?'

'The kids are out and I took the mother to *her* mother's. I'm on the way back to theirs now with a key, so I can make sure he hasn't broken in while we've been gone. It'd be as good a way out of the gardens as any other, with the added bonus of scaring the Gordons while he's at it, whether they're in or not. Dick and Jane are on the way over, but four of us can't search for him effectively. We need a drone up to contain the area.'

'When did he go to ground?'

'Ten…' He checked the clock as he reached the bottom of Franklin Street and turned in. 'Twelve minutes ago.'

'So, he could be anywhere by now.'

'Yes,' Pete admitted, pulling up at the kerb a couple of doors down from the Gordons' address. 'But he'll either have to go back to his car or abandon it and head away on foot. And before that, he's got to get back out onto the street. And I can't see him risking coming back out the way he went in, in case we're watching for him.'

Colin paused for just a beat. 'Leave it with me.'

The line went dead and Pete switched off the ignition and stepped out of the car. Looking up the street, he could see no pedestrians on the narrow pavements nor hear any alarms going off anywhere. That, at least, was a good sign.

He called Jane.

'It's Pete,' he said when she answered. 'Are you with Dick or on your own?'

'We're bringing both cars, just in case.'

'OK. When you get here, go past the bottom end of Franklin and far enough around the bend to see up Roberts, then wait and see if the suspect shows.'

'Right.'

Pete quickly described what the man was wearing. 'Talk later.' He ended the call and made another.

'DC Feeney.'

'Dick, it's Pete. I need you to turn up Radford Road and into the top of Roberts. Stop up there on the bend so you can see down the hill.'

'All right.'

'We don't know where he'll come out so we need to cover all exits. I'm on Franklin and Dave's watching his car, in case he gets back to it before we're all in position. The Guvnor's trying to arrange a drone for us on the basis of public safety trumping the NCA's paranoia.'

'What if he takes a hostage?' Dick asked.

'Then, we've got a whole new set of problems. But I can't see it, unless just as an escape plan. Which is why we need eyes all around him.'

'Or he could break into the Gordons' place and either hide up and wait for them or do Christ-knows-what in there while he's got free reign.'

'Except I've got a key.'

'Ah. We'll be there in a couple of minutes.'

Pete's phone buzzed with another call coming in. He glanced at the screen.

'Good. Got to go.' He switched calls.

'You've got your drone,' Colin said without preamble.

'Thanks, Guv. When?'

'They said twenty minutes.'

'I'll have Dick and Jane here in two, so we'll have him contained until it arrives. Then I'll get Dave back here and go into the Gordons'.'

'Right.' Colin hung up.

Pete sat quietly waiting, eyes peeled. What felt like much longer than two minutes later, he caught the brief flash of bright green in his mirror as Jane's car passed the bottom end of the road behind him. All else was quiet and still around him until his phone buzzed. He picked up.

'It's Jane. I'm in position.'

'Can you see the end of Temple Road in your mirror?'

'Yes.'

'Perfect. Stay put and call up on the radio if you see any movement.'

'Will do.'

He hung up and called Dave.

'No signs of activity round there?' he asked when he picked up.

'Quiet as the grave.'

'Good. Jane's up Roberts Road now. Dick will be...' His phone buzzed with another call coming in. 'That'll be him, I expect, up the top end. Come up Franklin and back me up while I go into the house, yes?'

'Will do.'

Pete switched calls. 'Dick?'

'No need to be insulting, DS Gayle. I'm getting there as fast as I can.'

He recognised the voice on the other end. Not Grey Man, but the drone operator from the photography unit. 'Hello, Greg. I was expecting someone else. Where are you?'

'I just passed the County Council offices.'

'Great. If you turn into Roberts Road then take the second on the left, I'm just up there. You'll see my car. And if I'm not in it, Dave Miles will be out here on his bike.'

'Bike? I didn't know we still used them.'

'Motorbike. Big, black number. His own, not an official one.'

'Right. I'll see you in a minute or two.'

'OK.' Pete hung up and, moments later, heard the growl of a big engine and Dave swung into view around the junction at the bottom of the hill behind him. He stood up out of the car to let Dave see him. As the leather-clad DC pulled in behind his car, his phone buzzed in his hand. He glanced at the screen and took the call.

'Hello?'

'It's Dick. I'm just pulling up at the top of the road. I can see you from here. Is that Dave?'

'Yes. Stay put and keep your eyes peeled. Now we're all here, I'm going into the house, to check it out. The drone operator will be here in a minute, too.'

'Right-oh.'

Pete ended the call and turned to Dave, told him to get the drone operator set up and flying and keep his wits about him, then he set off up towards the Gordons' house, taking the keys from his pocket as he went. Cathy Gordon had shown him which was for the front door and which the back. He selected the one he wanted as he walked so that, arriving at the door, he could slip it in and turn it without pause or hesitation.

He pushed the door open and went in fast.

Immediately felt a breeze coming through from the back of the house.

He stepped through the doorless opening in the corner, at the base of the stairs, into the back room.

It was set out as a dining room with a stubby kitchen extension off the opposite corner, covering almost the full width of the house so that this room no longer had a window. It had been bricked up when the kitchen was added. He crossed the room so he could see into the kitchen from the far corner as he stood beside a display and drinks cabinet. The back door was in the far end of the extension, a large window beside it, which was where the draft was coming from. White-doored units with pale wood handles were ranged under the window and along both sides of the little room.

Behind the wooden slatted window blind, he could see a neat hole had been made in the glass with a cutter, perfectly round and about five inches across.

The key was still in the lock of the back door, just a foot or so away from the cut in the double-glazed window. Pete had no doubt he'd find it unlocked. The question was, was the burglar still in the house?

If so, he'd have to be upstairs and Pete's brief glance as he passed the bottom of the stairs had told him the two doors at the top, off either side of the small square landing, were both open, allowing light into the stairwell.

If the man was up there, he'd have the advantage over anyone coming up towards him. Especially as Pete had no Taser, or even a baton, and was not familiar with the layout.

He drew a breath.

'If you're up there, you're going nowhere,' he called. 'If you get past me, I've got men outside. And the Gordons aren't coming back until I tell them it's safe so you might as well give yourself up now because not to will only add to the charges against you, and no clever barrister will be able to argue a way out of them.'

He waited.

No response came. No creak of a floorboard, intake of breath, rustle of clothing: nothing.

'OK. You want it the hard way, don't say you weren't warned.'

Rather than go up there defenceless, he stepped away from the stairs and crossed quickly to the kitchen. Here, he took a few seconds to find four tea-trays standing on their edges at one side of the cupboard under the sink, where the lack of a shelf allowed the height needed to accommodate them.

The one at the back of the stack was old-fashioned, made of white-painted thin plywood and deep sided with angled corners. In the ends were hand-sized cutouts for carrying it.

That would do.

Leaving the others on the worktop beside the draining board, he took it in his left hand by one of the handles and lifted it, shield-like, across his lower torso. It was far from perfect, but it would do the job if he was quick enough. There was no way the Chief was going to allow him to call in SWAT.

In any case, with any luck, the man wasn't even up there, he told himself. He'd probably just broken in to prove he could, and to scare Dale and his family, and walked straight through and out the front door while no-one was watching.

It would have taken no more than a couple of minutes to get in, using a glasscutter and a suction pad.

He headed back to the stairs and, without further warning, started up.

In these old houses, there was no way he was going to reach the top without at least one or two stairs creaking and, sure enough, the third, fourth and fifth all did. As he stepped up again, he was listening intently, but still heard nothing from the upper rooms. He paused, waiting for a couple of seconds before continuing upward.

He took a single step. Then two at a time. Another two and, raising the tray defensively, he ducked his head around to the left. Found a narrow corridor, just the width of a door, leading along to a bathroom in the upper floor of the rear extension. The door stood open, as did the one to the bedroom at his shoulder. A distinctly male enclave, he noted before switching his attention to 'his right. Here was a much more feminine space, most of it taken up by two single beds. Clothes, make-up, hairbrushes, pink and white décor all suggested a mother and daughter shared this room.

Pete stepped inside. He checked behind the door, in the two single wardrobes that filled the alcoves to either side of the chimneybreast and between and beyond the beds. There was no-one here. He crossed the tiny landing to Dale's room. The door stood flat against the wall. The far side of the bed – a divan like the others – was clear. He snatched open the wardrobe door and was, for the third time, greeted by only clothes. A floor-to-ceiling cupboard in the corner over the stairs was stacked with boxes, many of them for assorted brands of trainers, and contained the loft hatch in its ceiling, but there was no way anyone could have gained access to it without disturbing the boxes beneath, which clearly hadn't been moved in some time.

He checked the bathroom too, but the man wasn't here.

He was long gone, Pete realised with a sigh of mixed relief and disappointment.

He switched his radio and phone back on. Used the radio to contact his whole team. 'Any signs of him out there/?'

'No,' Jane replied.

'Nothing,' said Dick.

'Nothing on the drone.'

'Nope.' Dave completed the set.

'He's been in the house, but he's not here now,' Pete told them. 'It'll need a glazier for the kitchen window.'

'I know one,' Jane replied. 'I'll get onto him.'

'Thanks, Jane. I suspect our man's left the area, but we'll hold our positions for a while, in case he's holed up in another house and waiting 'til he feels like the coast is clear. I've got a view of the gardens from the bathroom window here so you can bring the drone down and conserve it's battery, Greg.'

'Or I could widen the search area while it's up and see if I can spot him on the surrounding streets.'

'If you can. But it's been twenty minutes now. I know he's broken in here and then left, but he could still have walked half a mile or more.'

'Or be hiding up somewhere close by, looking innocent, until we bugger off,' Dave retorted.

'Which you already have from where he parked,' Pete pointed out. 'If he knows the street layout, he could get back around there without being spotted, if he hasn't already. It might be worth a spin around and see if you can spot anything, Greg.'

'Right, I'll do that. Silver Golf, wasn't it?' He read out the registration.

'That's right.'

'On Temple Road?'

'North side, behind the nursery school,' Dave confirmed.

'Stand by.'

Less than a minute later, the radio hissed again.

'North side?' Greg asked. 'As in, opposite the back of the nursery school?'

'Yes, yes,' Dave replied.

'He's gone.'

'*What?*' Dave demanded.

'There is no silver Golf, on either side of that stretch of road.'

'Bastard!'

CHAPTER EIGHTEEN

'Hello?'

The woman's eyes were clear blue and curious as she opened the door to him. She was small and fine-boned with curly grey hair, wearing a peach-coloured polo-neck sweater under an open white cardigan with a pleated skirt.

'Mrs Lambert?'

'Yes.'

He held up his ID. 'I'm DS Gayle with Exeter CID. Could I have a word with your daughter?'

'You'd better come in.'

'Thank you.'

She stepped back and showed him into a typical 1930's semi with the stairs leading up on the left side of a narrow hallway, doors leading off to the right and at the far end, all of them now closed. She led him through the nearest, opposite the bottom of the stairs, into a sitting room with a flower-print three-piece suite, a TV in the far corner and a display cabinet against the wall to his right, full of ornaments and mementos.

Dale Gordon's mother was sitting on the sofa in front of the display cabinet. She moved to get up as he stepped in, then recognised him and went still, trying to read his face.

'What's happened?'

'You'd better sit down, Detective,' the older woman cut in. 'Would you like some tea? You look like you need something.'

Pete glanced down at himself. 'Yes, I had a bit of an issue with a telegraph pole earlier,' he said. 'Haven't had a chance to get cleaned up and changed yet.'

'A busy morning?'

'Mum!' Her tone was impatient.

'You could say,' Pete admitted.

'I'll get the kettle on,' she said with a small smile.

He returned the expression and sat in one of the easy chairs facing the bay window that looked out through net curtains onto a steeply sloping lawn with a low stone wall at the top, his car's roof just visible beyond it.

'So?' Cathy Gordon urged as the door closed behind her mother.

'She seems like a nice lady, your mum.'

'She is. Why are you here?'

Pete drew a breath. 'The man we're after broke into your house before we had a chance to get there. The only damage is the kitchen window,' he added quickly. 'One of my colleagues is getting onto a glazier, to fix it. As far as I can tell, he didn't take anything – or leave anything, for that matter. It was just a scare tactic. To prove he could. I don't know if he went back out the way he came in or walked out through the front door. I've got people checking with the neighbours as we speak, not that it makes much difference. What it comes down to is, he got away. For now.'

Her expression shifted yet again, settling into one of horror. 'So, he's still out there.'

'As I said – for now. We've got colleagues checking the traffic cameras and so on to try and track him.' *At least, Dick Feeney's getting onto Graham to see if there are any in the relevant spots now,* he thought. There hadn't been a couple of years ago when they wanted them on another case. 'So, for that reason – and I've already said this to Dale – you need to stay away from there for a while. All of you. Have a few days away. A cheap holiday somewhere.'

She snorted. 'Yeah, right. As if there is such a thing at this time of year.'

'It only needs a few days,' he said. 'Have you got any other relatives you could go to, if you can't afford anything else? Further away than here.'

She shook her head. 'No. And we've got lives. We can't just drop everything without any notice.'

'It's a couple of weeks yet until the new school year starts, so Becky won't miss out,' he said. 'And if you let me know who it is, we can get your GP to provide you with a sick note for work.'

'It's not as simple as that,' she argued. 'If I don't work, I don't get paid, and I've still got bills to pay.'

'Where do you work?' He was aware of the zero-hours contract system used so often in the NHS and elsewhere. Surely, something could be arranged.

'Hairdressers on South Street,' she said. 'I tried to get a job at the one on Roberts Road, but they'd got no openings, and haven't had since. So, I'm effectively self-employed, although the owner still treats us like staff. Slaves, more like,' she added with a grunt. 'So, we don't get sick or holiday pay and Becks needs new uniform and books and such. I need to work.'

He sighed. With a daughter of his own, he knew how expensive it could be to supply and clothe them for school. 'I suppose, if there's absolutely no other choice, you've got the one advantage that, having kept your married name, your mum's is different. Could the three of you stay here for a few days? Or Becky stay over with a friend?'

She frowned. 'This ain't a mansion.'

The door opened and her mother pushed through, a tray in her bony hands. 'What's wrong with this house?'

'Nothing, Mum. It's just not big enough for four people to have their own rooms.'

'Four? Why?' She set the tray down on the coffee table in the middle of the green and beige patterned carpet. 'What's going on?' She glanced at Pete. 'Or shouldn't I ask?'

'We were just discussing options,' he told her. 'There's a problem at Franklin Road. Your daughter and her kids need to stay somewhere else for a few days while it gets sorted, that's all.'

'Oh, what, a gas leak or something?'

'No,' Pete said. 'They'd have to sort one of those out the same day, definitely. Could cause all kinds of problems otherwise. But...'

'I suppose Becky could stay over with her mate, Mandy, who she's with this morning,' Cathy broke in. 'As long as it's only a few days. But then, there's only one spare bed here and Dale's in and out at all sorts of weird hours. Mum couldn't have that.'

'He'll have to just stick to the nine-to-five for as long as it takes,' Pete said. 'You never know, it might do him good. If it's all right with you, Mrs Lambert?' he added, looking up at the older woman, who was busy pouring three cups of tea.

'As Cathy said, Detective, there's only the one spare bed. But I suppose, if either she or Dale had the sofa...' She handed a cup to her daughter.

The younger woman took the cup and shrugged. 'A few nights, I could stand it, I suppose. As long as it is a few.'

'It will be,' Pete assured her. 'One way or another, we'll have it sorted.' He accepted a full cup from Mrs Lambert.

'There we are, then,' she said brightly.

'Good,' Pete nodded. 'That's one thing dealt with, at least.' He turned back to Cathy. 'So, what are your normal working hours?'

'I'm doing afternoons this week. I'll be off in fift... Ten minutes,' she corrected herself. 'A bit further to walk from here.'

'Don't worry, I'll give you a lift.'

'No, that's...' She caught his stern look and stopped. 'Actually, yes, OK. Thanks.'

'DS,' said the mother. 'Is that Detective Sergeant, like in the detective shows on TV?'

Here we go, Pete thought. *Awkward question time.* 'Yes, that's right.'

'So, what's a detective sergeant doing speaking to people about making alternative accommodation arrangements after an accident in the street?'

He tipped his head. 'It's down to whoever's free at the time, Mrs Lambert. I had a spare couple of minutes.'

'You look a bit worse for wear, if you don't mind me saying,' she said with a frown.

'Yes, I know. I feel it, too, if I'm honest. I slipped on the street and went a cropper. Caught my arm on the telegraph pole at the bottom of the hill as I went down. I was just going home to clean myself up and change when the need came up for someone to come and speak to Cathy, here.'

'Should I call Mandy's mum and arrange for Becks to stay?' Cathy suggested.

'Yes,' he said, and she took out her phone and dialled.

He heard the squeals of delight from across the room and gave her a smile.

'That's all set, then?' he said when she hung up.

She nodded and put the phone away.

They finished their tea and headed off a few minutes later. Pete waited until they were in motion, back along the road towards the cluster of streets where she lived before saying, 'You'd better tell Dale to wind his neck in for the duration. Normal rules still apply and if we're keeping a close eye...' He glanced across at her, raising an eyebrow. 'He doesn't want to get caught with anything he shouldn't be in possession of.'

'He doesn't...' She bristled, then slumped. 'Yeah, all right. I don't ask what he gets up to and I definitely don't get involved. Stay well out of it. But I know he must be doing some dodgy deals of some kind, to bring in the money he does. I'm just grateful for the input. And he's a good lad. Helps out with the bills, with Becky...'

'Maybe,' Pete said. 'But he needs to watch himself. Take what's happening now as a warning.'

She grunted. 'Life's going to get harder, then, financially, as if it wasn't hard enough already.'

Pete shrugged. 'At least you'll be safe. Talking of which – you'll need to stay in as much as possible. We'll do this for you each day. Take you there and bring you back. And Dale will need to be ultra-careful that he's not followed when he comes home. You really need to make that as plain to him as you can. His regular haunts are off-limits and he needs to do everything he can to make sure no-one can follow him back from wherever he does go. And none of you say anything to anyone about you and him staying with your mum, is that clear?'

'Jeez,' she grumbled as he drew up to the junction with Topsham Road, signalling to turn right, into town. 'It's like being back in junior school.'

'It's for your safety, not mine,' he said and, with the road clear, pulled out.

'Yeah, I know, but... What about picking up some clothes, toothbrushes – stuff like that?'

'We'll arrange it later, after you finish work. Have you got the card I gave you?'

'It's at home.'

He took another from his jacket and handed it over. 'Here. Put that in your purse and call me when you're ready to leave work. Someone will pick you up. Either me or one of my team.'

'Hadn't you ought to be concentrating on catching the bugger who's causing all this aggravation?'

Over the brow of the hill, he took the right fork, heading towards the city centre rather than down towards the twin bridges.

'Yes, but it's not as simple as that, unfortunately.'

'What's that mean?'

'Resources are limited and your immediate safety is the priority. There's other people concentrating on finding the suspect.'

'So, you're just a menial. Like Lewis to Morse or whatever,' she said as they drew up behind a short queue of traffic at a set of lights.

He tipped his head.

'So, who's your Morse?'

'DI Underhill.'

The lights changed and the traffic began to move. They went from a wide tree-lined multi-lane road into a narrower street, lined with buildings of various ages, mostly in use as shops.

'And where's he? Do I get to meet him?'

'Morse is fiction,' he said. 'In the real world, DIs don't come out of the office all that much. They send us DSs and DCs.'

She grunted. 'There's us,' she said, pointing across the road to a shop with a purple hoarding above the window, pink lettering labelling it as Shell's.

'OK.' He checked his mirror and pulled over. 'Remember – call me when you're due out.'

'All right. Thanks.'

*

He watched her cross the road, checked the street around them, then signalled and pulled away. Immediately, he called Dick Feeney.

'Anything useful from Graham?' he asked.

'No. I remember we found two or three private cameras in the area, last time we needed to, but that's it, still. Do you want one of us to go and get hold of any footage from them?'

'Yes, you go. I'll need Dave and Jane to stick to the Franklin Road address for now. Did you and Jane find anything on the PND before it all kicked off this morning?'

'Nothing we could tie to our suspect. We all know there's violence between – even amongst – drug gangs all the time. GBH. ABH. Very rare for anything to get solved, though, and nobody's been killed up to now. Not locally, anyway. It happens now and then in the big cities, of course.'

'This is a pretty drastic change of MO for our man, then.'

'Desperate times, maybe?'

'Maybe,' Pete agreed. 'How'd it go with the neighbours? Anyone see anything.'

'No,' Dick said as if it was a stupid question.

'Well, we had to check. How did Jane get on with her glazier?'

'He's coming within the hour.'

'Woah. What's that going to cost?'

'He'll just board it for now, measure it and get a new glazing unit made up. There's a place down on Marsh Barton that he uses. He'll do it for the price of the glass, he said, given the circumstances.'

'Wow. See, it's not only coppers that have hearts.'

Dick grunted.

'I need to call Dale, tell him not to go home. I'll talk to you soon.' Pete hung up and redialled.

'Yeah,' came the answer almost instantly.

'Dale. Pete Gayle. Message from your mum: do not go home. Go to your nan's instead. And while you're at it, make absolutely sure you're not followed. Got it?'

'What? What's going... You spoke to my mum?'

'Yes.'

'You told her what's going on?'

'Only part of it. The part she needed to know. Which is that you're all in danger until we can get this offender off the streets. And, for your info, his latest trick was to get past us, break into your house, and sneak back out again without being seen.'

'He broke into our house?'

'Yes. He didn't take anything. It was just to scare you, I expect. To prove he could do it.'

'And he got past you lot to do it? Twice?'

Pete pursed his lips. 'Don't rub it in, Dale. Remember how all this got started.'

'Yeah, with an innocent trip to Tesco's.'

'Which you knew damn well was for a far from innocent reason. You're not that slow on the uptake.'

'Oh, so this is all my fault now, is it? Well, thanks for bugger all, *mate.*'

'Just bear in mind that your actions can affect the safety of your sister, your mum and now your gran, too, all right?'

'Yeah, yeah. Did you call me just to give me a lecture or was there a useful purpose?'

Pete sighed. 'Just to tell you to stay away from Franklin Road until we take you round there with your mum and sister. And bear in mind that part of the process of keeping you safe for the next few days is going to mean us keeping an eye on you. Understood?'

'Shit, man! What are you trying to do, kill my business?'

'No, Dale. That's just an added bonus.'

CHAPTER NINETEEN

The next exit north along Topsham Road from Roberts Road led into a short cul-de-sac, little more than a parking area for the surrounding houses and flats. Pete parked there and walked down a long set of narrow brick stairs to another enclosed parking and garage area that served the block of flats between. This gave out onto the bend in Temple Road behind the nursery school. From here, he crossed Roberts Road and walked up Franklin to the Gordons' house.

He knocked on the door and it was opened by Jane.

'All quiet still?' he asked as he stepped inside.

'Yes.'

It had only been ten minutes since he left to take the Gordon family back to Fairpark Road after their brief visit to collect what they'd need for a few days away.

'You head off home, then, and get some sleep. I'll see you again about 1:00.'

Back on Fairpark, when he dropped Dale and Kathy off, he'd spotted Dick Feeney's car already in position, far enough along the road not to be obvious, though still close enough to give him a view of Mrs Lambert's house and the path that led down to it behind the low stone wall backing the street pavement. He would be relieved in the early hours by Dave, who was now at home, resting.

'It's a shame there aren't more of us,' she said. 'Spread the load a bit.'

Pete tipped his head. 'We can't risk Ben or Jill being seen by our suspect in the wrong context. If he recognised them, it'd screw everything up, as well as putting them at more risk than they are already with him.'

'Yeah, I know. Still, at least they can do desk work in the meantime. Frees the rest of us from that.'

He gave her a brief smile. 'Dick didn't find too much in the way of private CCTV from earlier but they're going through what he did get. It might give us a direction of travel, at least, with a bit of luck.'

'Yeah, trouble is, it seems like our suspect doesn't rely on luck too much. He's more of a planner.'

'Albeit a violent one.'

'Hmm. That window, by the way – the glazier did a special trick with the boarding.'

'Oh, yes?' Pete had noticed earlier that he seemed to have simply slotted a piece of OSB into the space that would otherwise have been occupied by the damaged glazing panel, rather than boarding over the whole window, which would entail making permanent holes in either the window-frame or the brickwork around it.

'Well, the piece of OS Board he put in to replace the glass until he can get a new panel made up, he drilled I think it was five different holes through, cross-ways, and put metal rods into them so that, if our man does come back and try the same trick again with a jigsaw or something, he said it would make a God-awful racket and bugger up his saw blade.'

Pete smiled. 'I like his style. Who is he?'

'Nikki French's brother.'

Nikki was a uniformed female police constable who they'd worked with a few times, on different cases over the past few years. 'Ah. Didn't he used to be in the job himself?'

'Yeah. He got invalided out a few years back. While you were off, I think. Went into a burning house before the fire crew got there to rescue a kid he heard screaming from inside. Got the kid out, but his lungs were buggered by fumes in the process. They reckoned it was from some old furniture in there. Pre-fire-safety. He couldn't abide desk-duty so he took a career change.'

'Shame. Sounds like a good man.'

'He is. Still, I'll get off. See you later.'

She left, leaving Pete alone to dwell on the many dangers of their job and the momentary nature of them. You could be minding your own business one minute and in mortal danger the next, from any number of means and directions, deliberate or otherwise. Their lives all hung in the balance at any given moment.

He wondered how Ben and Jill were getting on with the CCTV that Dick had found and whether anything would come of their attempts to force their suspect into contact with the two youngest members of his team. If it happened tonight, he'd soon know. The new phones they'd been provided with for the job had been set up to be monitored by all the other team members' phones, twenty-four-seven. If they rang, the rest of the team would know about it and the call would be recorded automatically. And there was no reason for them to ring unless it was with a contact from the suspect.

He couldn't see it happening tonight, but he hoped it would happen, in spite of the danger it represented to Ben and Jill – and the sooner, the better for all concerned.

*

Shock sparked through Pete at the buzz of his phone. He snatched it up, glancing at the time on the screen as his thumb reached for the green icon. It was just after 11:00pm. Fear mixed uncomfortably with anticipation. Had he been wrong? Was this the contact they'd been wating for? If so, why had the monitoring alarm failed to go off?

'Hello?'

'Boss? It's Ben.'

Just as he'd feared. 'What's going on?'

'We found the Golf.'

Pete slumped with relief.

'It was on the footage from the house on Wonford Road, heading south. But that's it. No sign of it on Barracks Road. Nothing on Magdalen Road or round the hospital. Nor Burnthouse Lane. It's like it vanishes.'

'What about St Leonard's School?'

'He'd already passed St Leonard's Road by the time we pick him up on Wonford Road.'

'Of course. Well, if he didn't go around the hospital or onto Magdalen, he either lives in the area of Wonford Road or he dropped down onto Topsham Road.'

'But he doesn't show up at the petrol station, either.'

'Well, that narrows the search even further, doesn't it?' Pete concluded. 'He didn't show up on the traffic cameras anywhere either, so he's somewhere in that area: Wonford Road, Topsham Road and the streets off them. We're closing in. We've just got to get out and search around there thoroughly. OK, Ben. Thanks for the call. Get some rest, all right? Or at least switch to watching martial arts or self-defence videos.'

Ben laughed. 'Night, boss.'

Pete hung up feeling better than he had when he took the call.

If they could find that Golf before its driver contacted Ben – or any other potential courier – it would be a hell of a lot safer for everyone concerned.

He thought about the part of the city they'd been talking about. Victoria Park Road, Matford Lane, the streets off Barrack Road between Wonford Road and the barracks as well as the streets leading down from the other side of Topsham Road into Countess Wear and towards Trews Weir, the Salmon Pool and Duckes Meadow, plus all the side-streets in that whole neighbourhood... The only way to search the area effectively would be on foot but that was a lot of ground to cover in a short time. Especially as there were so few of them and they were having to keep an eye on this place as well as the comings and goings of both Cathy and Dale Gordon twenty-four-seven. How they were going to manage it, he didn't know, especially as the car could well be hidden in a garage, but it had to be done. And it would be. Somehow. He was determined to see to that.

*

The shock came several hours later.

He was dozing on the sofa when he heard it and jerked up, instantly awake. A glance at the mantel over the gas fire told him it was approaching 6:30. He reached for the phone that was buzzing angrily on the coffee table, wincing as the sudden movement sent a spasm of pain through his shoulder. Grabbing it up, he swiped at the screen. Didn't recognise the number displayed there, but it had to be urgent at this time of day. He tapped the screen to accept the call and hadn't got the phone to his ear when he heard her panicked voice screaming.

'He's gone! You said we'd be safe here, but he's gone!'

He blinked, fully awake now. It had to be Cathy Gordon. 'Slow down,' he said. 'Tell me from the start. What's happened?'

'Dale's gone, that's what's happened,' she snapped, distress switching to anger.

'When? Where from? How?'

'I don't know! I just... didn't hear him snoring like he normally does, so I went to check on him and he's not here.'

'Have you tried phoning him?'

'Of course I have! It goes straight to answerphone.'

So it's switched off, he thought. *Or the battery's dead.* 'Did you leave a message?'

'Yes. Told him to come home, everything would be all right.'

He drew a breath. 'And I'm sure it will. We'll find him. I promise.'

'Like you promised we'd be safe here?' she snapped back.

'When did you last see him? Or hear him?' he added, given her comment about his snoring.

'When we all went to bed. Eleven-ish.'

'What does he wear in bed?'

'Eh? What's that got to do with anything?'

'Tell me, Cathy.'

'Pyjamas.'

'You've just come from his room?'

'Yes.'

'Were the pyjamas there?'

'Um... Yes.'

'Then he's got dressed, right?'

'Well, yes, but…'

'I'll be there in a few minutes. We'll figure it out and we'll find him. OK?'

'So, he's…'

'Probably just slipped off to stay with a friend, to avoid us so he can carry on his business uninterrupted. Didn't tell you in case you tried to stop him. I'll see you shortly.'

He ended the call and swiped down the contacts list. Tapped the one he was looking for and waited only two rings for it to be answered.

'Hi, it's me,' he said when she picked up. 'Can you get here early? Like now. Dale's done a runner so I need to go round there and start the search for him.'

'OK.'

'Thanks, Jane.' He ended the call and went through to the kitchen, to make himself a cup of strong coffee. Had drunk only about three-quarters of it before a tap came at the front window. He pulled back the curtain, saw Jane peering in at him through the nets and opened the front door.

'Thanks for getting here so quickly,' he said, letting her in. 'I'd better get round there and see what's up.'

'Either Grey Man nodded off or he went over the back fence.'

'Yes, but his mum's concern was whether or not he went by his own choice.'

'Or was snatched. Well, yes, I suppose it would be, given the circumstances, but he's a big lad. He can look after himself.'

'True, but if our suspect did find him, we know how ruthless he is. Just in case, get onto his mobile phone provider as soon as they're open for business and get hold of his call log and tracking data. I'd better go. See you later.'

She let him out and he heard the click as she locked the door behind him.

It was almost as far to walk to his car as it would have been to walk directly to Mrs Lambert's house on Fairpark Road, but he took the car, on the principle that he didn't know what he was going to find when he got there and what he'd need to do about it. The streets were still quiet. Even Topsham Road was deserted as he pulled out of the little side road, turning down the hill, past the stone gargoyle in its little alcove on the back of the building that formed the corner of Roberts Road, where he turned off again.

At this time of the morning, there were few spaces between the parked cars along here, and he saw no pedestrians.

He parked nose-to-nose with Dick Fenney's near-identical Ford to his own, the black car that had partially concealed it from Mrs Lambert's house having been moved at some point since last night. He could see Dick frowning as he pulled up and killed his lights and engine. Stepping out, he heard the buzz of the window going down as he approached.

'What are you doing here?' Dick asked.

'Have you been awake all night?'

'Yes.' Dick's frown sharpened in irritation.

'And you've seen nothing?'

Dick shook his head. 'Why?'

'Dale's gone. Stay put for a bit while I see what I can find out.' He turned away, striding swiftly towards the house where a desperate mother and, no doubt by now, grandmother waited for him.

The front door was snatched open before he reached it down the sloping concrete that provided access to the short row of semis behind their protective stone wall. Cathy Gordon was dressed in jeans and a plain white T-shirt, her hair pulled back into a short ponytail and no makeup adorning her face. It was a look that suited her, he thought, despite her expression.

'The back door's unlocked,' she said by way of greeting. 'I know we locked it before we went to bed, and took the key out.'

He nodded. 'That supports what we were saying before. He slipped out while you were asleep. Probably suspected we'd be keeping an eye on the front of the house. But let me have a look.'

He reached the front door and stepped inside. 'Where's your mum?'

'Front room.' She nodded towards it's closed door. 'She's in a right state.'

'Understandably,' he allowed, stepping past her towards the kitchen doorway.

In the small kitchen, he found the back door was on the side of the house, at his left shoulder. He removed the key and set it aside, opened the door and crouched to look closely at the lock. Taking out his phone, he used its torch app to shine a light into the mechanism. There were no obvious scratches or tool-marks inside or around the rim of the keyhole. It wasn't a definitive answer but it was indicative, at least.

He looked up at her. 'I can't see any sign it's been picked.'

'So, he unlocked it and went out?'

He tipped his head. 'Have you checked the windows?'

She nodded dumbly.

'All secure?'

She frowned suddenly. 'Why would he do it? He'd know it'd make me and mum panic. How could he be so bloody stupid and selfish?'

Pete shook his head. 'Maybe that's not what it's about,' he suggested. 'You said he was a big help with the bills. I know at least part of what contributes to that and he'll have customers that rely on him. Or have been doing. He won't want to let them down and lose them. And lose the income they provide.'

'Yeah, but...'

'He can't operate under our noses. We'd crowd him too much. Not let him get away with it.'

'So...'

He shrugged. 'I'm just guessing, but it all ties in. All we've got to do is find him. Make sure he's safe for you.'

She let go a deep sigh. 'Stupid, stupid sod. What's he thinking?'

'You need money. He's found a way to provide it.'

Her eyes flashed. 'Yeah, with... What? Drugs?'

He nodded. 'He's admitted that much to me in the past. We didn't charge him. We had more serious issues to deal with at the time. But he won't get away with it forever and, when he does come unstuck, he won't like the consequences, believe me. Prison is not a nice place for a lad of his age. Not nice at all. It's not designed or meant to be.'

'So, he's on the run from the police and this bloody criminal that he got himself tied up with.'

He reached out to briefly squeeze her upper arm. 'We'll find him.'

'How?' she demanded with a sharp frown.

Pete pursed his lips. 'To start with, what friends of his can you tell me about? Any names he's mentioned or people you've met, male or female. We can talk to them, ask if they've seen him or heard from him, if they know anywhere he might have gone for safety.'

'For…?' She stopped herself, shoulders slumping at the futility of the protest she was about to make. 'I don't know much about who he spends time with these days. I think he's pretty much moved on from his old school mates.'

'Was there anyone, even back then, that he was close to?'

'Gareth Smalley and Tony Merriman. But he hasn't mentioned them in a long time.'

'So, who has he mentioned?'

'Just a few nicknames. Pol – who I'm sure is a guy, not a girl. Gam.' She shook her head. 'None of them make any sense to anyone who doesn't know them.'

Pete smiled. 'That's the way it is with nicknames. We can search our database. It might come up with something. Any more?'

She shrugged. 'The only other one he mentions at all regularly is Carl, but again, I don't know a surname.'

'I wonder if Becky would?'

She grimaced. 'She might, but I doubt it. And it's a bit early to be disturbing anyone to ask her.'

Pete pursed his lips briefly. 'All right. We'll start with Gam and Pol, see if they pop up on the database and go from there.' Dale had somehow managed to avoid actual charges so his information on the PNC was limited, Pete knew. It wouldn't extend to known associates. He took out his phone and called Jane.

'DC Bennett.'

'Jane, you've got your laptop with you, haven't you?'

'Yes.'

'Can you do a PNC search on the nicknames Pol and Gam? Associates of Dale and possibly of someone called Carl, another friend of Dale's who we could do with identifying if he pops up in association with the other two.'

'OK. I'll call you back.'

She hung up and he turned back to Cathy Gordon, standing just inside the kitchen.

'We'll have an answer in a minute or two. In the meantime...' He tipped his head towards the far side of the small, square lawned garden space, where a wooden fence faced the expanse of Bull Meadow Park. A few steps and he could see that, although the fence was only four feet high from this side, the ground dropped away sharply so that, from the far side, it was at least six feet high and protected by a dense strip of thick undergrowth. Looking over, he saw a patch where the shrubbery was knocked down and flattened.

Dale had gone over there and left the area on foot – there was no telling whether towards Magdalen Road to the right or further down through the park and it's play area towards Topsham Road, a few streets away to the left.

His phone buzzed in his hand and he glanced at the screen and took the call.

'Hello?'

'It's Jane. Pol is Stefan Polanowski. He's got a record for possession with intent. Several convictions. Known associates include Dale Gordon and Gavin Michaels, neither with actual convictions against them. There's no Carl linked to him.'

'OK, thanks for that. It's a start, at least. Can you text me the addresses and phone numbers we've got for Pol and Michaels? Sounds like he might be Gam.'

'I'll do it now. Done a runner, has he?'

'Yeah. I can see where he jumped the garden fence into Bull Meadow. At least he was on foot, with our suspect having wrecked his bike.'

'Someone could have picked him up, though.'

'True. See if Pol or Michaels has a vehicle registered to them and, if so, if it was caught on camera overnight.'

'Will do.'

They hung up and, moments later, his phone pinged with an incoming message. He checked the screen. It was from Jane: two names with addresses and mobile phone numbers. He returned to the kitchen, where Cathy waited.

'We don't know who Carl is yet, but we've identified the other two and got numbers and addresses for them. You can see where he went over the fence, down there.'

Her face seemed to crumple. 'Oh, God. Why the hell didn't he just leave a bloody note?'

Pete shook his head. 'Who knows? It would have been a lot easier all round if he had. I'll track these two down and see what they can tell me.'

'Thank you. And sorry for… You know,' she shrugged.

He gave her a brief smile. 'I know.'

His mind went briefly back in time to his own son, who had gone missing seven years ago for several months. The panic and stress they'd suffered had almost broken his wife, Louise. She'd sunk into a deep and protracted depression. But he couldn't afford to dwell on that now. He shook off the memories.

'You do, don't you?' Cathy said. 'Personally.'

He met her gaze. 'Shows, does it?'

She tried a smile that failed.

'I had a son,' he admitted. 'He went missing. We found him, but... He died soon after.'

'I'm sorry.'

He blinked his thanks. 'I'm hoping we can still save Dale from going down a similar path. I'd better go and stir his two mates out of their beds and see what they can tell us.'

CHAPTER TWENTY

Dave had arrived to take over from Dick by the time Pete emerged from the house on Fairpark Road. As Pete approached Dick's car, he emerged from the unmarked black Volvo parked behind it and they opened the rear doors of Dick's Mondeo and sat inside.

'You're off the hook,' Pete told Dick. 'He went over the back fence into the park and away on foot.'

'Are we absolutely convinced that he isn't our suspect after all?' Dave asked. 'I mean, we've only got his word, up to now, that this other bloke exists. The silver Golf and the bloke on Franklin Street could be coincidental. Could be a bloke from the council or a debt collector or something. And the break-in could have been Dale himself. It was a neat job, after all.'

Pete turned on him. 'A debt collector wouldn't run from us.'

'A supplier after him for payment, then?' Dave persisted.

'You were there when we interviewed him. Both Jill and I thought he was telling the truth. And you know what I think about coincidences. As for breaking into his own house...' His mind flashed back in time to his own house, a few years before. A very similar scenario. His own son breaking in, in the dead of night. Proving Dave's point. 'If you're right, I'll... No, I don't think he's that callous. Or clever. He's just a kid in over his head.'

Dave grunted. 'It's an old trick, acting dumber than you are. Just ask Grey Man,' he added with a grin.

'Oi!' Dick protested.

'And psychopaths are perfectly capable of acting nice, innocent and empathetic when they need to,' Dave continued.

'All true,' Pete admitted. 'But if it's him, where's he doing the work?' Not in the house, that's for sure. And they haven't got a shed. Haven't got room for one.'

'What about the gran's? Or an uncle or something? Family friend, even..'

'Mrs Lambert hasn't got a shed,' Pete replied, nodding towards the house he'd just come from. 'Again – a tiny garden, though not as tiny as Franklin Street. I don't know about his other grandparents, though. His dad's side. He said he'd never had any contact with them.'

'He said,' Dick repeated. 'And it might not even be a family thing. Could be a partnership with a friend. Old schoolmate or something.'

Pete still didn't believe Dale was the man they were looking for. The timing of the silver Golf's arrival and the man in the suit asking questions was too coincidental. And if not the gunman, then who was it who'd ran from him and Dave? He couldn't see it being a disgruntled supplier, though he had to accept the possibility. And his own son had been proof of how disingenuous and calculating young people could be.

'All right,' he said. 'I've got names for a couple of his mates plus a couple of others from his school days that he hasn't talked about for some time. Whether you're right or not, we need to track him down. His phone's off at the moment. I tried it on the way here and his mum did before that. But Jane's getting the tracking data and call history for it. That might give us some clues.'

'If he's dealing, he can't leave it off forever,' Dave said.

'I expect Jane will get the provider to let us know when it pops onto the network again. Of course, that's presuming we've got the number for his only phone which, if he's as clever and devious as you're thinking, is unlikely. He'd have a separate one for his dealing, that he'd change fairly often and keep his customers updated on by text.'

Dave shrugged. 'I never said he was a genius.'

'Just possibly a psycho,' Pete agreed.

'Well, you've got to admit, we can't discount it.'

Pete tipped his head. 'If it's true, we'll have him. But first, we've got to find him.'

*

He drew up outside the row of decorative Edwardian terraced houses with their white-rendered bay windows and white brick trims around the doorways and switched off the engine, leaning back in his seat to give a deep yawn.

Only three minutes ago, he'd sent Dick off to his bed while Dave took over the watch detail on Fairpark Road. 'I'm going have a chat with a couple of his mates, then hand over to the guvnor and knock off myself,' he'd told them, and in this moment, he was looking forward to doing just that.

He drew a breath and got out of the car, heading for the address, a couple of doors down the hill that led off Topsham Road at the corner of a churchyard and down to the river. Reaching the address he was looking for, he stepped through the gate into a garden that was no more than six feet deep from the front wall to the angled window bay and reached for the doorbell.

It was answered by a woman in her fifties, in dressing gown and slippers. She wore no makeup but she'd brushed her hair. It was lustrous and dark, swept across to expose a high forehead and well-sculpted brows.

'Yah?' Her tone didn't match her look.

Pete held up his warrant card. 'DS Gayle, Exeter CID. I need a word with Stefan, Mrs Polanowski.'

'I figure.' She stepped back, allowing him to enter a hallway that still featured the decoratively tiled floor these houses would have been finished with when new. It gleamed as if freshly polished, he noticed as she yelled abruptly. 'Stefan! Come down.'

'Huh? Whassup?' Fron just those two blearily voiced words, Pete could hear that his accent, unlike his mother's, was pure Devonian.

'You have visitor.'

Pete didn't catch the muttered response, but he heard movement as the young man got up. In moments, a door opened and he showed at the top of the stairs, hastily dressed in jeans and a T-shirt with a band logo on that Pete didn't recognise, his hair still messed up from sleep.

'Who are you?' he asked, looking down at Pete.

'A friend of a friend,' Pete said. 'I need a word. Urgent.'

'At this time of day? It's not even eight o'clock.'

'I didn't think there was an off-time in your line of business, Stefan,' Pete said as the younger man started down towards him.

Stefan sneered. 'What line of business is that, then, Mr Copper?'

Pete smiled. 'I'm not interested in what you get up to right now, Stefan. I'm looking for a friend of yours.' He stepped back as Stefan reached the bottom of the stairs, noting that the lad had inherited not just his looks from his mother. He was also no more than five-feet-five tall. Stepping off the bottom of the stairs, he tipped his head for Pete to follow him into the sitting room opposite.

As Pete had expected, it was small but very well-kept, the furniture modern but comfortable.

'Where were you last night, Stefan?' Pete asked once they were seated – Stefan on the sofa, leaving him with a choice of the armchairs.

'I went into town for a bit.'

'Did you meet up with anyone?'

'Lots of folks, as it happens. Who are we talking about?'

'Dale Gordon.'

Stefan frowned quickly. 'No, he weren't there. Why?'

'He's got himself into a bit of trouble. Not with the law,' he added. 'Just the opposite. I'm trying to make sure he's safe.'

'Right.' He sounded and looked sceptical.

'It's true,' Pete assured him. 'He was reported missing less than an hour ago and you're the nearest of his known friends, so… Here I am.' He spread his hands.

'Well, I didn't see him last night.'

'OK. Have you got any idea who else I should talk to? Who are his other mates? Who might he go to if he's in trouble? Or where?'

'Gam. Carl.' He shrugged. 'I dunno of anyone else.'

'Who's Carl?'

'Carl Benson. Lives up St Leonards.'

'You're sure he's not kipping on your bedroom floor?' Pete asked.

Stefan's eyes widened. 'No way. You can check, if you want.'

Pete flashed him a smile. 'Whatever it takes at the moment, Stefan. His mum's worried to death and, bearing in mind who he's got himself tangled up with recently, I don't blame her.'

'Eh? Who's that, then?'

'I can't say right now, but if you do see him or get in touch with him, tell him to contact either me or his mum, eh?'

Stefan shrugged. 'Who are you? You never said.'

'Pete Gayle.' Pete handed him a card. 'CID, not the drugs squad.'

'What, so, like rapes and murders and stuff?'

Pete nodded.

'Jeez. What's he got himself into? He ain't no major criminal.'

'As I said – he's currently a missing person. Unless...' He glanced upwards.

'Go.' Stefan's expression turned defensive and resentful. 'Just 'cause I got a record don't mean I'm tied into every bloody crime in this city.'

Pete stood up. 'Putting my mind at rest goes towards doing the same for Dale's mum.'

Having confirmed that Dale wasn't in the house, Pete moved on. It didn't take long to discover Carl Benson's address, now he had a surname, and it was closer than Gavin Michaels' so he headed there first.

St Leonard's Road was lined on one side with houses that looked like they were built at the same time – and by the same builder, using the same architect – as the Polanowski's. Lots of white amongst the brickwork and tiny low-walled front gardens. On the other side, the houses were a little larger, with gardens just big enough that some of them had been converted to single parking spaces for their residents.

Carl Benson lived in one of the smaller terraced houses.

Pete parked and approached the address with his warrant card ready in his hand. He was about to reach for the doorbell when his phone buzzed. He took it out and checked the screen, stepped back to the other side of the short hedge – almost a square – of golden privet that stood between the address he was about to visit and its neighbour.

'DS Gayle.'

'They've found the Golf on the Heavitree Road footage,' Colin said. 'Confirmed it's the same one. At least, the same VRN. Comes down Devonshire, turns right, then left into Clifton. Barely two minutes later, a male walks out of the end of Clifton and up towards the old nick. Too distant to see any details, even when he comes back. You can judge his height and build, but that's all.'

'And they are...?' Pete asked.

'Five-ten, average build.'

Pete let go a sigh. 'So, matching the male that Dale Gordon got the SIM card for and the one who's been after him on Franklin Street. Nothing from Alphington Road or Cowick Street yet?'

'No. And the car heads out of town when it comes out of Clifton Road, afterwards. Turns off somewhere before it gets to Magdalen Road.'

Which left three or four possibilities, one of which Pete was now standing beside.

'We checked the security cameras at the vet's there,' Colin explained. 'Found Dale yet?'

'No. I've identified his third friend, though. I was about to knock him up.'

Colin grunted. 'On you go, then.'

*

Benson was small and wiry, like a feather-weight boxer, except his face was undamaged. He had a prominent chin and dark hair that was a little on the long side, constantly flopping down over his forehead. Dressed in navy slacks and a polo shirt just a shade lighter with a small but prominent logo on the breast, he lounged comfortably on the sofa across from Pete, arms spread along the top of it in his neat but clearly bachelor-styled living room.

'So, what can I do for CID?' he asked.

'I'm looking into a missing persons case and I'm hoping you might be able to help,' Pete told him. 'Where were you last night, from 11:00 pm onward?'

'Here.'

'You didn't go out at all?'

'Not after that, no. I went to bed about half-past. Alone, unfortunately.'

Pete raised an eyebrow.

'My girlfriend doesn't live here.'

I can see that, Pete thought, looking at the dark but stylish decoration. 'But you'd like her to?'

'Of course. That's the point of having a relationship, isn't it?'

Pete tipped his head. He couldn't disagree with that. 'When did you last see or speak to Dale Gordon?' he asked, changing the subject abruptly.

'Is that who this is about? He's missing?' He dropped his arms from the sofa back and sat forward.

Pete nodded. 'As of this morning, yes.'

'Shit, I bet his mum and sister are in bits. I haven't seen him in…' He paused. 'Two, three weeks, I suppose. Yeah, must be three, thinking about it. Time flies when you're having fun, eh? What's happened?'

'That's what we're trying to figure out. How do you know him?'

'He comes into the gym. I've been working odd shifts lately, so I've missed him, but we normally have a chat. Occasionally go out for the odd night on the town, you know?'

'Which gym's this?' Pete asked, thinking it wasn't something he'd imagined Dale being involved with.

'Tudor Street.'

'Ah.' He'd been within yards of it a couple of days ago, Pete recalled, when a call from the very young man they were talking about had changed his direction of travel, pulling him away from it. 'Sounds like you're a regular there.'

'I own it. It was my grandad's. He left it to me, along with this place.'

Pete's eyes widened. 'You're a very fortunate young man, then. Aside from the loss of your grandad, of course. Your dad or mum not involved?'

He shrugged. 'Dad. No, he's never been interested. More academic than physical. He works at the Met Office.'

'Ah. So, what else do you get up to? I see no games consoles and such,' he said, pointedly looking towards the large black TV and the satellite receiver beneath it.

Benson grimaced. 'Never was into that kind of stuff. I like to use my hands. Again, a legacy from my grandad. I've got a little set-up in the shed, out the back.'

'Oh, yes?' Pete asked, his interest piqued. Dick's words came back to him. *'Could be a partnership with a friend....'* 'What sort of thing is that, then?'

'Lathe, drill-press, hand-tools... Nothing fancy. Haven't got the room for anything too grand, but it does for what I want.'

'What sort of things do you make?'

'Bowls, mugs, plates, bread boards, salad utensils. Skipping rope handles are a good one. That's one of mine,' he added, nodding towards a wooden platter that sat in the centre of the coffee table between them, made of beautifully figured wood in a mix of pale honey and rich dark tones, turned and polished to a soft sheen.

'Nice,' Pete acknowledged, hiding the disappointment that had dropped like a weight into his chest after the mentions of a lathe, drill-press and other tools had sparked a rising excitement. 'I noticed a similar piece at Dale's. A salad bowl.'

'Yeah, that was for his mum's birthday last year.'

'From you?'

'No, Dale bought it off me for her.'

Pete nodded his understanding. 'Somebody said earlier that Dale might have a similar hobby to yours, only with metalwork.'

Benson chuckled. 'I don't know who that was, but I can't see it. I let him have a go out there, once.' He nodded towards the back of the house. 'Not his sort of thing at all. Awkward wasn't the word.'

Pete's mouth pulled down in a grimace. That was something he could check on with Dale's old school, now he thought about it. 'So, if you haven't seen him for a while, do you know where he might have gone or anyone he might be with if he's gone willingly? Or has he mentioned any problems he's been having and who with?'

'He hasn't said anything to me about any hassles. I know he gets a lot of phone calls but I can't say I know his other friends, apart from a couple we've met in the pub now and again.'

'Who are they?'

'One's called Pol, for some reason. Another's Gav or Gam or something like that. And then there's a guy that I haven't met, but phones him a lot: Chopper. I don't know who he is, though. Dale's never said – or called him anything other than that, that I've heard.'

'OK. One last thing. Could you do me a favour and just call Dale?' He nodded towards the mobile phone that was sitting on the coffee table between them. 'He doesn't pick up for me or him mum. Phone might be turned off or he might just be screening us. Just leave him a message to get in touch if he doesn't answer.'

'Sure, no problem.'

He leaned forward to pick up the phone, swiped it open and scrolled to the number he wanted. 'Dale,' he said, moments later. 'It's Carl. Do me a favour, mate? Call your mum, let her know you're OK. She's in a right state. Or call me and I'll let her know. All right?' He raised an eyebrow at Pete, who nodded his appreciation. 'See ya,' Benson said and ended the call.

'Perfect,' Pete said. 'Thank you.'

*

It didn't take long, once he got back to his car, for Pete to find out that Chopper was Charles Pearson, who had an extensive record for violence, possession with intent to supply Class A and Class B drugs, as well as driving offences including failing to stop for police.

Dale's supplier, he guessed.

Pearson's address was in Heavitree, to the north of the royal Devon and Exeter Hospital but Pete didn't head straight there from

Carl Benson's house. There was something else he needed to do first so he was heading out of town on Topsham Road again, passing the County Council offices behind their shroud of trees and hedges when Jane called.

'I've got Dale's phone records,' she said. 'First thing to note is, it's been off since he got to his gran's last night.'

'He hasn't switched it on at all this morning?' The rush-hour was well underway now, but he was heading out of the city, so against the main flow.

'Nope. Not up to half an hour ago, which is when the records go up to.'

'OK. So, he's either got a burner that we don't know about – which wouldn't be surprising, given his chosen occupation – or he didn't call anyone to come and pick him up when he left last night. Who were the last calls he did make to?'

'The last two calls he made were to un-registered phones, both short ones of a minute or two, and eight minutes apart, between 19:40 and 19:53 hours.'

'Two different numbers?'

'Yes.'

'Sounds like he might have been planning something.'

'Yeah, but what?'

'Evidently to drop out of sight for one reason or another. He could have been arranging a pick-up for a specific time with either of those calls. Or, come to that, he could have bought himself a new bike during the day and locked it to a lamppost to go back to later. Can you get onto finding out who those two numbers belong to? Maybe his mum or sister or one of his friends will recognise them. Or one of them might belong to Charles "Chopper" Pearson, who's another associate of Dale's that I've come across and has a fairly extensive police record. I'm going to pay him a visit in a bit, so if you text them to me, I can find out if either of them belongs to him.'

'OK, I'll do that now.'

'Thanks.'

Pete hung up and concentrated on driving. He was passing a high brick wall on his left, the metal footbridge at the bottom of Burnthouse Lane visible in the distance when his phone pinged with an incoming message. He left it for now as he was approaching the junction he wanted. He made the turn into the short road that led down towards the school, past large, smart-looking old houses, waiting until he'd stopped in the school carpark before taking out the phone and checking the screen.

It was a text from Jane with the two unlisted mobile phone numbers. He copied them into his notebook, then into the contacts list on his phone, labelling them as Anunknown 1 and Anunknown 2 so they'd be together near the top of the list and easily accessible.

With that done, he headed inside. Stopping at Reception, he waited for the two girls the receptionist was dealing with to leave and stepped forward, warrant card in hand.

'Hi,' he said to the woman behind the high counter. 'DS Gayle with CID.'

'Yes, I remember you.'

He nodded. He'd been here a number of times, a couple of years ago, when he was investigating the awful mob murder of a young disabled male on nearby Burnthouse Lane and the events that led up to it. 'I've got another case that's related to the school. A missing person. Former pupil. I need to access his records. Reports. I understand you keep them all.'

'We do. But there are very strict confidentiality rules that apply to juvenile records, Detective. Do you have a warrant?' She arched a well-manicured eyebrow behind her glasses.

'No, but I could easily get one in the circumstances. I haven't because it would take more time than can be spared on a case like this. Every second can be vital. Should we speak to the head and confirm that it's not necessary? If you remember me, you'll remember my dealings with him last time around.'

Her lips pursed as if he were a recalcitrant twelve-year-old. She sighed theatrically. 'Very well, I suppose it'll be all right. The records are through there.' She raised a hand to indicate the door behind and to her left.

'I remember,' he said, stepping around the horseshoe shaped counter.

She made a show of unlocking and selecting a key from the small metal cupboard on the wall behind the counter then lifted a section and stepped through to unlock the door and precede him into the archive room.

It was about ten feet by twelve with two walls covered with shelving. Up to waist height was filled with A4 sized books arranged by year and alphabetically. From there up to near the ceiling were what looked like old-fashioned wooden card-files, only a little larger. Again, they were labelled with dates and alphabetical ranges.

'I would very much prefer to do the searches for you, Detective, but I can't leave the desk for that long,' she said. 'So be very sure to only look at what's absolutely relevant to your case.'

Pete pursed his lips. 'I don't have the time or the inclination to treat the place as some sort of library. As I said, every second counts in a case like this. And I am a detective sergeant, not a random member of the public.'

'Yes, well… You hear all sorts of things about the police, these days, don't you? The news makes them sound worse than the general public at times.'

'That's the Met you're thinking of. That's a long way from Devon and Cornwall, in both distance and attitudes, I can assure you.'

She humphed. 'I hope so, Detective.' Turning away, she closed the door behind her, leaving him alone.

Pete quickly saw how the system worked and stepped across to the area he needed. From Dale's age, he calculated back to his last year of school and found the drawer that would contain his annual report. Pulling it out, he riffled through until he found what he wanted, pulled it out and lifted the one behind it to an angle so he could find where to return it quickly, then turned and leaned back against the shelf that divided the reports from what he knew were the annual school photo books below to read the contents of the five-and-a-half by three-inch booklet.

He quickly saw that Dale had not taken either metalwork or woodwork to qualification level, but he had studied technical drawing and computer science. His technical drawing teacher had observed that he showed good aptitude for the subject and his work was diligent and precise, though his attendance record left something to be desired. His overall mark was A-. Computer science had produced similar comments and an A score.

Pete raised an eyebrow at that and flicked to the next subject. Then the next. They all said the same thing about his attendance. He seemed to have been a bright lad, but with the idea that, for some reason, he had more important places to be than in school.

He replaced the report and was looking for the previous year's when his phone buzzed in his pocket. He took it out and checked the screen. The number was unlisted. Probably work. He tapped the screen to answer.

'DS Gayle.'

'They've found the Golf on Monday morning,' Colin said. '7:03, it comes onto the twin bridges and over to Frog Street.

Tracing it back, he must have left it on Church Road because he comes out of Cecil onto Cowick Street at 6:59.'

'So, he knows the back streets and pathways. Probably used the one that goes up from the corner of Ferndale. Cheeky bugger might even have had a kip in the car for a few hours while we were looking for him. Nice quiet street like that.'

'At least we know he's not a bloody ghost.'

'We never thought he was. Just didn't know where to start looking for him. Where'd he go from Frog Street?'

'Last sighting's on Holloway Street, out-bound.'

Holloway being the street that became Topsham Road. 'Right past the end of Roberts Road.'

Colin grunted. They were back on familiar territory with this man, whoever he was. He knew how to vanish within the city, popping up occasionally where it was absolutely unavoidable, but then slipping back into the darkness like the ghost Colin had mentioned a moment ago.

'OK,' Pete said. 'At least it confirms it's the same subject we're looking for in both cases. Thanks, Guv.'

Colin hung up and Pete returned to searching for Dale's school report from the year before the one he'd just read.

It took just moments and when he found it, it said pretty much the same as the one he'd read before. He checked back a further year, before the boy had had to concentrate on qualification subjects. Here, he found both woodwork and metalwork listed. For woodwork, Dale had scored C-. For metalwork, he had got another straight A and, at this point, there were no adverse comments about his attendance. Something had happened during the following school year to affect that. Pete wondered briefly what it might have been, but he was looking at an age when impressions were easily made and influences could be powerful for good or bad.

He put away the report and took out his notebook, flicking back to the mention that Dale's mother had made of his two schoolmates. Gareth Smalley and Tony Merriman. It would be worth checking on their reports while he was here. Then he would have to disturb the head of the school after all, to check on which teachers might still be here who might remember Dale enough to know who else belonged on his list of friends from back then.

CHAPTER TWENTY-ONE

After spending more than an hour and a half at the school, Pete visited Gavin Michaels, as he lived on one of the side-roads off Burnthouse Lane, but he got nothing useful from him. He did, however, discover by surreptitiously dialling them, that neither of the unlisted numbers Jane had given him as Dale's last two contacts belonged to Gavin. Or, if they did, the phones were switched off. From there, he headed north, towards Charles "Chopper" Pearson's last known address. On the way, as he drove down past the junior school on Burnthouse, he tried one of the unlisted numbers again.

It was picked up on the second ring. 'Yeah?'

Pete paused as if unsure. 'Is that Chopper?'

'No, it's Ade.'

'Sorry,' Pete said. 'Wrong number.' He hung up and dialled the other number. Again, it was answered promptly. 'Yeah?'

'Um… is that Ade?' Pete asked, his tone again doubtful.

'No, it's Chopper.'

'Oh, sorry. But I was going to call you next,' he added quickly.

'Who is this?'

'Pete,' he said. 'I'm a friend of Dale's. I've been trying to get hold of him, but his phone's off. I wondered if he'd been in touch lately or if you could connect me with him.'

'Not without his permission.'

'Fair enough. You don't know where I could find him, I suppose?'

'What makes you think he wants to be found?'

'Well, he can't do any business if he isn't contactable, can he?' Pete countered in an affronted tone as he passed the house where the victim in the case that had had him spending time on this estate a couple of years ago had lived. Philip Lawrence, he recalled, and blinked at the sight of kids' toys on the tiny front garden now.

'He could be on holiday,' Chopper suggested.

'Yeah, right,' Pete said. 'In his line of work, he'd have let his customers know, and given them an alternative supplier.'

'So, how did you get this number?'

'From Dale. For emergencies, he said.'

'There you go, then.'

'So, can I come and get what I need?' He reached the end of the road and turned left at the mini roundabout onto Wonford Street, sure by now that Chopper knew exactly where Dale was, if he wasn't actually there with him.

'I don't know you.'

'Nor does my local newsagent. Why d'you need to?'

'In this business, there's a question of trust involved.'

'And here I thought cash was king.'

'All right. But it's early yet. I could meet you in half an hour. What you looking for?'

'A couple of ounces to tide me over.'

'Of weed?'

'Well, not H.'

There was a tiny pause, Chopper perhaps not appreciating his flippancy though Pete didn't regret it. He had to stay in character.

'Outside the Wonford Inn.'

'Half an hour?' Pete checked, having just driven past it and noted, in doing so, that it was boarded up and surrounded by metal safety fencing. They certainly weren't going to meet inside the place.

'If Dale says you're all right. What's your name again?'

He smiled, Chopper's comment confirming that he was in contact with Dale or perhaps even with him. 'Pete. Miles,' he added, using Dave's surname as it was the first one that came to mind.

'Right,' Chopper said and ended the call.

If the PNC's information was up to date, he was now only a few hundred yards away, as the crow flies. Pete, of course, had to take the roundabout route dictated by the street layout, but it was still not too far. He'd be there in a minute or two, at most.

Chopper's address, when Pete got there, was in a short row of what looked like 1950s red brick council houses on the downside of a narrow street that ran across the face of a steep slope. Parking was on the other side of the road, at the base of a six-foot brick wall that fronted the houses on the upper side while those on the lower side were a few feet down from the road, with garden paths that were steep enough to be made up of concrete stairs with metal handrails. At six feet tall, Pete could practically look straight into the bedroom windows as he crossed the road after parking his car.

The only thing that stopped him was the grubby-looking net curtain that covered it.

With his tie and jacket left in the car and shirtsleeves folded back over his forearms, he went down the steps to the quarter-glazed front door and pressed the bellpush. It buzzed sharply from inside and Pete took out his warrant card in readiness.

Held it up to the balding man in white vest and dark joggers who opened it.

'DS Gayle, Exeter CID,' he said. 'Is Chopper in?'

'Yes.'

'Is he alone?'

A frown snapped into place. 'What's that mean?'

'Has he got a friend round? Or a girlfriend?'

'No.'

'Can I come in, then, and have a quick word? I'm not looking to get him into trouble. Just for some information.'

The man shifted his stance, making it more solid. 'Why should he help you lot?'

'For the sake of a mate of his who's in trouble. Not with us.'

The man grunted.

'You'll be Mr Pearson, right?' Pete checked. 'Stanley?'

He grunted again.

Pete drew a quick breath. 'Charley,' he called. 'Come on down. I need a word. Won't take a minute. No warrant involved. Or I could come back with one, as you're on parole.'

The older man's expression sharpened.

'Keep the bloody noise down,' came a voice from the upper floor that Pete recognised as Chopper's. 'Don't want the neighbours knowing all our bloody business.'

'Then talk to me.'

'Let him in, Dad.'

He grunted and stepped back, allowing Pete to enter as a younger version appeared at the top of the stairs with longer dark hair and a black T-shirt with a darkly gothic-looking image on the front worn outside a pair of faded black jeans. He was barefoot, Pete saw as he started down the stairs.

The older man showed him reluctantly into a sitting room with pale orange walls, a cheap display cabinet at the back and a three-piece suite in brown and greyish beige stripes that looked like it had been new in the 1980s or before. The only modern thing in the room was the large black TV on a stand in the corner between the old-fashioned gas fire and the curtained window.

He took a seat as Chopper stepped into the room with him, Pearson senior disappearing elsewhere in the house.

'So, what do the police want with me now?'

'We're looking for a missing person,' Pete told him. 'Don't worry, you're not being accused of anything. But you do know him, so we thought you might be able to point us towards where he might have gone.'

'Who's that, then?'

'Dale Gordon.'

Chopper shrugged. 'Ain't seen him.'

'But you spoke to him yesterday.'

'Who says I did?'

'His phone records do.'

'I don't see how.'

Pete smiled. 'You don't need to. But trust me – they do.' He took out his phone, found the contact listed as Anunknown2 and hit Dial. Upstairs, a phone began to ring. 'You might want to get that.'

Chopper grimaced.

Pete ended the call and the ringing from upstairs stopped. 'So, where were we? Right, you spoke to Dale yesterday. Was it to arrange somewhere for him to stay the night?'

'Why would you think that?'

Pete pursed his lips. 'You're aware that harbouring a fugitive is an offence, right? And you're on parole.'

'You said he was missing, not a fugitive. What'd he do?'

'He's wanted for questioning in regard to the distribution of firearms and ammunition.' That would make him take more notice than drugs, of whatever class, Pete guessed. It was far more serious.

'Firearms! Since when? He...' He stopped. 'He's never been into shit like that, that I know of.'

'I didn't say you knew of it, Charles. Just that you were harbouring him. Where is he?'

'I dunno. He ain't here.'

Pete raised an eyebrow. 'You're certain of that, are you? Because you definitely know how to contact him. That much, I can be sure of. And what I also know is that his phone's switched off, so...' He shrugged, hands spread wide. 'What am I to think, eh?'

'I don't care what you think. He ain't here. You can check if you want.'

'So, you figured out there's no need to stir your stumps over to the Wonford Inn.'

'It didn't take a genius. Es...' He stopped again.

'Especially when Dale said he didn't know Pete Miles,' Pete finished for him.

'I didn't say that.'

Pete sighed. 'OK, Charles, I'll level with you. He's in trouble. Not with us, but with a chap he's done some work for. A very dangerous and ruthless individual who is involved in the sale and distribution of firearms and who doesn't take kindly to anyone who gets in his way – in any way whatsoever. He has killed before and he doesn't care who, how or where he does it. Lads like you think you're hard. You've got nothing on this man, let me tell you. I'd rather see a dozen of you and Dale on the streets than one of him. So that's why I'm here. Dale is missing and he's in danger. And, as such, the fact that he's missing is terrifying his mother. She needs to know he's safe.'

'Well, like I said, he ain't here. But I should be able to get hold of him. Tell him to phone home. Except he won't want to let his phone get traced,' he added pointedly.

'There are ways around that,' Pete said. 'A different number. A borrowed phone. A callbox, even, as rare as they are, these days.'

'Jeez! That's a blast from the past. Where'd you last see one of them?'

'There are some at the hospital. And plenty of ways in and out of there, if he's worried about being seen.'

'Where?' he asked with a frown.

'A&E.'

'Oh, right. I didn't know that.'

'You learn something new every day,' Pete said as, beyond the closed door, a stair creaked.

'What's that – Confucius?'

'No idea, but if it doesn't apply in my job, I'm not doing it right. So, how about that guided tour of the premises you suggested, then we can both get on about our day?'

The door opened.

'No need, if you're looking for me,' Dale said.

Chopper and Pete both turned towards him.

'What the…'

'I've spent the entire morning doing that,' Pete told him. 'Instead of looking for the man who caused the problem in the first place. Why didn't you at least leave your mother a note to say what you were up to?'

'I figured the less anyone knew, the less likely they were to find me and the safer she'd be without me there.'

'What, you thought he wasn't the kind of bloke who'd hurt your mum or your sister if he couldn't find you?'

Dale's jaw dropped, his eyes widening in horror.

'Yes,' Pete said. 'He very definitely would. All you've done is waste my time and my team's and force me to look at you again as the primary suspect in this case.'

'But I…' He shook his head. 'What? I wouldn't know the first thing about making guns.'

'As I now know.'

'So… What happens now?'

Pete stood up and stepped forward, looming over the lad. 'I ought to arrest you for wasting police time, but it would only waste more. Phone your mother and tell her you're safe and well, at least. Then what you do is up to you. As long as it's legal.'

CHAPTER TWENTY-TWO

Pete was regretting having swapped locations with Dick Feeney for tonight's watch shift. At least, at the little terraced house on Franklin Street, all you needed to do was listen for any sign of an intruder. You could use your eyes and hands for something else. Here, on Fairpark Road, with Dale Gordon safely tucked up with his mother and grandmother once more, all he could do was watch the street. And there had been almost no movement since just after 11:00 pm, except for a couple of foxes, a few cats and the odd rodent.

There had been no human foot traffic at all and only three cars in forty minutes, only one of which had stopped, the driver getting out and entering a house further along towards Roberts Road.

After a night shift the night before and a busy morning spent searching for Dale, he was finding it hard to maintain his concentration, especially as he had to remain covert, as much as possible, which meant no music – not even with headphones as he needed to be able to hear as well as see his surroundings.

He squeezed his eyes tight for a count of two then leaned his head back and yawned widely.

Dick would at least be typing up the daily notes on his laptop round at the Gordons' house. Here, he could do nothing except sip coffee and wait and watch.

He jumped as the buzz of his phone broke the interminable peace of the night and snatched it up from the seat beside him. Turning it over, he saw the number on the screen and recognised it.

'Jill?'

'Contact,' she said. 'We're on for a meet-and-greet.'

'When?'

'Twelve.' She was keeping things brief and cryptic, as planned, as they were unsure of how tech-savvy their man was: whether he might have sent spyware to Ben's phone when he made contact.

'Midnight?'

'Yes.'

'Damn.' That was only… He glanced at the clock on the dashboard. Eighteen minutes. 'Location?'

'Bart's Terrace, north end.'

A carefully chosen spot, he thought. There was nowhere to set up observation from, especially at short notice. Bartholomew Terrace was a footpath leading along the side of the steep ravine that housed Bartholomew Cemetery far below the street level and on the near side of it was a small tree-covered green space. Its entrance was from a narrow street, opposite a block of modern flats with parking only in the northern direction right in plain view. And there was no saying that their man, having set the meet with such a short lead-in, wasn't already in place, waiting for Ben to turn up, with or without Jill.

'Both of you?'

'He said not, but it will be.'

'Good. Keep a safe distance and try to get him in the light.'

'Boss.'

She knew what she was doing. Pete knew that but it didn't stop him being worried for their safety or wanting to remind her of the policies they were working under. She would be wearing a tiny camera on a necklace, but they would need the suspect to come out from under the trees surrounding the stone gateway pillars at the end of the pathway in order to get a good enough image of him to be able to identify him. 'Be safe,' he said. 'I'll let the others know.'

He ended the call and immediately called Colin Underhill.

'Yes?'

'Guv, it's Pete. Ben and Jill are on. Midnight at the top end of Bartholomew Terrace.'

He heard the sharp intake of breath from the other end. 'All right. Who've you got covering the Gordons?'

'Dick and me.'

'We can't get too close, but I can get to Fore Street and park just up from West Street if Jane or Dave can get to Paul Street and wait by the bottom entrance to the shopping centre. That way, if he abides by the one-ways, we've got him covered.'

'I'll tell the others.'

'Right.'

There was a click and the line was dead. Pete redialled. Two more calls to make. He called Jane first and told her where she was needed and why. Then he brought up Dave's number and hit dial.

'Yes?'

'Dave, it's Pete. Sorry, but you're needed. Ben's had contact from the suspect. They're meeting at midnight. Can you get to Iron Bridge? Park up somewhere unobtrusive, ready to follow him if he goes that way?'

'Of course.'

'You'll be one of three. I've got Jane on Paul Street and the guvnor on Fore Street so, whichever way he goes, you can liaise between you and leapfrog or whatever's necessary.'

'I'm leaving now.'

And Pete relaxed.

He'd done all he could. Now, he had to just wait and hope. If their man turned up at the meeting, then he and Dick could join the hunt. If not, then they were made – and the suspect certainly knew they were looking for him, so he might well have guessed that Ben was a plant – and the whole thing was a ruse, either to test Ben's credentials or to draw them away from the suspect's real target of the night: either the Gordons' house, where Dick was waiting for him, or here, where the family, apart from Becky, were hopefully sleeping.

Time would tell.

At least it wasn't going to be a problem staying awake and alert from now on. He adjusted his position in the seat, getting comfortable again, and laid the phone back on the passenger seat, face-down so it's glow wouldn't show if it rang.

*

The phone pinged just before midnight. He picked it up. A simple text message from Jill's undercover phone read, "On." Their man was there. She'd have sent that as a group text to the whole team, including Colin Underhill. Pete hoped that the hidden camera she was wearing would be recording, and that the subject would be in a position with enough light to get an identifiable image. He set the phone back down and slipped out of the car.

Whoever was at the meeting couldn't be in two places at once. Whether it was Dale – which seemed highly unlikely, based on the morning's events – or not, they couldn't be here and there at the same time.

He crossed the street and headed down the path towards Mrs Lambert's house and around to the side, where the front garden met the back. In many similar houses, this space would have been either blocked off with a fence or occupied by a garage, but here neither was the case. He moved quietly around to the back of the house. Dale's new bike was leaning against the wall under the kitchen window. He stepped forward and very gently tried the back door. It was locked. Peering into the lock, he could see that they key was in it from the far side. He moved into the shadows at the back corner of the house and settled in to wait.

Five minutes passed. Another five. Dale certainly wasn't their man. At least, he wasn't going to be at Bartholomew Terrace.

This was a first meeting. An important meeting to both sides, for different reasons. The subject was there to make an assessment of Ben – of his potential reliability in the role he was hoping to fill. If the spiky-haired detective didn't create the right impression, their man would walk away, despite whatever he'd been told by whoever gave him Ben's number.

But, if they could follow him as he left, maybe that wouldn't be such a bad thing…

More time passed. Surely, by now, they must have come to a conclusion?

Then his phone pinged again. He took it out from his pocket and carefully shielded the screen from view as he checked it. Another text.

"Back to car. No golf seen."

The meeting was over. Jill and Ben were back on Mary Arches Street and hadn't seen the silver Golf. So their man hadn't parked on Mary Arches or Bartholomew Street, at least in sight of where they'd met. Which made sense, from his point of view, of course. Pete hoped the others were in position because Ben couldn't wait the subject out without looking suspicious.

On the other hand, it was highly likely that their man was waiting for Ben and Jill to leave before making his own move.

Pete would have to be patient a little longer.

Time passed.

Soft rustling and snuffling sounds reached his ears from between the houses but it was too dark to see anything. Minutes later, he caught movement at the edge of his vision and looked towards the front of the house. A hedgehog shuffled into view and wandered off across the neighbour's front garden and out of view.

He wondered how much time had elapsed. It felt like an age, but he couldn't check without his phone becoming visible. He resisted the urge. Stood there in the deep shadows until he figured that too much time had elapsed. Finally, he gave in and carefully checked, shielding the screen as best he could.

Thirty-five minutes had passed since Jill's last text.

Too long, surely? Their man was careful, but that was taking it to an extreme beyond normal patience.

And one of the essences of the type of mind that got involved in criminal enterprises of this kind was a lack of patience. A craving for money the easy way. The lazy way. "I want it now and I don't want to work for it."

On the other hand, if they gave up and moved a minute too soon, he could slip away unseen – and might even spot them in the process, putting Ben and Jill at further risk. They had to wait him out. And that included Pete.

After just over an hour he returned to the relative comfort of his car, but the others still hadn't reported anything. Ten minutes later, his phone finally pinged. He snatched it up from the seat beside him and turned it over. A text from Colin, this time. "Stand down. We've missed him."

But how? Pete thought. *Where did he go?* He pictured the location in his mind, recalling all the ways to and from it. Most of the options emerged onto Fore Street,, where Colin was waiting. There was Paul Street, from where he could have turned right into North Street, but Jane would have seen him. And if he'd gone towards her and turned left, he'd have passed Dave. The only other way…

'Damn,' he muttered as the realisation dawned.

The only other way out of the area was on foot along Bartholomew Terrace, then down Barbican Steps towards Exe Street. It was a narrow, unlit path that you could only take on foot, the longest pedestrian-only route away from the meeting point and therefore the one that would leave the subject exposed and vulnerable for the longest, but it had to be the one he'd used. And turning left onto and then out of Exe Street, he'd have been able to follow Bonhay Road straight past the twin bridges and, in less than a minute, be onto Topsham Road.

If, as they had surmised, he lived somewhere in that direction, he could be home in bed by now.

He lifted the phone again, called up the group text and began to type. "B terrace to steps to Exe St?"

CHAPTER TWENTY-THREE

Chief Inspector Christine Naylor waited while Pete poured the last of the coffees and Colin Underhill twisted the vertical blinds far enough to keep the low sun from lancing into the meeting room with its large table, ceiling-mounted projector and expensive-looking sideboard before making the introductions. It was just before 8:00 am and they were seated around a table big enough for three times as many people in a room on the top floor of the Sidmouth Road police station.

'Inspector Evan Maitland and Sergeant Diane Swift of the National Firearms Targeting Centre, meet DI Colin Underhill, DS Peter Gayle and PCs Ben Myers and Jill Evans. Where do we stand, as of this moment?'

She directed the question at Colin, but he nodded for Pete to take the floor.

He stood up. 'Ben and Jill are in play as our suspect's next couriers. As best we can determine, he chooses a new courier for each delivery or two, usually from the city's small-time drug dealers and possibly other ne'er-do-wells, though we managed to get Ben into the picture by eliminating – or at least drastically reducing – his opportunities amongst the drug dealers. We are aware of the vehicle he uses to move around the city. It's a silver VW Golf on cloned plates but we haven't yet been able to trace it. This is a rural city with only the amount of CCTV cameras that are deemed necessary in that circumstance, and our man seems to be adept at avoiding them, at least most of the time.

'As for his description, we have an e-fit of him. We know he's IC-1, approximately five-foot-ten, not bulky but strong, with dark hair.' He turned to Ben and Jill. 'You met him last night. Do you want to add anything to that?'

'He hasn't got a strong accent, but what there is of it is Devonian,' Jill said.

'And he's got brown eyes,' Ben added. 'But we didn't get to see much of his face. He was wearing a baseball type cap and a Covid mask and he stayed in the shadows apart from just briefly, when we were still at a distance, to let us know he was there.'

'You're scheduled to pick up the item at midday, correct?' the immaculately uniformed Chief Inspector checked.

'Yes, ma'am.'

'Where from?' asked Maitland; a tall, imposing figure, even seated, his back ramrod straight, dark hair looking like he'd just come from the barber's, his voice deep and resonant.

'From a small-time drug dealer on Queen's Terrace. Steven Judd, AKA Sour. He's the guy our suspect got my contact details from.'

'Have we got eyes on Judd?' Maitland asked.

'Dave Miles is watching from inside the Farmer's Union,' Colin said. 'The downside is, our man's seen him before, though only briefly and in bike leathers. But we've only got so many people to call on. You wanted it kept to a tight team.'

'As we said at the outset, given the suspect's history, we have no way of knowing if he's got connections within the force,' Maitland said. 'He seemed able to come and go at will, carry on his business with impunity.'

'One thing we can say,' Pete put in. 'Although we don't yet know who he is or where he's from, he knows the city like the back of his hand and even then, he must do a lot of reconnaissance. To be able to get in and out of Prince's Square like he did, and move around the city without passing traffic cameras, as well as knowing Temple Street and Barbican Steps, West View Terrace and the route through Denmark Road up to Heavitree... Some of them, certainly, are off the beaten track. Only locals would know about them.'

'I can confirm he parked on West View Terrace last night for the meeting with Ben and Jill,' Colin said, nodding towards the two younger officers, both back in uniform while they were in the station. 'I went down that way after we stood down, looking for doorbell cameras or whatever and saw the security company sign covering the Barbican Court car park. Got the CCTV from them and confirmed the Golf going in and out past there.'

'Only someone who knows the area would know they could park up there,' Ben said.

'Exactly.'

'So he's lived or worked in the city,' Maitland said. 'How does that help us?'

'Also, he's probably got some sort of link to the drugs trade, past or present,' Jill added. 'Or why would he choose dealers as couriers and messengers? The least trustworthy people you could think of, bar very few.'

'Maybe because he can create a reputation among them as someone not to be messed with and it would stay away from our ears?' suggested the slim blonde Diane Swift, making her first contribution to the conversation, one slender eyebrow arching on a face that was long, despite the low forehead she kept covered with a fringe.

Pete tipped his head. 'True, but he'd still have to know where and when to find them and which ones he could afford to rely on. And you only get that knowledge by experience or at least having someone you can trust who has that experience. Not that it helps us at this stage,' he acknowledged with a glance at Maitland.

'So that's where we are. What's your plan from there?' Colin asked the newcomers.

'We have a team of surveillance officers but it'll take longer than four hours to get them on the ground and in place,' Maitland admitted. 'We'd be looking at tonight, at the earliest.'

'Which is too late,' the station chief pointed out. 'Are you two trained in covert ops?'

Maitland gave a quick frown but Swift nodded. 'I am,' she said.

'Then I suggest you get over to Queen's Terrace and liaise with DC Miles ASAP so you can follow the suspect once the hand-off is completed. My people can only be in one place at a time. We have a witness and his family to protect and the whole team's already been up half the night or, in some cases, more. So if we can't bring in more people, you'll have to make up the shortfall. For now, you can follow on foot to wherever he's left his vehicle, then call in DC Miles to take over while you get back to your car and catch up to piggy-back him.'

She nodded and pushed her chair back to stand up.

'Have you got any civilian clothes with you?' Pete asked.

'I packed an overnight case.'

'Jill, show her the locker rooms. Then you can point her in the right direction and put her in touch with Dave.'

'Boss.'

Naylor turned to address Maitland. 'While they're doing that, perhaps you should get hold of your team and get them into place ASAP to keep a careful watch on PCs Myers and Evans once they get under way. Do we have confirmation of the destination, Ben?'

'Birmingham, ma'am,' he nodded. 'I've looked up the timetable. The first train after the noon pickup is at 12:27 and he'll expect us to catch it.'

Maitland gave a grunt, his face taking on a slightly sour expression. He'd been put on the spot here and he wasn't used to it, Pete thought.

Well done, Chief Inspector Naylor. And Ben.

Maitland stood up and took out his phone. Stepping across to the wide expanse of windows that looked out over the fields at the edge of the city, he dialled and spoke quietly and briefly before hanging up and turning back to face them. 'They're on the way.'

'And what are we doing about the weapon?' Naylor asked. 'We can't let a live firearm out onto the streets.'

'We'll take care of it on the train,' Maitland said. 'We've got a specialist who'll join the train at Bristol. He'll be able to inactivate it, just in case.'

'Really?'

Maitland nodded. 'He's very good. He'll find a way.'

'I hope so.' She turned to Ben. 'As soon as PC Evans returns, you'd better get back to the flat. We don't want you missing in action on today, of all days. I'm surprised he didn't make any attempt to follow you home last night.'

Ben shrugged. 'He gave us a mobile phone. It's got a tracker in it. I checked when we got back there last night but left it active. And I've got the details of the SIM card in case someone can trace it. Could be useful, given the short notice,' he added with a shrug. 'I left the phone in the flat for now, obviously.'

She frowned. 'Are you sure that was wise? What if he calls it and you don't answer?'

'He won't. He said just to use it to contact the buyer to let him know we've arrived and arrange the exchange, then to contact him to let him know it's done and we're on the way back with an ETA.'

'Give me the SIM card details, I'll follow it up,' Colin said.

'You'd better have a good excuse for being out and about at this time of day,' the station chief said to Ben. 'Especially after the meeting last night. Either drop the car off at a garage and arrange to pick it up tomorrow or stop off at a supermarket on the way back there and get some shopping.'

'We'll go to Aldi, up at Pinhoe, ma'am. It'd suit the characters and there'd be no need to take his phone out there with us. Why would we? Arrangements are already in place for the pick-up.'

'Fine. Talking of tracking devices, your official ones are in place, I take it?'

Ben nodded. 'They are.'

She glanced at Pete, who took out his phone and brought up the app. 'All four active, ma'am.'

'Good. So we're as prepared as we can be. Good luck, everyone. Let's hope this all goes smoothly and gives us the result we need.'

*

Pete sat silently waiting. He was parked on the double yellow lines just inside the entrance of Roberts Road, far enough back to allow other vehicles to move around him without blocking the other side of the street, but close enough to the junction to get an unobstructed view of anything passing on Topsham Road – and particularly of its vehicle registration plate.

His eyes were sore, his head beginning to get muzzy with fatigue, but he had drops for the former and a flask of coffee for the latter. Hopefully, he could stay sufficiently alert until the suspect passed on the way back out of town, having left the package with his chosen middleman. If, of course, he hadn't done that already – last night, for instance. But Pete didn't even want to think about that possibility.

Not that he could help it.

Doubts like that were inclined to creep in when you were tired. He knew that from long experience.

He checked the time.

9:52.

He'd been here almost an hour, having come straight from the police station when the meeting ended.

He was just about to reach for his flask when his phone pinged. He turned it over to check the screen. A text had come in. It was from Colin Underhill.

"SIM card bought with other one. Same time, same old lady."

'Damn,' Pete muttered. So that was what had happened to the second one in the buy-one-get-one-free deal the woman in the supermarket's back-office had mentioned when he'd been in there checking on the purchase Mrs Tranter had made.

He began to type a response, keeping one eye on the road in front of him. "One mystery solved." He hit send and set the phone aside. Moments later, it pinged again.

'Blimey,' he muttered. That was quick.

He flipped it over and saw that this text was from Dave, on the group text account they'd set up for the previous night's operation. "Target acquired."

Pete frowned and once again typed a quick response. "Not passed me."

If they were right about his normal direction of travel, then he'd taken a detour, perhaps up Barack Road and into the city centre along Heavitree Road. Thinking about it, it made sense, given that Richmond Road, which led into Queen's Square, was one-way – away from the square.

Again, their man knew his way around the city intimately.

And it would make sense for him to leave down Richmond Road, turn left and head straight out past where Pete was sitting.

Perfect, he thought.

He started typing again. "I'm waiting."

He was about to hit send when a horn honked behind him, making him jump. He looked up. A dark blue hatchback had stopped close behind him. The male driver saw him glance in the mirror and gesticulated for him to move. Pete tapped the screen to send his text and wound down the side window, putting out an arm to wave the impatient driver past.

The man revved his engine loudly, gears whirring in reverse, then clanking into a forward gear. Roared past him and hit the brakes hard for the junction no more than ten feet in front of him. Pete shook his head, wishing not for the first time that he had a display unit on the parcel shelf so he could put up warnings in the back window like traffic cars could. At times like this, it would make things a lot easier.

With his eyes gritty and his brain fogging with fatigue, he wasn't at all sure he had the patience to deal with idiot drivers this morning. He left the window down to make it easier to wave people past as well as get some fresh air into the car and keep him alert.

Their man wouldn't spend long dropping the package off with his chosen middleman and Pete needed to be ready for him.

He'd barely finished the thought when his phone pinged again. Dave. "Moving. Swift in pursuit."

Moments later, another text arrived. A new name in the group; Sgt Swift. "Left out of Richmond."

If she could stay with him in the unfamiliar city, it would save the risk of getting Dave involved, who their man might recognise despite the different surroundings. The downside was that, not knowing the sometimes complicated road layout, she couldn't give him warning of their approach to his position.

His thumbs set to work again. "What car are you in?"

"Black BMW," was the response. "U?"

"Silver Mondeo. Let me know when over gyratory."

Another ping, almost immediately, gave him a thumbs-up.

He heard another car engine from behind him, looked up and waved it past. It would have been useful to be able to switch on his hazard warning lights but, given what he was here for, it was hardly appropriate. He'd just have to stay alert.

The car pulled out past him, stopped for the junction and turned right, towards the city centre. Then another one came past, heading in the same direction.

His phone pinged again.

Another thumbs-up from Sgt Swift.

They were no more than a minute away.

He switched on his engine and waited, hoping no-one else was going to come past him and block the junction so he couldn't turn out behind her.

Then another car did come past him but its left indicator flickered and it pulled out, heading towards Topsham. Pete gave a sigh of relief and slipped the Ford into gear, easing forward so he could see better up the road to his right.

There. The silver Golf was followed by a small red hatchback, then a black saloon.

He eased up to the junction, flicking on his left indicator and waiting for the Golf and the two cars behind it to pass. Pulling out, he picked up his phone and opened the speech recognition app along with the group text. This operation would have been a whole lot simpler with radios, but they didn't know if he had a scanner in that car and they couldn't afford to do anything to alert him to their presence so the whole exercise had to be conducted in radio silence.

Watching the road carefully, he spoke into the phone. 'I'm behind you. Peel off when you can and rejoin a few cars back.' Quickly checking on the screen that the translation was correct, he hit send, waited a moment and, when he saw her glance in her driving mirror, waved briefly. She raised a thumb and, as they passed the bus stop at the bottom of St Leonard's Road, flicked on her left indicator.

Pete raised a thumb to her as he passed and continued to follow the little red hatchback along Topsham Road past the high hedge of Abbott's Park on his left, glad of the cover it was providing him from the driver of the silver Golf in front of it.

Then he grunted with disappointment as its indicator started to flicker and it slowed to turn into the County Council offices leaving him directly behind the target vehicle, albeit several yards back. He made no effort to close the distance between them as he continued to follow. At this range, there was no way the driver would be able to recognise him.

But then, with a clear, straight road in front of him, the Golf driver accelerated. Pete swore. He had to stay with him or risk losing him. But to stay with him could well mean blowing his cover.

There was no choice.

He put his foot down.

They sped past expensive houses, a tree-lined park, the high bricks walls of Wyvern Barracks. Pete checked his speedometer. They were doing forty-three miles an hour in a thirty zone. Clear of the barracks and its grounds, they passed more houses. The man in front slowed at last, coming up behind more traffic. Which left Pete with another quandary: should he close the distance between them now, as would be natural, or stay back so as not to be recognised?

He chose a compromise. Close up a bit but maintain a good stopping distance between them. The man had no more reason to expect to be followed now than he would at any other time and, even if he recognised Pete, no reason to suspect it was anything other than a chance encounter. He hoped.

They passed a speed camera in the middle of the road. Pete could now see the footbridge at the bottom of Burnthouse Lane in the distance ahead.

They slowed again and one of the cars in front of the Golf turned left into the junction. Now large houses loomed over them from behind high shrubs and trees on the left while, on the right, a retirement village stood back behind iron railings and manicured lawns. Another car turned off in front of them leaving the Golf following a bus past trees growing out over an old stone wall on the left, a higher stone wall now enclosing the road on the right. Then the space opened out on the right, the wall giving way to a wide grass verge around a side-road. The Golf's driver abruptly signalled and pulled out, speeding past the bus.

'Shit,' Pete muttered as a car rolled down the side-road, signalling left, towards him.

The Golf driver had made his move just in time. The bus signalled to pull over. The car came out of the side-turn opposite, forcing Pete to wait behind the bus, which now signalled out into the carriageway again.

As soon as he could, Pete pulled out and gunned the engine, but the Golf was a dot in the distance now. He accelerated hard, determined to keep it in sight. Had closed the gap only slightly when he was sure it swung across to the right. He looked for a landmark as he climbed the tree-lined hill but all he could say for sure was that the silver car had emerged from the trees' shadows, then turned.

As he got closer to the top of the rise, he could see that the first option was the junction that led into the old village of Countess Wear, but immediately after that, on the other side of a high, ragged hedge, was the off slip leading to the front of a couple of shops, one of which he remembered was a funeral parlour. He took the gamble, braking hard, and turned into School Lane. Now where? There was a turn immediately on the left, going up behind the shops or he could go straight on over the brow and down towards the river. Either way, the Golf was out of sight.

He sucked air through his teeth, but there was no real choice to make. Reluctantly, he pulled over.

CHAPTER TWENTY-FOUR

Running back around the corner, Pete checked that the Golf hadn't passed the junction he had stopped in and nipped up into the parking area in front of the shops. It hadn't. Walking back to his car, he brought up the group text and began to type rapidly.

"Need all hands ASAP at Countess Wear. Sgt Swift go on to RA," – the standard police acronym for roundabout – "and take right, Bridge Rd. Go under ftbridge n plot up at TLs to cover exit from Countess Wear Rd on rt. Photo all emerging and folw Golf if among them."

He hit send. She could figure out when she got there that she'd have to use her blue lights to cross the central reservation and go through a no-entry in order to do what he'd asked, as the exit from Countess Wear was a left turn only. She was the only one in a position to get there in time. Then he started a new text. "All others to school lane, CW, to search, inc Dick n Jane."

Again, he hit send. They had their man contained, one way or another. He couldn't be here and going after the Gordons at the same time.

He was about to get back into his car when his phone pinged with an incoming message, Seargeant Swift simply typing, "OK." Back in the driver's seat, he kept his phone in hand. He, too, would photograph any vehicles – or, indeed, male pedestrians – emerging from the old village.

More messages followed. Dick, Jane, Dave – even Colin Underhill – all saying the same thing: "On way."

It took no more than a couple of minutes but it felt like a lot longer before the first of the team arrived. It was Colin's dark green old-style Range Rover that pulled around the corner into view from behind the hedge and rolled past him to stop just beyond the junction on the left. Pete stepped out of his car and walked towards the big SUV, hearing a motorbike engine behind him as he approached. A glance told him Dave was turning in from the city-ward side of the junction.

Colin rolled his window down and they nodded to each other as Dave swung the big bike into the kerb in front of the Range Rover and cut the engine. Moments later, Dick's silver Ford arrived, then Jane's little green Vauxhall. They congregated outside the senior man's car and Colin nodded once more for Pete to begin.

'I was some way back, but I'm sure he turned in here,' he started. 'I checked the front of the shops and he wasn't there. But although there's only one other way out of the place, which Sergeant Swift is covering, there's a few different ways through it and some turn-offs and dead ends too. Of course, if he lives here and he's put the car in a garage, we're stuffed, but if it's outside, with a few of us trawling the streets and both ends covered, we're bound to find him pretty soon. I thought if one of us stays here, phone out, photographing any vehicles and any male pedestrians coming out of the village, and Swift's doing the same at the far end, on Bridge Road, then the rest of us can split up and cover a street each.'

Colin nodded agreement.

'Sounds like a plan,' Dave said.

Pete took out his phone and called up an on-line map. Zooming in on the area in question, he made sure everyone could see. 'Best bet's probably for Jane to stay here. If the Golf passes, then follow it. Otherwise, as I said, just record anyone on the way out. You're probably the most credible-looking amongst us for doing that innocently. Plus, the suspect hasn't seen you before, as far as we know. He has seen Dave and I.'

'What about me?' Dick asked.

'Age,' Dave told him bluntly. 'You look like an old fart who wouldn't know which way up to hold a mobile phone, never mind how to take pictures on it surreptitiously.'

'Bloody cheek!'

'He did say "Look like,"' Pete reminded him. 'Anyway, someone needs to go up the side-road there, Exe Vale, not forgetting that little dead-end off the side of it. Someone else can go down to the next one, Countess Wear Road, and along to Bridge Road. And the two others down past the pub and around, back up to the junction with Countess Wear Road, one of them checking the cul-de-sac down there that crosses the river.'

'Dave, you and me down Mill Road,' said Colin. 'You can have Mill Lane. Pete go along Countess Wear Road and link up with Swift. That leaves you to cover Exe Vale, Dick.'

'I don't know if I can remember that cul-de-sac by the time I get there, at my age,' Dick said, looking at Dave.

'You'd better,' Colin said. 'We'll meet back here unless someone finds something. If not it'll be time to start checking garages and knocking on doors, see if anyone recognises the Golf or the e-fit.'

'Thanks, Guv.' Pete headed back to his car. He let Colin and Dave lead off and followed them up over the brow and down as far as the old, stone-built community hall that he thought looked like the only possibility for having been the school that gave the road its name, unless the school had been pulled down decades ago and replaced with one or more of the 1970s-built houses on the other side of the road. As the bike and the 4x4 continued straight on past the pub, he slowed and turned left around the community hall and past the church behind it.

Beyond the church, the road narrowed. Houses on the left were set back behind long gardens, raised up from the road, while on the right, they stood close to the roadside, some with garages opening directly off the street. After a short distance it opened out again on the left around a crossroads where Exe Vale came down and through between two high, blank whitewashed walls on the right. Narrowing again beyond this, the road he was on curved to the right between a high hedge and a stone wall before opening out again where Mill Road came up to meet it from the right. He continued past the junction and a small open area of grass leading down to the river opposite a pair of sixties-style bungalows before the road closed in again with homes on both sides. Angling away from the river, it went up a rise. He had to be getting close to the far end by now, he guessed as he crested the rise and saw low bungalows and garages extending away along the right side of the road while the left pulled out again, several cars parked along that side.

And one of them was a silver-coloured Golf, its distinctive shape recognisable even though it was between two other cars, only the top portion visible.

'Yes,' he said, lips tight as he resisted the urge to punch the air in the confines of the Ford. He kept going, easing off the accelerator to let the car roll steadily down the incline and past the stationary vehicles, slow enough to recognise the number plate as he passed. He continued a few yards further, away from the Golf and the houses it was parked outside, before pulling over and picking up his phone.

He used the group text again.

"Found it."

Pressing send, he started typing again. "Opposite garages toward far end of CW Rd. Continuing on to check with Swift."

Again, he pressed send before doing just that.

The road narrowed again and curved to the left before emerging towards the junction with Bridge Road, where he saw

Swift's black BMW pulled up on the right, outside someone's driveway.

She was sitting on their wall, the laurel hedge behind it brushing the back of her top as she pretended to play with her phone while waiting for someone. He had to admit, she didn't look out of place in her sleeveless salmon-pink blouse and skinny jeans, blonde hair loose down onto her shoulders.

There was just room in front of her car on the combined pavement and cycle path that led down Bridge Road, past the junction, for him to pull over and get out to go and speak to her.

Before he could get out of the car, his phone pinged with an incoming message.

Colin: "Dick and Jane return to watch on Gordons. Dave join Pete door knocking around car location. I'll take over on School Lane."

Pete nodded to himself. That all made sense and required no response from him. He stepped out of the car and approached Sergeant Swift.

'I saw your texts,' she said by way of greeting.

'Have you seen our man, though?'

'No-one's walked through here. A few cars and vans have passed since I got here but no-one looking flustered. I've got pictures so we can check them out later.'

'Perfect. You stay put awhile. I'll stroll back there and meet up with my DC, see if we can find out anything useful.'

'Right.'

*

They met at the junction of Countess Wear Road and Mill Road, the latter barely wider than a car as it came up at a sharp angle past the peeling black-painted doors of the detached garage of an old white rendered cottage with high hedges around its garden.

Pete had pulled into the widened space opposite, in front of a substantial 1960s dormer bungalow fronted by a raised garden of shrubs and lawn with a drive leading up. Dave parked behind him and flipped up his visor.

'How d'you want to play it?' Dave asked.

'Well, we can't just go knocking on doors randomly in case one of them belongs to our suspect,' Pete said. 'Ideally, we could do with talking to someone who's outside already, mowing the lawn, washing their car or whatever. At least we know what our man looks like so we can avoid talking to him direct if we do it that way. And we know he's male.'

'Yeah, but if we dropped on his Mrs by mistake, she wouldn't help much, would she?' Dave countered.

'Not if she knew what he was up to,' Pete admitted. 'We just need to find someone and ask if they can tell us about the Golf. If they know who it belongs to, if they've noticed it and how long for – things like that to start with.'

'It's a bit bold to leave it on the roadside, bearing in mind how careful he's proved himself to be otherwise,' Dave pointed out.

'Yes, but he might not have a choice. Not all the houses along here have got garages and if he has, that might be where he's doing his work. And this isn't exactly a major thoroughfare, is it?'

'True.'

'Plus, it's parked end-to-end between two other vehicles so, at normal driving speed, you wouldn't pick up on the number plate. I only did because I was looking for it.'

'Hmm.' Dave didn't look or sound convinced. 'Still…'

'So, what are you thinking – he lives a distance away and just leaves it there? Or found a spot and left it? But then, where did he go? A relative or friend? Because he hasn't walked any distance away from it.'

'OK, so the cautious approach.'

Pete nodded. 'Even if someone comes out to another vehicle, we can't be sure our suspect hasn't got more than one. We need to talk to a male who doesn't resemble him and who hopefully can tell us about the Golf. In which case, I don't suppose it needs more than one of us out here, to be fair,' Pete concluded. 'It's not exactly densely populated along here.'

'You want to go and look after Annie if Louise is working?' Dave asked.

'No, that's OK. She's at my parents. Coming back tomorrow to get ready for the new school term. And year.'

'You're fetching her?'

'We'll see. If not, my old chap can bring her back. Or keep her for another day or two.'

Dave chuckled. 'I'm sure she'll love that.'

Pete tipped his head. 'She's getting to an age where she might get bored with them, I suppose, but she hasn't yet. At least, she hasn't admitted it if she does. She was talking about teaching him how to play chess this time. If he takes to it, that'll keep 'em occupied.'

'Is he likely to, do you think?' Dave didn't know Pete's parents. He was Exeter born and bred while Pete had been raised in Okehampton, where his parents still lived.

'He might. He's got a sharp mind. Was a joiner until he retired. No, you get off, get some rest. If we don't find him today, the watch will have to be kept up on the Gordons tonight.'

'Yeah, that's me. What about you?'

'If I can't make it, you can always cover the old lady's address tonight and we can check the other place in the morning. There's no-one there, at least.'

'OK,' Dave allowed with a shrug. 'But stay sharp, yeah? Don't want you walking into any trouble that you don't need to on account of being too tired.'

Pete grinned. 'It's nice to know you care.'

Dave grunted. 'I care about who might take over from you, if you get retired through injury or summat.'

Pete laughed. 'Go on, get out of here. And tell Sergeant Swift she can get off back to the nick, too.'

He waited while Dave dropped his visor, kicked the motorbike into life, exhausts rumbling with suppressed power, and dropped it off the stand to roar away. Then he ambled after him along the narrow road.

A couple of minutes later, he walked past a big old redbrick house with a clock and bells in a miniature tower over its black gates and rounded the turn that allowed him to see along to where the Golf had been parked. It was still in the same position at the side of the lane, pulled up tight against a hedge-topped brick wall opposite a short row of garages. No-one was in sight. This could be a long wait, he realised, but he had to play it out. It was the only way to go.

In the meantime, at least he could take the opportunity to let his wife know what was going on and why he wasn't home yet. He took out his phone and dialled.

*

It took longer than he'd hoped. Text messages had informed him that Ben and Jill had collected the weapon and boarded the north-bound train some time before he finally saw what he needed.

A man emerged from an entrance just beyond the short row of garages opposite the Golf and approached one of them, key in hand. He was grey-haired, slim, around Pete's own height but stooped with age, smartly turned out in a lemon-yellow polo shirt that contrasted with his tanned complexion and khaki slacks.

Pete hurried forward, long strides covering the ground quickly while he tried not to look rushed to anyone watching. He waited until he got close, the dark blue garage door now open, before speaking. With his warrant card raised subtly, he said, 'Excuse me. Have you got a second?'

The man turned as he was about to enter the garage beside a small red sports car.

'I'm with Devon and Cornwall Police,' Pete said. 'Do you know anything about that silver Golf over there? Who owns it or where they live, for instance?'

The man frowned. 'Can't you look that up or something?'

Pete tipped his head. 'We could if the number plates were real.'

'Ah, right. Well, no, I'm afraid I don't know who's it is.'

'Have you seen it around here before?'

'Yes, it's been around for a few weeks. It comes and goes occasionally, as you'd expect, but that's about all I can tell you.'

'You haven't seen the driver?'

He shook his head.

'OK, thanks for your time.' Pete backed off. He was getting nothing useful here.

The man turned away into the garage and Pete headed back towards his previous position to wait for someone else to appear. He was only part-way there when he heard the roar of an engine behind him. He glanced back. The man had driven the sports car out of the garage and stopped just clear of it to get out and close the up-and-over door. As Pete continued along the road, he heard the car drive noisily away.

He had to wait only a few minutes longer before someone else emerged, though, from one of the bungalows on the left. A woman – again, grey haired – in jeans and a jacket came down the wide drive with a slim long-haired dog straining ahead of her on the end of a lead. She headed towards him and he stepped forward, walking purposefully. When the gap closed sufficiently between them, he took out his warrant card and spoke.

'Excuse me,' he said. 'Sorry to trouble you. I won't keep you a minute – I can see the dog's eager for his walk. I'm DS Gayle with Exeter CID. Can I ask your name?'

A slender eyebrow rose. 'Maureen. Harper. How can I help?'

He nodded towards the car parked further along the road behind her. 'We're making enquiries about that silver car, parked outside your neighbour's. It's been brought to our notice that it's got incorrect number plates on. I was wondering if you'd seen anything in the way of its comings and goings, or those of its driver that might be helpful?'

She grimaced. 'The silver one? I've seen it around here over the past couple of weeks or so, I suppose, but I can't really say I've taken a lot of notice of it. Illegal plates, you say?'

He nodded. 'What we term clones. The same as those carried by another, similar, car that we know is the correct bearer.'

'Oh, dear! Why would someone do that?'

'Sometimes to avoid paying road-tax or insurance. Other times it could be a stolen car or it's done to hide their identity while they're on the road, committing other offences. Burglaries or drug dealing, for example.'

'I see,' she said, nodding. 'And that's one of those? You're sure?'

'We are. What we're not sure of yet is where the person driving it lives and, rather than just seizing the vehicle and leaving them free to potentially commit the same crime again, we'd like to find out who they are first.'

'Yes, that makes sense.'

'So, you've seen it around here for a couple of weeks or so. Have you seen the driver?'

She shook her head. 'Sorry, no.'

'No problem.' This was getting him nowhere and might not, if he spent all day here. But something sparked in his mind, following on from what he'd said to her. 'Is your husband at home? I noticed you're wearing a ring.'

'Yes. He sometimes comes out with Meg and I, but he's feeling a bit under the weather at the moment. Did you want me to fetch him out to speak to you?'

'No, no. That's OK. You go on and have your walk. I'll go and speak to him. He's on his own there, is he?'

'Yes. I don't suppose he'll be able to tell you any more than I could but be my guest.'

'I expect you're right but we have to cover all bases, as they say.'

'Hmm.' She went on her way and Pete headed for the drive she'd emerged from. Walking up the steep dark red tarmac, he rang the bell. Waited a few moments before movement showed behind the rippled glass of the door.

It was opened by a man of about the same age as the woman he'd just spoken to, but where she was slender and smart, his considerable belly bulged over the waistband of his dark trousers, stretching the fabric of his blue polo shirt, worn under a cardigan that almost matched the trousers.

'Yes?'

Pete raised his warrant card. 'Mr Harper? DS Gayle, Exeter CID,' he said. 'I was just talking to your wife along the road with the dog and wanted to ask you basically the same questions.'

'Oh, yes?'

'Can you tell me anything about the silver Golf parked outside your neighbour's?' He pointed to the roof of the car, just visible between the low evergreen shrubbery lining the top of the retaining wall at the far side of the neatly mown lawn.

'Not really. I just figured they must have got a new one. Haven't spoken to them for a while. Nothing deliberate. We just haven't crossed paths, that's all.'

Pete nodded. 'You haven't seen the driver, then?'

'No. Sitting room's at the back of the house. This one here's a bedroom,' he said, pushing a thumb towards the room that overlooked the front garden from his left while the space to his right was mainly taken up with the built-in garage.

'What can you tell me about the neighbours? What are they like?'

'Pleasant enough. Couple in their fifties or so. No kids. Keep themselves to themselves.'

'And the man of the house – what does he look like?'

The man frowned. 'Why? Is there some sort of problem I ought to know about?'

'We suspect the car's been used in a number of crimes around the city.'

He grunted. 'Well, I can't see Dom being a master criminal. He doesn't seem to have it in him. But I suppose you never can tell, eh? He's – like I said – in his fifties. Shorter than you. Maybe five-nine or so. Stocky. Dark hair, going grey, still a bit on the long side for military purposes, but you know...' He gave a shrug. 'What more can I say?'

'That's perfect,' Pete said. 'It confirms he's not who we're looking for at least. Thank you.'

The man nodded and Pete stepped away.

Back down on the street, he took out his phone and dialled.

'Yes?'

'Guv, it's Pete. I've spoken to a few people along here, where the car is, but got nothing useful yet except that the car's been around here on and off for the last couple of weeks. The question is, which way do we play it from here? Keep on as we are or call in a tow truck and haul the car off to Forensics to check it for DNA and prints in the hope our suspect's already on record? Trouble is, that leaves him out there, still potentially unknown and now certain that we're onto him. Or we could place a hidden camera somewhere here – perhaps in a garden with the permission of one of the home-owners – and wait for him to hopefully come back and use the car again.'

'*If* he comes back to it. He was chased there, so he knows we're after him and he'll expect us to have found the car.'

'So, you reckon it's a lost cause?'

'There's always a chance, but in this case it's a faint one.'

'So we let Forensics have it and knock on all the doors around here, see what reaction we get? Hope someone knows something or saw something and we don't end up talking to the man himself, or his Mrs?'

'That's about the size of it,' Colin confirmed. 'At least we've got the e-fit to use. See if anyone recognises him. Meantime, get the VIN from the car and run it. Find out where it came from.'

'All right. Will do.'

'Forensics will be there in… fifteen minutes. Once that's all done, we'll clear out and leave a couple of cameras just in case while Forensics process whatever they get.'

'Right.'

'And I'll take your nightshift. Franklin or Fairpark?'

'Oh,' Pete said, surprised. 'Franklin. But we'd thought it would be OK to leave it overnight, pick it up in the morning.'

'With Jane?'

'Yes.'

'Don't want to be sexist, but it's better she knows what she's walking into.'

'Ideally, yes, but…'

'That's settled, then.' He cut the line.

'OK,' Pete said to the dead phone. 'Appreciated.'

CHAPTER TWENTY-FIVE

While he waited for the tow-truck that would take the Golf off to Forensics at the force headquarters in Middlemoor, Pete went to the house beyond the Harpers' – another similar property, the last of the short row, its garden fronted with a mix of tall, thin conifers, small deciduous trees and strappy-leaved phormiums, a substantial hedge of dark conifers bordering the far side from the road to the corner of the house.

Hearing music from within, he knocked on the door.

The woman who answered in a lightweight V-necked pink sweater and mid-length skirt was still smiling and suppressing dance moves as she opened the door, her blond pony-tail swinging.

'Yes?'

Pete held up his warrant card. 'DS Gayle with Exeter CID,' he said. 'Could I have a quick word in relation to an investigation we're conducting?'

'Of course. What do you need?'

'The silver car you can see down there: is it yours?'

'No.'

'Did you see it arrive, by any chance?'

'No, but I saw it leave earlier. It was here overnight. It's been around here for a little while.'

'You saw the driver?' he checked.

'Yes.'

'Did you recognise him?'

'No, but that doesn't mean much, these days, even out here. People come and go all the time.'

Pete nodded. 'True. What does he look like?'

'Tallish. Dark hair.' She looked him up and down. 'A bit like you, actually. Maybe not quite as tall. Why? Has he done something wrong?'

'Well, yes. The car's stolen.' He ignored her gasp of shock. 'Did you see which way he came from?'

'Along that way somewhere.' She pointed along towards the centre of the village with a long, red fingernail.

He nodded. 'What time was this?'

'Oh, about half past nine, twenty to ten.'

Which tied in with the time Dave spotted him in Queens Square, Pete realised, especially if he'd been as careful as usual and taken a roundabout route to get there. He took his copy of the e-fit from his pocket and showed it to her. 'Do you recognise this male?'

She looked at it carefully, lips pushing up. 'No, sorry. Is that him?' She glanced up. 'I never saw him from that close.'

Pete nodded. 'It is. But that's OK. We'll find him. All right, thanks for your time. I'll let you get back to your music.'

*

Once the car had been removed from the roadside and taken away, he began door-knocking in earnest, working his way from the car's location back along the road towards the junction with Mill Road. An hour later, though, he'd reached the junction by the little green and gained nothing. Apart from a couple of alarms on detached garages, there was no sign that anyone around here bothered about security. Half of them probably still didn't lock their doors at night, he guessed. And no-one he spoke to recognised the picture of the suspect or recalled a vehicle arriving on the street around 9:30 that morning.

Pete reported in to Colin and headed home for a well-earned rest.

Despite how exhausted he felt, it took him a long time to get to sleep, thoughts and scenarios running round and round in his mind until finally he drifted off. And was woken after what seemed like hardly any time at all by his phone.

Groggily, he registered the light coming in through the closed curtains. A glance at the clock on his beside cabinet told him it was 7:12. His phone screen told him it was pm – and that the caller ID was blocked.

He answered it. 'Hello?'

'I know you're resting, but you'll want in on this,' said Colin Underhill. 'Get yourself to the nick.'

'What, now?'

'No, next Tuesday.'

'What's going on?' Pete asked, swinging his legs out of the bed.

'We're aiming to get the gunman's collar felt tonight. Need everyone in on it.'

'Right, I'm on the way. What about the others?'

'I'll call them.'

The phone clicked dead. Pete drew a breath, set it down and got dressed, blinking and shaking his head to rid it of the hangover of sleep. He left a note for Louise and was out of the door in less than five minutes.

They met in the incident room that Pete and his team had vacated just a few days ago. Colin, Evan Maitland, Diane Swift and

Christine Naylor were already there when he arrived, along with Ben and Jill. Maitland appeared to be chairing the meeting. At least, he was on his feet in front of the whiteboard while the others sat around the cluster of desks in front of it. Pete joined them, noting gratefully that there was already a steaming mug of coffee on the desk in front of him as he sat down.

He picked it up and took a gulp.

'Right,' said Maitland. 'Now we're all here, there's no time to waste. Our man isn't hanging around this time. He wants to take the return package – his money – tonight. Which we have to suspect means he's preparing to do a runner.' He nodded to Ben who placed his phone upright on the desk in front of him and plugged it into a speaker block. He tapped the screen and his voice came from the speakers.

'Yes?'

'Be at Bury Meadow Park at eleven-thirty tonight. Go to Aldi and get a bag for life. Put the package in it. I'll have a similar one with your money in it. We'll swap and be on our way. Don't leave by the same entrance as you entered. And come alone, this time.' He chuckled. 'Your girlfriend would be about as welcome there as a fart in a lift, that time of night.'

'We're not attached at the hip,' Ben retorted. 'She came along last time because I didn't know you.'

'Well, now you do. Enough, anyway. And we've got a contract. Meet me where the paths cross on the north side.'

'OK…' The call ended abruptly.

'You've been to Aldi?' Pete checked with the spiky-haired constable, who was in black jeans and a black V-necked T-shirt with a leather waistcoat.

Ben nodded.

'We've also opened the "package,"' Maitland added. 'And added a little something to it. A tracking device tucked carefully inside one of the wads of cash it contains. We then sealed it up again, as it was before. We're talking about a sandwich box, basically, wrapped in packing tape.'

'Isn't that a bit risky?' Pete asked. 'If he opens it...'

Colin tipped his head in response.

'He said not to leave by the same entrance as you entered,' Maitland continued. 'How many entrances are there to this place?'

'Four official ones, plus a gap in the hedge down Woodbine Terrace,' Jill replied.

'So, five,' he concluded, looking around the table. 'And we know where he's going to be tonight, so I'd say your guard duty on the Gordon family could be done without. The more boots we've got on the ground around that park, the better. One thing confuses me: why did he make the comment about PC Evans?'

'Bury Meadow is known for a certain type of visitors after dark,' the chief inspector told him.

'It's a gay hook-up spot,' Colin said.

'Ah. That could complicate things.'

'Yeah, we'd be about as welcome as Jill,' Colin agreed, nodding towards her.

'Nevertheless, in all other ways, it's the ideal opportunity to pick him up,' Maitland maintained. 'If we can cover all five exits, stop anyone coming out – Aldi bag or not – and search them...'

'Really?' Colin asked. 'When did you last pull a stunt like that and have it work? You'd have half of them legging it before you could finish the introductions and your suspect probably either hiding up in there until morning or slipping away quietly while you're busy running after some idiot with a few illicit pills in his pocket.'

Maitland turned on him. 'We have done this before, DI Underhill. The question is, given those factors, what can we do to ameliorate them?'

'Ben, you'd better get off back to the flat,' Naylor said.

'Ma'am.' He stood up to leave. He could see where she was coming from, just as Pete could. They didn't know the suspect's current location or how much background research he'd been able to do on Ben's alter-ego. Far better to err on the side of caution at this stage. He could be filled in with the necessary details by phone later.

'Right, let's get down to details,' Maitland suggested, opening up the computer in front of him. 'Can I throw the screen from this up onto the whiteboard?'

*

'Oi! Oh, it's you.' Ben's voice came through the earbud in Pete's left ear which trailed up from his phone, on a conference call that included Ben and the four other team leaders spread around the park.

A response came faintly through the tiny speaker. He couldn't make out what the other male said, but the hand-over was clearly taking place. It would be minutes now before they needed to start stopping anyone and everyone who left the park.

He could hear Ben's voice again. 'See for yourself. I haven't touched it. It's wrapped up like a damn mummy in parcel tape or something.'

A response.

'Drone target acquired,' a different voice came through: the drone operator who'd attended Franklin Street just a couple of days before. Pete glanced upward. Somewhere up there was a police drone looking down on them with an infra-red camera, the operator tucked into a dark corner close to Colin Underhill's location at the other side of the little grey gothic-looking Bury Meadow Lodge in the corner of the park nearest to the city centre. CI Naylor had asked Pete to arrange that after the meeting, earlier. But he could neither see nor hear it from here. Which had to be a good thing.

'It'd better be all there.' Ben's tone had changed, was now challenging – even threatening. 'If it ain't, I've got enough friends around here to be able to find you, and you won't want me doing that.' He paused. 'Right, then.'

That was it. The suspect would be heading out of the park at any second. Pete focussed his gaze on the gap in the high hedge bordering the park, a few feet away from where he crouched in the shadows behind a car on the short, narrow cul-de-sac. A row of Victorian terraced houses faced the hedge, in front of which were parked several vehicles. The gap was just a few steps along from the gate at the far end that gave access to the rear of the Lodge.

This was probably the least likely egress point for their suspect, but Pete wasn't surprised at having been allocated it. This wasn't his case. Wasn't even Colin Underhill's, who was covering the small gateway that gave legitimate access to the park from the other side of the Lodge, on New North Road, which was a main route northward out of the city centre, leading down to Cowley Bridge Road and out towards Crediton and Tiverton. No, the more likely exit points, including the one Ben had entered by, at the far corner of the park, were being covered by Swift, Maitland and one of his other sergeants, a stocky bald-headed male called Brian Tolliver.

He focussed his attention on the gap in the hedge.

As if on cue, a head appeared through the dense leaves. The male looked around. Deep in the shadows, Pete held still as the head ducked back and a leg appeared, then the head again and the body between them as the male stepped through onto the street. He moved between the two vehicles that almost covered the gap and was taking a first step out across the clear tarmac when Dave stood up from the street-side of the vehicle beyond the gap and grabbed him.

'Police. Have you got a minute?'

Almost before the male could react, Pete stood up and moved into sight, blocking his escape, warrant card held up in view. 'We won't take up too much of your time,' he said.

The male in Dave's grip appeared to relax, though his narrow, clean-shaven and acne-dotted face showed an expression of sour resentment. He was small and skinny, his blond hair dishevelled, but deliberately so. He was dressed in a white T-shirt and joggers that looked grey in the dim light from the single streetlight at the far end of the street. Trainers were fashionably – and stupidly, in Pete's mind – unlaced on his feet.

'A quick search. Everyone leaving the park tonight is undergoing it. We're looking for a murder suspect. If you'll step over here, against the car…'

'Have I got a choice?'

Pete shrugged. 'No really. But it's for your own good. Submit to this, it's a minute of your time tonight. Don't and it could be your life, tomorrow night.'

He rolled his eyes and turned towards the big 4x4 that Pete had been concealed behind.

'Best not lean on it,' Pete said. 'It's not ours. The alarm might go off.'

The kid raised an eyebrow and Pete could see he was tempted to do just that.

'Do, and you'll be arrested for obstruction of a police investigation and aiding and abetting.'

He gave a theatrical sigh and stood in the street, arms lifted outward, hip cocked to one side as Dave patted him down.

'Thank you,' Pete said when it was done. 'On you go.'

He gave a disgusted 'Humph,' and flounced away as Pete and Dave resumed their positions to wait for the next one.

It didn't take long. Another head appeared through the gap only a minute or so after they'd regained their hiding places, another young male stepping through. Pete was about to move when he saw something that stopped him. Another figure following the first one out of the park. Older, taller, and dressed smartly in a suit, albeit without the tie, this was a man in his forties or fifties, Pete guessed.

'Hang on, Dave,' he murmured into his phone. 'There's two.'

He let the second figure emerge and step into the gap between the cars, then stood up and moved to cut off his retreat.

'Evening, gents,' he said.

The older man's head snapped around in shock.

'Police,' Pete told him and saw, over his shoulder, his companion looking ready to bolt. 'You might dodge my colleague's Taser, but you won't get past the dog at the end of the street,' he said.

And he wasn't lying. Every officer involved in the operation tonight was armed with a Taser and there was indeed a dog van parked out of sight, around the corner from the end of the little street, in case anyone decided to try and avoid the pat-down he was demanding they submit to.

Other dog handlers were located close to the other exit points from the park, too, waiting in case they were needed. As Diane Swift had suggested in the meeting earlier, a carrot and stick approach was their best option. Making it clear why the searches were required – that the police weren't interested in why the subjects were there, as long as they weren't connected to the crime they were investigating – would suffice in most cases. But there were bound to be a few who decided not to cooperate.

Not many people, though, however desperate they might be to conceal their sexual proclivities or any illicit drugs they might be carrying, would be prepared to defy a police dog.

Pete had thought when she suggested it that, every time he interacted with her, he liked Swift more.

'What is this?' the older male demanded. 'We're not doing anything illegal.'

'Then you've got nothing to worry about,' Pete said. 'Move over that way.' He nodded towards the right – the blocked-off end of the street. 'A quick search and you can be on your way unless you're involved in the case we're investigating.'

'Which is?'

'Murder and arms trafficking.'

'What?' the man spluttered. 'Do you know who I am?'

'No, and I don't care unless I find you lied to me about not breaking the law.'

'I am a member of the police oversight committee.'

'And I told you: I don't care. Lift your arms.' Pete demonstrated quickly.

The man pursed his lips but complied and Pete reached for his cuffs to begin patting him down when a shout came through his earpiece. He recognised Colin Underhill's dull bark.

'Runner.'

'It's him. The suspect.' That was Jane. 'Stop! Police with Taser.' Then: 'Damn! Are you all right, Guv?'

'Go,' Colin gasped.

'Suspect fleeing on New North Road,' Jane reported. 'Crossing the road.'

Pete's movements got quicker, more cursory. He thought he heard a dog's frantic barking from beyond the brick wall and the wooden gates that gave access to the Lodge. Then he definitely heard a car horn and the screech of tyres.

'Barny!' An unfamiliar female voice.

'Dog's been hit.' Colin sounded a little stronger this time.

'Suspect heading north on New North Road,' Jane reported.

Pete finished what he was doing and stepped back. 'Go,' he told the man and turned to Dave. 'Are you hearing this?'

'Yes.'

'Let's go.'

They both ran for their vehicles. As Pete unlocked the unmarked Ford, he saw Dave grabbing up his helmet and swinging a leg over the big bike. He kicked it into life while Pete sat into the car and hit the engine start button. They sped off, Dave just yards ahead, both turning right at the end of the short terrace, towards the Clock Tower.

'Turning into Hele Road,' Jane gasped.

'Target confirmed,' said the drone operator. 'Locked on.'

'Thank God.' Jane's voice was quieter, speaking almost to herself.

'In pursuit,' came another voice. That was Maitland's other sergeant, Brian Tolliver, Pete thought. He'd been manning the main entrance to the park off New North Road, along with a constable from the National Crime Agency. They'd be closing in on Hele Road from the opposite side from Jane. They'd be a few yards behind her going down there, he guessed.

'Suspect crossing the grass towards Queen's Terrace,' Jane reported, the juddering of her running clear over the open phone line.

Pete had the advantage of blue lights and sirens in the car, which Dave didn't on his motorbike. He hit the switch and they both turned out around the clock tower on its little roundabout outside the grey bulk of the Farmer's Union Hotel, heading after the fleeing suspect. Pete gunned the engine, following Dave. It was just a few yards to the entrance to Hele Road, on the left. As he passed, he saw Colin dusting himself off, having picked himself up off the pavement on the right while, on his left, a uniformed female officer crouched beside a German Sheppard dog that was lying on its side at the edge of the pavement. He hit the indicator for the left fork immediately beyond the traffic lights as, in front of him, Dave leaned into the turn, brake light flaring.

'Left, left, into Queen's Terrace,' Jane said.

Pete braked, wondering where the suspect was thinking of going. He seemed to be heading around in a circle. Had he parked his car in Queen's Square or Richmond Street, which led off it?

'Subject crossing the road,' Jane said. By now, he could see her in the distance, almost past the wide open churchyard on the right, her red hair flying, distinctive even under the streetlights as the time approached midnight. Two more figures were running after her, one of them in uniform, the other shorter, stockier, his bald head gleaming under the lights as he passed them.

Pete knew there was a footpath that led down behind the churchyard, all the way to St David's Hill. If the suspect took that, Jane and the two NCA officers were on their own. It was too narrow for a motorbike, never mind a car.

'Passing the church path,' Jane said. She was beginning to breathe more heavily and speak more quietly, he noticed.

Dave braked again for the bend in the road just beyond the location she'd mentioned. He was closing in, just three or four yards behind her now.

Pete began to slow for the same bend in the narrow road.

'Right, right, into Little Silver,' Jane said.

'Dammit,' Dave cursed. This, again, was no more than a narrow footpath.

Pete sucked air through his teeth. His only option – and Dave's – was to carry on past, up to the square, and turn across the bottom end of it and into Richmond Street, to try and cut their man off there. Unless he went on down to St David's Hill, where the jumble of footpaths that made up Little Silver emerged just along from the church path.

He rounded the bend, the street narrowing even further as it led up towards the back end of the tree-lined square, now no more than a car width between the pavements on either side, both edged with double yellow lines to prevent anyone parking along here. Ahead of him, Dave slowed for the right-hand turn at the square and went from sight.

Though only yards behind him, by the time Pete reached the square, Dave was still out of sight, no doubt having turned right again onto Richmond Road. Pete followed. Reaching the corner, he glanced right and saw Dave's taillight in the distance. He'd obviously had the same thought as Pete. He was going to head their man off at the far end of Little Silver, if he went that way, leaving Pete to cover the exit onto this long, narrow street with its row of Regency-style white-rendered town houses on the left, vehicles parked in front of most of them despite the little car park off to the right, part-way down.

'Subject right and then left,' came the voice of the drone operator.

Probably not going on through to where Dave will be waiting for him, then, Pete thought. He could go to ground or he could come out down here, where the little car park marked the access to the jumble of houses and flats that made up Little Silver. There was nowhere to pull in until a few yards beyond the car park entrance.

Pete stopped there, killed his lights and engine and stepped out of the car.

A figure ran out of the carpark and across the road just as Pete pressed his key fob to lock the car.

'Stop,' Pete shouted as the man angled away from him, back up towards Queen's Square. 'Police.' Then, in a lower tone, 'Shit.'

As he set off after the man, Jane appeared, the uniformed officer now alongside her.

'Sod that,' Pete muttered. 'I'll go on round and try to cut him off,' he said more clearly for the benefit of those listening on the open group phone connection. Turning back to his car, he unlocked it and hopped back in, gunning the engine. There wasn't room to turn it around on this narrow street, so he flipped on the blue lights and sped down to the far end, turning left on St David's Hill. He was about to take the narrow off-slip that led down the side of the Iron Bridge when Jane's voice sounded in his ear again.

'Subject right, right, into Richmond Court.'

Again, he was going off-road, Pete thought. Either he knew his way intimately around the city centre, as they already suspected, or he was just dodging hither and thither and hoping for the best. Pete gunned the car down the narrow slip-road to the junction at the bottom and turned left, up the long stretch of Northernhay with its jumble of houses, cottages and old brick commercial premises towards Queen Street.

'He's gone through under the trees into another section,' came the voice of the drone operator before Pete was a quarter of the way up the long hill.

Seconds later, Jane responded. 'He jumped over the Armco.'

'Heading north,' came the response.

'OK, following.'

'Now east, past a garage or something.'

'Received.'

There was no need for that on a group phone line, Pete thought. She much be tiring.

'Turned left, left, up the steps towards Queen Street.'

Pete was almost there. He signalled left, not sure if he'd be close enough to cut the suspect off, but he wouldn't be far behind him.

'Left again,' the drone operator reported.

By now he'd gone around in almost a full circle. What was he playing at?

Pete slowed for the junction.

'He's into a taxi,' the drone man reported. 'A black... Prius. Standby for registration.'

Pete pulled out and saw the car several yards ahead, pulling out from the roadside.

'Whiskey Foxtrot seven two... He's turned right at the Clock Tower.'

Pete had seen him do it as he gunned the Ford along the road, seeing Jane and the uniformed constable appear at his left as he passed the end of the stepped footpath that came up from Richmond Court. He couldn't stop. He was just yards behind the taxi. He flipped on his sirens, blue lights already reflecting off the windows of the buildings around him.

'Joining pursuit,' Colin said through the little speaker in Pete's ear. He glanced left as he made the right turn around the Clock Tower and saw Colin's big old range Rover bearing down on him. Pete had a few yards' lead and a much newer engine so he kept position. Saw the taxi ahead, accelerating away from him past the hedges and trees in front of the big old houses on the left, opposite a stretch of much more modern university buildings that looked like blocks of flats though he knew they weren't.

As he watched, the Toyota's brake lights flashed but then it seemed to accelerate harder. He pushed down on the accelerator, gaining a little despite the taxi driver's efforts. There was less than eighty yards between them when the Toyota reached the mini roundabout in front of the old prison, where the road angled away to the right onto the brick-sided bridge over the railway lines coming out of the back of Central Station, another road coming in at a steep angle on the left so that it looked almost straight on from Pete's viewpoint.

It looked as if the taxi was aiming for the left fork, but then it suddenly whipped right, pulling too far around, tyres squealing as it tilted dangerously. Pete hit the brakes as the Toyota came to a halt in the middle of the roundabout and the driver's door opened, the cabbie in his shirtsleeves, rolling out onto the tarmac.

CHAPTER TWENTY-SIX

Pete slammed on his brakes, dropping the clutch to let the ABS bring the car to a shuddering halt with its bonnet no more than a foot from the boot of the Prius. He cut the engine and shoved open the door, heard an impact from inside the other car as he hopped out and around the door. Another impact and glass shattered at the far side of the taxi. He ran around it, drawing the yellow plastic weapon from its holster on his right leg.

At the far side of the car, a pair of legs were emerging from the opening where the passenger-side rear window had been. Feet hit the ground, crunching on tiny pieces of shattered glass as Pete shouted. 'Police with Taser. Move slowly and keep your hands in view.'

The man froze briefly then wriggled out of the car and straightened. Left arm out to the side he turned to face Pete, his right arm folded upward over his shoulder. Pete caught the glint of steel, the bulk of a knife handle sticking out, and fired the Taser. Fifty thousand volts crackled along the twin wires. The target went rigid. The knife fell from his hand, rattling on the tarmac. Then he crumpled.

Pete stepped in quickly, kicking the knife away as he drew his cuffs, snapping on one side before flipping the man over and cuffing him at the rear.

'You were warned,' he said as he stood up and took a step back. 'Now you're nicked. Possession of and attempted assault with a bladed article, assaulting a police officer, resisting arrest, suspicion of dealing in illegal firearms and murder. For now. Roll over and sit against the car.'

He heard Colin's deep, gruff voice from the far side of the Prius and glanced up. The DI was helping the driver up onto shaky-looking feet. Then he lifted his radio. 'This is DI Underhill. We need transport for one, vehicle recovery and a paramedic ASAP outside the old prison.'

Pete looked down at the man staring coldly up at him and suspicion hit him like a bolt of electricity. He'd intended to leave the man seated there. He couldn't run from that position. But something made him want to search him now. 'On your feet,' he ordered.

'You're taking my car?' the cabbie protested.

'You're in no condition to drive,' Colin pointed out. 'And the car's in no condition to be driven. Especially not as a taxi. We'll fix it while we've got it and you'll have it back soon enough.'

Pete glanced over again. The cabbie's shirt was shredded where he'd hit the tarmac and rolled. Blood showed around the tears in the fabric.. There was nothing he could charge the man at his feet with, in that regard, except... He looked down at him. 'You're further under arrest on suspicion of kidnapping. Up.'

Beyond the cars now parked all across the little roundabout, blue lights showed as other police vehicles approached from the direction of the park.

Pete stayed clear, the Taser ready in his hand as the man turned onto his knees and came reluctantly upright.

'Face the car,' Pete told him before finally holstering the weapon and stepping forward to search him.

'Where is it?' he demanded when he'd finished and the man's wallet, keys and a bundle of change were on the car roof.

'What?'

'The money.'

The man grinned over his shoulder, the flashing blue lights from the police cars positioned all around them now to block off the roads, glittering in his eyes. 'What money?'

'The money you were in that park to collect.'

'Don't know what you're on about.'

Pete spun him around and grinned back at him. 'Spike's one of us,' he told the man. 'So we know that's not true. In the car, is it? Or did you dump it while you were running?'

'I'm telling you nothing. Except I recognise your voice,' he added with a sneer.

'What does that mean?'

'Spike will need to watch his back.'

'Another charge,' Pete retorted. 'Threatening a police officer.'

He shrugged. 'In for a penny... Every minute of every day. And night.'

Pete shook his head. 'Empty threats will get you nowhere, matey. Especially where you're going.'

'Wherever that is, I'll have connections. Guaranteed.'

'Which doesn't say a lot for how effective they are,' Pete pointed out. 'Think about it. If they were any good, they wouldn't be in prison, would they? Sit down again.'

The man's lip curled briefly. 'I'll stand, thanks.'

'You'll sit. One way or another.' Pete took a step back, his hand hovering close to the Taser.

The man shrugged and let his legs fold, his back sliding down the door of the car with a horrible ripping sound of metal on metal until he was seated on the tarmac once more. 'Oops,' he said as Pete looked above his head and saw the deep gouge down the door panel that he'd made with the cuffs.

He shook his head. 'You really do think you're a bad bugger, don't you?'

'You know I am.'

'What I don't know yet is your name. But now we've got your wallet, we'll soon fix that, eh?' He reached for the black leather folder on the taxi roof. Stepping back, he opened it. A bank card, a credit card and a driver's licence filled the slots in front of the thin wad of cash. He took out the bank card and the driver's licence. Examined them closely. The names matched, and the photo was of the man at his feet.

'So… Raymond Collier of Lower Lane, Ebford… As I said before, you're under arrest on suspicion of resisting arrest, assaulting a police officer, possession of a bladed article in a public place, attempted assault with a deadly weapon, dealing in illegal firearms, kidnap and murder. You do not have to say anything but it may harm your defence if you do not mention when questioned something which you later rely on in Court. Anything you do say may be given in evidence. Do you understand?'

Collier stared at him silently.

'Do you understand what I've just told you?' Pete asked again.

He nodded once.

'Good.' He glanced up and around as more blue lights began to flash behind him and the sound of an engine signalled a new arrival. A white van with a riot shield folded up above the windscreen and the Devon and Cornwall Police logo on the side was moving past the patrol car that was parked across the road. 'Here's your ride.'

*

It was barely 8:00am but the sun was already high enough to cut across the tops of the houses opposite Mrs Lambert's and directly into the bedroom windows, which were at Pete's eye level as he stood up out of his car in front of it.

He walked along to the entrance at the end of the short row and down the path that gave access to them. He hadn't seen anyone inside, but they'd clearly seen him because the front door opened before he could reach for the bell.

'Morning, Detective. Have you got some news for us?'

The old lady was up and dressed, as he'd expected she would be, as smartly as ever in a thin sweater and pleated skirt.

'Actually, yes,' he said. 'But I'll speak to your daughter and your grandson as well, all together, if that's OK, Mrs Lambert.'

'I don't know if Dale's awake yet. We'll have to check.'

'If you could…'

She pursed her lips, pausing for a moment as she peered up at him. 'He's a good lad, basically, Detective, and he does his best, but…' She shrugged. 'You'd better come in.'

'Thank you.'

She moved aside, indicating he should go ahead and enter the sitting room.

Dale was sitting up on the sofa as he stepped in. He pushed the quilt away and swung his feet to the floor. 'What time is it?'

'Just after eight,' Pete told him as the old lady pulled the door closed behind him.

He heard the creak of a floorboard from the hallway and a female voice followed by another. 'Sounds like you mum's up and about,' he said. 'I'll get her and your gran in here.'

'Hang on! Lemme get some trousers on first.'

He scrambled up as Pete reached for the door. With Dale scurrying for his trousers behind him, he called out, 'Cathy, Mrs Lambert, have you got a minute?'

The kitchen door opened and Dale's mother stuck her head through. 'What is it?'

'I've got some news that affects you all.'

'Yes, Mum was just saying.' She stepped through, followed by her mother. Pete inclined his head towards the room behind him and stepped back as Dale cinched up his belt and grabbed the duvet to fold it roughly. By the time the two women stepped into the room, the duvet was on the floor in the corner behind the sofa and both men were seated.

'What is it?' Cathy asked again.

'Sit,' Pete instructed and waited until they'd complied. 'All right. This morning, about five past midnight, we arrested the man who's been threatening you. His name is Ray Collier. He comes from Ebford, out near Topsham.'

'So…' Cathy started. 'We can go home? We're safe?'

Pete nodded.

'How long for?' Dale demanded. 'Are you sure you're going to keep him locked up?'

Pete drew a breath. 'I'm not going to lie to you. There's no guarantee what a jury will do until they've done it. But we've got him for murder, kidnap and a whole lot of other things. There's still work to do, but I think there's a solid case and, given the charges and his skill-set, he'll be remanded while we build it so, for now at least, he's where he needs to be. We'll keep you updated on the progress of the case. If nothing else, we may need you to testify. Both of you,' he added, looking at Cathy.

She dipped her head in a definite nod. 'Whatever it takes.'

'Good. Dale?'

'If it keeps mum and Becks safe.'

His mother, on the sofa next to him, reached up and placed a hand on his shoulder, squeezing it lightly.

'Right. In that case, I'll go and get on with building the case.'

Dale nodded gratefully. 'Thanks, man.'

Pete nodded. 'Just stay inside the law or you'll end up in there with him.'

'Hey!' he protested.

'Look after your mum,' Pete told him. 'And your sister.'

CHAPTER TWENTY-SEVEN

Pete was still struggling to believe that he'd been given this opportunity as he pulled up his chair in the interview room opposite Raymond Collier and his solicitor, who Pete had dealt with several times before, with other clients.

He'd noted the slight pinching of the suited man's lips as he entered the room and now gave him a tight smile. 'Morning, Mr Davidson. How are you?'

Davidson nodded reluctantly. 'Well, thank you, Detective Sergeant.'

Pete switched his attention to the man's client as he reached for the recorder and switched it on. 'Mr Collier. Raymond. You remember me, I take it? Detective Sergeant Peter Gayle. We met last night. This is Detective Inspector Colin Underhill,' he added as Colin sat down beside him. 'We're here to interview you regarding the charges I listed to you when you were arrested. You're still under caution.'

Collier stared at him flatly, not responding.

'I gather you chose not to say anything to our colleagues from the National Crime Agency. But maybe you'll be more conversational with us locals, eh?' Pete suggested. 'I mean, it's not as if there's any reason not to be and we all know it's a lot harder to not join in a conversation than it is to say your piece.'

'My client has every right to maintain his silence,' Davidson said.

'Of course he has,' Pete agreed. 'I'm just saying there's no point in making that effort. We've got more than enough forensic and witness evidence to make our case.' He returned his attention to the suspect. 'So, the point of this interview is two-fold. One: it's required as part of our transparency responsibilities. So you're aware of the case we're putting forward. And two: to give you the opportunity to respond with any explanations or extenuating circumstances that might be relevant: why things happened the way they did. Any reasons that the charges perhaps ought to be reduced. You do that now, it makes the whole process simpler and quicker and cheaper for the taxpayer, so you potentially get a reduced sentence in acknowledgement of that. Like the well-known thing of getting up to half the sentence shaved off for pleading guilty before the trial starts.'

Collier didn't respond.

'OK, so let's begin, shall we? You'll have guessed that we found your car. I say your car: the Golf. Forensics have been busy on it, confirmed that you're the person who was driving it. And the VIN told us where it came from, along with the original plates, tucked away in the spare wheel well, under the boot space. With your fingerprints on. So, in addition to the other charges against you, we can add handling stolen goods. I don't imagine you went over to a village just outside Plymouth to steal it yourself so, again, you could help that by telling us who you got it from...'

Still, Collier didn't say anything. Didn't move. Simply stared at him.

'No?' Pete asked. 'Nothing to say on that? OK. Moving on, then: there's also the B&E on Franklin Street. Dale Gordon's address, along with his mother and sister. You're aware that you were seen there by myself and a colleague prior to the act. One of the occasions when you resisted arrest.'

'Allegedly,' Davidson put in.

Pete glanced at him but resisted the temptation to reply. 'You wore gloves for the B&E, of course, Raymond, but you still left some DNA. Why did you go there? What for?'

Collier gave him the slightest hint of a cold smile. 'No comment.'

'That was one of the few points we're here to raise that we don't actually have the answer for already,' Pete admitted. 'I mean, was it in the hope of finding the family there? To scare Dale into silence? Or had you got more than that in mind?'

He grunted derisively. 'No comment,' he repeated.

'One of the charges already levelled against you is kidnapping. Another is murder. Things can't get any worse than that, in terms of sentencing, even if you were planning other offences of the same type.'

'I thought we were here for you to question my client, Detective Sergeant?' Davidson said.

'We're here for a conversation, Mr Davidson, as you well know, and as I already explained to your client,' Pete reminded him. Then turned back to Collier. 'Anything you want to say on the break-in at the Gordons' address, Ray?'

'No comment.'

'All right. Talking of Plymouth, I gather you lived there for several of your younger years. We looked you up. You had a bit of a reputation over there. And a fairly extensive charge sheet, mostly gang-related. So, how did you go from that to a backwoods village outside of Exeter?'

'I was left the place. An uncle.'

'And, rather than sell it, you moved in?' Pete nodded. 'A fresh start, eh? So, what happened? What went wrong, to lead you back into the lifestyle?'

'Covid. Business went tits-up. Had to make a living somehow.'

Pete nodded sympathetically. 'Hit a lot of people hard, that did. So, you had a skill set and connections and decided to put them to use?'

He nodded.

'For the benefit of the tape, Ray...'

Collier glanced at the recorder and back at Pete but said nothing.

'OK. So, the car – the Golf – came from your old connections too, did it?'

'No comment.'

'You'll be expecting us to search your place at Ebford, of course. That's under way now. Had to wait for the guys from the National Firearms Targeting Centre in Birmingham to get down here, to join our forensics team. They'll no doubt be discovering all sorts out there, eh?'

Collier let a smile spread slowly across his unremarkable features. 'They can search all they want. They'll find nothing illegal.'

'What, you don't keep any stock? Just make to order?'

He didn't respond.

'You don't keep one for yourself? For self-defence?'

'No... Comment.'

Pete chuckled. 'Prefer a knife, eh? Or a spike. Close quarters. See the look in their eyes. Feel the life slip away.'

Again, that smile, slow and easy, never reaching the eyes.

'We found it, along with the cash, in the taxi. The driver's business card tucked in with them was a nice touch. Subtle but effective. "I know where to find you."' He paused to let that sink in.

'You didn't expect us not to search the taxi, did you, knowing that you'd got the cash only a few minutes before you got in it? I mean, there were limited possibilities, weren't there? You could have handed it off, but then why be there in the first place? Or you could have stashed it while you were running around the city centre last night with my colleagues on your tail, but the opportunities were kind of limited, eh? So, it made sense. Under the backrest of the back seat there was neat, though. Out of sight but quick to access by folding it down and lifting that bit of carpet that goes under it to keep the dirt out.'

He tipped his head but said nothing.

'Of course, modern cash being what it is – basically plastic – it's a lot better than the old stuff for us. Holds fingerprints nicely. And the tracker we put in with it helped us find it and identify it.'

Davidson had been about to say something, but now clamped his mouth shut, his argument killed before it was made.

'See, there's the other thing I don't get,' Pete continued. 'Why keep the weapon? I mean, most people would have wiped and dumped it. Keep their distance and create doubt – in a jury's mind if nowhere else. Was it the weapon after all? Was it yours or not? But you kept it. I mean, I know it's a nice tool. Well-balanced, effective and all that, but still dangerous to keep it after you've used it for killing someone.'

'Says who?'

Pete tipped his head once more. 'I dare say you stuck it through the dishwasher, eh? Make sure there were no prints or blood traces left on it?'

'No comment.'

'The only trouble with a tool like that is that they come in a sheath,' Pete said. 'And you know how it is. You use it, maybe wipe it off, and put it away for safety. It's automatic. Reflexive, almost. And you may have wiped it, but not necessarily as thoroughly as you'd have washed it. So, there is a degree – albeit tiny – of transfer. Of blood.' He allowed himself a tiny smile. 'And guess what we found on the inside of that sheath, Ray? Exactly that: blood. Just a tiny amount, but these days, with modern methods, it'll be enough to be identified.'

The smile was gone from Collier's face now, leaving it cold and blank.

'So, there's the murder charge,' Pete said. 'My only question on that…' He glanced at Davidson. '…is, how did you manage it without being seen or heard?'

Collier stared at him silently for a stretch of several seconds. Pete was about to assume he wasn't going to respond when he finally spoke. 'What murder's this?'

Pete's eyebrow rose. 'There's more than one? OK, for now, we're talking about the death of Shane Gallagher last Sunday night.'

He grunted. 'That waste of space? World's better off without him.' He paused. 'Whoever killed him, I'd imagine they heard someone coming and just stayed put until they'd gone, then slipped away in the opposite direction.'

'What, into the square?'

He smiled, saying nothing.

Pete nodded. 'It's what we suspected, but the whole area was searched.'

'Obviously not well enough. Or not soon enough.'

'Well, nobody's perfect, eh? So, what was your problem with Shane? You said the world's better off without him. Why?'

'He was a drug dealing leech.'

'Well, there's plenty of those in the city. We keep trying to get rid of them, but it's like a huge game of whack-a-mole. You swat one and another pops up. So, why him, in particular?'

He shrugged. 'Convenience. Got to start somewhere.'

'What, so you were helping us out, doing the city a favour?'

He smiled. 'You can thank me later.'

'It was nothing to do with the gun you sent him up to Birmingham with or the fact that he was arrested when he got back, then?'

His eyes narrowed briefly. 'Don't know what you're on about.'

'So, how did you know he'd been brought in? You weren't waiting for him at the station, were you?'

He smiled. Seemed about to speak but stopped himself. 'No comment.'

'Which leaves the question of whether the rumour being put about is true. That you've got someone feeding you information from our side of the fence. A mole. Or is that just a story you've encouraged to make yourself look more invincible than you are on the streets? We've been working on the assumption that it's true, which is why it's taken us a little bit longer to catch up with you. Limited resources to throw at the job when you've got to keep things quiet in case the wrong set of ears picks up on what you're doing. Until the National Crime Agency got onboard. So, out of interest, is it true? Or is it just a fairy tale put about to scare people, make yourself seem like more of a nightmare than you really are?'

Another tight smile. 'I couldn't possibly comment.'

'No matter. Now the immediate concern's dealt with – you're here with us – we can concentrate on finding out. Weeding out any possible information source you might have on the force. Not going to go well for them when we find them, mind. Losing their job and their pension will be the least of it. Ex-coppers don't do well inside. Not well at all.'

He glanced at Colin, sitting quietly beside him.

'It's in hand,' the senior man said.

Pete raised an eyebrow. 'Yes?'

Colin nodded. 'Made the first move last night, soon as you'd booked him in.'

'OK.' Pete hadn't known about that. 'We'll see what comes of it, then. It'd have to be someone with a connection. A relative. Neighbour. Someone he's dealt with in the past. On a previous case or whatever...'

'Dapper's checking that angle.'

'We'll soon know, then.'

Pete had been watching carefully for a reaction from Collier as they discussed the subject, but there was none. He remained stony-faced.

'Nothing to say, Raymond?'

'Why would I help you out?'

Pete shrugged. 'As I said before – cooperation potentially reduces your sentence. Sign of remorse, potential rehabilitation.'

He gave that small, brief smile again.

There would be no reforming this man, Pete knew. He hadn't got it in him. But he had to offer the concept. The possibility. To try to get him on-side, to see the benefits of playing ball.

'No comment.'

'OK. We'll get onto Plymouth, get them to send some uniforms out to ruin some of your old buddies' days and see what they can stir up in connection to you. I'm guessing, for one thing, you'll have reached out to someone for a replacement for that Golf, since you knew it was on our radar. Which reminds me – how did you get away from there without being spotted?'

That brought a wider smile. 'I'm surprised you hadn't already sussed that. Been in touch, even. I was waiting. Saw that…'

'I'd advise you not to say anything more on that subject, Mr Collier,' the solicitor beside him cut in.

Collier looked at him and back at Pete. 'I'm not going to tell them anything they don't already know.' He turned back to Pete. 'Yeah, I saw that pretty redhead up the end of School Lane, taking pictures with her phone. Might have been in plain clothes, but she was obviously a copper. I was tempted to do something about her, but I didn't know if she might be sending a live feed back to your HQ or something. And anyway, I'd got a reason to be there.'

'Oh, yes? What was that?'

'Was in the Tally Ho! the night before. Left my car down there, as a responsible citizen. Got a taxi home instead of drinking and driving.'

'Really? What taxi firm did you use?'

He chuckled. 'Don't recall. I was a bit tiddly.'

'Oh, well. There's only so many in the city. We can check.'

'Hmm. You do that. You might find him. Or it might have been his knocking-off time so he'd have done it as a cash job on his way home.'

It was Pete's turn to smile. 'That's illegal. He could lose his licence. And we do have ways of finding out.'

Collier stared at him, saying nothing.

'OK,' Pete said. 'Is there anything we haven't covered?' he asked Colin.

'That'll do for now.'

Pete nodded. 'No doubt there'll be more to discuss when the search is completed out at Ebford. We'll talk again then, Raymond. For now, interview terminated at...' he checked his watch. 'Twelve-sixteen.'

*

Pete turned left out of the police station and headed out of the city with the taste of a surprisingly good shepherd's pie still fresh on his tongue from the canteen. There was no point in going home this afternoon. No-one was there with Louise having headed up to Okehampton to fetch Annie back from her week with his parents. He'd have gone himself – would have cherished the opportunity – if it hadn't been for this case, but Louise would spend most of the day with them and head back in the late afternoon, so he wanted to make the best use of the time he had available.

Ebford was a small, loose collection of houses and cottages on narrow twisting lanes clumped off the Exmouth Road, just south of Topsham, less than five miles from the Exeter police station. Early on a Sunday afternoon, he covered the distance in less than ten minutes, turning off the main road into a narrow lane between two old white-rendered buildings. He drove through the heart of the village, passing a variety of homes, old and new, large and small, cottages, bungalows and larger houses until, towards the far side, with the properties well spread out, another lane came in on the right, signposted as Lower Lane. He turned down it and hadn't gone far when a gateway on the right revealed signs of police activity. A white Forensics van and a pair of patrol cars plus a handful of other vehicles were spread around the gravelled drive and the rough paddock it ran through towards a substantial stone house with a garage beside it and outbuildings behind, one of them almost barn-like in proportions, though it was built solidly of breezeblocks with big double doors on the front, a smaller man-sized one cut into one of them. The small door stood open as he stopped his car next to the boxy forensics van and killed the engine. A uniformed officer appeared from somewhere to his right as he stepped out.

'Sarge.'

Pete nodded in response. 'How's it going?'

The man, a few years older than Pete and a few inches shorter, but at least as heavy, shrugged. 'There's plenty to do.'

'Who's in charge?'

'The folks from Brum think they are, but as far as the rest of us are concerned, it'll be Sar'nt Jackson.'

Pete nodded his thanks and stepped across towards the heavy black front door which stood ajar behind the man. Inside, with no-one in sight as he stood facing the stairs with closed doors on either side of him, he called out. 'Craig, where are you?'

'Who the hell let you in here?' a familiar voice thundered from somewhere within the ground floor. 'I'll have his bollocks on a necklace before the day's out.' The door to Pete's right opened and Craig Jackson stepped through. An inch taller than Pete, he was also six inches wider; an intimidating presence to anyone who didn't know him, especially in the heavy black uniform of an Ops Support sergeant. Pete had known him for several years. They'd patrolled together many times before Pete switched to CID and Jackson to Ops Support.

'The DI not come out here?' Jackson asked, seeing Pete alone.

Pete shook his head. 'To be fair, I only did because I wanted to be sure in my own mind that I can go home and tell the Mrs that we're definitely going to nail the bugger. How's it going?'

'All right. We've left the NFTC guys to it in the workshop out the back. We're concentrating on the house and garage for now, with the forensics guys.'

'Anything in the garage? I see the door's closed.'

'Yeah, done and dusted long since. An old Subaru Outback estate car from 2001.'

'OK, that could help. Have you found his phone yet? He wasn't carrying it when we picked him up last night.'

Jackson shook his head. 'Not yet. Unless he dumped it while you were chasing him.'

'I didn't chase him. I just caught him,' Pete grinned. 'But it's possible, I suppose. You want an extra pair of hands in here?'

'Not without gloves on,' Jackson said. 'But yeah, if you like. Forensics are upstairs. We're down. But we haven't started on the room behind you yet.'

Pete reached into his jacket pocket and came out with a pair of gloves. 'I'll just give Jane a quick bell, then see what I can find in there, then. What colour's the Subaru?'

Jackson nodded. 'Dark Green. Give us a shout if you need a hand.'

As the uniformed man turned to go back the way he'd come, Pete stepped outside and took out his phone to place the call.

'DC Bennett speaking.'

'Jane, did you happen to see – or better yet, get a photo of – a dark green Subaru estate car coming out of Countess Wear yesterday?'

'I'll check through and call you back.'

'All right.'

He ended the call and returned inside, turning left in the small entrance hall and stepping into a room that was a good seventeen feet by fifteen with a high ceiling and two tall sash windows with shutters folded back against the thick walls to either side as well as curtains. The room didn't appear to have a cohesive function. There wasn't even a carpet covering the floorboards which had greyed with age. An old table stood in the far corner with a laptop computer and a 3D printer on it and a chair in front. In another corner was an upright freezer. A few old pictures were haphazardly arranged on the walls and, in the corner directly across from the doorway, the space between the front wall and the chimney breast was filled with a built-in cupboard that looked to be almost as old as the house, the double doors painted a muddy brown that was chipped and dulled by age. There were two sections to it: above and below roughly waist height, the lower section standing out a few inches further than the upper.

It wasn't going to take long to search the space.

He started with the built-in cupboard. Crossing in front of the windows, he pulled open the doors. Inside, the contents were neatly stacked and contrastingly modern. Files, books, boxes and bags of the substrate materials for the 3D printer. The books – around twenty of them lined neatly on a shelf at eye level – all seemed to be about two subjects: engineering and guns. There were three box-style files, none of them labelled, on the next shelf down. He was about to pull the first one out when his phone buzzed in his pocket. He took it out to answer.

'Gayle.'

'It's me,' said Jane. 'That Subaru: have you got the VRN?'

'Hold on.' He headed out of the room and the house, crossing to the uniformed man standing guard outside. 'Have you got a note of the registration number of the car in there?' he asked, jerking a thumb towards the garage.

'Yes.' He took out his notebook and flipped it open, turning it for Pete to see.

Pete read out the number.

'Yep,' Jane said. 'I've got him leaving about three minutes after you all disappeared into the village.'

'Excellent,' Pete said. 'That's one more nail in his coffin.'

He thanked the officer and headed back inside. 'I'm helping on the house search at the minute. I'll let you know if we find a smoking gun.'

'Ho, ho, ho,' she retorted.

He grinned. 'At least you're getting most of the day off.'

'And enjoying every minute.'

'Make the most of it while it lasts,' he shot back, 'I might call you in yet, just to be awkward.'

'Huh,' she grunted.

'See you later.'

'I hope not.'

He hung up and returned to what he'd been doing, lifting out the first file and opening it on the narrow shelf that was formed by the outstanding lower section, where the printer substrate was kept.

The file was filled with household bills. He found electricity, landline telephone, water and council tax as well as TV licence. Setting it aside, he took out the next file and opened it.

'Oh,' he muttered. It contained – was filled by – a large hardback book. In old-fashioned gold lettering on the worn-looking embossed leather cover was printed, *Holy Bible* in fancy script. He almost set it aside, but something made him pause. He took the file across to the desk and tipped the old book out. It slid out of the box onto the Formica surface and, as it landed, he realised what had made him pause. It landed a lot more gently than might have been expected. It was too light for what it purported to be. And now that he could see the edges, something else caught his eye.

'Now, isn't that interesting?'

Set into the gilded false page edging down the side was a keyhole. 'I wonder where the key's going be that fits in there?' He ducked down to check the underside of the old kitchen table for a drawer, but there wasn't one. Yet, the key wouldn't be far away, he guessed. Unless it was five miles away, among the bunch that Collier had had in his pocket when he was arrested.

He grunted. That would be a pain, if it were true. He decided to finish searching in here first. Reaching up, he slid his hand along the empty top two shelves but found nothing but dust. Careful to handle them in a non-typical way so as to minimise the risk to any fingerprints present on them, he next began to remove the bags and boxes of printer substrate from the lower cupboard, lining them out on the floor between the windows in the order he removed them. He was lifting the last bag out from the bottom shelf when he saw it. Sitting on the floor of the cupboard where the bag had been was a small, flat key.

He set the bag aside and reached for the key. Took it across to the table and tried it against the escutcheon in the side of the hidden lockbox. It was the right size. He slid it in and turned it.

Nothing.

He tried turning it the other way.

'Ah,' he muttered as it slid around like a well-oiled machine. He opened the cover.

Inside was a block of dark grey foam. Looking closely, he could see a slight indentation at the top edge. He gently pushed a gloved finger in and levered upward. An inch thickness of the foam folded stiffly away under his pressure and he lifted it out. Took a breath.

'I've found the mobile,' he shouted.

An inexpensive smart-phone in a leather-look case was slotted neatly into a cutout in the lower layer of foam. In a separate smaller and shallower cutout was a spare SIM card, brand new and unopened, and in a third was the phone's charger.

Turning back towards the cupboard, he started to replace the bags of printer substrate. Was lifting the first when a thought struck him. He took out his phone and placed a call.

'Maitland.'

'DS Gayle,' he said in reply. 'Those two guns that you've confiscated from our man here – what are they made of?'

'Mostly plastic of some kind with metal essentials – barrel, firing pin and so on.'

'Plastic as in 3D printed plastic?'

'Yes.'

'I wonder if that can be chemically matched.'

'Why? Where are you?'

The door opened and Craig Jackson stepped in. 'You bellowed?'

Pete nodded and tipped his head towards the table in the corner. 'In the spare room in his house,' he said into the phone. 'There's a 3D printer here, and all the stuff that goes with it.'

'Well, yes, it can. I'll send someone in there to get samples.'

Maitland cut the call as abruptly as Colin Underhill would have.

'Well, thank you, too,' Pete muttered and put his phone away. 'Maitland,' he said in reply to Jackson's querying glance. 'He's sending someone in here for that stuff.' He nodded towards the contents of the lower cupboard.

'Ah.' He nodded towards the phone still nestled in its hiding place. 'Nice find. Have you tried it?'

'Not yet. Be my guest.'

Jackson lifted the phone out, opened the case and pressed the power button. As Pete stepped across towards him, the distinctive opening jingle sounded. Jackson swiped the screen and held it out for him to see. 'This'll have to go to the techy boys at Middlemoor.'

'Yes. He won't give us the code, that's for sure,' Pete agreed. 'Even if he knows we'll crack it, he'll make us do the work.'

'Awkward bugger, is he?'

'You could say that. Wouldn't talk to Maitland at all, apparently.'

'Yeah, well… Who would, given a choice?'

Pete chuckled. 'Not keen?'

'Arrogant sod, isn't he?'

Pete tipped his head. 'I'm not going to disagree. Tell you what: I'll take that to Middlemoor, see if anyone's in Technical and feeling helpful, now I've done the hard part of your job for you.'

'Ooh!' Jackson chortled. 'Cheeky sod. You ain't changed, have you? One bit of blind luck and your head gets all swole up like a pumpkin.'

'Some of us have just got it,' Pete said with a grin. 'And you know what they say – if you've got it, flaunt it.'

Jackson sealed the phone into an evidence bag and filled in the details. 'Here. Bugger off out of here while you can still fit your head through the door.'

CHAPTER TWENTY-EIGHT

He used the car's comms system to dial through as he drove back towards the gate of Collier's property,

'Dave, it's me,' he said when it was answered. 'What have you found out about Collier and his connections in the force, if they exist?' He stopped at the twin five-bar gates before pulling out into the lane, which was no wider than the driveway he'd been on.

'Well, there's nothing at Sidmouth Road.' The police station they were based at, now three years old, was finally becoming known, as its predecessor had been, by its location rather than simply, "The new station." Pete's mind went immediately to the neighbouring force HQ, known as Middlemoor. 'What I did find was a link at Crownhill,' Dave continued.

'Plymouth?' Pete turned left at the T-junction, heading into the village.

'Yep. One of Collier's old gang buddies switched sides, came over to us.'

'Have they been in contact recently?'

'That, I don't know. Have we got his phone yet?'

'Yes, but it's locked. That's why I called you: to see if you'd found anything in the way of a clue to the possible access code. A four-figure number that might be significant to him.' He slowed for a cyclist in black and orange Lycra who was too intent on pedalling to pay attention to his surroundings. He was tempted to tap his horn or flick the sirens on and off but resisted.

Dave grunted. 'Could be anything, couldn't it? His dog's year of birth, the phone number where he grew up, the calibres of the first two guns he ever fired. Who knows?'

'Yes, well, I'm on the way to Middlemoor, to visit Tech Support, see if they can crack it, if there's anyone in there on a Sunday. I just thought, if you'd got anything, it might save time. But they'll get there.'

Dave chuckled. 'There's only ten thousand possible combinations. How hard can it be?'

Pete grunted. 'You try it. You'd have bruises on your fingertips long before you ever got into it, I bet.'

'Yeah, but they'll hook it up to a computer. Shouldn't take long that way.'

'I hope not,' Pete grumbled as he passed through the narrow neck of the village street where it met the main Exeter to Exmouth road, white-rendered building crowding in on either side.

'So, where was it, being as he wasn't carrying it?'

'In a hidden lock-box in the house here.'

'So he left it at home so he couldn't be tracked with it. I wonder how often he's done that.'

'He was using it the night of Shane Gallagher's murder. To lure him out, apart from anything else. What I'm hoping is that it's still got the same SIM card in it.'

'That really would nail his arse to the wall, wouldn't it? And he has been kind of busy since then, between dodging us, going after Dale Gordon and making a new gun from scratch. So here's hoping. But even if it hasn't, we've got Gallagher's phone records, we can get whatever number he contacted him from and take it from there.'

'That's the sort of spirit we need. Leave the negative vibes to Grey Man.'

'What should we do about his buddy in blue?'

'Pass the details on to the guvnor. He can follow it up as he sees fit. But keep hunting. The more info we can collect, the more we can hit him with, next time we have a sit-down.'

'Will do.'

Pete ended the call as he approached the roundabout at Clyst St Mary, keeping to the left of the three lanes to head westward, under the motorway and into the outer portion of the city.

*

It was almost twenty-four hours later when they sat down again in the same interview room that they'd used before with Ray Collier and his solicitor.

Pete switched on the voice and video recording system and made the introductions. 'I'll remind you, just so there's no possibility of doubt: you're still under caution while you're here in the station, Ray, so anything said in this room can be used in court. Talking of which, you know the judge is going to want you to plead guilty, to save him the time and effort of a trial, don't you? So will the prison service, so they won't have to feed and house you for as long. By the same token, you'll no doubt want to plead guilty, too, because then you won't have to be locked up for as long. A win-win, all round, right? Except for us and the general public.' He indicated himself and Colin Underhill, who was once again seated beside him. 'Personally, I want you to go to trial and get the full dose of what you deserve. But I'm obliged to give you the opportunity to plead guilty, just in case you're one of the tiny minority that can be rehabilitated. And the process of pleading guilty starts here, in this room, with admitting what you've done, fully and honestly. So, with that in mind, let's make a start, shall we?'

'Want a drink, first, won't you, after all that spiel?'

Pete smiled. 'I'll manage. Don't want to break the flow. I had a run out to your place in Ebford after we spoke yesterday. Nice place.'

Collier shrugged. 'It does the job.'

'Must be a bit of a pig to keep warm, though. I didn't see any radiators in the rooms I went into.'

'No gas out there, is there?'

'You could use oil. Or there's enough space for a ground-source heat pump if you want to be green about it.'

He shrugged. 'We'll see. Fires do, for now.'

'I helped out the search team a bit while I was there. Make myself useful, you know. I've got to say, I like the old family bible. Great idea. Especially fitting so well in the box file.'

Collier's eyes narrowed as he waited to see where Pete was going.

'The foam inside's a bit of a giveaway, though. Too light. You'd have been better with a block of wood, carved out to take what you want to put in it. More work, I know, but much more effective. I took the phone to our tech support guys. They've got all sorts of fancy gadgetry and programming to get into them. Wasn't a problem. So, we've got the data from it, including the call you made on Sunday night to Shane Gallagher, to tell him to go and meet you.'

'You can't know what was said during a phone call, Detective. We all know that,' the grey-suited solicitor interrupted. 'Texts, perhaps, but not calls.'

'Not calls, no,' Pete agreed, glancing at him briefly. 'But locational data. Even if you'd switched it off as soon as you made the call, you'd already placed yourself in the vicinity with that, Ray. Between that and the blade... They've got the DNA off the sheath, by the way, as we expected. So that seals that.'

'Except that you can't say for certain that my client was in possession of the weapon at the time of the crime,' Davidson interrupted again.

Pete tipped his head at him. 'His car was there – correction, sorry: the stolen car he was in possession of was there – his phone was there, the spike was there and he was found in possession of it a few days later,' he said. 'What do you think a jury's going to add that up to?' He turned back to Collier. 'I'll tell you, Ray: guilty as charged, that's what. Oh, and talking of cars, you were right: we did get a photograph of your Subaru leaving Countess Wear after you dropped the Golf off there on Saturday.'

'I explained that.'

Pete nodded. 'You did. Or you tried to. Trouble is, I followed you there along most of the length of Topsham Road. And before that, you were seen by another officer getting into the car and followed by them to where I took over. And there's footage of you the night before, driving up to West View Terrace, to park it there while you went to meet our undercover officers. So, with all that in mind, would you like to change anything you've said so far?'

He stared at Pete for a stretched second, his face expressionless, then shrugged. 'No comment.'

'Really? OK, we'll move on. I didn't go into your workshop personally. No need. There was a bunch of guys from the National Firearms Targeting Centre busying themselves out there.' He used the full title deliberately, to emphasise their area of expertise. 'They were very interested in some of the tools you've got out there. They found everything you'd need to make the parts of a gun that need to be metallic. Specific and unusual drill bits. 5.6mm. 6.35, 9.65, 10.16, 11.43, 12.7. As the son of a carpenter and joiner, I know what the standard sizes are, and none of those are standard. Except as gun-barrel diameters. And then there were the broaching bits to match. They tell me they're to create rifling in barrels. I gather they're easy enough to get hold of, but not many people would have a use for them. Not in this country.'

He shrugged again. 'What can I say? I'm a collector. Bit of an obsessive.'

'Have you ever heard of tool marks?' Pete asked.

'Course.'

'Very distinctive, they tell me. You can match a specific tool to a piece that was created with it. Especially those broaching bits. A bit like ballistics. And now, they've got those two weapons you sent up to Birmingham for comparison.'

'Allegedly,' Davidson put in.

'He sent the second one with our undercover officer, Mr Davidson. Pay attention.' He turned back to Collier. 'And I understand they can chemically match the 3D printed parts to those substrate packages in the cupboard under where your phone was, too. So, the only issue we've got left to resolve is the question of whether or not you've got a man on the inside. A buddy on the force. And we've been looking into that, as we said we would. Do you recognise the name of Brent Tolliver?'

Collier blinked.

'I see you do. We ran across him as an old associate in your PNC file. And guess where we discover he is now. Our side of the fence. One of us, over at Crownhill nick. So, what are we to make of that, eh? A case for the IOPC?'

He frowned. 'What the hell's that?'

'The Independent Office for Police Conduct. What they'd call Internal Affairs on the other side of the pond.'

Collier shrugged. 'Please yourself on that. You won't find nothing against him. Not on my account, anyhow.'

'And yet you spoke to him just last week.'

Another frown brought a quick grin from Pete. 'We accessed your phone, remember?'

He grunted. 'Yeah. He called me. Just social. Catching up. Or checking up, maybe.'

Pete shook his head. 'Not on our account. We hadn't identified you at that stage. But the good news is, no-one's tried to access your file or find out anything about you that shouldn't since your arrest. So we can only conclude from that, that Tolliver's an innocent coincidence and the legend of the man on the inside is just that – a legend to scare the boys and girls on the street.'

Collier smiled. 'I couldn't possibly say.'

Pete shrugged. 'No problem. We will make sure, obviously. What it does, though, is it leaves you in here, on your own, with no backup and a case against you that's about as solid as they get. So, what's it to be? When DI Underhill here calls the CPS is he going to tell them to get ready for a trial or that you're going to plead?'

'Seems like the sensible option is to take a plea.' He turned to the man beside him with one eyebrow raised.

'I think this might be an opportune moment for us to have a brief recess, Detectives,' the suited man said. 'So that my client and I can have a discussion.'

'Hmm. We could go and find that drink you suggested, Ray,' Pete agreed. 'Ten minutes enough?'

He nodded.

'That should suffice,' the solicitor agreed.

'Right. Interview suspended, then.' He checked his watch and quoted the time. Colin reached for the recorder to switch it off.

*

They returned in twelve minutes. Pete was tempted to wait longer, let them sweat, but Colin vetoed the idea. 'Let's get it over with and have an early finish for the day,' he said. 'Paperwork can wait for tomorrow.'

'Fair enough,' Pete agreed.

Retaking their seats, Colin switched the recorder back on and Pete made the standard introductory announcement. 'So, have you reached a decision?' he asked.

Collier nodded. 'I'll plead.'

'OK. So, you're admitting that you're guilty of the crimes you were arrested for?'

'Yeah.'

'Why? I mean the crimes, not the admission, obviously. How did you get involved in gun-making?'

'Accident, I suppose. And fascination. The lads knew about my uncle, that I could do stuff like that. I was asked if I could fix a piece that was jammed. So I took it, fixed it, and while I had it, I copied it. Not the right calibre. Hadn't got the tools for that. But it looked the part and it was just for me, at the time. To have it. No good taking it out anywhere: you got something like that, sooner or later you're going to have to use it or look like a twat. And I couldn't, obviously. It was a dud. But...' He shrugged. 'I wasn't very old. Seventeen, eighteen.'

'And you'd done it once so you got asked to do it again?' Pete suggested.

Collier nodded. 'Not asked, so much. It was... required. I was... I'd got onto drugs, to where I couldn't say no.'

Pete nodded. 'I was going to ask about that. What have you got so strongly against dealers? And if you hate them so much, why use them?'

He shrugged. 'Disposable, ain't they? If necessary. Nobody will miss 'em. Well, the users will, briefly, but they'll soon find another.'

'But, if you were one of those users, you dealt with them regularly. What set you against them so much?'

'Had a bad experience, didn't I?'

Pete tipped his head. 'Go on.'

Collier sat looking at him silently.

'If you're going to do this, Ray, it's all or nothing.'

He grunted. 'There was a time over in Plymouth they come calling and I couldn't pay. There was three of 'em. They decided to take it in kind. I was big enough, but I was Jonesing. Couldn't defend myself. They thought they'd have a laugh. Teach me a lesson and make it known on the streets as an example.'

'So, they roughed you up?'

Again, that flat stare was his only response.

Davidson saw which way it was going and took a breath, setting down his pen. 'My client was severely assaulted, Detective. In a way that, normally, only women are subjected to.'

Pete looked at him, then back at Collier, who hadn't moved, his expression stony. 'I see.' He took a breath. 'You know, I've read your file and done some background research. There's no mention of this. You didn't report it?'

His lip curled. 'What do you think? No, I didn't report it. I was nineteen and on the streets more than I was at home. Not that I was welcome there, by then. So, no, I waited until I could and dealt with it myself. After that, I got a reputation. I could do work instead of pay cash. Gun repairs. And that's what I did until I got off the gear. Don't know how many. They came from all over the place. Easier to fix one than replace it. If you know how.'

'Getting clean is a major achievement,' Pete acknowledged. 'Most of those who try don't manage it. How long has it been?'

He pursed his lips. 'I started cutting down after… The attack. Took me a couple of years to get fully off it.'

'But you kept doing the work? The repairs?'

'For a while. Then I did one too many. My uncle found out. And there was nowhere I could set up my own workshop, so that was it.'

'But now you've started again. And not just repairing but making from scratch.'

He shrugged. 'Like I said, Covid cut my income. Had to do something and I saw an opportunity. Crime don't stop, does it?'

Pete allowed him a small smile. 'That's a fact. So, you were out of the life, by then, but you'd kept up your connections?'

He frowned, not keen to go there.

'We got into your phone, remember. And that list, along with the Police National Computer makes it relatively easy to put two and two together. Like you and Noah Green.'

His lips pressed briefly together. 'What about him?'

'I gather he's into nicking cars. Allegedly,' he added with a glance towards the solicitor seated beside Collier. 'And you were in touch with him about three weeks ago. Right before that Golf started appearing in Countess Wear. And again after you left it there, the day before yesterday. After a replacement for it, were you?'

He shrugged. 'Doesn't hurt to keep in touch with an old mate now and then. See what he's up to. No law against that.'

'There is against incitement, though.'

A frown flashed across his brow.

'To commit burglary or theft, for instance,' Pete expanded.

He chuckled. 'There's no way you're going to prove that.'

'But it is part of the deal. Part of what we're doing here now. I said full and honest disclosure, remember?'

'Of my crimes, yes. I can't speak to what other people get up to, though. Especially forty-odd miles away.'

'My client's not going to speculate on your behalf, Detective,' Davidson put in. 'That's not part of the deal.'

'But you did know the Golf was stolen, didn't you?' Pete said, addressing Collier directly.

'I might have suspected.'

Pete shook his head. 'We found your fingerprints on the original plates in the spare wheel well under the floor of the boot. As well as on the back of one of the false plates you replaced them with.'

'They were just to throw off anyone trying to follow me.'

'And the fact that the car hasn't been re-registered in your name?'

He shrugged. 'Haven't got around to it yet.'

Pete shook his head. 'And I thought we were doing so well here, Ray.'

He paused then let out a sigh. 'All right, I knew it was nicked. There's no saying where he was going to get another one from, though.'

'OK,' Pete conceded. 'The other night,, then, while I think of it – when you went to meet Spike at Bury Meadow. You hadn't got the Golf and you weren't in the Subaru, so how did you get there?'

'Taxi,' he said.

'What, from Ebford?'

'From there to the RDE, then another from there into the centre.'

Pete nodded sagely. 'Careful as always, eh?'

Collier gave him a quick smile.

'So, was the Prius we caught you in pre-booked to go home in, or was that just a convenient coincidence?'

'He was pulling up as I come up off the steps, so I took the chance while it was there.'

Pete nodded. 'We'll check your phone records, of course. And those of the taxi firms. But thank you for the admission.'

Collier didn't respond.

'Back to the three who attacked you, then. You said you dealt with them yourself. How, exactly?'

That cold smile flashed again. 'They won't be raping anyone else. Or dealing to anyone else.'

'They're dead?'

He nodded slowly.

'For the tape…'

'They're dead.'

'Again, how? And when?'

'With a knife. Slow. One at a time. First one was easy. Wasn't expecting it. Last one took a bit of finding. He'd gone into hiding by then.' He grunted. 'Wet hisself when he saw me. Gibbering wreck, he was. Screamed like a little girl when I got going on him. In the end, I had to cut his tongue out to shut him up. Made him swallow that, too. And it worked, sort of. Didn't stop him screaming but he choked on his own blood after a bit. Shame, really. I was hoping to make him last a lot longer but there you go.' He shrugged, unfazed by what he'd said although Pete noticed Davidson had turned pale, next to him, sweat beading on his forehead as he swallowed reflexively.

'I'm not aware of any bodies being found in those sorts of condition,' Pete said.

'They weren't. I got rid of 'em.'

'How? Where?'

'There was an old disused abattoir on the west side of the city. It was in a rival gang's territory, but they didn't use it. So I did. Took them there, cut them up, put the bones through a garden shredder that I got off the online auctions and fed them to the wild boars round Burrator and Colliford lakes. There's more of them around than the authorities like to admit. Like them big cats. Don't want to scare the poor public, I suppose.'

'No, they leave that to the likes of you,' Colin said.

Collier raised an eyebrow. 'Thought you'd forgotten how to speak.'

'He's not known for wasting words,' Pete said.

'Leaves that to you, eh?'

Pete allowed himself a brief smile. 'Just trying to get you talking, Ray. And it's worked, hasn't it?'

Collier shook his head. 'Self-preservation. Simple as that.'

'Exactly,' Pete agreed. 'The strongest instinct we've got. Appeal to that and you're onto a winner every time. But back to the dealers. You called them disposable yesterday. You killed Shane Gallagher, but you didn't tell us why.'

He flashed his thin smile again. 'Because he was busy trying to set me up.'

'How did you know that?'

'Like you said – you'd had him in here. He came out, free as a bird and with the package still in play. Only one way that was going to happen, wasn't there? Then he turns up with a tail. As it turns out.'

Pete glanced at Colin, beside him.

'You didn't know it was a tail at the time?'

'No, but the timing was suspicious and when I asked him, he started blabbering and couldn't look me in the eye, so...' He shrugged.

'What about the other couriers you've used? What happened to them?' Pete asked.

'Nothing. Used each one a couple of times and moved on. No good letting 'em get comfortable. They might think about taking advantage.'

'So, how many have there been?'

'What, couriers or guns?'

'Guns.'

His lips pushed briefly upward. 'Over the last three years... Eleven.'

Pete gave a low whistle. 'At twelve grand a pop. That's a nice chunk of change. And all by word-of-mouth?'

'Well, I haven't got an ad in Guns and Ammo or Shooting Times.'

'Which reminds me – how did you find Sean Gallagher? And Dale Gordon?'

His lips pushed upward. 'They're not hard to find. Right time of day, right sort of place, you're pretty much guaranteed to come across one, aren't you?'

'So, they were just random selections?'

'Yeah.'

'And the others, before them – they were the same, were they?'

He nodded.

'And you did your research on them before approaching them?'

Another nod.

'How did you go about that?'

He shrugged. 'It's easy enough to follow 'em home when they've done what they're there for. An address can get you a name, easy enough. Ask the neighbours about them. Or, if there's time and the space, just sit and watch, see who comes and goes and take it from there. It's not like I need to be anywhere else unless I've got a job on in the workshop.' He smiled. 'They say patience is a virtue.'

Pete suppressed a derisive snort.

'All right,' Colin decided. 'That'll do. Let's wrap it up and see what the CPS decide.'

Pete nodded. 'Unless you've got anything else you want to tell us, Ray?'

He shook his head.

'In that case, interview terminated at...' He checked his watch 'Perfect time for tea and a bun. 15:58.'

Colin reached over to switch the machine off and they stood up to leave. 'Someone will be along in a minute to take you back to your cell,' Pete told Collier. 'Mr Davidson.' He nodded to the solicitor.

Outside, in the wide, white-painted corridor, he turned to Colin. 'You going to join us for a donut, guv?'

Colin shook his head. 'I'll let you have your five minutes of fun. Then tomorrow, the paperwork starts.'

'Yeah,' Pete replied. 'And, on this case, there's going to be a lot of it.'

THE END

AUTHOR'S NOTE

The level of gun crime in the UK is one of the lowest in the world. The National Crime Agency operates on several levels to counteract it. Its National Firearms Targeting Centre coordinates the national intelligence picture on firearms. They work closely with police and other investigative and forensic agencies, such as the National Ballistics Intelligence Service (NABIS), to share intelligence and capabilities. They also work with several foreign agencies to target the importers directly.

The majority of shootings in the UK are committed by street gangs involved in many types of criminality, such as armed robberies and drug distribution. Victims of gun crime are generally known to the police, criminals using firearms in feuds with other criminal groups, for protection, punishment or to extend their criminal enterprises.

Illegal firearms are usually obtained through criminal networks and armourers, often exploiting cultural or family links to source regions. Most come from eastern Europe, often via Belgium, the Netherlands and France. They can be concealed in vehicles on channel ferries or through the tunnel, but an increasing number are coming directly from the USA. Bought on the dark web, they can be simply sent by parcel post.

The trade in smuggled guns is largely driven by gangs who traffic drugs from cities to smaller towns and rural areas — known as "county lines" gangs, although these gangs still primarily use knives as their weapon of choice. Only 33 people were killed with guns in 2019 in the UK, despite over 10,000 firearms offences being recorded, but the problem is an increasing one.

One former London gang leader and gun trafficker said that he had handled more than 50 firearms and sold many more to gangs across Britain. Sometimes, he said, the smuggled guns had arrived in the country inside boxes containing infant highchairs.

"I got my first gun from one of my elders when I was like 13, 14," he said, speaking anonymously to avoid arrest or retribution from his old associates. He had since stepped away from the gang with the help of Gangsline, a London-based organization that helps gang members leave crime.

His gang trafficked dozens of new and used weapons, including American Glocks, he said, with prices reaching £15,000. Today, investigators say the smuggling pipeline is well established.

The presence of American guns in the UK was highlighted in July 2019, when officers with the National Crime Agency raided a rusty blue container ship as it arrived at the port of Ambarli in northern Turkey after traveling from Florida. In some of the shipping containers were old American cars inside which 57 firearms and 1,230 bullets were hidden, on their way to gangs in Britain and Bulgaria. The guns had been purchased legally at antique gun fairs in Florida and then smuggled to Turkey to be illegally reactivated before sale.

And not all the guns on Britain's streets are imported. In October 2022, officers from the Metropolitan Police's Specialist Crime Command discovered a 3D firearms factory at a home in London and made one of the largest seizures of 3D printed firearm components in the UK, though this is not the only such source of the weapons that has been found.

The head of the National Firearms Targeting Centre said the latest 3D weapons are "stuff that you definitely wouldn't want to see on the streets in the UK". While early versions were unreliable single-shot weapons, the latest ones are extremely sophisticated and there are plans for them, including for automatic weapons, available freely on the Internet.

However, new guidelines for sentencing offenders convicted of firearms offences ranging from the unlawful possession of weapons to manufacturing illegal guns came into force in England and Wales on 1 January 2021, including sentences of 10 years and even life in prison. It is hoped that this will act as a deterrent. In the meantime, most of us can take at least some comfort in the fact that almost all gun crime in the UK is perpetrated by gang members on other gang members rather than against innocent members of the public, and while guns are used to frighten victims, they are very rarely actually fired even by the most violent criminals.

*

I hope you enjoyed this book. If so, please do go to whichever platform you purchased it through and leave a review to help other readers make an informed buying decision.

https://www.amazon.co.uk/JackSlater/e/B003X8IMEC/ref=dp_byline_cont_ebooks_1

https://www.kobo.com/gb/en/search?query=jack%20slater&fcsearchfield=Author

https://www.barnesandnoble.com/s/jack%20slater/_/N-8qa

If you have any other comments or observations on the books, you can contact the author on jackslaterauthor@mail.com or see the website https://jackslaterauthor.site123.me He can also be found on Facebook: https://www.facebook.com/crimewriter2016 where you will find the latest updates on his writing and lots of other relevant content.

Pete and the team will be back soon with another case to solve.

ABOUT THE AUTHOR

Raised in a farming family in Northamptonshire, England, Jack Slater had a varied career before settling in biomedical science. He has worked in farming, forestry, factories and shops as well as spending five years as a service engineer.

Widowed by cancer at 33, he remarried in 2013, in the Channel Islands, where he worked for several months through the summer of 2012.

He has been writing since childhood, in both fiction and non-fiction. *No Second Chance* is the fourteenth crime novel in the chart-topping DS Peter Gayle mystery series.

Other books by the same author:

Nowhere to Run (DS Peter Gayle crime thrillers, Book 1)

A missing child. A dead body. A killer on the loose.
Returning to Exeter CID after his son's unsolved disappearance
Detective Sergeant Peter Gayle's first day back was supposed to be
gentle. Until a young girl is reported missing and the clock begins to
tick.

Rosie Whitlock has been abducted from outside her school that
morning. There are no clues, but Peter isn't letting another child
disappear.

When the body of another young victim appears, the hunt escalates.
Someone is abducting young girls and now they have a murderer on
their hands. Time is running out for Rosie, but when evidence in the
case relating to his own son's disappearance is discovered the stakes
are even higher...

No Place to Hide (DS Peter Gayle crime thrillers, Book 2)

A house fire. A suspicious death. A serial killer to catch.
When a body is found in a house fire DS Peter Gayle is called to the
scene. It looks like an accidental death, but the evidence just doesn't
add up.

With only one murder victim they can't make any calls, but it looks
like a serial killer is operating in Exeter and it's up to Pete to track
him down.

But with his wife still desperate for news on their missing son and
his boss watching his every move, the pressure is on for Pete to bring
the murderer to justice before it is too late.

No Way Home (DS Peter Gayle crime thrillers, Book 3)

A dead body. A mysterious murder. A serial killer on the loose.
A taxi driver is found murdered in a remote part of Exeter. He is a family man, no enemies to be found. There is no physical evidence, except for dozens of fingerprints inside the cab. How will DS Peter Gayle ever track down his killer?

Then another cab driver is found dead. Now this isn't just a case of one murder but a serial killer on the loose, once again…

No Going Back (DS Peter Gayle crime thrillers, Book 4)

A gruesome find on a woodland walk. A body posed and naked, the killing savage and frenzied. Was the victim known to her attacker? Or is a serial killer emerging in South Devon? With no clues at the scene, DS Pete Gayle and his team must identify the victim before they can even start looking for a suspect.

No Middle Ground (DS Peter Gayle crime thrillers, Book 5)

A missing father. A desperate daughter. A terrible discovery.
A new case is the last thing DS Pete Gayle needs right now, but when it falls right into his lap, he has no choice. Justice is crying out to be served. With a career-making trial about to begin and his son in imminent danger from a pair of psychopathic brothers, Pete goes on the hunt in what could turn out to be the biggest case of his life.

No Safe Place (DS Peter Gayle crime thrillers, Book 6)

His young son is recently dead, his traumatised daughter is going through hell and his station chief is out for his blood – or at least his career – when DS Pete Gayle is called to a murder scene on a residential street in Exeter.
A body has been found, horrifically tortured and left outside a women's refuge. She is quickly identified as a resident, the victim of domestic abuse.
But the obvious suspect was three hundred miles away, so who did this? And why?
Haven't these women been through enough?
Touched by the plight and the resilience of the shelter's residents,

Pete must track down a vicious and sadistic killer before more can fall prey.

No Compromise (DS Peter Gayle crime thrillers, Book 7)

A brutal murder. A man jailed. A new witness who claims he couldn't have been there.

Already in the middle of a violent and complex case, DS Pete Gayle gets entangled in a tangled web of lies and intrigue. With a man in jail for a murder he may not have committed, the reputation of the station and the whole force is on the line. Pete has to face one of the hardest choices of his life. To break ranks and go against another officer risks losing friends, colleagues and career, but if he ignores the case, will he be able to live with himself?

No Compassion (DS Peter Gayle crime thrillers, Book 8)

A vicious rape, a woman left traumatised. A previous victim is
quickly identified. Then more come forward.
A serial rapist is attacking the women of Exeter in their beds at
night.
There are fingerprints and DNA but no matches, CCTV but no
identification.
With the press clamouring for answers DS Pete Gayle and his team
must work through a maze of conflicting evidence to identify and
arrest the offender before he can commit another brutal attack.

No Stone Unturned (DS Peter Gayle crime thrillers, Book 9)

A murder in mysterious circumstances.

A woman is brutally slaughtered just feet from her sleeping family.
But no-one hears a thing and none of them belong in this grand and
expensive home. Who are they? Why are they here? And why was
this woman killed?

DS Pete Gayle must draw on all his skills as an investigator to figure
out what went on here and why.

No Good Deed (DS Peter Gayle crime thrillers, Book 10)

A young woman sits quietly compliant at a sea-front bus-stop as a
police officer takes a bloody knife from her hand. 'I'm safe now,'
she says.

But safe from whom? Who is she, where has she come from and
whose blood is on that blade? These are just a few of the questions

DS Pete Gayle must answer in the latest book in this top-selling series.

No Fair Hearing (DS Peter Gayle crime thrillers, Book 11)

A young man with special needs is beaten to death by a vicious mob on an estate where the residents live in constant fear. When DS Pete Gayle begins to investigate all he finds is a rumour about the victim that is quickly proved false and a wall of silence more solid than the stones around the city's old prison. Was this just pointless spite that went too far or is there more behind the horrific death? Pete must battle a mini-crime wave designed to keep him in the dark as he seeks justice for an innocent victim and his distraught family.

No Fear of Consequences (DS Peter Gayle crime thrillers, Book 12)

A student disappears in broad daylight just yards from the university. With potential witnesses beginning to disperse across the country for the Christmas break, DS Pete Gayle is under extra pressure to figure out what happened as quickly as possible. Did she leave of her own accord, unable to cope with the pressures of university? Was she snatched by an ex-boyfriend, a stalker or a random attacker? Or was she targeted because of the way she'd chosen to supplement her student loan?

One disturbing discovery after another draws Pete and his team through a minefield of sensitive information, much of which he is all too aware, as a father himself, would be horrifying to the victim's parents. But he has to follow the evidence, wherever it may lead.

No More Than Bones (DS Peter Gayle crime thrillers, Book 13)

Exeter-based DS Pete Gayle is already busy with a child-snatching case when pathologist Dr Tony Chambers calls CID to report that a body has been found in Exwick cemetery. And this burial, in a shallow grave among the trees bordering the graveyard, is not an official one. With nothing but the skeletal remains to go on, Pete must find out who the dead man is, how he got there and, most importantly – who put him there?

Nowhere to Run: The Dark Side

The other side of the mirror from DS Pete Gayle's investigation in Book One of the series, Nowhere to Run – this is The Dark Side.
A young girl is snatched from right outside her school.
While she fights to survive in the clutches of her abductors, her family is ripped apart by guilt and recriminations. And, with no demand or even a message to go on, they are forced to rely on the police to find her. But not even the officer in charge of the case is aware until it's too late of just how close he is to the kidnappers.

The Venus Flaw

Murder and corruption in the Maltese government combine with the concealment of a horrific secret in a minefield of intrigue and violence.

When Dan and Wendy Griffin find a cave full of prehistoric artwork on the coast of Malta they are plunged into a living nightmare. Someone is trying to keep something hidden, but who? And what? Unable to trust the police or the British Embassy and with no clues other than the cave itself and the fact that one of the men trying to keep them from it works for the National Security Service, they must try to figure out what is going on before one or both of them are killed.

Printed in Great Britain
by Amazon

32801108R00194